CRITICAL MASS

CRITICAL MASS

DAVID HAGBERG

A Tom Doherty Associates Book
New York

CRITICAL MASS

Copyright © 1992 by David Hagberg

This book was printed on acid-free paper.

A Tor Book
Published by Tom Doherty Associates, Inc.
175 Fifth Avenue
New York, N.Y. 10010

Tor® is a registered trademark of Tom Doherty Associates, Inc.

Library of Congress Cataloging-in-Publication Data

Hagberg, David.
        Critical mass / David Hagberg.
                p.   cm.
        "A Tom Doherty Associates book."
        ISBN 0-312-85255-X
        I. Title.
        PS3558.A3227C75   1992
        813'.54—dc20   92–3621
                                                        CIP

First Edition: June 1992

Printed in the United States of America

0 9 8 7 6 5 4 3 2 1

This novel is for Dominick Abel and Tom Doherty. It's nice to be believed in, and even nicer to have such friends.

ACKNOWLEDGMENT

Special thanks to Robert Roningen,
my friend and weapons expert, for vetting
the manuscript. His help is appreciated.

PROLOGUE

Hiroshima
AUGUST 6, 1945

The electric lights dangling from the hospital ward ceiling paled to nothingness in the morning sun streaming through the tall windows. A man dressed in what appeared to be a uniform, but without any insignia of rank or unit, stopped at the swinging doors and forced himself to look back. The hospital was nearly full just now, and all but two of the beds in this ward were occupied. An old man sat, head bowed, beside the last bed on the right. He held the hand of the dying old woman beneath the covers. The man in the uniform looked at them, he suspected for the last time, then turned.

A floor nurse seated at the desk smiled consolingly, but she said nothing. There was no shame or dishonor in dying well. And the old woman in the last bed on the right was accomplishing her dying in an orderly, quiet, dignified fashion. She was well respected in the Red Cross Hospital because of it.

Isawa Nakamura pushed through the swinging doors and walked out into the corridor where he hesitated a few moments longer. The windows here looked downtown, toward the prominent dome of the Industrial Promotion Hall. It was a little after eight, and he was still early for his appointment. No use, this morning, being early. He would gain face by arriving one or two minutes late.

Life was for the living. The dead were not to be forgotten, but time just now was becoming terribly important to those who were going to survive. And if nothing else could be said about Nakamura, he was a survivor. As a child he and his brother had been ice skating on a pond at their family retreat near Sapporo on the northern island of Hokkaido when the ice broke and he went in. His brother jumped in after him and pushed him out of the icy water. Instead of running the mile or so home for help, Nakamura went to the nearby shelter hut where he changed into dry clothes. When he came back to the pond his brother was gone, drowned, so he calmly walked home to report the tragedy. A great many people had died that year of influenza, which was brought on by a chill. No use taking a chance.

At thirty, Nakamura was one of the rising stars in the Japanese industrial-technical revolution. A self-taught electronics engineer, he was as ruthless with his body as he was with his mind. At five-foot-four he was a compact, well-muscled man with deep-set obsidian eyes and jet black, luxuriously thick hair. Given six months he and his people could develop a small, powerful radar that could be installed in fighter aircraft, giving the Japanese airman the decided advantage.

Given a year, the air force would be flying jets, which along with radar and new developments in rocket armaments and guidance systems, could turn the tide.

It would depend on the spirit of the people. If they were willing to defend the homeland on the beaches, in the hills and forests, and in the cities, street by street, house by house, it might buy them the development time. But only just.

There was no time for the dead or dying because Japan would surely lose the war unless the living—all the living—dedicated themselves to the struggle.

He looked again toward the swinging doors. It had been the matter of the estate that had brought him down here. As soon as his mother and father were dead he stood to inherit money and land. He wanted to see with his own eyes the state of their health. She was dying, and his father didn't look well. The strain of her death would probably kill him within a month or two.

He'd also come down to meet with the colonel of the Hiroshima Defense District, who fancied himself a businessman, and who was willing, for a price, to supply Nakamura's firm with the needed copper wire and gold leaf for switch contacts. Both metals were virtually impossible to obtain these days.

"Isawa-san," someone called for him in a small voice at the end of the corridor.

He turned in irritation as Myeko Tanimoto, dressed in a crisp white and red flowered kimono, held up a delicate little hand for him. She traveled as his secretary. In reality she had been a maiko, which was a geisha in training, until Nakamura bought her from the school. At fifteen, she was a perfectly formed porcelain doll. But she frightened easily, and just lately she had begun to get on his nerves.

"Return to the car and wait with Kiyoshi," he said as she hobbled in tiny steps toward him.

"There has been another air raid signal, Isawa-san. Didn't you hear it?"

"It is like the others last night. There is nothing this time. You heard the all clear."

"But it is said that they have seen B-san. Three of them to the northeast over Lake Biwa."

"They will bomb some other city. It is their rendezvous point. Now return to the car, Kiyoshi will be getting worried."

"May I remain here with you?" Myeko asked. She had stopped halfway along the corridor. A nurse came out of one of the wards, looked at her, then at Nakamura, and left.

"Do as I say," Nakamura told her.

"But I am frightened . . ."

"Obey!" Nakamura roared.

Myeko stumbled backward as if she had received a physical blow, then, lowering her head, she turned and hobbled back to the stairs the way she had come.

Dr. Masakazu Saski came to his office door, a disapproving scowl on his deeply lined face. "What is the trouble here?" he demanded.

"There is no trouble, *sensei*," Nakamura said. "But I wish to have a word with you about my parents."

The doctor's eyeglasses were perched on top of his head. He flipped them down and peered myopically at Nakamura. "Who are you?"

"Isawa Nakamura."

"Ah, the young lion." The doctor shook his head. "Come in then," he said, and he turned and disappeared into his office. Saski had a bad reputation for being overly Western in his brusque, to-the-point manner. But he was a good doctor and he worked cheaply.

The doctor's office was small, and in complete disarray, with medical supplies, journals, books and files scattered everywhere.

"You want to know how your mother is doing," Dr. Saski said gruffly.

"She does not look well."

"No. Neither is your father. Both of them will be dead within a few months. Your mother soonest, I should think."

"What is wrong with them?"

"Age. Heartache. They talk about your brother almost all the time."

"I see. What are you doing for them?"

"Keeping them comfortable . . . and together. Something you could do, Nakamura. It would free up valuable space here."

"I have no time . . ."

"You could hire a nurse to care for them. You are young and wealthy. For that matter your parents have money, and property. They speak often of their place on Hokkaido. From what I understand it has not been visited since your brother's accident. They would like to go there now, to die and be at peace with their son."

Nakamura said nothing.

"Surely you can understand this, Nakamura-san. You have a wife and children of your own in . . ."

Nakamura slapped an open palm on the doctor's desk. "There will be time after the war for holidays. I will hear no more of this."

"The war is over, you young fool," Dr. Saski said, harshly. "All that is left is for the profiteers. And later, the gallows. The Americans will not honor *seppuku*. Perhaps it would bring more honor to your family to commit *hara-kiri* now."

"The war is not over until the Emperor Tenno concedes defeat, a move he will never make."

"Or until we are all destroyed."

"I could have you shot for treason."

Dr. Saski snatched up his telephone and held it out to Nakamura. "Call your military friends, Nakamura-san. Call them now, if you are not a coward. But let me tell you that the great empire is gone. Up in flames with our cities. Tokyo is in ruins. Soon we will join her. Maybe sooner than you think. So it doesn't matter. Go ahead and call your friends in their high places. Maybe they will come down to deal with me. Maybe they will tell you to go away. Who knows. I am willing to see. Are you?"

"Perhaps I will kill you myself."

"You are certainly capable of it."

Nakamura suddenly had no idea what he was doing here, wasting his time like this. Yet he found himself wondering about the doctor. He didn't understand the man. "You would rather die than fight back?"

For the first time Dr. Saski's expression softened. "We speak of being Japanese. There is no honor left in it. Believe me, I have seen as much as you, maybe even more. The misery, the starvation, the wounds, the open, festering sores. Where is the honor, Nakamura-san? I ask you."

Nakamura felt as if he were standing at the very edge of an extremely dangerous precipice. If he made the wrong move he would fall over and plunge to his death. By sheer dint of will he stepped aside, away from the doctor's desk. The sunlight streaming through the windows across the hall illuminated the room. "You are no Japanese. You are nothing but scum."

"I am not a murderer . . . like you."

"Bastard . . ." Nakamura said, when a tremendous flash lit up the corridor at his back, as if someone had let off a gigantic photographic bulb.

There was no noise, but Dr. Saski's eyes turned an opaque white almost instantly, and he staggered backward.

Instinctively Nakamura, who'd survived a number of bombing raids on Tokyo, dove for the floor, protecting his head with his arms. His first thought was that the Americans had dropped another *Molotoffano hanakago*—what the public called Molotov Flower Baskets, which were cluster bombs. But this flash was much too bright. And there was no explosion.

Nakamura started to raise his head when a huge shock wave hit the hospital as if a loaded freight train going full tilt had slammed into the building's foundation. Window glass flew through the open office door like pellets from a shotgun's barrel, slicing Dr. Saski's face into ribbons. In the next instant the desk lifted up on unseen hands and fell on top of the doctor.

Ceilings and walls were falling with horrible grinding crashes, and moments or seconds later people began to scream.

Nakamura pulled himself upright, scattering pieces of wood and glass and papers that had fallen on him, and staggered over to where Dr. Saski lay beneath the heavy oak desk. Blood streamed from hundreds of slashes on the doctor's face and chest, and his eyes were bleeding, both corneas milky white. He was still alive, but it was obvious he would bleed to death unless he got help soon.

"Can you hear me, *sensei*?" Nakamura shouted.

Dr. Saski grabbed for Nakamura's shoulder with his one free hand. "What was it? A bomb?"

"Yes, I think so. Are you in pain?"

"My patients."

"You are in no position to help them now. You must save yourself. I will see if I can lift the desk off you."

"No," Dr. Saski cried, desperately clutching Nakamura's arm. "You must help organize the evacuation before there is fire."

"Don't be a fool. There is nothing to be done for them."

"Damn you, Nakamura, they need your help."

Nakamura pried the doctor's fingers from the material of his jacket and backed away. Scrambling to his feet he went to the corridor door. Everything was different. A big section of the floor above had collapsed, dumping beds and bodies in a bloody heap all tangled with wooden beams, boards, glass, electrical wires and plumbing pipes and even surgical equipment, bottles, bandages and other debris.

None of the window frames held any glass, and the scene outside toward the center of the city nearly a mile away was unbelievable, like something out of a nightmare. A hellish cauldron of smoke and fire in dozens of unreal colors rose straight up into a gigantic column the top of which was lost in billowing clouds of dust.

This was no cluster bomb. It was something else. Tearing his eyes away from the fantastical scene outside, Nakamura looked back in at the doctor. Japan had lost the war. There was absolutely no doubt of that now. Afterwards, when the Americans occupied the homeland, there would be war trials. Those who had fought hardest and with the most bravery for Japan would be the first to go to the gallows . . . as Dr. Saski had predicted.

Evidence would have to be gathered. There would be witnesses, even from his own factory where he had used Korean slave labor since 1938.

There would be no extenuating circumstances. Isawa Nakamura would be found guilty as charged: Crimes against humanity.

"I pleaded with him to help save my patients, but he ignored me, running away to save himself instead.

"He came to visit his parents, but not out of some filial duty. He came to see how long it would be before they were dead. He wanted the inheritance, you see."

More people were screaming and moaning. A woman's voice came from beneath the pile of rubble in the corridor. *"Tasukete! Tasukete!"* Help! Help!

Nakamura went back to the doctor, his shoes crunching on the broken glass.

"Nakamura, is that you?" Dr. Saski cried.

Nakamura looked down at the doctor for a moment or two. He could definitely smell smoke. The hospital was on fire. There was no doubt of it.

"Can't you hear them crying for help, Nakamura? You must help them. They will die otherwise."

Nakamura picked up a long, dagger-like shard of glass from the floor, and kneeling down beside Dr. Saski, blotted out the screams of the dying and helpless. Life was for the living, and he intended to live. At all costs.

"Nakamura!" Dr. Saski rose on his free elbow.

Nakamura grabbed a handful of Dr. Saski's hair, yanked his head back, and with the shard of glass hacked through the man's carotid artery, and windpipe, blood spurting everywhere, before he reared back.

The doctor struggled desperately for a full minute before he took a last, gurgling gasp and his head thumped back on the floor.

The glass shard had cut deeply into Nakamura's hand. Tossing it aside he bound up the wound with his handkerchief and hurried out into the corridor. It was very dark, almost as if night had fallen. Looking through the gaping windows he could see that the sky was completely covered with swirling masses of dark clouds and dust.

He was confused. There'd only been the one flash. One bomb. But how could it have done so much damage?

Much of what he could see of the city was gone; either flattened by the blast or burning furiously. There seemed to be fires everywhere. And the street directly in front of the hospital was choked with debris. He'd been saved because he'd moved away from the open doorway at the last moment. He'd been lucky. Those caught outside would not have fared so well.

For the first time he remembered that he had a car waiting for him. Kiyoshi Fukai, his driver, was downstairs with Myeko. He had sent her back outside just before the bomb. They were both outside, exposed.

Nakamura was suddenly angry and frightened. He did not want to be stuck in Hiroshima. And without a car and driver it would take them days to make it home to his wife and children and business. There was too much to be done, too many records to be destroyed before the enemy landed, too much to be dismantled and hidden, for him to be delayed.

Sprinting down the corridor, he scrambled over piles of debris and beds and bodies, mindless of the cries for help, panic suddenly rising inside him. The Americans had targeted Hiroshima for some reason. They had bombed it once, they would almost certainly bomb it again. He had to get away before the bombers returned.

At the far end of the corridor the stairway was surprisingly undamaged and free of debris, though the smoke became heavier as he raced down from the third floor.

At street level the pharmacy was burning furiously, but no one was doing anything to put out the flames. A few nurses were helping patients escape from the hospital, but there appeared to be no organized efforts at rescue yet. Everyone seemed to be in varying states of shock.

Outside, directly in front of the hospital, a dozen people sat or lay on the grass, the clothes scorched off their bodies, their skin flash-burned and blistering.

The only thing that Nakamura could think was that the American bomb had touched off an ammunition dump nearby, or perhaps ignited a gas works. But there seemed to be no fire concentrated in one area.

An ambulance was overturned in the middle of the driveway, on fire as was a big, black car behind it. An American car, Nakamura realized, his stomach clutching as he pulled up short.

His car. A Chrysler.

"No," he shouted, leaping forward.

He had to swing wide of the ambulance, the heat was so intense, and on the other side he had to pull up short again. There was no possibility of getting close to the Chrysler. Its gas tank had evidently ignited, spewing the synthetic fuel in the tank forward into the passenger compartment. Black, greasy smoke rose up into the dust-filled sky, and flames completely engulfed the big car.

Suddenly enraged, Nakamura stood ten yards away from the

burning car, and began hopping from one foot to the other. Burned and wounded passersby paid him absolutely no attention. People were crying for help, or for *mizu*—water, and others were screaming, *Itai! Itai!* It hurts! It hurts! It was a scene from hell.

Gradually a familiar voice began to separate itself from the others in Nakamura's ears. A man crying "*Tasukete! Tasukete, kure!*" Help, if you please!

Nakamura turned in time to catch his driver Kiyoshi stumbling from behind the overturned ambulance. The back of his jacket and trousers had been completely burned away, as had some of his flesh. Part of his spine and a few ribs were exposed, obscenely white in contrast with his beet-red skin.

Kiyoshi fell backwards onto the pavement, and immediately lurched onto his side, a high-pitched inhuman keening coming from the back of his throat, his burned hands outstretched as if in supplication.

Nakamura reached him. "What happened, Kiyoshi? Where is Myeko?"

Kiyoshi's eyes focused on Nakamura. "Nakamura-san, what has happened?"

"Where is Myeko?" Nakamura shouted, grabbing Kiyoshi by the shoulders and shaking him. "Myeko?"

"In the car," Kiyoshi cried. "She is dead. I could not save her. She is dead. Help me, Nakamura-san. Please help me."

Nakamura sat back on his haunches and looked down in contempt at his driver. There was absolutely no hope for the man. No medical science in the world could help him. Life was for the living.

He looked up at the destruction all around him, then back at the ravaged body of his chauffeur, who had served him well for nearly ten years.

Life was for the living, and Nakamura knew that he would be one of the survivors. At all costs.

Somehow he would return to Nagasaki to his wife and children and to his factory and laboratory to do what had to be done before the enemy arrived.

BOOK ONE

1

Police Sergeants Pierre Capretz and Eugène Gallimard watched as the Air Service panel truck bumped toward them along the dusty ILS access road. In the distance to the east, runway 08 was flattened in perspective because of a slight rise in the ground level, and because of the thin haze that had hung over Paris and her environs for the past two days. Farther in the distance, windows in the Orly Airport terminal building glinted and sparkled in the morning sun.

The stink of burned Kerojet was on the breeze because an Air Inter L-1011 had just taken off for Montpellier with a tremendous roar that rattled the windows of the maintenance gate guard hut. The silence in the aftermath was so deafening that Capretz had to shout.

"He's not on the schedule."

Gallimard shrugged, but as he watched the van through narrowed eyes his left hand went to the strap of the Uzi slung over his shoulder. A driver, but no one else so far as he could see. The van was familiar, or at least the logo on its side was, but they'd been warned about a possible terrorist attack on a European airport within the next ten to twelve days, and he was nervous.

"Call Central," he said.

"Right," Capretz replied, but for a moment he stood where he was watching the approaching van.

"Pierre," Gallimard prompted.

"*Mais oui,*" Capretz said. He turned and went into the hut, where he laid his submachine gun down on the desk. He picked up the phone and dialed 0113 as the van pulled up to the gate and stopped.

Gallimard stepped around the barrier and approached the driver's side of the van. The driver seemed young, probably in his mid- to late-twenties. He had thick blond hair, high cheekbones, and a pleasant, almost innocent smile. His white coveralls were immaculate. He was practically *un enfant*, and Gallimard began to relax.

"*Bonjour. Salut,*" the young man said, grinning. There was something wrong with his accent. He was definitely not a Frenchman, though the nametag on his coveralls read: Léon.

"Let me see your security pass."

"Yes, of course," Léon said pleasantly. He reached up and unclipped his badge from the sun visor and handed it out. "You need to see the work order?"

"Yes," Gallimard said, studying the plastic security badge. It seemed authentic, and the photograph was good, yet something bothered him. He glanced back at the hut. Capretz had his back to the window, the phone to his ear.

Léon handed out the work order for an unscheduled maintenance check on one of the ILS transmitters. The inner marker. The document also seemed authentic.

"Problems?"

"You were not on our schedule," Gallimard said. "And we have been warned about a possible terrorist attack."

Léon laughed. "What, here? Maybe I've got a bomb in the back and I mean to blow up some runway lights."

"Maybe I'll just take a look in the back, if you don't mind."

"I don't care. I get paid by the hour."

Gallimard stepped back as Léon got out of the van, and together they went around back where the young man opened the rear door.

"Take a look."

Gallimard came closer and peered inside the van. Nothing seemed out of the ordinary. Tools, some electronic equipment, and what appeared to be bins and boxes of parts.

A metal case about five feet long and eighteen inches on a side caught his eye. "What's in the big box?"

"A VHF antenna and fittings."

Gallimard looked at him. "I'll open it."

Léon shrugged.

Gallimard climbed into the van and started to unlatch the two heavy clasps on the box when a movement behind him distracted him. He looked over his shoulder, as Léon raised what looked to be a large caliber handgun with a bulky silencer screwed to its barrel.

"*Salopard* . . ." Gallimard swore as the first shot hit him in the left side of his chest, pushing him backward, surprisingly without pain. And the second shot exploded like a billion stars in his head.

Léon ducked around the side of the van and looked over to where the other security guard was still trying to get through on the phone. He'd apparently seen or heard nothing. Concealing the nine-millimeter Sig-Sauer behind his leg he started waving and jumping up and down.

"Hey, you! Inside there! Help!"

Capretz turned around.

"Help me!" Léon shouted.

Capretz came to the door, a puzzled look on his face that turned to concern when he didn't see Gallimard.

"It's your partner. He's down. I think he's had a heart attack."

The Orly terminal was a madhouse. July and August were the traditional months when Parisians took their vacations, and they streamed out of the city in hordes.

No one paid any particular attention to the three men who entered the main departures hall and went up to the offices on the mezzanine level. Two of them, Bob Roningen and Don Cladstrup, were field officers from the CIA's Paris Station. Beyond the fact they were both bulky, well-built men in their mid-forties, there was very little to distinguish them from the average businessman. Nor, apparently, was anything bothering them at the moment. They were doing something totally routine.

The third man, however, was extremely nervous, glancing over his shoulder from time to time as if he suspected someone was following them. He was Jean-Luc DuVerlie, an electro-mechanical engineer for the Swiss firm of ModTec, GmbH, and he was frightened that the information he'd come to Paris to give the CIA would cost him his life. He was having second thoughts about it.

They went down a short corridor, and at the far end Cladstrup knocked at the unmarked door.

DuVerlie looked back the way they had come, and Roningen shook his head.

"There's no one back there. We came in clean."

"But it is not your life at risk," the Swiss engineer said, his English good, but heavily accented. He was barrel-chested with a square face and extremely deep-set eyes beneath thick, bushy eyebrows. He looked like a criminal, or an ex-boxer who'd been beaten too many times in the ring.

"You came to us, remember?" Cladstrup said evenly.

DuVerlie nodded. "Maybe this was a mistake."

"Fine," Roningen said, holding out his hands. "Why don't we just call it quits here and now? You go your way and we go ours."

"They would kill me. Within twenty-four hours I would be a dead man. I have explained this. You don't know these people."

"Neither do you."

"I know what they are capable of doing. I told you, I saw it with my own eyes."

"When you show us, we'll go from there," Cladstrup said, as the door was buzzed open. They went inside where they turned over their plane tickets and passports to the French passport control officer behind a desk. A second policeman, armed, stood to one side.

"You're booked on flight 145 for Geneva, is that correct?" the passport officer asked stamping the exit visas.

"That's right," Roningen said.

The cop looked up at DuVerlie with mild interest, then handed back their documents. "It leaves in thirty minutes. There is coffee and tea in the waiting area. Maurice will show you the way and he will stay with you until it is time to board. You will be the last on the aircraft. And please do not try to leave the waiting area until you are told. *Comprenez-vous?* Do you understand?"

"Yes, thank you," Roningen said, and they followed the second officer out where they took another corridor nearly the length of the terminal building to a small but pleasantly furnished VIP lounge. The windows overlooked the flight line where the plane they would board would be pulling up momentarily. No one else was using the lounge this morning.

A telephone on the wall buzzed, and the cop answered it.

"After you have seen their weapons cache, as I have, then you will have to believe me," DuVerlie said.

"It'll be a start," Roningen said. "And the body."

"It's there unless the police have discovered it. Leitner was an important engineer. Perhaps the best at ModTec."

"What was he giving those people?" Cladstrup asked, looking over toward the cop who was still talking on the phone.

"First I will prove to you that they mean business. And then we will discuss what you will do for me."

"We'll see."

"You know they killed him because he was stupid. He threatened to go to the police unless they gave him more money. But the police couldn't help him."

"So he told you instead."

"We were friends," DuVerlie said. "I was supposed to be his insurance."

"Right," Roningen said wearily. Already he was getting tired of the man, but Langley thought DuVerlie's story was interesting enough for at least a preliminary follow-up. Depending on what they found or didn't find in Lausanne, they would decide what to do next. But the Swiss engineering firm built, among other things, electronic triggers for nuclear weapons.

Capretz had the presence of mind to grab his weapon from the desk before he rushed across to the van. Something was drastically wrong but he couldn't put it together. The phone was out of order; no matter what number he dialed he was connected to a recording asking him to wait. And now this.

Thumbing the Uzi's safety to the off position he came around to the open door at the rear of the van. Léon was a couple of yards off to his right.

Gallimard was down and not moving inside the van. Something was definitely wrong. "Eugène," Capretz called out. He didn't know what to do.

"Something happened to him and he just collapsed," Léon said, excitedly. "Maybe it's his heart. Do you know CPR?"

"He has nothing the matter with his heart."

"Well, I don't know. He didn't say anything. He just fell down."

"Eugène," Capretz called and stepped closer. There was something on the side of Gallimard's head, but the interior of the van was in relative darkness and Capretz couldn't make it out. But he understood that he was going to have to call for help somehow.

He turned to ask the Air Service man if there was a two-way radio in the van in time to see a large pistol suddenly materialize in the man's hand. The first shot hit him in the right arm, driving him nearly off his feet. He started to bring the Uzi around, when a thunderclap burst in his head.

Shoving the pistol in the belt of his coveralls, Léon safetied the Uzi, laid it in the back of the van and then hefted the security guard's body in the back as well.

Closing the door, he scuffed dirt over the bloodstains on the road so that if anyone came along they would not notice that anything had happened here.

Around front he raised the road barrier, then went into the hut where he took the phone off the hook, listened, then replaced it. He wore thin leather gloves so that he would leave no fingerprints, and the patterns in the soles of his boots were common. He'd purchased the boots at Prisunic, a discount store in Paris, five days ago. They were untraceable, as was the van which was nevertheless legitimately registered to Air Service here at the airport, though the company did not own it.

He drove beyond the barrier, then went back and lowered it.

Behind the wheel he checked his watch before he headed the rest of the way to the ILS installation just off the end of the main east-west runway. He had twenty-eight minutes to go.

2

Kirk Cullough McGarvey had always had bad luck with women, especially saying goodbye to them. This instance was no different, except that it was the second time he was saying goodbye to Marta Fredricks.

"I don't understand why you don't just come back to Lausanne with me now," she said. They sat together in the back seat of a taxi heading out of Paris to Orly Airport. She was tall, athletically thin and wore her dark hair long, nearly to the center of her back.

"I have a few more things to take care of here first," he said. "And I think it'll be better all the way around if you pave the way."

She looked into his eyes and smiled. "You're probably right. And then?"

They'd avoided that subject for the week she'd been with him in Paris. And then what, he asked himself. He was quitting Europe, and returning to his ex-wife Kathleen in Washington, D.C. Or at least he and she were going to give it a try.

Tall and husky, McGarvey was a good-looking man with wide, honest eyes that sometimes were green and other times gray. He was in his mid-forties and had lived in Europe for a number of years, including a time in Lausanne where he'd run a small bookshop as a cover. He'd been in hiding then, as he supposed he still was. Once a spy, always a spy.

He'd been a loner for the most part, though in Switzerland he and Marta had lived together. Ex-CIA assassins made the Swiss nervous, and Marta, who worked for the Swiss Federal Bureau of Police, had been assigned to watch him. "Watch you, not fall in love with you," she told him once. "That I did all on my own."

She was looking at the passing scenery, and he studied her profile. A blood vessel was throbbing in the side of her long, delicate neck. She'd come as a complete surprise, showing up on his doorstep last week.

"I heard you were in Paris. Thought I'd drop by to say hello while I was in town."

She'd moved in with him, of course. They'd had no discussion about that, because she was still in love with him.

But she had brought, besides her presence, a flood of memories for him. Some of them good, or at least tolerable, but most of them difficult. What spy looks back on his past with any joy? Or what soldier, for that matter, looks back at past battles with any fondness? They had been at war. And he had killed in the fight. Not a day went by without some thought for the people whose lives he'd ended. Sometimes he'd been close enough to see the expressions on their faces when they realized they were dying. Pain and fear, of course, but most often their last emotion had been surprise.

He especially remembered the face of the general he'd been sent to kill in Santiago, Chile. The man had been responsible for thousands of deaths, and the only solution was his elimination. But McGarvey's orders had been changed in midstream without him knowing about it. He returned to Langley not a hero but a pariah, and the CIA had released him from his contract.

Switzerland had come next, and then Paris when the Agency had called him out of retirement for a "job of work" as his old friend John Lyman Trotter, Jr., had once called an assignment.

More death, more destruction, more pain and heartache. He'd lost a kidney in the war. He'd nearly lost his life. He'd lost his wife, and the loneliness, that at times was nearly crushing, rode on his shoulder like the world on Atlas's. He figured he could write the book on the subject.

"Good thoughts or bad," Marta asked, breaking him out of his morose thoughts.

He focused on her. She was studying his face, a bemused expression on her's.

"I think I'll miss Paris."

"You're leaving for good, aren't you," she said. "And somehow I don't think you'll be resettling in Lausanne."

"I haven't decided yet," he lied, and he managed a smile. "Besides, I don't think your boss would be very happy having me on his turf again."

"Something could be arranged."

"Maybe I'd get called up."

She shook her head in irritation. "You're getting too old for war games, Kirk. And you must have noticed by now that the Russians have gone home. The Wall is down, the Warsaw Pact has been dismantled—they're holding free elections in Poland, for God's sake—and all the bad guys are in jail."

"No fool like an old fool."

"The CIA can't afford you," she said. "Maybe it never could." She searched his eyes earnestly. "Didn't Portugal teach you anything?"

"How did you hear about that?"

"I'm a cop, remember? I see things, I read things. People confide in me."

"Is that why you came to Paris, Mati? To save my life?"

"And your soul."

"It's not for sale. Maybe it never was." Every spy has his own worse nightmare. Arkady Kurshin had been his. But the Russian was dead. He'd seen the man's body just before it was lowered into a pauper's grave outside of Lisbon seven months ago.

"I love you, Kirk, doesn't that count for something?"

It had been his fault, of course, allowing her to set up housekeeping in his apartment. But the excuse he'd made to himself was that he was tired, gun-shy, rubbed raw, vulnerable, even, and he needed her warmth and comfort just then.

"It counts for a lot, Mati. But maybe it would be best if I didn't come to Lausanne after all. You're right, I have no intention of staying there, or anywhere else in Europe, for that matter."

"You're going home?"

"For awhile."

Marta was silent for a moment. "But I thought you might want to come to Switzerland at least to visit your daughter. She's still in school outside Bern, isn't she?"

"She'll be home for Thanksgiving. I'll see her then."

"What are you telling me now, Kirk? That you're going back to your ex-wife? I thought she was going to marry her lawyer, the one who was always suing you."

"Stay out of it."

"She dumped you once because of the business. Are your hands any cleaner now?" An hysterical edge was beginning to creep into Marta's voice. She'd changed over the past few years. She'd lost some of her old control.

"Let it rest, Mati," he said gently.

"They why did you let me move in with you? To make a fool of myself?"

"Could I have stopped you?"

She started to reply, but the words died on her lips. He was right, and she suddenly knew it. Just as she knew that indeed it was over between them. He could see how the light and passion faded from her eyes, and she slumped back.

"What will you do with yourself in Washington?" she asked after a couple of minutes.

"Maybe I'll open another bookstore. Maybe teach at a small university somewhere."

"You'll get bored."

"All the bad guys are gone, remember?"

She looked at him again. "Somehow I think you'll manage to find some. Or they'll find you."

"I'll leave that to cops like you."

The cabbie pulled up at Orly's Departing Passengers entrance for Swissair, and McGarvey helped Marta out with her single carryon bag. The day was warm and humid, and out here the air smelled of car and bus exhaust, and burned jet fuel.

"I'll leave you here, Mati. I hate long goodbyes."

Marta looked at her watch. It was past eight. "My plane leaves in fifteen minutes. You can give me that much time, can't you? After all, it'll probably be years before I see you again."

McGarvey shrugged. "Go ahead. I'll pay the driver and catch up with you."

"Don't stand me up."

"I'll be right in," McGarvey said, and he watched as she crossed the sidewalk and went into the terminal. He turned, and as he was paying the cabbie he noticed a brown Peugeot parked across the way. The diplomatic plates were of the series used by the U.S. Embassy. He'd had lunch with Tom Lynch, the Paris chief of station, last week, and Lynch had been driving a car with the same series.

"*Merci, monsieur*," the driver said, but McGarvey just nodded and went inside where he caught up with Marta. What the hell was the CIA doing out here this morning, he wondered?

3

At 8:20 A.M., the man whose nametag read Léon got out of the bogus Air Service van and studied the distant airport terminal through a set of powerful binoculars. The end of this morning's active runway was a little more than a half mile to the east. The wind, light but steady, was coming almost directly out of the west. Swissair flight 145 would be taking off directly toward him.

In the past eighteen minutes, five jet airliners had taken off or landed. Orly was busy this morning, as usual at this time of year. None of them had been the flight he was interested in. He knew that for a certainty because he could see the Swissair jetliner parked at its boarding gate in the distance.

Léon was not his real name. In fact he was Karl Boorsch, who had been employed by STASI, the East German secret service, until late in 1989 when the Communist Party in Eastern Europe had begun to fall apart. He had managed to get out of the Horst Wessel Barracks in East Berlin just minutes before a crowd of angry demonstrators had broken in and started tearing up the place.

Most of the others had been rounded up in the next few months, but Boorsch went to ground, not lifting his head even to sniff the air until the first call had come from Monaco in the form of a brief advertisement for H.W. to come home, all was forgiven.

He smiled, recalling that day. Since then there had been plenty of work for all of them. Especially over the last year when they'd started the project.

Old alliances, he thought, were the best. Or in this case certainly the most interesting and rewarding. And when the project was completed, there would be other work. A lot of work.

He tossed the binoculars in on the seat of the van, then went around to the back and opened the door. Climbing in, he had to crawl over the second French cop, getting a little blood on the side of one of his boots. It didn't bother him. He'd seen enough blood in his ten years with STASI, since his eighteenth birthday right out of *Gymnasium*, to be totally inured to it.

Pushing the first cop's body out of the way, he pulled the long metal case back to the open door. The box was heavy, and it took an effort to drag it that far.

He jumped down and looked back the way he had come, and then toward the active runway. Nothing moved along the dirt access road, but what looked like a French Air Inter jetliner had pulled away from the terminal and was moving slowly along a taxiway. That would be flight seventeen. It and one other were scheduled for takeoff before the Swissair flight left for Geneva.

Around front he studied the taxiing plane through binoculars to make sure he'd identified it correctly. He had. Next he got the secure walkie-talkie from beside the seat and keyed the READY TO TALK button.

"One," he said. He pressed the TRANSMIT button and his digitally recorded word was encrypted, compressed into a one-microsecond burst and transmitted. The on-air duration of the transmission was so short that even automatic recording equipment picked up nothing, not even a brief burst of static.

"Clear," the man watching the highway turnoff to the access road responded.

"Two."

"In place," the second man replied. He was somewhere within sight of the terminal's front entrance.

"Three."

"Quiet," the third man answered. He was on the N7 somewhere between here and Paris, monitoring the French Police frequencies for any unusual traffic. There was none.

Replacing the walkie-talkie, Boorsch again studied the jetliner, which had reached the end of the runway and was slowly turning. Seconds later the big aircraft seemed to lurch forward as if the pilot had suddenly let up on the brakes, and it started its takeoff roll.

Boorsch watched a couple of seconds longer, then put the binoculars down and stood back as the American built DC-10 thundered directly at him, its nose finally rotating, its main landing gear lifting off the pavement, and suddenly the huge bird was passing directly overhead, the noise so loud rational thought was all but impossible.

He thought he caught a glimpse of a few passengers looking down at him from the tiny windows, but then the plane was climbing, seemingly straight up into the blue, cloudless sky, the sounds from its engines fading in the distance.

Already Air France flight 248 was bumping down the taxiway, the last before the Swissair flight.

Boorsch watched as it reached the end of the runway, hesitate for a moment, and then turn, accelerating even before it was completely lined up.

This was an A-320 Airbus, the same type of aircraft as Swissair 145, and Boorsch watched it with critical interest as it lumbered heavily down the runway toward him. Its nose gear rose from the pavement, and the big airliner seemed to hang there like that for a long time before the mains lifted off, and then it was roaring overhead and climbing.

Boorsch turned and watched as its landing gear retracted, and when it was only a tiny speck in the sky he glanced back toward the distant terminal—the Swissair jetliner was still at the boarding gate—before he went to the rear of the van.

Unlatching the lid on the long metal box he flipped it open. For a moment or two he just stared at what the case contained, but then he reached inside and ran his fingertips lovingly over the nearly four-foot-long Stinger ground-to-air missile, and smiled.

4

In the Orly Airport's Security Operations room the direct line from the control tower buzzed.

Police Sergeant Marie-Lure Germain answered it. "Security, Germain."

"Ah, Marie-Lure, there's an Air Service truck parked by the inner marker just off the end of zero-eight. What are you showing in your log?"

"Just a moment, Raymond," she said. Raymond Flammarion was the day shift tower supervisor. He was a stickler for detail. No one liked him but everyone respected his abilities.

Nothing appeared on the situation board which showed activity in and around the airport. She turned back to her console. "Nothing here."

"Well, I am looking at the van through binoculars this very moment, *ma cherie*. The rear door is open, but I don't see anybody out there. And you know, considering Interpol's warning . . ."

"I'll check it out."

"Please do, and get back to me. There's not an aircraft in or out today that is not completely full, if you catch my meaning."

"Give me a minute, Raymond. Somebody probably forgot to file." Marie-Lure hung up, and punched up the number for the gate guard hut out there on her operations phone. The connection was made immediately and the number began to ring.

At twenty-three, Marie-Lure was one of the youngest members of Orly's security staff which, augmented as it was just now from the Police Contingency Pool out of Paris, numbered nearly one hundred people. But she was conscientious and professional. She'd been trained at the Academie de Police in Paris, and had graduated in the top five percent of her class.

After five rings without answer, she broke the connection and redialed. Again there was no answer. It was possible the phone was out of order, and it was possible that both officers had stepped away from the hut. But just now it was bothersome.

She put down the phone and beckoned the shift supervisor, Lieutenant Jacques Bellus, who ponderously got up from behind his desk on the raised dias and came over. He'd accepted an early retirement two years ago as a Chief Inspector with the Paris Police to take this job. It was much safer.

"Have the bad people finally arrived?" he asked.

"Flammarion has spotted an Air Service maintenance truck off the end of zero-eight. He wants to know what we have on it."

Bellus glanced up at the situation board.

"We show nothing," Marie-Lure said. "And now there is no answer from security out there."

"Who is on duty this morning?"

Marie-Lure brought up the information on her computer. "Capretz and Gallimard."

Bellus grunted. "Have you called Air Service?"

"I didn't want to alarm anyone yet."

"Well, call them, and I'll try the guard hut again," Bellus said and he picked up the operations phone.

Marie-Lure telephoned the Air Service Dispatch Office across the field at the Air France Service Hangar. The dispatcher answered on the first ring.

"Air Service."

"This is Orly Security. What are your people doing out at the inner marker off zero-eight this morning? We're showing nothing on our board."

"There shouldn't be anyone there, so far as I know," the young man replied. "*Moment.*"

Marie-Lure could hear the shuffle of papers, and a couple of seconds later the dispatcher was back.

"The work order is here. Apparently some *mec* stuck it in the wrong order. Looks like an unscheduled adjustment on the marker frequency. Sorry, but I didn't know a thing about this. Someone will get the axe."

"Send a runner over with a copy of the work order, would you?"

"As soon as possible. We're busy this morning."

"*Merci.*" Marie-Lure hung up.

Bellus shook his head and hung up. "Still no answer. What'd Air Service have to say for itself?"

"The work order was apparently misplaced. They'll send it over as soon as they can."

"Have we got anybody nearby this morning?"

"I think Dubout might still be over by one-eight. He could get over the back way, but he'd have to cross the runway."

"Get him on the radio, and then get authorization from the tower."

"Do you want to delay air traffic for a few minutes?" she asked.

Bellus pondered the suggestion for a moment, but then shook his head. "As long as it's a legitimate Air Service order, I don't think that's necessary."

"Yes, sir," Marie-Lure said, and she got on the airport security frequency to raise Sergeant Dubout.

The passengers on Swissair 145 would be in the final boarding process by now. Boorsch stood out of sight from anyone who might be looking this way from the tower or the terminal, and studied the plane with the binoculars. The boarding tunnel was still in place, but the baggage compartment hatches in the belly of the Airbus had been closed, and the baggage handlers had withdrawn.

The air was suddenly very still and thick with the odors of the airport and of Paris. French smells, somehow, that Boorsch found offensive. Frogs were filthy people, even worse than the sub-human Polaks or Kikes, although France itself was a pleasant enough country.

Boorsch lowered the glasses, then raised them again to study the tower, and then the maintenance hangars across from the main terminal. Normal activity, so far as he could see. Nothing out of the ordinary. If any alarms had been sounded, they were not outwardly visible.

Sooner or later, of course, airport security would realize that something might be wrong with their access road guards out here, though the presence of this van would cause no real questions. He'd personally taken care of that earlier this morning during the shift change at the Air Service Dispatch office.

Someone would come out to investigate. That was why his timing had to be so tight. Only minutes now and he would be finished here and he could make his escape.

Laying the glasses aside, Boorsch carefully removed the Stinger missile and its handheld launcher from its metal container. The unit, which was about four feet long and a little less than four inches in diameter, weighed thirty-one pounds, including the reusable launcher and the rocket with its solid-fuel propellant, high-explosive warhead and infrared heat-seeking guidance system.

In theory the missile was simple to use. Point it at a heat-emitting target. Uncage the firing circuits, and when the missile's sensing circuitry locked on to a viable target a steady tone would sound in the operator's ear. At that moment the user pushed the fire button, and the Stinger was away, accelerating almost immediately to a speed of one thousand feet a second, with an effective range of four thousand yards.

In practice however, first-time users almost always missed even the easiest of targets. Like using a shotgun to shoot clay pigeons, the operator needed to lead the target . . . especially an accelerating target such as a jetliner taking off.

Of the six ex-STASI comrades who'd trained with the Stinger in Libya, Boorsch had been the best, so when this emergency had developed, he'd been the natural choice for the assignment.

"Don't let us down, Karl," he'd been instructed. "This is important to the project. Very important."

The walkie-talkie in the front of the van came to life. "Three," the man patrolling the N7 transmitted.

Carefully laying the missile down, Boorsch hurried around to the front, and snatched up the walkie-talkie. "Three, go," he radioed.

"Trouble on its way across the field from one-eight."

"ETA?"

"Under five minutes."

"Understand," Boorsch responded. "One?"

"Clear."

"Two?"

"Clear."

Boorsch laid the walkie-talkie down and went to the rear of the van where he grabbed the binoculars and scanned the field in the vicinity of the end of north-south runway. A jeep was just crossing the runway itself.

He turned the glasses toward the Swissair flight. The boarding tunnel had still not been withdrawn. There was time. But not much of it, he thought as he laid the binoculars down and pulled out his pistol.

5

McGarvey had to show his passport to follow Marta through security to the boarding gate, and it struck him that everyone out here seemed a little tense. It was probably another terrorist threat. The French took such things very seriously.

Most of the passengers for the Swissair flight had already boarded, leaving the waiting area empty except for one flight attendant and two boarding gate personnel, one of whom was making the boarding announcement over the terminal's public address system.

"Ladies and gentlemen. All passengers holding confirmed seats for Swissair flight 145, non-stop service to Geneva, please board now. Flight 145 is in the final boarding process. *Mesdames et messieurs* . . ."

"I don't want to go like this, Kirk," Marta said, looking up into his eyes. "I have a feeling I'll never see you again."

"I'm not what you think I am, Mati. I never was."

"I knew what you were from the beginning," she said earnestly. "And I love you despite it."

McGarvey had to smile. "Not a very good basis for a relationship."

The flight attendant was looking pointedly at them as the gate person finished the final boarding call in German.

"I'm not proud. I'll take you any way I can get you."

Something was wrong. Some internal warning system was ringing bells at the back of McGarvey's head. It was the CIA car outside, he couldn't put it out of his mind. What were they doing here now? Watching him?

"Listen, Mati, do me a favor and wait right here. I don't want you getting aboard that plane for a minute. I need to make a call first."

Marta glanced over at the attendant by the open door to the boarding tunnel. "What is it?"

"Probably nothing," McGarvey said. "Just hang on." He went over to the counter. "May I use your house phone?" he asked the attendant who'd just finished making the boarding announcement.

"The lady must get aboard now, sir, or she will miss her flight," the young man said.

"May I use your house phone? It's very important."

The attendant hesitated a moment, but then sighed and handed over the handset. "What number would you like, sir?"

"The airport security duty officer."

A look of alarm crossed the attendant's face. "Sir, is something wrong?"

"I don't know. Get me the number, please."

"Yes, sir."

A moment later the call went through. "Security, Bellus."

"Monsieur Bellus, my name is Kirk McGarvey. I am an American."

"*Oui, monsieur*, what can I do for you?"

"One or more of my countrymen, from my embassy . . . security officers . . . are presently somewhere here at the airport. It is imperative that I talk with them. Immediately."

"I don't know what you are talking about, Monsieur McGarvey, but I am very busy . . ."

"You do know. Call them, and give them my name. Please, this is important."

"Where are you calling from?"

"Boarding gate E17."

"Swissair?"

"Yes, please hurry."

"I will require an explanation."

"Yes, of course."

The line went silent. Everyone was looking at him. Marta came over.

"What's wrong?" she asked.

He shook his head. The flight attendant had come over from the boarding tunnel door and was watching.

Bellus was back a minute later. "Monsieur McGarvey. The answer is that unless your message is extremely urgent, they'd ask you to contact the appropriate . . . office at your embassy."

"I see."

"Is it extremely urgent?"

McGarvey looked out at the Swissair jetliner. "No. I thought they were friends and I just wanted to say hello."

"Pardon me, monsieur if I find that odd, since you will be flying to Geneva aboard the same aircraft. You are at E17?"

"Yes," McGarvey said. "Actually I didn't know if they'd arrived. I'm terribly sorry to have bothered you."

"Are you a resident of Paris, Monsieur McGarvey?"

"Yes," McGarvey said. He gave the cop the number of his apartment on the rue Lafayette in the tenth Arrondissement.

"And you are known at this address, and by your embassy?"

"Yes, of course."

"I will verify this, Monsieur. Have a good flight."

"*Oui, merci.*" McGarvey hung up.

"Well?" Marta asked.

"It was nothing," he said and he kissed her. "Goodbye, Mati."

"Just like that?" she asked, her eyes filling again.

He nodded. "Have a good flight." He turned and walked off without looking back.

"What was that all about?" Cladstrup asked as Roningen came back from the telephone. DuVerlie was across the room out of earshot if they talked softly.

"Does the name Kirk McGarvey ring any bells?"

Cladstrup had to laugh. "You'd better believe it. I was just coming into the Company when he was being booted out. Late seventies. Something to do with Chile, I think. He screwed up."

"He's living here in Paris, and he was involved with that incident at our embassy this winter."

"That's what I heard."

"Well, he's apparently here at the airport, and he called security and asked to speak to us."

"By name?" Cladstrup asked.

"I guess not, but I told Bellus that I'd speak to him if he had something urgent for us. Apparently he didn't, because he backed off. But get this: Bellus thinks he might be on this flight. He called from E17 next door."

"Is his name on the manifest?"

"No, but that doesn't mean anything."

"What the hell?" Cladstrup glanced over toward DuVerlie. "Do you suppose there's any connection?"

"Would you recognize him if you saw him?"

"I could pick him out of a crowd."

"Go see if he's aboard, and I'll call Lynch and find out if he knows what's going on."

DuVerlie jumped up from where he was seated, but Cladstrup

waved him back. "It'll be just a minute," he told him, going over to the French cop at the door to the boarding tunnel. "I'm going to check out the plane before we board."

"As you wish," the cop said, stepping aside.

Cladstrup entered the boarding tunnel and hurried out to the plane, where he showed their tickets and his identification to the stews. "We'll be just a minute," he said. "Is everyone else aboard?"

"Yes, sir. I believe so," one of the women said. "The preliminary headcount tallies except for you and the other two gentlemen with you. You'll be the only three in first class."

"Every other seat is taken?"

"Yes, sir."

"Mind if I look?"

The captain was watching from the cockpit. "Have we got a problem?" he asked.

"Not at all, Captain. There's a possibility someone we know may be aboard. I'd like to check it out."

"Make it snappy, I want to get out of here on time."

"Will do," Cladstrup said, and he turned and made a quick walkthrough. McGarvey was not among the passengers.

"Is your friend aboard?" the head stew asked.

"No," Cladstrup said. "I'll be right back." He hurried back up the boarding tunnel to the VIP lounge. Roningen was just getting off the phone.

"He's not aboard," Cladstrup said. "What'd Lynch have to say?"

"He hasn't heard anything either, but he'll check it out."

"In the meantime?"

"We go to Geneva. What else?"

The American-designed but French-built jeep bumped along the dusty road just off the end of the active runway. From where Boorsch watched from the back of the van, he could only see the one man behind the wheel, and no one else.

This one was probably a supervisor and had been sent out to check on the gate guards. There'd be no reason for him to bother with a maintenance man on an apparently legitimate call.

But the cop would have to pass right by the van, which was exactly what Boorsch wanted. He couldn't afford to have a cop at his back, cutting off his escape route.

When the jeep was about twenty yards away, Boorsch stepped out from behind the van, and waved. The jeep slowed almost immediately.

He knew that he was in plain sight now of anyone with a good set of binoculars who might be watching from the tower, but it could not be helped. He could see with the naked eye that the Swissair jetliner had been backed away from the boarding gate and was now turning out toward the taxiway. Time was running short.

Boorsch walked up onto the road as the jeep pulled up. "Hello. Good morning."

"Good morning," the cop said. His name tag read Dubout. "How is it going out here?"

"I have a little problem. I'm happy that you came along. I need a second set of hands for just a moment. It's that damn antenna assembly."

"It'll have to wait. First I have to check on my people."

Boorsch glanced back in the direction of the guard hut about two miles away. "What, you mean those two at the gate? I don't think it's their fault."

Dubout's eyes narrowed slightly. "You saw them?"

"Of course. How'd you suppose I got out here?"

"What did you mean: Their fault?"

"The phone, that's why you're out here, isn't it? Their phone is out of order. They asked me to have a look, but I think it's something wrong with the line. Probably at the box out on the highway."

"I'll check it out."

"Could I just get you to lend me a hand here? It'll only take a minute. Maybe less. I need someone to hold a pair of pliers while I tighten a bolt from the other side of the antenna case."

Dubout hesitated a moment.

"It won't take any time at all."

"All right," Dubout said, setting the parking brake and getting out.

"It's in the back of my van," Boorsch said. "Only take a few seconds."

"Well, let's get on with it."

"Sure," Boorsch said, letting the French cop come around the back of the van first. He pulled out his pistol at the same time Dubout reared back.

"*Mon Dieu.*"

Boorsch shoved him forward with his left hand so that they would both be out of sight of anyone watching from the control tower, and shot the man three times in the back of the head.

Dubout fell forward onto the missile's carrying case. Pocketing his gun, Boorsch shoved the man's body the rest of the way into the van.

He grabbed the binoculars and studied the far end of the runway. The Airbus had nearly reached the end of the taxiway. It would be taking off within the next sixty to ninety seconds.

Laying down the glasses he snatched up the walkie-talkie. Ordinarily he was calm under pressure, but he'd never had a chance to shoot down an airliner filled with people before. He was getting excited, and nervous.

"One," he keyed the transmitter.

"Clear."

"Two."

"Clear."

"Three."

"Clear. What about you?"

"It's good here," Boorsch said. The Airbus had turned onto the runway. "Stand by."

6

"Swissair one-four-five, you are cleared for immediate takeoff, runway two-six. Wind two-eight-zero at eight. Barometer two-niner-niner-seven. Switch to departure control at one-two-niner-point-zero-niner out of the pattern. Have a good day."

"Roger, tower, thank you," Captain Josef Elver said, advancing the throttles so that the big jetliner could make the turn onto the runway.

"The numbers are green," his first officer, Claude Piaget, said.

"Roger," Elver responded as the bird came around onto the runway's centerline. "Here we go." He advanced the throttles to the first position.

"Rolling," Elver said as the A-320 started down the runway, ponderously at first, like a lumbering ox. Ridiculous to think that anything so huge, that weighed so much, could possibly fly.

"On the numbers," Piaget said calmly.

The runway marker lights began to flash past them in a blur. Captain Elver quickly scanned the flight instruments in front of him, taking his eyes off the view outside the windscreen for only a moment.

"Vee-one," Piaget warned to his right.

The Airbus was gathering speed rapidly now, and instead of sluggishly responding to his touch the rudder pedals and side-stick controller had come alive. They were flying, almost.

"Vee-R," Piaget said.

"Rotate." Elver eased back on the jet fighter-type stick to his left, and the jetliner's nose came smoothly off the surface of the runway. With his right hand, he maintained the throttles all the way to their stops, and the plane seemed to surge forward.

"My numbers are green," Piaget said.

The jetliner's speed was approaching one hundred sixty knots, well into the partial flaps-down flying speed envelope for their weight. The runway markers were a complete blur.

"Vee-two," Piaget announced.

"Lifting off," Elver said, easing the stick back and the Airbus came off the runway, almost by itself, the bumpy ride instantly disappearing.

"On the numbers," the first officer advised.

"Begin reducing flaps," Elver ordered, and Piaget began retracting them. Their speed immediately started to increase and Elver eased the stick farther back, the plane barreling up into the cloudless sky.

Once out of the pattern, flaps up and landing gear retracted, Elver planned on turning over control to Piaget so that he could go back to the head. He was picking up a bug of some kind, and frankly, he felt like hell.

Boorsch's stomach was tied in knots. He'd known excitement in his life, and he had been anticipating this moment ever since he'd gotten the call forty-eight hours ago. But he'd never expected anything could give him such a lift, such intense pleasure as this.

The Stinger missile and launcher were comfortably heavy on his right shoulder where he stood behind the Air Service van. He could hear the roar of the huge Airbus, and he knew that it was off the ground now.

It was time.

Stepping away from the rear of the van, he raised the Stinger, finding and centering the jetliner's bulk in the launcher's sights. The plane was climbing directly toward him, impossibly loud and impossibly huge.

He no longer cared if he was visible from the tower. At this point no power on earth could prevent what was about to happen.

He lost the aircraft in the Stinger's sights, but then got it again, centering the engine on the portside wing in the inner ring.

With his cheek on the conductance bar, he thumbed the missile's activation switch and the launcher began to warble.

"A miss almost always comes from too early a shot," the words of their instructor echoed in his ears. "In this business one must have the patience of Allah."

Allah had nothing to do with it, but Boorsch did understand timing. The Stinger was a fine weapon, but it could not produce miracles.

"Give it a chance and it will perform for you as you wish."

The jetliner was climbing now at an increasingly steep angle, its engines producing their maximum thrust and therefore their maximum heat.

He pushed the forward button, uncaging the missile's infrared seeker head. Almost instantly the tone in his ear changed, rising to a high-pitched scream as the missile locked on to its target.

Still Boorsch waited, certain that by now someone in the tower must have spotted him and called security. Soon the airport and surrounding highways would be crawling with cops.

The Airbus passed directly overhead, and Boorsch led it perfectly.

At the last moment he raised the sights slightly, pulled the trigger, and the missile was off, the launcher bucking against his shoulder no harder than a 20-gauge shotgun.

7

"*Mon Dieu*! Raymond," one of the tower operators shouted in alarm.

The moment they had spotted the lone figure emerging from behind the Air Service van, with what even at this distance was clearly recognizable as some sort of a missile, Flammarion had gotten on the phone to security with one hand and on the radio to flight 145 with the other.

The Swissair copilot came back first. "Swissair one-four-five."

For an instant Flammarion stood with his mouth open, hardly believing what he was seeing with his own eyes. The missile had been fired.

"Abort! Abort!" he screamed into the microphone.

"Security, Bellus," a voice on the telephone answered.

"Say again, tower?" the Swissair copilot answered calmly.

The missile's exhaust trail was clearly visible in contrast against the perfectly blue sky. About one hundred feet above the ground it made a slight loop before it began its graceful curve up and to the west directly behind the departing jetliner.

In that short instant it struck Flammarion that the weapon was a live thing; a wild animal stalking its prey, which in effect it was.

But it was so incredibly fast.

"Abort!" he shouted as the missile suddenly disappeared.

For a split second Flammarion's breath was caught in his throat. Something had happened. The missile had malfunctioned. It had destroyed itself in mid-air. It had simply disintegrated, the pieces falling to earth much too small to be seen from this distance.

A fireball began to blossom around the engine on the left wing. Suddenly it grew to tremendous proportions, and pieces of the jetliner—these big enough to easily be distinguished from this distance—began flying everywhere.

Something had struck them on the port side, and the Airbus began to sag in that direction, slowly at first, but with a sickeningly increasing acceleration.

Alarms were flashing and buzzing all over the place, and Elver's panel was lit in red.

"We've lost our portside engine," Piaget shouted.

"I can't hold it," Elver shouted. "She's going over!" He had the stick and right rudder pedal all the way to their stops, but still the jetliner continued to dive as she rolled over to port.

He thought it was almost as if they had lost their left wing. *The entire wing!*

His co-pilot, Piaget, who had been on the radio with the tower, was speaking loudly but calmly into the microphone. "Mayday, mayday, mayday! This is Swissair one-four-five, just off the end of runway two-six. We've lost control. We're going in. We're going in. Mayday, mayday, mayday!"

Elver reached out and chopped all power to the starboard engine. The powerful thrust on that wing was helping to push them over.

Piaget should be given a commendation for his coolness and dedication under pressure. It was just a fleeting thought, replaced by the certainty that none of them were likely to survive beyond the next fifteen or twenty seconds.

The reduced thrust on the starboard wing seemed to have the effect of slowing their port roll, but only for a moment or two. Then they continued over.

"Mayday, mayday, mayday . . . !" Piaget was shouting into the microphone.

The ground was very close now. Looking out the windshield Elver estimated their altitude at less than one hundred feet.

He could hear people screaming in utter terror and hopelessness back in the passenger compartment, but a moment of calmness came over him now that he knew for sure he was going to die.

It was happening too fast, Elver thought. And much sooner than he'd ever expected.

The moment before impact he reached out for the master electrical switches.

"*Putain,*" the cabbie swore, and he suddenly jammed on the brakes and hauled the taxi over to the side of the highway.

McGarvey, seated in the back, had been thinking about the last

time he and Marta had parted. That had been Lausanne, several
years ago. She'd been sitting in their kitchen, and on his way out
with his suitcase, he looked back in at her. A pistol lay on the table,
but she made no move to reach for it.

He wondered what he would have done had she picked it up and
pointed it at him. He supposed he would have done exactly as he had
done.

He was shoved violently forward. At first he thought they'd hit
something. The driver was looking back the way they had come even
before he'd brought the taxi to a complete halt.

"*Qu-est qu'il-y-a?*" McGarvey shouted, irritated, but then he
turned and looked in the same direction as the driver, and his gut
instantly tightened.

An airliner was down. A huge ball of fire and smoke billowed up
into the clear sky to the southwest. He'd heard no noise, partly
because of the distance, partly because of the traffic noises, and
partly because the cabbie had been playing the radio very loud.

Traffic on the N7 was coming to a standstill as McGarvey jumped
out of the cab. It was definitely a downed airliner, and he knew in his
heart of hearts that it was the Swissair flight he'd just put Marta on.

The cabbie got out of the taxi and crossed himself. "They are all
dead," he muttered half under his breath.

A big puff of black, oily smoke was slowly dissipating in the air
not too far to the east, about where McGarvey figured the main
east-west runway ended. Below that, and a little farther east, the
faint traces of what appeared to be a small jet contrail also hung in
the air.

The trail was distorting on the very slight breeze, but it was still
identifiable.

McGarvey stared at it for a full second or more, willing himself
not to come to the conclusion that had formed almost instantly in
his mind. But it was inevitable.

The Swissair flight was down because someone standing near
the end of the runway had shot it down with a handheld ground-
to-air missile.

Either a Russian-made SA-7 *Strela*, or the American Stinger.
Both were readily available on the market for a couple of thousand
dollars each. And either would be effective in bringing down a
jetliner.

In the next minutes all efforts would be concentrated on the
crash site in a desperate effort to rescue anyone who might have
survived the crash. Allowing the man or men who had fired the
missile a chance to escape in the confusion.

Not if he could help it.

McGarvey shoved the cabbie aside, jumped behind the wheel
and took off, back toward the airport, the wrong way down the
highway.

8

Lieutenant Bellus finally made some sense of what Flammarion was screaming, and his blood went cold.

"It's crashed! It's down! Oh, God, there's fire everywhere! It's horrible!"

"Scramble the crash units," Bellus shouted.

"They're on their way! But I tell you no one can survive down there. Don't you see, the wing was off. It was gone, in pieces. They didn't have a chance."

"Calm yourself, Raymond, and tell me what happened," Bellus shouted.

Marie-Lure was taking a call, and her console was lit up like a Christmas tree, but she was staring at the shift supervisor.

"Oh, it's horrible! Horrible!"

"What happened to that airplane?" Bellus demanded. "Raymond, pull yourself together. Other lives may depend on this. Do you understand?"

"Yes, I see," Flammarion responded, calming down a little. "The fire units are halfway across the field. We're diverting all traffic to De Gaulle and Le Bourget."

"Very good. Now, exactly what happened?"

"It was a rocket, I think."

"What do you mean, a rocket? Was it a warplane? What?"

"No, from that Air Service van. I saw it with my own eyes,

Jacques. He held it on his shoulder, and fired it when one-four-five took off. Just after she lifted off."

"The Swissair flight?"

"Yes, yes. I thought it would be all right . . . but then there was a flash and the wing started to come off. They didn't have so much as a chance, Jacques."

Bellus held a hand over the telephone mouthpiece. "Is there any word from Capretz or Gallimard?" he asked Marie-Lure.

"Nothing yet."

"What about Dubout? He should be out there by now."

"He doesn't answer his radio."

"Who else is on the apron?"

"Péguy, Bourgois and Queneau."

"Tell them I want that Air Service maintenance man picked up. But tell them to be careful, he'll be dangerous."

"Sir?"

"He shot down the Airbus, and it's got something to do with the Americans."

"My God."

Bellus turned back to the phone. Flammarion was babbling something. He had gone to pieces again.

"Listen to me, Raymond," Bellus said. "Listen. Can you still see that Air Service van out there?"

"What . . . the van? Yes, it's still there. I'm looking at it now. But your jeep is gone."

"Jeep? What jeep?"

"Your office asked permission for it to cross one-eight."

It was Dubout. "You say the van is still there. Do you see anybody there? Anybody nearby?"

"No, there's nobody."

"Do you see any bodies, Raymond. Any bodies in the vicinity of the van?"

"No."

"Anything lying on the ground?"

"Nothing."

"All right, Raymond. Now look around out there. Is there anything moving? Any sign of that jeep?"

"Are you crazy? Of course there's movement. Jeeps, ambulances, fire trucks."

"All going toward the crash. But look now, Raymond. Is there anybody *leaving* the scene? Is there anybody going in the opposite direction?"

"I don't know."

"Look," Bellus shouted. "This is important if we want to catch the bastard who did this."

"There are people dying out there. Burning to death."

"That's right. Now, can you see any movement *away* from the airport? That jeep?"

"Wait."

"Hurry, Raymond. There may not be much time," Bellus said, and he held his hand over the telephone's mouthpiece again.

Marie-Lure looked over. "They're on their way."

"*Bon.* Get my helicopter here on the double. Have Olivier pick me up just outside. Then get your weapon, you're coming with me. Marc can take over here."

"There it is," Flammarion shouted excitedly.

"Is it the jeep, Raymond?" Bellus asked.

"Yes, it's just beyond the crash. South."

Bellus looked up at the situation map on the wall, and visualized where the Airbus had gone down, and therefore where Flammarion was telling him the jeep was headed.

"He's headed toward the highway. The N7. Can you see that far?"

"No. He's gone. The fire and smoke. He's on the other side now."

"All right, Raymond, thank you very much, you have done a fine job. Go back to your duties now," Bellus said, and before Flammarion could reply he broke the connection.

"Three-minutes," Marie-Lure said.

"Go out and hold it, I'll be right there," Bellus said, and he punched up an outside line and dialed the confidential emergency number he and all French security people were supplied with for the American embassy in Paris. He had such a number for every embassy. The number was answered on the first ring. "Seven-eight-one-one."

"This is Orly Airport Police Lieutenant Jacques Bellus. Swissair flight one-four-five has crashed. I believe two or more of your people may have been aboard."

"One moment please," the woman said.

Two seconds later a man was on the line. "Lieutenant, my name is Tom Lynch. I'm a special assistant to the ambassador. What's this about Swissair one-four-five?"

"It has crashed, monsieur. Did you have people aboard? Messieurs Cladstrup and Roningcn, along with a third, unidentified gentleman?"

"Yes," Lynch said heavily. "What has happened?"

"Apparently someone shot that airplane out of the sky on takeoff."

"Shot . . . ? What the hell are you talking about?"

"With a missile."

"I'm on my way out."

"Yes, monsieur, your presence will be most helpful. There will be some questions, among them the name of another man who may have been aboard that airplane."

"We'll discuss that third man later . . ."

"No, monsieur, this is a fourth man. Kirk McGarvey."

Lynch said nothing.

"Is this name familiar to you?"

"Yes," Lynch said. "I'm on my way." The connection was broken.

As McGarvey raced back toward the airport, dodging traffic the wrong way on the divided highway, he tried to work out how the terrorist or terrorists had gotten through Orly's tight security, and then how the shooter expected to get away.

Another part of him forcefully held off any thought about Marta and the other people aboard the downed airliner, except for the CIA officers aboard. He didn't believe it was a coincidence. The shooter wanted those officers dead. Why?

The N7 throughroute ran south directly to the airport, with on-off ramps leading up to the terminal, before it plunged under the airport itself for 1400 yards, coming out on the opposite side of the east-west runways.

Traffic had come mostly to a standstill by now, but several accidents had occurred and he had to drive around the wrecks. In one case a large articulated truck had jackknifed across the highway apparently in an effort to avoid slamming into the rear end of a car that had stopped short. The truck had tipped over and blocked almost the entire width of the highway. No police were on the scene yet, but as McGarvey passed, the driver was crawling out of the cab. He looked unhurt.

The shooter had been positioned somewhere near the end of the active runway, which meant he'd been in plain sight of anyone in the tower.

But apparently no alarm had been raised, which meant the shooter must have been disguised to look as if he belonged there. Airport security, most likely. Or as a runway inspector, or a maintenance person working on one of the approach systems.

Afterward he would have simply driven off. Possible to a rendezvous point where he would transfer to another vehicle for his escape.

Check that, McGarvey thought.

If he had been in plain view of the tower before the shot, then he would have remained in plain view afterward. Only then he'd be known for what he was.

In addition, any movement at that end of the field *away* from the downed airliner would come under immediate suspicion.

Approaching the terminal ramp leading off the N7, McGarvey turned that last thought over. Something was there. Something he was missing.

He visualized what the situation had to be like across the field. The shooter brought the Airbus down. Then he got into his vehicle and went . . . where?

Toward the crash, of course. Where he would merge with other rescue units.

Or, if he had put the burning wreckage between himself and the tower, he would have disappeared for all practical purposes.

Long enough for . . . what?

To drive down to the N7, and come back this way, beneath the airport, back to Paris where he could easily meld into the background.

The logic was thin, McGarvey had to admit to himself, passing the terminal ramp. The highway dipped into the tunnel, no traffic whatsoever now. All of it must have been stopped on the other side of the crash site. But if the shooter had done anything else, if he had gone in the opposite direction, there'd be nothing McGarvey could do.

An Orly Security Police jeep with blue and white markings came directly toward him at a high rate of speed, its lights flashing, its siren blaring.

McGarvey had to swerve sharply to avoid a head-on collision, and as the jeep passed he got the distinct impression that the lone man behind the wheel wasn't dressed as a cop. He'd been dressed in white coveralls.

Definitely *not* a police uniform.

McGarvey slammed on the brakes, hauled the Citröen taxi around in a tight U-turn and accelerated after the jeep.

9

"It's gone now," Marie-Lure said as their Dassault helicopter broke through the thick cloud of greasy black smoke.

"Did it go into the tunnel?" Bellus demanded, angrily. They had spotted what they took to be the jeep heading down onto the N7, and Olivier Rambaud had cut through the dense smoke on the security chief's orders. He'd expected the terrorist to head south—*away* from the airport.

"It must have," Marie-Lure answered. She was studying the southbound lanes of the N7. "There's no sign of it now."

"Where the hell does he think he's going?"

"Paris?" Marie-Lure suggested.

"He wouldn't get far in that jeep."

"Maybe it wasn't him."

"Who else?" Bellus asked. He leaned forward and shouted to their pilot. "Cross the field . . . I want to get to the front of the terminal . . . the jeep is in the tunnel."

The pilot nodded and they peeled off to the north as he contacted the tower and told them his intentions. Nothing commercial was taking off or landing at Orly, but other helicopters were streaming toward the crash site from city hospitals and morgues. The tower was directing their movements to avoid any further tragedies.

"Lieutenant Bellus, are you there?"

Bellus wore a headset connected to the police frequency radio. He keyed the mike. "Here."

"They're dead, Jacques. All three of them." It was Queneau. The man sounded shook up.

"Where are you?"

"We're at the end of zero-eight. They're all in the back of the Air Service Van. They've been shot to death."

"Who are you talking about?" Bellus shouted, although he knew exactly who was in the back of that van.

"Capretz and Gallimard . . . and Christian. *Merde*. He was shot in the back of the head."

Bellus forced himself to calm down. "Is there anything else there, Phillipe? Anything we can use?"

Queneau didn't answer.

"Phillipe!"

"The missile launcher is in the back of the truck as well. The American Stinger."

"Secure the area," Bellus ordered. "No one is to touch anything. Anything at all, until the evidence team gets there. Do you understand?"

"*Oui*," Queneau said.

"Don't worry, Phillipe, we'll get the bastard!" Bellus said, and he pulled off the headset. Marie-Lure was watching out the windows, but her complexion had paled.

"We're taking no chances," Bellus told her.

She looked up.

"He is a killer. So we will shoot to kill if necessary."

She nodded, and looked back out the windows as they came over the top of the big terminal building just above where the N7 emerged from the tunnel. She stiffened. "There!"

Bellus followed her gaze. The jeep, its blue lights still flashing, was pulled up in front of the departing passenger entrances into the terminal. So far as he could tell it had been abandoned. The terrorist was either inside the terminal or someone had picked him up in front.

"Down there," he ordered the pilot, and as they descended he got back on the radio. "Security Central, Bellus."

"Security Central," his dispatcher answered.

"The bastard may be inside the terminal. I want it sealed. Now!"

"Yes, sir."

"And, Marc, did you hear Queneau?"

"Yes, sir."

"Spread the word."

A Citröen taxicab pulled up behind the jeep, and a man jumped out, glanced up at their helicopter, and then raced across the sidewalk and entered the terminal.

"Who the hell was that?" Bellus swore.

* * *

Boorsch knew that he was being followed, so he'd decided at the last moment to lose himself in the confusion in the terminal instead of trying to make his rendezvous outside Paris.

It was the taxicab in the tunnel, in the wrong lane. The cabbie had made a U-turn and had come after him. So far as he'd been able to tell, there'd been just the driver, no passenger in the back seat. But he couldn't be sure.

He'd peeled off his coveralls. He was dressed in tan slacks and a light sweater, but he was conspicuous in the terminal for his lack of luggage, even a briefcase or small bag. And the big Sig-Sauer stuffed in the waistband of his trousers made a telltale bulge beneath his sweater, which he had to cover with one hand.

Steeling himself to act normally, as if he was not on the run, as if he belonged here, Boorsch calmly made his way across the main passenger hall, past the ticket and checkin counters to the escalators leading up to the mezzanine level where the shops, restaurants, lounges and money changing booths were located. There were a lot of people in the terminal, and there seemed to be a general movement toward the windows that faced south, where the Airbus had gone down. The paging system was abnormally silent, and there was a muted hum of tense, and in some cases nearly hysterical conversations.

On the escalator Boorsch watched the front doors. A well-built man dressed in dark slacks and a tweed sportcoat entered the terminal, stepped to one side and waited, apparently studying the crowded arrivals hall.

The same one from the taxi? Boorsch hadn't got a clear look, but whoever this one was he was a professional, and he had cop written all over him. Boorsch could almost smell it from here.

Just before Boorsch stepped off the escalator, the man looked his way, hesitated for just a moment, and then started forward.

Boorsch knew he'd been made. The bastard was definitely a cop. Either that or CIA.

He hurried left, along the broad concourse, immediately losing himself in the crowds. When he was certain that he was out of sight of anyone down on the main floor, or coming up on the escalator, he sprinted around the corner down a corridor to the public restrooms and a bank of coin-operated storage lockers.

The blond hair and light blue sweater were unmistakable. McGarvey had got only one brief glimpse of the man's shoulders and head as he'd started to take off his white coveralls in the tunnel, but it was enough.

But the bastard had been sharp enough to put himself in a position to spot anyone coming after him.

He was armed, no doubt, while McGarvey was weaponless. The

balance of power here had definitely shifted. If the terrorist had the presence of mind to stage an ambush somewhere above, or if he had help, McGarvey wouldn't have one chance in ten of surviving the encounter.

But Mati had been on the flight that the son of a bitch had shot down. There was little doubt she was dead. All of them were probably dead. It wasn't likely anyone could have survived the kind of fire that had produced that much smoke.

The bastard's target had been the CIA. But he'd been too much of a coward to face them one-on-one. Instead he'd opted for the methods of the terrorists. Mindless violence against mostly innocent people. McGarvey's jaws tightened with the thought of it.

He reached the escalator, and raced up the moving stairs, taking them two at a time, shoving people out of the way. At the top he darted across the broad concourse, out of any possible line of fire.

Pulling up just within a nearly empty cocktail lounge he scanned both ways, but there was no sign of the man nor any indication which way he had gone.

The bartender had come out from behind the bar. "What is it? What is happening?"

"Did you see the blond man wearing the blue sweater get off the escalator just a moment ago?" McGarvey demanded.

The bartender, an older man with long handlebar moustaches, shrugged. "Who are you? What is going on?"

"I'm an American policeman. There has been a plane crash, and the blond man may have had something to do with it. Did you see which way he went?"

"*Mon Dieu*," the barkeep shouted throwing up his hands. "He was holding his stomach, as if he were about to be ill."

"Which way did he go?"

"*A droite.* To the right, with everyone else."

"*Merci*," McGarvey said, then stepped back out onto the concourse and headed toward the right.

A large crowd had gathered along the broad expanse of windows about one hundred feet farther down the corridor. The windows looked south, toward where the Airbus had gone down.

It was possible the terrorist had merged with that crowd, or was trying to do so now. All he needed was a little time. To do what? Go where?

The man knew that he was being followed. He'd been looking directly down at McGarvey, and for a moment their eyes had locked before he'd disappeared onto the concourse.

The question was, had he spotted McGarvey in the cab, or the police helicopter overhead and run here to the terminal in blind panic, or had this been planned? Did he have a bolt-hole, or perhaps help standing by? There were a thousand places to hide here, and as many escape routes.

A slightly built man wearing a cap and jacket, its collar turned up to cover the back of his neck, emerged from a corridor fifty feet away and without looking back headed immediately toward the crowd in front of the windows. He carried a small overnight bag slung over his shoulder.

The same man? There was no way of making sure, short of catching up with him and pulling the cap off his head. But if he was armed, he would probably not hesitate to open fire. More people would be hurt or killed.

McGarvey pushed his way through the people and hurried into the corridor the man had just come out of. A bank of coin-operated lockers and public telephones lined one wall, while on the other side were the doors to the men's and women's restrooms.

No one was around. Everyone was rushing to the nearest windows to catch a glimpse of the crash.

Shoving open the men's room door, McGarvey stepped inside. There was no one there, and he was starting to back out when he spotted something on the floor in front of the last toilet stall at the end, and he went back in.

It was blood, he could see that as he approached. The lock on the stall door had been forced, as if someone had put his shoulder to it.

Pushing the door open, McGarvey looked inside. The man seated on the toilet, his trousers and shorts down around his ankles, had been shot in the middle of the forehead at close range. The bullet had exited the back of his head, and a good deal of blood had run down the tiled wall and across the floor.

It was him! The green jacket and black overnight bag to help him blend in, and the cap to hide his blond hair. He'd come in here, taken the man's things and killed him.

McGarvey raced back up the corridor to the still-crowded concourse, and, trying to be as inconspicuous as possible, worked his way to the big knot of people gathered in front of the line of windows.

The fire was almost out and the smoke was clearing, leaving behind a long line of debris in the distance at the far end of the airport. The tail section from the Airbus jutted up in silhouette on the horizon, and seemingly everywhere there were hovering helicopters, firetrucks, ambulances, police units, and hundreds upon hundreds of people.

McGarvey just caught a glimpse of the scene and he was brought up short. No one could have survived, as he had feared. But the thought that Marta's body was down there, possibly burned beyond recognition, or damaged so massively that a positive identification might never be made, made him shiver.

He stepped back a pace as an older man, dressed in a three-piece gray suit, suddenly stumbled and fell down.

For an instant McGarvey thought the man might have suffered a heart attack or a stroke, but then he saw the line of blood down the side of his face, and he reared to the left in time to see the man in the cap and green jacket disappear around the corner at the far end of the concourse.

10

The shot had been fired from a silenced pistol, and there was enough background noise on the concourse so that only a handful of people nearest the downed man had any idea that something was happening.

"Someone call a doctor," McGarvey ordered and he pushed his way through the crowd and started after the gunman. He was not familiar enough with Orly's terminal to know exactly what was back here, except that the boarding gates were off to the right somewhere.

Possibly offices, no doubt with a rear exit or exits from the terminal down to the employee parking area. But how did the man expect to get clear from the airport? He had to know that by now security would have sealed the entire area.

Unless, of course, he did have help. Someone waiting for him, in which case McGarvey, unarmed, would be rushing into a definite no-win situation.

He pulled up short at the end of the concourse, and eased around the corner in time to see the shooter disappear down a corridor about fifty feet away without looking back. The man definitely knew where he was going.

McGarvey sprinted after him, running up on the balls of his feet, careful to make as little noise as possible. Out here in the open corridors like this he'd have no chance against an armed man or men, whose shots would be framed by the walls, just like a shooting gallery. But if he could get the man in a situation where a clear shot was difficult or impossible, there might be a chance of stopping him.

He pulled up again at the corridor the shooter had gone down and took a quick look around the corner. The man had reached the far end where he was knocking on a door.

Another door halfway up the corridor opened and a woman stepped out.

"Get back," McGarvey shouted to her.

The gunman half-turned and fired at McGarvey, the shot smacking into the wall at head height just as McGarvey ducked back out of sight.

He heard a second shot, what sounded like the woman, grunting or crying something, and then a buzz. For a split second McGarvey couldn't identify the sound, but suddenly he understood that the gunman had knocked at a security door, which was being buzzed open for him.

"*Arrêter!*" McGarvey shouted, looking around the corner again.

A man had come out of one of the offices and was kneeling down over the woman, as the same moment the gunman fired three shots through the open doorway at the end of the corridor and then disappeared inside, the door closing behind him.

McGarvey rushed down the corridor and the man kneeling over the woman looked up and then reared back in alarm.

"She's been shot!"

"Call an ambulance," McGarvey shouted, racing past him, to the end of the corridor.

The door the shooter had gone through was of heavy steel construction, with an electric lock operated from inside. He put his shoulder to it only once, realizing immediately that there was no way for him to break it down.

Another man wearing a white shirt, the sleeves rolled up, his tie loose, had come out of the same office as the woman.

"What's behind that door?" McGarvey shouted hurrying back to them.

Both men moved back as if they thought they were going to be the next victim.

"Where does it lead?"

"It is security," the man standing stammered.

"Security for what? Where does it lead?"

"The VIP boarding lounge."

"How do they get out there? Is there a service corridor?"

"Ghislane is dead," the kneeling man cried.

"*Oui.* Yes, there is a service corridor at the rear."

"Is there another way of getting back to it? Without going through security?"

The man was shaking his head, but then he nodded. "Yes, yes, from Armand's office. He is our public relations *Chef de Service.*"

"Show me!" McGarvey demanded. Precious seconds had passed and by now the killer could be long gone.

"She's dead," the man on the floor cried again. "Why? Why has this happened?"

McGarvey followed the second man into a large office furnished with a half-dozen desks. Two women were huddled together in the corner behind a few filing cabinets.

"Just here," the Frenchman said opening a door at the rear. A plaque read: *M. Coteau. Chef de Service. Publicité.*

The office was fairly small but very well appointed. A middle-aged man with graying hair was seated at his desk, speaking on the telephone. He looked up in surprise.

"Armand, there has been a shooting," the Frenchman who'd led McGarvey in, sputtered excitedly. "It's Ghislane."

McGarvey went directly across to a door at the rear of the Chef de Service's office, and just eased it open so that he could look out into the long corridor. A door to the right, at the far end of the corridor, one hundred fifty feet or more away, slammed shut.

McGarvey looked back. "Which boarding gate does the door at the end serve?"

"E17 . . ." Coteau said, suddenly realizing the significance. "My God . . . the Swissair flight."

"Call Security. Tell them that the man who shot down that flight just entered the VIP lounge down there. He's blond, but he's wearing a dark cap and green jacket. Hurry."

McGarvey stepped into the corridor and raced down to the far end, aware that once again he was presenting himself as a perfect target. By now the gunman would have to suspect that his pursuer was not armed. McGarvey only hoped that the man would be so intent on making his escape that he wouldn't take the time to wait in ambush. It was also possible that he didn't know that there was an alternate way into this service corridor, other than through security. He might not be expecting company this soon.

At the end of the corridor McGarvey hesitated only long enough to listen at the door. There were no clear sounds from within.

Stepping to one side, out of the line of fire, he turned the knob and carefully opened the door.

He got a brief glimpse of the gunman, his green jacket off, holding his pistol on a policeman who was taking off his uniform. The cop looked up in surprise, and the terrorist turned and snapped off a shot as McGarvey ducked back.

Someone shouted something, and there was a crash and another silenced pistol shot. McGarvey looked through the door again as the cop, his arms wrapped around the gunman, blood streaming down his face, started to fall backward.

Someone was coming down the corridor in a great rush behind McGarvey as he leaped into the room.

The terrorist, knowing what was about to happen, was desperately trying to free himself from the already dead cop when McGarvey reached him, batted the pistol out of his hand, and hauled him off his feet, slamming him against the wall.

Boorsch. Karl Boorsch. McGarvey knew the man! Until a few years ago he'd worked in East Berlin as a STASI hitman. McGarvey had had a brief encounter with him about eight years ago. It had been a situation in which neither of them had had a clear shot, but McGarvey never forgot a face.

Boorsch whipped out a switchblade knife, flicked the blade open and lunged. McGarvey managed to sidestep the thrust, but the ex-STASI triggerman was younger and faster, and ducked McGarvey's swing.

Suddenly recognition dawned in his eyes. "You," he said, and an instant later a man in civilian clothes a big pistol in his hand appeared in the doorway.

"Put it down!" he shouted.

Boorsch stepped back and started to toss the knife under-handed, when Bellus fired three times, all three shots catching the East German in the chest, destroying his heart and left lung.

McGarvey stood perfectly still. His back was toward the door so he could not see what was going on in the corridor, but there were definitely several people out there now. Undoubtedly airport security; all of them armed, all of them jumpy because of what was happening. He wanted no mistakes.

"Are you carrying a weapon, Monsieur?" the cop in the doorway asked.

McGarvey recognized his voice from the telephone before Marta had boarded the plane.

"No, I am not, Monsieur Bellus."

"Who are you?"

"Kirk McGarvey. We spoke on the telephone earlier."

"Search him," Bellus ordered. "And get the medics in here to see to Allain."

McGarvey moved his arms away from his body as a uniformed cop came up behind him and quickly patted him down.

"Nothing," the cop said.

Another uniformed cop came over and was feeling for a pulse at the downed cop's neck. But it was clear that the man was either already dead or soon would be. His head wound from the large-caliber pistol Boorsch had used was massive.

"You may put your arms down," Bellus said coming the rest of the way into the lounge.

McGarvey turned to him. "This is the one who shot down that plane, I think."

"You led me to believe that you were on the flight."

"No," McGarvey said. "I came to see a friend off."

"Who?"

"A Swiss Federal Police officer named Marta Fredricks."

"Did she board?"

McGarvey nodded.

"Then I am truly sorry. You must know that there is little possibility of any survivors."

"I didn't think so."

"What are you doing here, Monsieur? Exactly?"

McGarvey told the security supervisor everything from the moment the cabbie had suddenly pulled over to the side of the highway, until now, leaving nothing out except the fact he'd recognized Boorsch.

"Are you a police officer?" Bellus asked. A young, attractive woman in a police uniform stood at his elbow taking everything in with wide eyes.

"No."

"American Central Intelligence Agency?"

McGarvey shook his head.

"Do not toy with me, Monsieur. A great many people have died this morning. I will not play a guessing game here. You telephoned asking about two men who worked for the Agency, and minutes later the flight they boarded was shot out of the sky."

"I used to work for the Agency," McGarvey said. "Some years ago."

"Yes?" Bellus prompted.

"I spotted their car out front and I wanted to speak to them."

"About what?"

"Why they were here at the airport."

Bellus looked at him through lidded eyes. "A curious question from a man who no longer is in their employ."

"He is dead," the doctor said looking up.

Bellus nodded. "What about the other one?"

"Also."

"Then there is nothing here for you," Bellus said. "Go back out on the field. Maybe there will be a miracle today after all."

The doctor left.

"I was asking a question, Monsieur McGarvey."

"One which I don't think I could ever adequately answer for you."

"But you will try."

McGarvey hesitated, looked down at Boorsch and the French cop who had died fighting . . . what? The Cold War was over. The two Germanies were reunited. The STASI had been completely dismantled. What the hell was this one doing here?

He looked back up at Bellus and the young girl at his side. "Old habits die hard," he said.

"That's no answer," Bellus countered.

"I didn't think you'd believe it was."

It was noon before the French authorities allowed McGarvey to speak with a representative from the U.S. Embassy. A special investigative team from La Sûreté had taken over the opening moves, and they had been anything but friendly or gentle.

They cleared out from the small room adjacent to the airport's Security Operations center where McGarvey had been held, and an older, balding man in a well-cut suit came in. He had career diplomat written all over him.

"I'm Greer Adams, Mr. McGarvey. Deputy consular officer from the embassy."

They shook hands. "Can you get me out of here, Mr. Adams?"

"Yes, of course. You merely have to sign two statements for the French authorities. The first is your sworn statement that you had no involvement nor any prior knowledge of the terrorist attack on Swissair flight 145. And the second is that you promise to show up at a preliminary hearing in Paris at a time and place to be announced."

"No problem," McGarvey said. "I'll need a ride back to my apartment."

"We have a car waiting just outside," Adams said, producing the two French documents.

McGarvey signed them both, then followed Adams through security and outside. No one even bothered to look up as he left.

Tom Lynch was waiting in the back seat of the car. "Trouble seems to have a habit of following you around, McGarvey," he said.

"So it would seem," McGarvey replied, getting in.

"Who was the shooter?"

"I don't know."

"Somebody said he recognized you just before Bellus shot him to death."

McGarvey looked at the CIA chief of Paris station with a straight face, but said nothing.

11

It was a few minutes before eight in the morning, Washington time, when CIA Deputy Director of Operations Phillip Carrara answered the phone on his desk.

"Yes," he said sharply. It had been a long night.

"He's here, are you ready?" Lawrence Danielle asked in his soft voice. Danielle was the deputy director of the CIA.

"No, but I'll be right up, Larry. How's his mood?"

"What do you think?"

"I'll be right up."

Carrara replaced his phone, and cinching up his tie went to the door. His secretary Mildred Anderson was at the copy machine. "Are you about finished, Millie?"

"By the time you roll down your sleeves and put on your coat, I will be," she said without turning around.

She'd been here since 4:00 A.M. in response to the emergency call, and would probably be here until midnight, as would most of the others on the European desk. Gathering a crisis management team had never been a problem for Carrara. He was a well-liked DDO, despite the fact he was tough. "An Hispanic has to work three times as hard as a WASP to achieve the same rate of advancement. And that's a fact of life you cannot sidestep." He would tell that to anyone who asked, though he was not a proselytizer, nor was he bitter. He was, however, diligent, and he expected nothing less from his staff.

Cuffs buttoned and coat on, Carrara took the half-dozen copies of the hastily prepared report his secretary had readied up to the seventh floor where he was immediately ushered into the director's large, well-appointed office. Big windows looked out onto the rolling Virginia countryside.

The DCI, Roland Murphy, was seated behind his desk watching the morning news programs from the three major U.S. networks plus CNN on a bank of monitors to his left. A retired Army major general, he was a large man, with a bull neck, hamhock arms, and thick Brezhnev eyebrows over deep-set eyes. He was one of the toughest, most decisive men to have sat behind that desk since Dulles. And when the general barked, his people jumped.

With him were the Company's general counsel Howard Ryan and the Deputy Director of Intelligence Thomas Doyle as well as Danielle.

Danielle was a small, pinched man, just the opposite of Murphy. He'd been with the Company for twenty-five years, and had even served briefly as interim DCI a few years ago. Ryan, who had come over from the National Security Agency at Murphy's request a couple of years ago, was a precise man whose father ran one of New York's top law firms. No one in the Agency had ever seen him dressed in anything but three-piece suits. Doyle, on the other hand, looked like a rumpled bed, but he was probably the smartest man in the room. He and Carrara, who'd also never paid much attention to his clothing, were good friends.

Murphy and the others looked up when Carrara came in. All four television monitors were showing pictures of the downed Airbus.

"I hope you know more than these jokers," Murphy said sharply. "Because no two of them can even agree on the number of people killed."

"One hundred fifty-seven," Carrara said. "Including six French security officers—three on the field and three in the terminal—a female employee in the Orly Public Relations department, and two other innocent civilians—one in the men's room at the airport, and the other standing in a crowd on the mezzanine level. Plus, of course, the terrorist himself."

Carrara handed the copies of his report around, then poured himself a cup of coffee from the sideboard before he took his seat across from the DCI.

As they were reading, Carrara's eyes strayed to the CNN monitor. He'd been working with Tom Lynch and their people in Paris since early this morning, but this was the first opportunity he'd had to see actual pictures of the crashed airliner. He didn't like to fly, and seeing the news reports live and in color did nothing to dispel his fears.

Ryan looked up sharply from his reading, and moments later

Murphy did the same, slamming his open palm on the desk top. "McGarvey?" he roared.

"At this point it looks as if his presence at Orly was purely coincidental," Carrara said, expecting the reaction. Neither the DCI nor Ryan had any love lost for McGarvey, though for completely different reasons. "But if you will read on, General, you'll learn that he was instrumental in catching up with one of the terrorists."

"Who is dead, no doubt," Ryan said.

Carrara nodded, but before he could continue Ryan turned to the DCI.

"Our Mr. McGarvey strikes again, conveniently eliminating everyone in his path. But I'm willing to bet that it was no coincidence, his being there."

"I'm sorry, Howard, but I disagree. Carrara cut in. McGarvey was apparently saying goodbye to an old friend of his."

"Who?"

"A woman by the name of Marta Fredricks."

Danielle looked up from his reading. "Wasn't she the Swiss cop who lived with him in Lausanne a few years back?"

"Yes . . ." Carrara said, but again Ryan interrupted.

"Need more be said?"

"That's a little pat, don't you think?" Danielle asked.

"On the surface, yes," Carrara admitted. "But McGarvey did not kill the terrorist, the chief of Orly security did that. And at this point he seems willing to cooperate with us and the French authorities."

"I mean about Lausanne, that connection. It's where DuVerlie was leading us. Same city, same flight." Danielle glanced at the report. "And you say here that minutes before the flight McGarvey telephoned Orly security to ask about our people. On the surface, as you put it, Phil, couldn't it be construed that McGarvey wanted to make sure they were actually aboard one-four-five?"

"He's gun-shy," Carrara said.

"What's that supposed to mean?" Ryan asked.

"It means that everytime he spots our people hanging around we come to him with one of our dirty little insoluble problems. And each time he agrees to help, it nearly costs him his life. He wanted to find out what was going on. In his mind *our* people being there was the coincidence."

"What do the Swiss authorities say?" Danielle asked.

"They haven't replied to our query about Miss Fredricks, except to confirm that she is a Federal Police officer."

"On assignment to Paris?"

"Unknown at this point," Carrara said.

"Which brings us back to our original problem," Murphy said. "DuVerlie's fantastic story."

"It would seem that he was telling the truth after all," Danielle put in.

"Have the French identified the terrorist?"

"Not yet," Carrara said. "But they're working on it. He was carrying no identification."

"What about the rocket he used to bring down the airliner?"

"One of ours, a Stinger. I just received the serial number of the launching device. My people are checking it out, but I don't think it'll get us much. The Stinger is a fairly common item on the open market. But we might have another lead. Orly security found some kind of a walkie-talkie in the back of the van the terrorist used to get out to the end of the runway. Which means he may have been communicating with someone."

"So?" Ryan asked. "We didn't think this would turn out to be a one-man operation."

"It may not be so simple," Carrara said. "The French have invited us to take a look. The walkie-talkie is evidently special, its signal not monitorable by normal means. They weren't clear on that point, probably because they didn't have it figured out themselves. But there are no manufacturer's labels or markings on the device. No way of determining its origin."

"So they used a high-tech toy," Danielle said. "The French are cooperating with us, that's the main thing."

"Another piece out of our French operations," Ryan said. "We might as well take out a newspaper ad announcing our presence."

"How about DuVerlie's story?" Murphy asked, bringing them back on track. It was clear that he was not happy.

"Tom Lynch thinks he might be able to put an asset into ModTec within thirty days. It's possible that Leitner talked to someone else. Or DuVerlie might have said something. He was nervous enough."

"What about the Swiss authorities?" Ryan asked. It was his job to keep the Agency out of legal trouble, so far as that was possible. He was an expert on international law, and certified to practice before the International Court at The Hague.

"I suggest we keep them out of this for the moment," Carrara said. "They would only slow us down."

"We're treading on dangerous ground here, General," Ryan warned, turning again to Murphy.

"Until today I might have agreed with you," Murphy replied. "But shooting down that airliner was no random act of terrorism, and I don't think we need to discuss that possibility. Which means DuVerlie was telling us the truth . . . at least that part about their ruthlessness and apparent organization."

"There weren't many people who knew that DuVerlie was going to be aboard one-four-five," Carrara said.

"No. Which means we're dealing with professionals. Well disciplined, and well financed. And when someone like that goes after a key component for a nuclear weapon, it makes me nervous. Extremely nervous."

"Takes more than an electronic switch to make a bomb," Danielle pointed out. "Even if they've already got the device, which we're not sure about, they'll need a sufficient quantity of fissionable material."

"Eighty pounds of plutonium would be enough," Doyle said, speaking for the first time. "Along with a component called an initiator, to get the chain reaction going once the critical mass was achieved."

"Yes," Murphy said. "But we'll assume for the moment that if they're after the switch, they're after the rest."

"I'll give Lynch the go-ahead," Carrara said.

"I want you directly involved with this, Phil. Tom Lynch is to have every resource available to him."

"Yes, sir."

"What about McGarvey?" Ryan asked, his hate obvious.

"As soon as the French are through with him, bring him here to Washington," Murphy said.

"He may not want to return," Carrara said.

"That wasn't under discussion. As soon as he's free, *bring* him here."

12

The evening was warm and exceedingly humid, and as usual traffic throughout the gigantic city of Tokyo was horrendous. People seemed to be everywhere; omnipresent in crushing numbers; endless streams of bodies scurrying back and forth almost as if they were ants intent on some mysterious, unknowable purpose.

Within a twenty-mile radius of downtown lived thirty million people crammed into twenty-three wards, twenty-six small cities, seven towns, and eight villages. Stretching fifty-five miles east to west, but only fifteen miles north to south, everything about the megalopolis was outrageous and contradictory. Prices were astronomical while average salaries were low; space which was at a premium was squandered—land was sold by the square yard, yet the Japanese preferred to build outward, rather than upward; the culture of the people was stylish and elegant, yet the city on the whole was ugly, a monstrosity by Western standards.

A tall, well-built American got out of a taxi in front of the Roppongi Prince Hotel about a mile and a half from the Imperial Palace and paid off his driver. He wore a well-cut dark business suit, and as usual for meetings such as the one he'd arranged for this evening he wore a wire.

His name was James Shirley, and he worked as chief of station for CIA activities in Japan, a post he'd held for nearly five years. Both he and his wife (they had no children) loved the country, and had no intention of ever returning to Washington, no matter what the Company desired. If and when his reassignment came, he'd decided to resign rather than accept it. He was nearly fluent in Japanese, so he didn't think he would have much trouble finding a well-paying job with a large Japanese corporation that did business in the West.

He waited just within the main doors into the lobby for several minutes after his cab left, making certain that he'd not been followed. He'd taken great pains with his tradecraft to get here tonight.

Satisfied at length, he crossed the lobby and went out to the courtyard where on a lower level tables were placed around the acrylic swimming pool, the sides of which were transparent so that the swimmers looked like fish in an aquarium. The man he'd come to meet was seated alone at a small table, his alligator-hide attaché case open in front of him, his dark horn-rimmed glasses pushed up on top of his head.

Shirley went directly across to him. "Monsieur Dunée? Armand Dunée?"

The short, swarthy Belgian looked up with a scowl. "Who is it wishes to disturb me? Are you English, or American?"

"American," Shirley said. "I believe we met last year in Brussels."

Dunée nodded toward the empty chair opposite. "Anything is possible."

Shirley sat down, and a waiter came over immediately. He ordered saki, cool.

"You were not followed?" Dunée asked when they were alone.

"No. Did you bring it?"

"Yes, but I'm not going to hand it over here. I think I may have been followed."

Shirley stiffened slightly, but then smiled. "By whom?"

"I don't know for sure. It was the same two cars behind me all the way across town."

"Japanese?"

"I think so."

"Are they here at the hotel?"

"I don't know. I doubled back on the subway, then walked a half-dozen blocks before I caught a cab here. But I'm no spy."

Shirley glanced across the room. Two other men had come in behind him, but neither of them seemed suspicious. He kept talking.

"It sounds as if you did all right. But the next time I'll want you to abort the meeting if you think you're being watched. I'll explain how to make the proper signal."

Dunée seemed concerned, but so far as Shirley could tell the man was holding together. It was a good sign this early into the recruitment—although Dunée had come to him, not the other way around.

The Belgian worked for a consortium of seven Japanese companies that did extensive business in the West. His job was to act as liaison between them and banks in Europe and the U.S. In actuality he claimed to work for the Banque Du Credit Belgique as an undercover man here in Tokyo. His real employers, he claimed, were concerned that these Japanese companies were planning a series of currency manipulation raids on the West—a theory that just now was getting a lot of play in Washington. He was a spy after all, but of a different type than Shirley.

They had arranged to meet this evening so that Dunée could hand over a series of documents that outlined the consortium's plans concerning eighteen U.S. savings and loan institutions. He said he'd not told his Japanese or his Belgian employers about his contact with the Americans, and he had refused up to this point to tell Shirley what he wanted in exchange. But that would come tonight, at or just before the handover.

What would happen afterwards remained to be seen so far as Shirley was concerned. Japan was his home now, and he wasn't about to do anything anti-Japanese unless the Belgian's charges were very serious, and completely substantiated. Shirley was not a traitor, merely cautious.

The waiter returned with the saki, and Shirley paid him. "You leave first," he told Dunée. "I'll be one minute behind you."

"Where shall I go?"

"Out front. If it looks clear we'll get a cab together."

"How will you know?"

"Leave that to me," Shirley said, and after a hesitation Dunée closed his attaché case, and left without looking back.

Shirley remained seated, sipping his rice wine. No one had seemed particularly interested in them, or in Dunée's departure. In all likelihood the Belgian had managed to lose his tail, if there'd even been one in the first place.

After one minute, Shirley followed the man outside. Two taxis were waiting in the long driveway. One of the drivers had gotten out and was speaking with the doorman and a bellman. Just ahead of the first cab, two workmen in white coveralls, hard hats on their heads and paper air filters covering their faces, were unloading five-gallon paint cans from the back of a small, open truck. No one else was around at that moment, except for Dunée, who stood to one side a few yards from the lead cab. Shirley went down to him.

"Let's go."

"It's them, I think," Dunée said excitedly. "Below, on the street."

Shirley stepped around the Belgian to get a better look, and he stupidly tripped over the man's feet and went down heavily, a sharp pain stabbing at his right ankle.

For a dazed moment or two he didn't understand what had happened, except that he'd probably broken his leg. He looked up as Dunée walked back into the hotel, and a second later he was completely doused from behind with something very cold and wet.

Gasoline, the horrifying thought crystalized in his brain. Burned like acid.

He turned around in time to see one of the men from the open truck lighting a book of matches.

"No!" Shirley shouted at the same moment the workman tossed the burning matches. "No!"

The gasoline and fumes ignited instantly with an explosive thump. Shirley reflexively took a deep breath as the first massive pain struck him, drawing burning fumes deeply into his lungs. Mercifully a red haze began to blot out his vision, his hearing and his other senses, and his last thought was that he was too ridiculously young to be dying.

13

CIA operations had been moved to the U.S. Consulate until a new embassy could be built a couple of blocks away on the Avenue Gabriel. Just around the corner from the Tuileries Gardens, the building was old and very French with slow iron cage elevators, creaking wooden floors and terrible plumbing.

It was past lunch by the time McGarvey arrived with Tom Lynch, and they went immediately up to a small conference room on the fourth floor. The Station had been on emergency footing all morning because of the air crash, and its effects could be seen on the faces of everyone they met. This was the second serious attack on the CIA's French operation in seven months.

The French were starting to ask some tough questions, for which there were no answers that were satisfactory to either side. It was a common understanding that the CIA operated within the country, as did the SDECE—the French secret service—in the U.S. But as long as neither side attracted too much attention to itself, the status quo could be maintained.

McGarvey, however, was a common denominator between this attack and the one that had destroyed the embassy seven months ago. A lot of French citizens had died in each event, and now the Sureté National, which headed the French Police, had taken notice.

"It's only a matter of time before the SDECE takes an interest in you . . . an official interest," Lynch told him on the way back from the airport. The chief of station was a slender man with light brown hair and delicate, almost English features. He'd been with the Company for nearly ten years, and was one of the rising stars. He was a corporate man; a team player.

"It had nothing to do with me, Tom, and you know it," McGarvey said. "They were after your people."

"Possibly. But why the hell did you call airport security about them?"

"Because everytime I look over my shoulder it seems like one of your people is back there. And I'm starting to get tired of it."

"Then go back home, McGarvey. Nobody wants you over here. You make people nervous. You make me nervous."

"As soon as the French are done with me, I'll leave Paris."

"Good," Lynch had said, and they'd driven the rest of the way back to the city in silence.

McGarvey went to the windows which overlooked a courtyard. Two women were seated on a bench, the remains of a late lunch spread out beside them. He and Marta had often brownbagged it in the parks of Lausanne. It was an American custom she'd found particularly charming.

"Wait here," Lynch said. "I'll be back in a minute and we can get started with your debriefing."

McGarvey didn't bother to reply, staying instead with his thoughts about Marta. There was no reason for her or the others aboard 145 to have been killed. And there especially was no reason for an ex-STASI hitman to have committed such an act of terrorism.

But it had happened, and like the crash a few years ago at Lockerbie, the official investigation might drag on for a very long time before producing any results. Most likely the real reason for the attack would never be known for sure, because any official investigation was of necessity ponderous, allowing the terrorists ample time to sidestep any move made against them.

It was one of the reasons he'd not told anyone about Boorsch. The French had his body. If they identified him, well and good, but in the meantime McGarvey would have some autonomy of movement as soon as he was finished with his testimony.

His other reason, of course, was Marta. She'd wanted to stay with him in Paris for a couple of days longer, but he had insisted she leave. He'd forced her on that flight, and it had cost her her life. He owed her something, and it was a debt he meant to repay.

His starting point would be Boorsch. It was unlikely that the man had worked alone. STASI, as a secret police organization, had been dismantled when the East German government fell. But not all of its officers had been caught. It was possible they had linked up with each other to do . . . what?

Lynch came back a couple of minutes later with an attractive woman in her early to mid-forties whom he introduced as Lillian Tyson, a special assistant to the ambassador.

"Are you with the Company?" McGarvey asked her.

"Actually she's in charge of legal affairs here," Lynch said. "For all American interests in France."

"I'm going to try to keep you out of jail, Mr. McGarvey, if that's all right with you," she said. Her voice and manner were sharp and self-assured, as was the smartly tailored gray suit she wore over a ruffled silk blouse and textured nylons.

"Los Angeles?" McGarvey asked.

"Chicago," she said, taking a small cassette recorder out of her purse and laying it on the table. "Please sit down, Mr. McGarvey. I want you to give us your statement, and afterwards we'll see just what we'll want you to tell the French authorities when they question you on Monday."

"Who will it be, the Sûreté National?"

"No," Lillian Tyson said. "The SDECE wants to interview you at Mortier."

The compound just off the Boulevard Mortier on the northeast side of Paris housed the SDECE's Service 5, known simply as *Action*. It was the counterespionage branch of the agency.

"The bully boys," Lillian Tyson said. "They're particularly interested in you." She turned to Lynch. "What was it Colonel Marquand asked? 'Why is it this bastard's name keeps cropping up?'" She turned back. "Pay attention and you'll come out of this in one piece."

"Why are they involved?" McGarvey directed his question to the station chief.

"The attackers weren't French."

"Do they have an ID already?"

"I only know what was waiting on my desk for me, and what Lillian told me."

"They went directly to the ambassador about you, Mr. McGarvey, which is why I'm here."

"You said attackers, Tom. Plural."

"They apparently found a walkie-talkie."

"May we get started now?" Lillian Tyson asked.

McGarvey ignored her. "What were they after? Who did we have on that plane?"

"I can't tell you, but I'm sure you'll be told something in Washington. The message was on my desk. You're wanted as soon as the French are finished with you."

"Sit down," Lillian Tyson said sharply.

"I don't think so, counselor," McGarvey replied. "Not unless you and Tom would like to answer some questions as well. I had a friend on that flight."

"Yes, we know, and we'd like to ask you about her, as well."

"Tell Murphy, not this time," McGarvey said to Lynch, and he started for the door.

"Hold it right there, mister," Lillian Tyson shouted.

"Am I under arrest?"

"Not yet," Lynch said. "But I'm sure the general will order it if you refuse to help out."

"Step out that door, McGarvey, and I'll turn you over to the French authorities," Lillian Tyson warned.

"Then I'd have to tell them everything I know, counselor. *Everything.* I'd suggest you talk that over with your boss."

McGarvey opened the door and stepped out into the corridor.

"Goddamn you . . ." Lillian Tyson swore.

"I'll be in touch, Tom," McGarvey said, and he left.

"Who in the hell does that son of a bitch think he is?" Lillian Tyson asked.

Lynch was shaking his head. What little he personally knew, plus what he'd been told and had read about the man, all added up to the same thing. He looked at the woman.

"I don't believe you'd really want to know that."

McGarvey's apartment was in a pleasantly quiet neighborhood just off the rue Lafayette a few blocks from the Gare du Nord. He paid off his taxi at the corner and out of old habit, went the rest of the way on foot, watching for the out-of-place car or van, the odd man or woman lingering in a doorway, the telltale flash of sunlight off a camera lens in an upper-story window.

There was nothing this time, though the feeling that the business was starting all over again for him was strong. No doubt Murphy was convinced that McGarvey's presence at Orly this morning had been no coincidence. And the fact that the general had taken a personal interest meant the presence of the CIA officers aboard that flight had been very important.

But the Cold War was over. It was a line he'd told himself over and over for the past seven months since he'd killed the Russian, Kurshin, in Portugal. He'd been a soldier, but all the battles were done. He was retired.

It was time now for him to return to his ex-wife Kathleen in Washington and try to pick up the threads of his former life before he'd joined the Company. Before he'd become . . . what?

He stopped across the narrow street from his building. He had killed, therefore he'd become a killer. He'd killed silently, and from a distance, on occasion, which meant he'd become an assassin. Ugly, but the business had been necessary.

No night went by without the memories of the people he'd killed parading through his sleep, like macabre sheep to be counted before he could rest. Those memories would never stop haunting him until he was dead. It was one of the prices he'd paid for becoming what he'd become.

The other price he'd paid, and continued to pay besides the estrangement of his wife and daughter, was the enmity of his own government. The general had called him a "necessary evil" and despised him. Yet when there'd been trouble, of a nature that the CIA couldn't or wouldn't handle itself, McGarvey was pushed into the corner in such a way that he could not refuse to help.

Complicated, he thought. His life had never been easy, on the contrary, it had been complicated.

Waiting for a small Renault to pass, McGarvey crossed the street and entered his building. The concierge's window was closed, so he went directly up to his third-floor apartment. If there was mail he would get it later.

For now he wanted to finish packing. Most of his things would go into temporary storage here in Paris until he knew for certain where he was going to end up, while the rest, except for an overnight bag, he was sending ahead to Washington.

His apartment door was wide open. Two uniformed French policemen were in the corridor talking with a broad-shouldered man in civilian clothes. There seemed to be a lot of activity inside.

The civilian turned around as McGarvey came up. "Who are you?" he demanded.

"My name is McGarvey, this is my apartment. Now who the hell are you and what do you think you're doing?"

A short, very dark, extremely dangerous-looking man, also dressed in civilian clothes, appeared in the doorway. "Searching your apartment, Monsieur McGarvey. Do you have any objections?"

"You're damned right I do."

"Then come in please, and we will discuss them. I'm sure something can be worked out."

"First of all, who are you?"

"Phillipe Marquand," the swarthy man said. He was built like a Sherman tank. "Are you presently carrying a weapon?"

"No," McGarvey said. Marquand was with the SDECE.

"Then it is only the one automatic pistol which we have found in your apartment—for which you apparently have no French permit to carry—that you own. Is that correct?"

"I would like to speak to Tom Lynch at my embassy."

"In due time, Monsieur. First you and I will have a little chat."

"Monday . . ."

"Now. By Monday you will be out of France in good health, I assure you. That is, if you cooperate."

"There's nothing I can tell you, Colonel. If you know who Tom Lynch is, and what I was, then you will understand."

"Ah, but you have it wrong," the SDECE colonel said. "I don't have many questions for you, rather it is I who am going to answer your questions."

McGarvey's eyes narrowed, and Marquand smiled.

"The man's name was Karl Boorsch, and he had been a field officer for the East German Secret Service. Both facts you know, of course. But what you may not know is that Boorsch had help, a great deal of help, and a great deal of money."

"What do you want from me?" McGarvey asked.

"Your help in tracking them down and eliminating them, of course."

BOOK TWO

14

WASHINGTON, D.C.
JULY 5, 1992

A thick haze had settled over the Washington area as night fell, lending the city a mysterious air that Kelley Fuller found intimidating. She paid off her cab in front of an eight-story apartment building near Howard University Hospital, and hefting her single overnight bag, hurried into the lobby and impatiently punched the elevator call button.

She was a thin woman in her mid-thirties with long, dark hair, delicately proportioned Oriental features and a soft, yellow cast to her skin. She wore a white blouse, dark skirt and high heels, not exactly traveling clothes, but she'd been in a hurry.

The elevator was on the sixth floor, and as she waited for it to descend to the lobby, she put down her bag, went back to the glass doors and looked outside.

No one had followed her so far as she could tell. But she was certain that it would only be a matter of time before they came for her like they had Jim Shirley.

She closed her eyes tightly for just a moment, Shirley's screams echoing in her head. She'd seen everything from where she'd hidden in the shadows in front of the hotel, and when Dunée had calmly walked past, she'd been frozen, unable to take her eyes off the horrible spectacle below for more than a split instant.

Shirley had screamed for such a long time, but no one even attempted to help him or stop the two delivery men who'd simply gotten back into their truck and driven off. By the time someone brought a fire extinguisher from the hotel it was all over, Shirley's body burned to an unrecognizable charred mass where it had fallen to the left.

She had run, and had kept running without sleep for the past forty-eight hours, hoping that once she reached Washington everything would be better, that she would be safely among friends. But now that she was here, she wasn't so sure that anyplace would be safe for her ever again.

She'd gotten a clear, if brief, look at Dunée's face as he'd passed. He'd been smiling. Behind him, a man was being burned alive, his screams inhuman, and Dunée seemed to be enjoying himself.

The elevator dinged, but Kelley lingered at the glass doors for a moment longer, wondering if she'd done the right thing coming back. But she was so frightened she couldn't go on. Not after what she'd witnessed. She needed to talk to someone. She needed to be among people she knew and trusted. She needed to be told what to do next.

Kelley had telephoned from the airport, and Lana Toy was waiting in the corridor as the elevator opened on the fifth floor, a look of puzzled concern on her small, round Oriental features. They'd been friends for a number of years, working together as translators for the State Department.

"What happened to you?" she demanded, taking Kelley by the arm and leading her back to her apartment.

"You didn't tell anybody I'm back, did you?"

"No, but what are you doing here? You're supposed to be in Tokyo. What happened?"

"I can't tell you that," Kelley said. "But I might have to stay with you for a little while, if that's okay."

"Of course it is. But are you in some sort of trouble?"

"Just lock the door, Lana, and get me a drink," Kelley said. She put down her bag and went to the window where she carefully parted the curtain and looked down at the street.

The cab was gone, and as she watched, a city bus passed, but there was no other traffic. No movement. But God, she could almost feel that someone was down there, watching from the darkness, and she shivered.

Jim Shirley's screams would stay with her for the rest of her life. One of the reasons she'd not been able to sleep for the past two days was because she'd been on the run. But the other, even darker reason was because she was afraid to sleep. Afraid what her nightmares would be. She knew that she was going to relive the experience. She was frightened that she might relive it from another point of view, from someone else's perspective.

Lana Toy, a bottle of vodka in one hand and two glasses in the other, came back from the kitchen. She stopped short. "You *are* in trouble," she said, her face serious.

"I'm going to need your help, Lana. But I don't want you to ask me any questions. Please. It's for your own sake."

The other woman nodded her reluctant agreement, then came the rest of the way into the small but nicely furnished living room and set the bottle and glasses on the coffee table.

"I need to use your phone."

"Sure," Lana Toy said, pouring the drinks as Kelley went to the phone and dialed a number.

It was answered on the first ring, by a man who simply repeated the number.

"This is Yaeko Hataya," Kelley said softly. "I'm here in Washington."

"We've been worried. Can we come for you?"

"No," Kelley said sharply. She glanced at Lana Toy, who was watching her. "I'll call back in . . . five minutes."

"Are you safe?"

"For the moment," Kelley said. "Five minutes." She hung up. "Now I'll take that drink," she told her friend.

Phil Carrara was one of four men in the small third-floor briefing room listening to Sargent Anders, the director of Technical Services, explain what they had learned from Tokyo. Actually, he thought, they had nothing concrete yet, and the way things were going they might never find Shirley's killers or their actual motives.

Within three hours of the attack a team of four forensics people from Technical Services had been sent over, along with two of the best covert operations muscle currently in house and not on some field assignment somewhere.

During the thirteen-plus hours it took to get to Japan (they'd gone via commercial carrier to attract less attention) Tokyo Station had all but closed down. The Japanese were extremely sensitive about spies in their midst.

Shirley's cover had been as a special economic affairs adviser to the ambassador, the actual day-to-day work of which fell naturally to his staff. The Japanese CIA and Federal Police accepted this ruse so long as there was no trouble. With this incident, everyone over there was keeping a low profile, and would continue to do so for at least the next few days.

The other three men with Carrara were his Assistant Deputy Director of Operations, Ned Tyllia, the Chief of the Far East Desk, Nicholas Wuori, and the Chief of Operations Covert Action Staff, Don Ziegler.

"The delivery truck has been found abandoned in a parking area near the Ikebukuro train station in northeast Tokyo. About five miles, as the crow flies, north of the Roppongi Prince," Anders was saying.

It was something new. Carrara sat forward. "Who discovered the truck, Sargent, certainly not one of our people?"

"No, sir, it was Tokyo Police. The call came from a local *koban* after one of their officers stumbled across the truck. Its license tag had been removed. A mistake on their part, I'd say. Naturally we monitored the call, as we do all police and military calls, and once the truck had been picked up and brought to the impound yard, one of my people got in for a quick look."

Anders looked more like a bookkeeper than a cop, which is what he'd been with the New York City Police Department for eleven years before coming to the CIA. He was a precise little man, who sometimes affected a British accent because he thought it made him sound like James Bond. (Ian Fleming had been and still was the most widely read author by CIA employees.)

"Did we get anything?"

"Unknown yet, but there's the possibility. According to eyewitnesses, the two bad guys wore hard hats and paper air filters. We recovered two used filters and one plastic hard hat from the truck. The items are enroute to our lab in Yokosuka where we should be able to come up with a DNA profile from hair out of the hat and from saliva off the filters. Won't give us a name or names, but we'll have something to match if they're eventually bagged."

"Fingerprints, anything like that?" Carrara asked.

"No time, it was a quick in-out. But we managed to get a sample of the gasoline they used. It was normal unleaded, but it was laced with hydrochloric acid. Ten percent."

Everyone was shaken.

"Even if the fire hadn't killed Jim, the fumes would have burned out his lungs," Anders said.

"Determined bastards," Tyllia commented.

"And ruthless," Anders agreed.

The telephone at Carrara's elbow buzzed softly and he picked it up. "Carrara."

"This is Tony. Kelley Fuller just called."

Carrara raised his hand for Anders to hold up. "Where is she?"

"Apparently here in Washington. But she used her workname, and she sounded strung out, though she says she's safe. She'll call back at 8:32."

Carrara glanced up at the wall clock. Four minutes. "Did you get a trace?"

"I brought it up, but she was too fast. I'll get her when she calls back. I offered to send someone for her, sir, but she refused."

"We'll keep her at arm's length for the moment. I don't want her contaminated."

"Yes, sir," the communications man downstairs said, and Carrara hung up.

The Resource and Evaluation Committee for most deep-cover operations in which a blind asset (an agent unknown to the local station) was used included the men in this room along with the Director of Central Intelligence and his deputy, and sometimes the Deputy Director of Intelligence and his assistant.

"Kelley Fuller has surfaced," Carrara told the others.

"Where?" Wuori, the Far East Desk chief, asked sharply. He'd known Kelley since she was a little girl growing up in Honolulu, his home town.

"Here in Washington. She's made initial contact and her next call comes in a few minutes." Carrara picked up the phone and punched the number for the DCI's locator service. It was Saturday. Murphy had left his office at noon.

"She's on the run, then. Must have seen something."

"Presumably," Carrara said, waiting for his call to be patched through.

"How'd she sound? What'd Tony say?" For a time Wuori had been like a father to Kelley. It hurt now that she was in Washington, apparently in trouble, and had not called him.

"Shook up, but safe." Carrara's call was going through. It rang, and Murphy's bodyguard answered gruffly.

"Yes."

"This is a yellow light for the general."

A moment later Murphy was on the line. "Murphy."

"She's surfaced here in Washington," Carrara said without preamble. Murphy would recognize his voice, and there was no doubt who he was talking about. "She'll be calling again in a couple of minutes."

"Is she all right?"

"Tony said she sounded strung out, but she was safe."

"Any sign that she's been compromised in Tokyo?"

"We've seen or heard nothing," Carrara said, knowing what was coming next.

"Then send her back, Phil. The bastards hit Jim, there's no telling if they'll be content to stop at that."

"It's a warning . . ."

"You're damned right it is," Murphy growled. "Considering the billions in foreign trade that's at stake, you and I both know they won't stop."

"I'll meet her tonight."

"Don't queer it by being spotted with her," Murphy said. The instruction stung a little because Carrara was enough of a professional to know as much.

"Sure thing."

"Listen, Phil, there's more than just money at stake here. Tokyo Station, among its other troubles, leaks like a sieve. Everytime we sneeze, the Japanese have the handkerchief out even before we start."

"But this is something new," Carrara said. Murphy disagreed.

"You're wrong. Murder is one of the oldest of crimes. Read your Bible."

"Yes, sir."

Carrara hung up, thought for a moment, then looked at the others. "If she's not blown her cover by running, we're to send her back."

"For God's sake, Phil, we'd be signing her death warrant," Wuori argued.

"We have no evidence that whoever hit Jim was also after her, have we?" Carrara asked.

Anders shook his head.

The phone at Carrara's elbow buzzed.

"We'll do what we can to insure her safety, but she goes back," Carrara said, and he picked up the phone.

"She's in an apartment on the north side, leased by Lana Toy," Tony said. "A friend of hers."

"Right," Carrara said. "Put her on." A moment later the incoming call was transferred to the briefing room. "Is that you?" he asked.

"Phil?" Kelley Fuller asked, her voice small and shaky.

"Yes, it is, but listen to me, don't use names now. Do you understand?"

"Yes."

"Okay, listen carefully. I want you to stay right where you are for one hour, let's say until 9:30 sharp. Then I want you to leave the apartment and take the first right."

"On foot?"

"Yes. I'll pick you up as soon as I'm sure it's safe. Do you have that?"

"Yes."

"All right, I'll see you in a bit."

Kelley Fuller had put a light sweater over her shoulders, and Carrara spotted her walking alone north on Second Street toward McMillan Park and the reservoir. He passed her, and swung around the block to come up from behind her again.

So far as he was able to tell, no one was watching her. It had been a few years since he'd been in the field, but some skills were never lost.

He pulled over to the curb before the corner, reached across and opened the passenger door as she was passing. "It's me," he called out.

She came immediately over to the car, and got in. "I saw you pass the first time," she said.

Carrara pulled away, and turned the corner on W Street toward the hospital. "Do you think you were spotted in Tokyo?" he asked.

"It was horrible, Phil. He never had a chance. By the time he knew what was happening it was too late."

"Were you spotted?"

"If they were watching him they had to know we were seeing each other," she said. She was very frightened. It was obvious by the way she held herself and by the shakiness in her voice.

"They were pros, Kelley. If they'd thought you were significant, they would have killed you before you had a chance to run."

"What are you telling me, Phil?"

"We want you to go back to Tokyo, to your job at the embassy."

Kelley reared back, a horrified expression coming to her face.

"The problem is not going to go away," Carrara said. "It was a warning to us, and one that'll probably be repeated. He was playing on their turf, and evidently he got out of hand."

"Me next."

"Not you. But there's a good chance they'll go after Ed, if they believe he was involved with Shirley's . . . extracurricular activities." Edward Mowry had been the assistant chief of Tokyo Station. For the moment he was acting COS, his cover now the same as Shirley's had been, as special economic affairs adviser to the ambassador.

"Then we have to warn him."

"We'd lose everything we worked for, Kelley. Think it out." Carrara had fought the entire project, but it had the personal blessing of the entire seventh floor: Murphy, Danielle and Ryan—the unholy trinity.

"He's a sitting duck," Kelley cried in anguish.

"I sent a team over to watch out for him, but they're going to stick out like sore thumbs."

"What can I do?"

"Keep your eyes and ears open, just as you have been doing. You're still the unknown quantity."

Kelley looked at him with disgust. "I can't believe you're saying that to me. Now, of all times."

Carrara concentrated on his driving for the moment. No one in operations had liked what they'd sent Kelley to do. Some of them had daughters nearly her age. But she had been recruited for the project without much persuasion. It was being called PLUTUS . . . after the god of wealth, and greed.

"I want you to keep your eyes and ears open, just as you have been doing."

"You want me to go to bed with Mowry to find out if he's been bought by the Japanese," she shouted.

"I want you to watch him."

"I didn't see anything that would have helped Jim."

"Yes you did, we just didn't listen. You spotted Dunée and

warned us, but we took too long to find out that the real Armand Dunée was not the man who made contact with Jim."

Kelley closed her eyes. "At first I thought it would be interesting," she said. "Necessary. But I'm in over my head here."

"We all are."

She reopened her eyes. "It's only money, Phil. We're only talking about balancing foreign trade, or buying out Rockefeller Center, or MCA, or Disney World. Nothing earth-shattering."

"That's what we *were* talking about. But now we're discussing murder. A horribly brutal murder, with the possibility that there's more to come."

"Not me," Kelley cried.

"We want you to go back to Tokyo, back to your work with the USIA. If you spot something—anything, no matter what it is—that looks wrong, let us know immediately."

"And then what?"

"We'll pull you out."

"What if I'm the target?"

"You won't be."

"What if I am?" Kelley insisted, her voice rising with anger.

"Then we'd have to protect you . . ."

"Like you protected Jim Shirley," she said disparagingly.

"If they want to kill you, they won't stop trying simply because you return to Hawaii, or here to us," Carrara said harshly, hating himself for what he was doing to the woman. Yet he didn't think that she was anyone's prime target. Whoever was gunning for the Company's Tokyo operation wouldn't be interested in a USIA translator and sometime companion of the chief of station. They were after bigger fish than she.

Jim Shirley had been a good man, though over the past few years his loyalties had gotten slightly muddled. He didn't deserve to die that way. And Carrara was going to do everything within his considerable power to catch his murderers.

15

The lights of Monaco were brilliant against a black velvet backdrop as Ernst Spranger, a tall, ruggedly built, handsome man, pointed the bow of the powerful speedboat toward the ship just visible in silhouette on the horizon to the south. The night was gentle and warm, the sea almost flat calm.

Spranger was impeccably dressed in evening clothes, as was the beautiful woman seated beside him, indifferently humming the melody from the opera they'd just left. Like the others who'd come at Spranger's command three years ago, Liese Egk had worked for the East German STASI as an assassin, a job at which she was an expert. She was a complete sociopath, totally without conscience. Combined with her intelligence, training and aristocratic good looks, she was lethal.

"I think I will miss Boorsch," Spranger said, not bothering to raise his voice over the roar of the engines.

Liese was looking at him, a contemptuous expression forcing her full, sensuous lips into a pout. "He was a good shot with the Stinger, but he was an idiot. He would have caused us considerable trouble."

Spranger couldn't hear her voice, but he got most of what she'd said. They spoke in German, which was much easier to lip-read than English because of its regular pronunciations.

"Maybe you will cause us trouble in the end," he told her, and she laughed.

"Then you better watch your back." She glanced toward the ship on the horizon. "At least we're not going out as failures."

"No," Spranger said to himself. Yet he still wasn't clear in his mind exactly what had happened at Orly. The Airbus was down, everyone aboard dead, including Jean-Luc DuVerlie. But something had gone wrong at the last moment.

Bruno Lessing, who'd remained in front of the terminal for just such a contingency, reported that Boorsch had shown up in a big hurry, and moments later he'd been followed by a thickly built man dressed in what had appeared to be a British-cut tweed sportcoat. Directly after both men had entered the terminal a French police helicopter had touched down, and Lessing had of necessity driven back into Paris.

The police were understandable. But who the hell was the man in the tweed jacket?

And why had they been summoned again, unless it was bad news? It was possible, he thought, that somehow British intelligence had gotten onto them, though it was unlikely unless the CIA had asked for help.

But there was no reason for such a thing to have occurred. If the Americans had requested help from anyone it would have been from the Swiss, who still hadn't discovered the first engineer's body.

DuVerlie had come as a surprise. And except for the fact that they'd already gotten what they'd needed from ModTec, no one wanted the Swiss or the Americans to suspect they had.

Question was, how much had the Swiss engineer told the CIA, and exactly why was it they were returning to Lausanne?

Puzzles within puzzles. But it was a part of the business that Spranger had one way or the other lived with for all of his life. His father before him had been an agent (though not a particularly good one) for the RSHA—the Nazi intelligence service—before and during the war.

Spranger and his mother had hidden themselves in Switzerland for eight years before returning to West Germany. Within one year she was dead, and he had slipped into East Germany offering his services to the STASI. The Russians, not as squeamish about former Nazis as they led the world to believe, accepted the young man with open arms, and his real training had begun.

He slowed the speedboat as they approached the 243-foot cruiser *Grande Dame* out of Monaco. The sleek, white-hulled pleasure vessel lay still in the water, all her lights ablaze, her portside boarding ladder down. There were no movements, the only sounds from the ship's generators. Except for the lights the ship could have been abandoned, or everyone aboard dead. It had been the same each time they'd been called for a rendezvous.

Spranger maneuvered the speedboat close, then chopped the

engines, so they would drift the last few feet. He tied a line to a cleat on the platform and helped Liese up, scrambling onto the boarding ladder directly behind her.

Reaching the main deck they went aft and entered the spacious, well-furnished main salon. Music was playing softly and champagne had been laid out for them, as usual.

A white coated Italian waiter appeared. "*Accogliere cordialmente, signore e signorina,*" he said pleasantly. "Champagne tonight?"

Spranger nodded.

Outside, the speedboat was started and left, and seconds later the *Grande Dame's* engines came to life and they began to move.

"Please," the little waiter motioned for them to take a seat.

The telephone next to Spranger rang once. Putting his champagne down, he lit a cigarette then sat down and picked up the phone. "Yes?" he said English.

"Tell us about the gentleman in the tweed coat at the airport." the Japanese voice said in clear English.

"I don't know for certain," Spranger answered, surprised that they knew about him. It meant they must have had one of their own people watching the airport. "My guess would be that he is an intelligence officer. British or American."

"What is being done about him?"

"Nothing. I don't consider him a threat at this point. Although Boorsch will be identified and probably traced back to us, we can handle the inquiries. And your position with us is very well insulated."

"What about Switzerland?"

"We have the parts."

"I see," the Japanese man said after a brief hesitation. "And why have you not delivered them?"

Spranger had been expecting the question. He'd hoped it would not have come so soon, but he wasn't going to hedge. "The parts are in a safe place, where they shall remain until we have gathered everything you contracted for. Only then will we make delivery."

"Why?"

"Insurance," Spranger said bluntly. He looked over at Liese. She was watching him, a faint smile on her lips.

"Against what?" the man asked.

"You."

"Do you consider us a threat to your well-being? We are, after all, allies once again."

"Allies, but not friends," Spranger said. "Is there anything else?"

"We could replace you, if you refuse to cooperate."

"No one else could do the job."

The man laughed. "I believe we could find someone capable. A person such as Miss Egk, for example."

"She could do the job," Spranger said, once again surprised.

"Unless I killed her first. Then you might never get your little toys."

Liese's smile broadened. She was seated on a low couch across the salon from him. As he watched, she crossed her long, lovely legs.

"Do we still have a contract?" Spranger asked after a moment.

"Yes, of course. But I am worried about the man in the tweed coat, and I believe you should be worried as well. Look into it."

"If you think it's important."

"I do."

"I will have to divert some resources. It will cost you . . ."

"Money is no object. I have already made that quite clear."

"Very well," Spranger said.

"How soon do you expect to be in a position to fulfill the terms of our agreement?"

"Soon."

"How soon? Days? Weeks? Months?"

"Soon," Spranger repeated, and he hung up.

16

On Sunday morning Swissair quietly reinstituted its flight 145 to Geneva, and though Orly had reopened almost immediately, passenger traffic on all airlines was sharply down.

McGarvey had spent most of Saturday in the clippings library of *Le Figaro*, France's leading daily newspaper, looking for background information on the STASI and what had become of its top officers. But he'd not found much beyond a series of articles published last week in which a French journalist reported that there were still thousands of KGB men and officers operating throughout what had once been East Germany, and that only the East German secret service itself had actually been dismantled by the mobs.

Early this morning he had checked out of the Latin Quarter hotel where he'd holed up out of Tom Lynch's way, and took a cab out to Orly.

Mati was dead. That irrevocable fact began to settle over him like a dark, malevolent cloud as his taxi came within sight of the airport. In his mind's eye he could see the big plume of smoke rising into the morning sky. And he could see the Stinger's contrail. No one aboard the Airbus had so much as one chance in a million of survival. The destruction had been so complete that authorities were admitting they might never be able to properly identify even half the bodies.

Poor Mati. She could never have envisioned that her life would end that way. Or that her death would be so misused.

"Frankly, the sooner you are out of France the better I will feel," Marquand had told him bluntly.

"Are you so sure I'm interested?" McGarvey asked.

The French intelligence officer nodded. "Had you continued to Paris after one-four-five was destroyed, I would have not been so certain. But your own actions have betrayed you, as they do all of us in the end."

Mati had come from Lausanne. The CIA had been sending its people at least as far as Geneva. And Marquand told him that the organization of ex-STASI officers (if such an organization existed) maintained its bank accounts in Bern and Zurich. All roads, it seemed, led to Switzerland.

"Show your face in Lausanne, and if you are spotted by Boorsch's friends they will assume that you are investigating them. They will come for you, then, no matter where you go or what you do."

Even Marquand had known about poor Mati. Everyone had, and somehow she was being used as the key, or as a lever to pry him loose from . . . what?

He was out of the business. He'd told them that a dozen times. He had nothing left to give. He was, like the Cold War, an anachronism. A man whose time had passed. An idea that no longer fit. An ism that had become too dangerous in what was being called the "new world order."

McGarvey paid off his driver and went directly through the terminal to the Swissair boarding area. He'd made his reservations yesterday at the airline's downtown office under his real name, giving the opposition, if there was any, time enough to react.

Tom Lynch was waiting for him across from the gate, and he pulled McGarvey into the cocktail lounge that was half-filled with travelers. They got a table where they could watch the boarding.

"What the hell do you think you're doing?" the Paris chief of station asked. "We've turned this town upside down looking for you."

"I'm going to Lausanne," McGarvey answered, watching Lynch's eyes. The COS was an organization man. He put the Agency before personal feelings.

"The Swiss will kick you out," Lynch said, betraying nothing.

"I'm going to pay my respects, Tom. Any other reason I'd be going there?"

"I don't know. But Murphy is screaming bloody murder for you. He'll have your head on a platter if you don't show up in Washington."

"He doesn't have the authority."

Lynch looked at him with a smirk. "You've been around long enough to know better than that, McGarvey. The man has a long reach."

McGarvey leaned forward. They were calling his flight. "So do I, Tom."

"Are you threatening me?" Lynch demanded.

"I had a friend aboard that flight. I'm going to Lausanne, as I said, to pay my respects. Afterward I'll go to Washington to see Murphy. I was leaving Paris in any event."

"Yes, I know. We've been to your apartment. Your concierge said you gave it up. She also said the police had been there."

McGarvey waited.

"Marquand is suddenly unavailable. Did you happen to see him, by chance?"

McGarvey nodded. "He told me to get out of Paris."

"What'd you tell him?"

"That I was leaving this morning."

"You know what I'm talking about."

McGarvey's flight was called again.

"I didn't tell him much, Tom, other than about my relationship with one of the passengers."

"And about me? About our little talk?"

"No."

"It would be too bad if I found out differently."

"What about the pair you sent to Geneva? Care to comment?"

"I don't know what you're talking about," Lynch said with a straight face.

"That shooter wasn't gunning for Marta. My guess is that he was after your people."

"What'll I tell the general?"

"Tell him that I'll drop by in the next couple of days," McGarvey said getting to his feet. "Soon as I'm finished with my business in . . . Lausanne."

The COS flinched, but the reaction was too slight to draw any conclusions from. McGarvey suspected, however, that the general would know he was on his way to Switzerland probably before his flight cleared the Paris Terminal Control Area.

Had Mati not been aboard flight 145, McGarvey knew he could have turned his back on the situation. But Marquand, the man's cynicism notwithstanding, had read him correctly: McGarvey's actions *had* betrayed him.

McGarvey's flight touched down just before 10:00 A.M. at Geneva's busy Cointrin Airport, and he was among the first passengers to deplane and pass through customs. No one bothered to check his bag, in which he had hidden his disassembled pistol in his toiletries kit. Passengers traveling under U.S. documents were almost never checked. It was a long-standing tradition in Switzerland, probably because of the billions of American dollars on deposit in Swiss banks.

It would not take very long, however, before his name on the passenger manifest rang some alarm bells and the Federal Police would begin looking for him. Before that he definitely wanted to show his face. And Lausanne was as good as any city to show it in.

He rented a Ford Taurus from the Hertz counter and within the hour he had cleared Geneva and was heading the thirty-five miles on N1 along the north shore of Lake Geneva, the morning bright and warm.

It had been a long time since he'd last been here, and coming back like this was dredging up a lot of memories, some pleasant, and others not quite so pleasant. And now his daughter Elizabeth was in country, attending school outside of Bern. He wanted to see her, or at least telephone, but if he was being watched she would be endangered.

"The business has ruined our lives," Kathleen had told him at the divorce hearing eight years ago. "I've got to get out, Kirk, before it completely swallows Elizabeth and me."

By that time the CIA had already fired him, and he'd had every intention of getting out. But he'd not protested the divorce, and it hadn't been too long afterward that Trotter had come to Lausanne looking for him, asking him for help. "We can't do it without you, Kirk," he'd said. "Believe me, if there'd been another way, we would have taken it."

And so it had began, again, for him. And, he supposed, it would never stop until he got a bullet in his head.

He pulled into a wayside park along the lake shore between Nyon and Rolle, about halfway to Lausanne, shortly before noon and reassembled his Walther PPK. Apparently no one had followed him from Paris, though he suspected Marquand's people would be somewhere nearby. Nor were the Swiss on his tail yet. At least not outwardly.

But, if the French intelligence officer had been correct in his assessment of the ex-STASI organization, they might have already spotted him. He did not want to become a sitting duck for some fanatic still fighting the Cold War.

If someone shot at him, he was definitely going to shoot back. If, on the other hand, the Swiss Police caught up with him first, they would deport him immediately whether or not he was armed.

Lausanne was a city of some quarter-million people, and the traffic was horrendous, partly because of the narrowness of the streets, and partly because at all times it seemed that the city was being torn down and rebuilt.

McGarvey locked his bag in the trunk and had the Lausanne-Prince Hotel valet downtown park his car, before heading the two blocks over to the Place Saint-François on foot.

He stopped at the news kiosk and bought a newspaper and the latest copy of *Stern*, the German newsmagazine. A photograph of the downed Airbus was on the cover.

Across the square his old bookstore, International Booksellers, still occupied the same two-story yellow brick building. Marta had told him that his former Swiss partner, Dortmund Füelm, to whom he'd sold the store, still ran the place. Füelm had been one of the Federal Police watchdogs assigned to him, but when McGarvey had left, Füelm had retired, and stayed on at the store.

No one had followed him from Geneva, and no one in the busy square seemed to be paying him or the bookstore any special attention, so, folding the newspaper and magazine and stuffing them under his arm, McGarvey crossed with traffic and went inside.

Füelm, an old man, stooped and white-haired, was at the back of the small shop, speaking with two men about an expensive art book. He looked up, spotted McGarvey and did a double take, his eyes growing wide.

He hurried over. "*Gott in Himmel,* I can scarcely believe my senses," he cried, and he and McGarvey embraced.

"You look fit, my old friend," McGarvey said.

"And you do as well," the old man replied, the smile fading from his face. "I just learned last night about our little Mati." He shook his head. "I'm so sorry, Kirk. We all are. She was so full of life."

"It's why I came back. I thought perhaps I might speak with her parents, maybe her friends. She was in Paris to see me, you know."

Füelm nodded. "Yes, I know, Kirk. And believe me, I wish that you could stay in Switzerland, but it's just not possible."

McGarvey stepped back, careful to keep his hands away from his jacket.

"He's armed," Füelm told the two men who'd put down the art book.

"We wish for no trouble, Herr McGarvey," one of the men said. They both looked like professional boxers.

"I didn't come expecting trouble," McGarvey said.

One of the Federal cops took the pistol from McGarvey's belt at the small of his back. Füelm had felt it during their embrace.

"Then why are you armed, Kirk?" Füelm asked.

"Old habits."

Füelm nodded sadly. "You must leave Switzerland immediately. These gentlemen will escort you back to Cointrin. Where do you wish to go? Back to Paris?"

"Washington."

"Very well."

"I left a rental car at the Lausanne-Prince. My bag is in the trunk."

"The car has already been taken care of, Kirk. And your bag is on its way to the airport."

McGarvey smiled. "You Swiss can't be faulted for lack of efficiency."

"No," Füelm said. "And I'll pass along your condolences to Mati's people. She often spoke of you to them, and they always wanted to meet you. Her father especially."

"I'm sure they're good people."

"Yes, they are," Füelm said.

He and McGarvey shook hands. "Take care, Dortmund."

Füelm leaned in close and lowered his voice. "Find the monsters who did this to our little Mati, Kirk. Find them, and kill them!"

17

McGarvey thought about Otto Rencke all the way across the Atlantic from London, and by the time his Northwest flight touched down a few minutes before eight at Washington's Dulles International Airport, he'd decided to use the man.

No one was waiting for him at customs or in the Arrivals Hall, which was surprising. He thought that the Swiss would have sent word that he was coming in, just as an interagency courtesy.

There was little doubt in his mind that Murphy wanted him involved in the Swissair business, just as the French did. But before he made any decision he needed more information than he expected the DCI would be willing to give him.

He'd thought a lot about that between Geneva and London, and then on the long flight across the Atlantic, and he had come to the conclusion that if he could find Rencke and convince the man to help, he would go through the back door. With any luck he would learn what he had to know for his own safety before anyone out at Langley knew what was happening.

Although he was getting no sense that anyone was behind him, or that anyone was watching, he thought it would happen sooner or later. "Trouble has a way of finding you," he'd been told more than once. And it was true.

He took a cab to the Marriott Key Bridge Motel and after it was gone he took another cab across the river to Union Station, where he took still another cab to the Holiday Inn Georgetown where he registered under the name of Tom Patton, paying with some of the cash he'd changed at the airport. For the moment, at least, he wanted anonymity here in Washington.

As of a couple of years ago, Rencke lived with his computers and a dozen cats in an ancient brick house that had once been the quarters for the caretaker of Holy Rood Cemetery. Then he had been a computer systems consultant on a freelance basis for the Pentagon and the National Security Agency. His particular talent was an almost superhuman ability to visualize entire complex systems, including supercomputers, satellite links, data encryption devices, and all the peripheral equipment and connections that linked them, and make them user friendly.

But at thirty-nine he was already a has-been from a dozen different jobs and callings. Trained as a Jesuit priest, he'd been, at twenty, one of the youngest professors of mathematics ever to teach at Georgetown University. But he liked women too much, so in 1974 he'd been fired from his job and defrocked all in the same day.

From there he'd enlisted in the army, as a computer specialist, but he'd been given a bad conduct discharge nine months later, because he also liked boys if there were no girls immediately available.

For a year he'd dropped out of sight, but then had shown up on the CIA's payroll, his Jesuit and Army records apparently wiped completely clean, so that he passed the vetting process with ease.

McGarvey had run into the man on several occasions at Langley, where Rencke had taken charge of the Agency's archives section, bringing it into the computer age.

They'd worked together again in Germany, and once in South America where Rencke had come to straighten out the station's electronic equipment.

In his spare time, Rencke had updated the Company's entire communications system, standardized their spy satellite input and analysis systems (so that CIA machines could crosstalk, thus sharing information, with NSA equipment), and devised a field officer's briefing system whereby pertinent, up-to-date information could be funneled directly to the officer on assignment when and as he needed it.

His past had caught up with him a few years ago, and like McGarvey, he'd become a pariah across the river.

It was after ten by the time McGarvey had reassembled his pistol (the Swiss had returned it to him on condition he show them how he'd gotten it through Cointrin's X-ray equipment) and he walked across the street into the cemetery. The evening was dark, the sky overcast and the air extremely humid. A light fog had formed from the river, muffling sounds and forming halos around the streetlights. It was a Sunday night; nothing much was moving in Washington.

The small, two-story house at the rear of the cemetery looked to be in reasonable condition, but deserted. There were no curtains or blinds in any of the windows, except one large bay window on the ground floor, nor was there a car in the carport, or a lawnmower, or paint cans, or anything else that would indicate Rencke was still in residence.

McGarvey stood in the shadows across a narrow lane watching the front of the house for any signs of life. As he remembered, Rencke had been a night person, preferring to sleep during the day. Of course there was no reason to believe that he was still here, or that something else in his past hadn't caught up with him and landed him in jail. But there also was no reason to believe he wasn't still here.

"Boo," someone said softly behind him.

McGarvey, startled, reached for his pistol, but then relaxed and turned around. It was Rencke; he'd recognized the voice, even in that one word.

The computer whiz looked like a twenty-year-old kid, with long, out-of-control frizzy red hair, wild eyebrows, and a gaunt, almost ascetic frame. He was dressed in Nikes, ragged blue jeans and a Moscow State University sweatshirt, its sleeves cut off at the shoulders. He was grinning.

"So, Mac, what're you doing wandering about in a cemetery in the middle of the night?" Rencke asked. "Let me guess. You're looking for bad guys. You're working freelance, still. And you've come to ask for my help. Is that about it?"

McGarvey had to smile. "You could have gotten yourself shot, you stupid bastard."

Rencke's head bobbed as if it were on springs. "Your control is better than that. I'm not stupid. And I'm not a bastard. Oh, well, I figure one out of three isn't so bad under the circumstances."

"I am here to ask for help, but what were you doing sneaking around in the cemetery at this hour? I thought you'd be at your computers."

"I had a Twinkie attack." Rencke wasn't carrying a bag. He grinned sheepishly. "Couldn't wait, so I ate them already. Bad me."

"I need to get into Langley archives, and maybe an operational file or two," McGarvey said. "Possible?"

Again Rencke's head bobbed up and down. "Anything is possible, Mac. Weren't you taught that in school? Come on, let's see how tough they've made it these days." He winked. "Of course it depends on whether they've discovered my screen door."

"Screen door?" McGarvey asked, as he followed Rencke across to the house and inside. The front door wasn't locked.

"We can put a screen door into a computer program . . . most of them leak like a sieve, you'd be surprised . . . but no one's figured out how to successfully install a screen door in a submarine. Especially a Los Angeles class boat. Right? Right?"

Rencke was almost bursting with suppressed humor and enthusiasm.

"So you've kept up with me," McGarvey said. He'd been involved with an incident over a hijacked Los Angeles class sub a couple years ago. "Why?"

Rencke led them into the living room, packing paper taped up over the bay windows. Soft lights automatically came on, as did a half-dozen monitor screens. He stopped and turned back to McGarvey.

"Do you want me to tell you something, Mac?" he asked, but didn't wait for an answer. "Okay. I find you endlessly fascinating. You're like a computer, only I can't figure out the CPU. I haven't even got your clock speed yet. So I keep watching. It's better than the Dodgers used to be."

"The man's name is Karl Boorsch. He was the shooter at Orly on Friday. Did you hear about it?"

"The Swissair flight. It was in all the newspapers. I'm not a hermit here."

"He's ex-STASI, I recognized him, and the SDECE made him as well. They suggested that he might be working for a well-funded organization of ex-STASI officers on the run from the new German government."

"Just like the Odessa," Rencke said. "The organization of former Nazi SS officers, you know. Big thing in the fifties and sixties. They mostly all died off, though."

"There were a couple of Agency types aboard that flight. Probably Boorsch's target."

Rencke's head was bobbing. "You want to know about this STASI outfit. You want to know who funds it. You want to know who they are, where they're hiding these days, and who their leaders are." He took a deep breath. "And, you want to peek at operations to see what they had cooked up. That about it, Mac?"

McGarvey nodded. "The general wants to see me, and I wanted to be prepared before I went over there. I don't like surprises."

"I see what you mean," Rencke said knitting his eyebrows. His complexion was very pale, his lips red. "Surprises are fun unless they start shooting at you." He dropped into a chair in front of a terminal and pulled up a telephone line.

"Can you help?"

"Go away," Rencke said, his voice already distant. "Come again another day." The Central Intelligence Agency's logo, a shield topped by an eagle's head, appeared on the screen. "Bring some Twinkies when you come back. A lot of Twinkies."

18

"I hate pigeons. They shit over everything and yet the city protects them."

Tom Lynch looked up from where he was seated on a bench in the Jardin du Luxembourg as a heavily built, swarthy man approached and sat down next to him. It was a few minutes after nine in the morning, the day already pleasant. It was Monday so there weren't any children around.

"Squab."

"Nothing but an overpriced dead pigeon," Phillipe Marquand said. He'd brought a small paper bag of cracked corn and he tossed out a handful for the birds who immediately flocked around.

"I thought Frenchmen were all gourmands."

"I'm a Corsican," Marquand flared. "And I didn't come here to discuss food."

"I didn't think you had," Lynch said mildly. He didn't like the SDECE colonel, but this was a friendly country in which the CIA had to walk with care. His instructions from Langley were to meet with the man, but give him nothing. The official line was that our people were making a routine trip to Switzerland, and that the terrorist attack had been nothing more than just that . . . a random act of violence.

The U.S. State Department's Anti-Terrorism Task Force was

working hand-in-hand with the French, which was as far as the White House wanted it to go for the moment.

"The Swiss kicked McGarvey out yesterday, did you know that?" Marquand asked. "We tracked him through London as far as Dulles, but then lost him. You wouldn't happen to know where he is now?"

"No," Lynch said. "Should I?"

"I would think that someone would want to ask him a few questions about Friday."

"I understand you and he spoke."

Marquand nodded.

"Is that why you knew he'd gone to Switzerland? It was an old flame of his aboard that flight. He'd known her from Lausanne. Said he was going to pay his respects."

"He is apparently a generous man, your McGarvey. But it was not the only reason he went to Switzerland."

"No?" Lynch said quietly.

"He was showing his face, hoping that the friends of Karl Boorsch might show themselves."

"Should I know this name?"

"He's the man who shot down one-four-five," Marquand said. "Former East German STASI hitman. Belongs to an organization of ex-STASI thugs who've gone freelance."

The information given so freely was breathtaking, but Lynch managed to maintain his control. "Have you any other names?"

"Not for now. But obviously Boorsch and his people want to stop your inquiries in Switzerland. Would you care to share anything with me?"

"Not at this moment," Lynch said looking the Frenchman straight in the eye.

Marquand's jaw tightened. "There were Frenchmen aboard that flight. Vacationers, most of them. Some with their families. In one case it was the mother and father, twin five-year-old girls, and the old grandmother. They will be buried in a common grave, what bits of their bodies were found, that is."

"I'm sorry."

"Yes, we all are. But it was no random act of terrorism, as you would like us all to believe."

Lynch started to object but Marquand held him off.

"Two of your people were escorting a Swiss citizen to Geneva. It is our belief that the STASI group wanted them stopped. We simply want to know why. What are you investigating?"

"I can't say, Phillipe," Lynch replied carefully, realizing by even telling the SDECE colonel that much he was giving away more than Langley had wanted him to give away.

Marquand nodded. "I told McGarvey this . . ."

"He is a civilian."

"But a special man. I also told him that we believe the ex-STASI group is well financed, maintaining its bank in Switzerland. Did you know this?"

Lynch held his silence, but he was seething inside. McGarvey should have told him about his meeting with Marquand. But he had lied.

"What we didn't know . . . or I should say suspect . . . is who has provided the bulk of their financing." Marquand looked away. "In the old days we might have suspected the Soviet Union. Perhaps the PLO, they sometimes fund outside groups. But it was none of these."

"No?" Lynch said.

Marquand turned back. "No," he said. "Our sources in Switzerland tell us that the currency paid into those accounts was in the form of yen. Japanese money. Now, what do you think about that?"

Seventy-five yards away, a man dressed in a French police uniform stood at an open window on the second floor of the School of Mines main building. He'd followed Marquand from Action Service Headquarters off the Boulevard Mortier, and it was only by happenstance that he spotted Lynch seated alone on the park bench in time to get into position.

He'd put it together that Marquand had come here to meet with the American CIA chief of station, and he knew that whatever those two men had to say would be of extreme importance.

He had missed the opening chitchat, but not the meat of their conversation. Lowering the four-inch parabolic antenna, which he'd carried in a leather haversack, he watched as Lynch walked off.

Spranger would pay well for this information, especially because it was the worst of all news.

19

The Director of Central Intelligence's chauffeured Cadillac limousine headed down Pennsylvania Avenue toward the White House a few minutes before 9:30 A.M. As usual, Monday morning traffic was heavy, but the day promised to be beautiful.

Murphy was in a puzzled, almost pensive mood. For the first time in his long government service career he was running up against a situation for which he had no clear answers. They could provide the President with the data—speculations, actually, because that's all they really had to this point—but it would be up to him to make the decisions.

In the transition period between the Cold War and what the politicians were now starting to call the "new world order," there was no predicting what could and would happen.

"Look at the war with Iraq and the subsequent fallout in the Gulf region," he'd told a gathering of U.S. military intelligence chiefs at the Pentagon. "There was no way in which we as an intelligence-gathering service could have foreseen even in broad strokes what came to pass.

"We can provide the raw data. We can provide spot analysis. And we can even point out what we believe are the current trends. But when the leadership of a foreign power we're monitoring doesn't even know where it is going, there is no chance for us to provide any realtime recommendations."

The unspoken crux of the situation, however, as all of them that day knew, was that their customers—the leaders who made use of the intelligence information they were provided—wanted the real-time advice.

As the President would today, he thought. Only this time there were no answers, not even any clear speculation.

Murphy's limo was passed through the White House gate to the West Portico, where he was ushered immediately upstairs to the Oval Office, his bodyguard waiting downstairs.

It was precisely 9:30. The President rose when Murphy came in and went around to the serving cart. He poured two cups of coffee and handed one to his DCI.

"You know, whenever you come in here with that look on your face, Roland, I automatically brace for the worst," the President said. He was a tall man whose face showed the strain of the office. But his eyes were penetratingly sharp, and he seldom if ever missed a beat. His staff had to keep up with his schedule, not the other way around.

"You haven't had the messenger shot yet," Murphy said, setting down his coffee cup. He took a leather-covered folder from his briefcase and handed it to the President. "This is the latest from Paris."

"Have a seat," the President said, putting down his coffee and sitting in his rocking chair. Murphy settled onto the leather couch across the coffee table.

"My chief of Paris Station met this morning with a colonel in the SDECE's Action Service, and was given some information. What I would call startling information."

"You've not pussyfooted before, General, don't start now," the President said, not yet opening the report. "Spell it out for me."

"The terrorist attack on the Swissair flight out of Orly on Friday may have some deeper, more ominous significance than we first suspected. The French intelligence service has identified the attacker as a man by the name of Karl Boorsch. An officer in the old East German intelligence service. We have him in our files as missing, and presumed still at large somewhere in Europe."

"You don't think he went to the Soviet Union?"

"No, sir," Murphy said. "But he wasn't working alone. The French found a walkie-talkie of an unusually advanced design in the van Boorsch used to penetrate Orly security."

"Go on."

"We haven't been able to figure out exactly how it works yet, but we know that it encrypts the signal, compresses it into an incredibly brief duration, and sends it out. Virtually undetectable by any equipment we currently have in the field."

"Who built it?"

Murphy shook his head. "There are no manufacturing plates or marks anywhere on the device."

"German?"

"Possibly. But it means that Boorsch had help."

"Which tends to verify the Swiss engineer's story," the President said.

"The French believe that an organization of ex-STASI members has been formed, presumably somewhere in Europe, perhaps even Switzerland, which tends to confirm the reports we've been hearing."

"Just what we need." The President shook his head and looked away for a moment. His presidency had been a successful one to date, but definitely anything but quiet. Someone in the media had begun calling him "America's crisis president," and the moniker seemed to be catching on.

"Apparently they're organized well enough to maintain at least two bank accounts; one in Zurich, and the other in Bern."

"What do they think they're trying to do? Retake East Germany? What's their purpose?"

"It's unknown at this point, Mr. President," Murphy said.

"Where are they getting their money? Who is supplying it?"

"Also unknown," Murphy said, girding himself. "But the French Action Service officer told my Chief of Station that they had identified the currency in which payments had been made into at least one of the STASI organization's accounts."

The President's left eyebrow rose. "Is this fact significant?"

Murphy sighed. "Well, Mr. President, if it is, I think we're in big trouble."

"As I said, spell it out."

"The payments were made in yen. Japanese yen."

"It's a stable currency," the President said. "I'm told that there's a small but growing movement to suspend trade on the international marketplace in dollars. The yen might be the next logical choice."

"Japan may be the country of origin for the payments into the STASI accounts."

"Could also be a ploy to throw off the investigation."

"I don't believe so, Mr. President, although it's a possibility."

"Because, Roland, God help us if what I think you're suggesting has even the slightest grain of truth."

Murphy said nothing, allowing the President to come to the same conclusions he'd come to earlier.

"If this group of ex-STASI officers is the same group who went after the engineers at ModTec, and from what you're telling me it looks as if that's the case, and if they're being funded by the Japanese, possibly the government . . ."

"I'm sorry, Mr. President, but there's no evidence to that effect."

"If that's the case, Roland, then it could mean that the Japanese are in the market for nuclear weapons technology."

Murphy sighed deeply and sat back. "I simply don't know."

The President had another thought. It was clear from his expression that he was still on the same path Murphy had gone down.

"Could this walkie-talkie the French found have been designed and manufactured by a Japanese company?"

"It's possible."

"Is it likely?" the President pressed.

"I can't answer that, sir," Murphy said. There was more to come.

The President's eyes narrowed. "What was Jim Shirley involved with when he was assassinated in Tokyo?"

"He was meeting with a man who claimed to be a Belgian banking adviser to a consortium of businesses in Japan. But he was an imposter, and there is no such consortium."

"Coincidence?"

"On the surface one would have to say no. But only on the surface. There is absolutely no solid connection between Japan and this STASI group. Nor has there been the slightest hint that the Japanese, that anyone in Japan, has the slightest interest in nuclear weapons technology."

"Give me a reading on this, Roland," the President said.

Murphy shook his head. "I'm sorry, Mr. President, but I can't do that."

"What is being done?"

"We're investigating ModTec to see if anyone else has been approached, and to see if the technology has already changed hands. We're also looking into the French assertion that the STASI accounts exist and that they've received Japanese currency payments."

"And in Japan?"

"We're investigating Jim Shirley's murder, of course. But beyond that . . . I'll need your authorization. Considering the pending trade agreement between our countries, if it were to come out that the CIA is spying against Japan it would go badly."

"You have my authorization, Roland," the President said. He sat forward. "Let me make myself perfectly clear. You are to take this investigation to its logical conclusion. No matter what resources you have to use to do it, and no matter which nation you're led to scrutinize."

"Yes, Mr. President."

"I want results, Roland. Soon."

Carrara came up as soon as Murphy returned from the White House. The DDO has harried. He'd been on the job, or at least in the building, for more than seventy-two hours. Ever since 145 had been shot down.

"We've got the green light to step up the investigation in Tokyo," Murphy said.

"How far can we go?" Carrara asked.

"All the way, Phil. You've got carte blanche on this one."

"If we're caught there'll be a lot of political trouble, not only from the Japanese, but from the Swiss as well."

"This is your operation . . ." Murphy said, but Carrara interrupted, which in itself was a mark of his tiredness.

"Yes, it is, sir. But I just wanted to make sure that everyone understands exactly what we're up against. Lynch thinks that the Action Service is playing us both ends against the middle, and although Kelley Fuller is going back over, she's going to be hard to control."

Murphy was impatient.

"What I'm getting at, Mr. Director, is that so far as I see it, either operation could blow up in our faces."

"We'll take the risk," Murphy said. "Now, where the hell is McGarvey? Is he here in Washington or isn't he?"

"He came through Dulles last night, but then he disappeared."

"Find him," the DCI ordered.

"We're watching his ex-wife's house. He'll show up there sooner or later."

"Good. The minute he does, I want him up here."

20

Otto Rencke thought in colors. He had been doing so for seven years, ever since he'd stumbled across a series of tensor calculus transformations concerning bubble memories that he could not visualize.

He'd hit on the notion of thinking of his calculations in a real-world fashion, coming up at length with the question of how to explain color to a person who'd been born blind.

With mathematics, of course. And he'd devised the system, which turned out to be his bubble memory transformations. If it worked in one direction, there was no reason to think it couldn't work in the other.

Lavender, for example, was among the simplest of all. In his mind's eye he could visualize an entire multidimensional array of complex calculations that described a many-tiered and interlocking series of traps leading into the CIA's computer system.

Someone had found and negated his old screen door program, which would have allowed him fairly easy access, replacing it with a complex system of fail-safes. Enter the program from the outside, or in an improper manner, and the incoming circuit would be seized, traced to its source, and an alarm automatically issued . . . all without the intruder knowing he'd been discovered.

A few minutes after ten in the morning, Rencke suddenly smiled.

On his main monitor, which glowed lavender, the CIA's logo

appeared in the upper left hand corner, beneath which the agency's computer asked him:

WELCOME TO ARCHIVES
DO YOU WISH TO SEE A MENU?

He jumped up and went into the kitchen where a half-dozen cats swarmed around him, meowing insistently. "Yes, my little darlings, I hear you," he cried. "Patience. The color is lavender and you dears must have patience."

Opening several cans of cat food and distributing them around the kitchen floor, he took a nearly full half-gallon carton of skim milk back into the living room, drinking from it as he went, milk spilling down his front and soaking his sweatshirt. But he didn't give a damn.

"The sonsabitches thought they could fuck me," he shouted, dancing around the lavender screen. "But they were wrong. Hoo, boy, they were wrong!"

McGarvey paid off his cabby and stood for a moment or two at the end of the long driveway leading up to his ex-wife's house in Chevy Chase. The country club was across the street, and in the distance he heard someone shout: "Fore!"

The house was an expensive two-story colonial set well back on a half acre of manicured lawn. A half-dozen white pillars supported a broad overhang protecting a long front veranda.

Whatever Kathleen was or was not, he thought, starting up the walk, she was a classy woman. They'd been divorced for eight years now, after a twelve-year marriage, and it was often difficult for McGarvey to remember clearly what their life together had been like, but it had been stylish.

Stormy at the end, though, in those days when he was gone more than he was at home. She'd guessed, in an offhanded way, that he actually worked for the CIA, that he was, in her words, a macho James Bond spy. But she'd fortunately never guessed the true extent of what he did, the fact that he had killed people in the line of his assignments.

But she'd always maintained a lovely, proper home (she had come into their marriage not wealthy, but certainly independent), and in public she presented a self-assured, dignified image. Not aloof, or snobbish, simply well put together.

It had come to a showdown: He'd had to choose either her, or his career. He'd just returned from Santiago where'd he'd taken out a Chilean general who would have probably taken over the country by coup. But his orders had been changed in midstream. The general was not to be killed. Even though the change in orders reached McGarvey too late, he'd been fired from the CIA.

On that night, not knowing what had happened, Kathleen had issued him the ultimatum. Even though her demand that he quit the business had been a moot point at that moment, he'd turned her down.

"We cannot have a marriage in which one of us dictates the other's life," he told her.

"You're right," she said, and he'd turned around and walked out, not even bothering to unpack his bag from his trip.

He'd been younger then, more sure of himself, more arrogant, and yet in some respects more frightened that something out of his past would be coming after him now that he no longer had the backing of the Agency.

What he hadn't counted on was the loneliness, and the missing his daughter, who when he had left was eleven years old.

Kathleen answered the door almost immediately. She was dressed in a pair of blue jeans and a T-shirt, her feet bare, her hair pinned up in back, and no makeup, yet she looked like a model out of a fashion magazine. Her neck was long and delicate, her features precise yet not hard. But it was her eyes that most people noticed first. They were large beneath highly arched eyebrows, and were a startling, almost unreal shade of green.

She smiled. "Hello, Kirk. When did you get back?"

"Last night. But it was too late to call."

She stepped back. "Come in," she said.

He followed her through the house to the large kitchen overlooking the swimming pool. The sliding glass doors were open, the odor of chlorine sharp.

"Sorry about the awful smell, but the poolman was just here," she said. "Coffee?"

"Sure," McGarvey said, sitting at the counter. "What have you heard from Liz lately?"

"Elizabeth," Kathleen corrected automatically. "Everything is fine. She loves school, but she misses home a little. That I got between the lines."

"Does she need anything?"

"No," Kathleen said, bringing their coffee over. "She called Saturday. Said everyone at school was talking about the Swissair flight that was shot down . . ." She stopped in mid-sentence.

"Everybody in Paris was talking about it too," McGarvey said, sidestepping Kathleen's next question. "There'll always be crazies out there."

"The news said that the terrorist had been cornered by an unidentified American."

"So I heard."

Kathleen was staring at him. "Are you home for good this time?" she asked stiffly.

"Almost."

Her eyes narrowed. "Almost?" she asked. "Almost, as in, not yet?"

"There's something I have to take care of first . . ."

"No," Kathleen said simply.

"I'm sorry, Katy, but it's important."

Kathleen reared back. "My name is Kathleen," she screeched. "Not Katy."

The doorbell rang.

"I want you to leave," she said. "Now! I want you out of my house, and I don't ever want to see you back here!"

The doorbell rang again.

"All right," she screamed. She spun on her heel and stormed back out to the stairhall.

McGarvey got up and went to the kitchen door as Kathleen opened the front door, and he just caught a glimpse of two men dressed in light slacks and sportcoats standing on the veranda.

Kathleen said something that he couldn't quite catch.

McGarvey ducked back. They definitely were Company. The Agency would have to know that he would show up here sooner or later. They'd merely misjudged their timing, but not by very much. Whatever Murphy wanted, it had to be important to go to these lengths.

In the old days, Kathleen had always kept the car keys on a hook by the garage door. It was tidy, she said, and the keys would never be misplaced.

He hurried silently across the kitchen and into the laundry room. A set of car keys was hanging on a hook next to the door into the garage. Snatching them, he slipped into the garage and got behind the wheel of Kathleen's 460 SL. With one hand he started the car, while with the other he hit the garage door opener.

As the service door slowly rumbled open, he watched the door from the laundry room.

It was snatched open a couple of seconds later, and McGarvey got a brief glimpse of a man in a sport coat. He dropped the gearshift into drive and slammed the gas pedal to the floor, the low-slung car shooting out of the garage, just clearing the still-opening main door by no more than two inches.

At the bottom of the driveway, he turned east, the opposite direction that the plain gray government Chevrolet was facing, and was around the corner at the end of the block before the two men who'd come after him even had a chance to cross the street.

The Agency knew for sure now that he was in Washington, and that he was on the run from them. They would be pulling out all the stops to find him. Nobody said no to the general.

McGarvey parked the Mercedes near Union Station, leaving the keys under the floor mat, then walked a half-dozen blocks down to Constitution Avenue where he caught a cab, ordering the driver to take him back to Georgetown. The police would find the car and would return it to Kathleen.

"I want you to stop at a grocery store, or corner market on the way," McGarvey said.

"Sir?"

"I need to pick up some Twinkies."

21

McGarvey had a fairly high degree of confidence that Rencke's intrusion into the CIA's computer system would not be detected. Nevertheless he approached the house in Holy Rood Cemetery with precautions, passing twice from different directions to make certain the place wasn't being watched.

There were a few people visiting graves, and a grounds-keeper was mowing the lawn near the Whitehaven Parkway entrance, but no one seemed interested in the house. Nor had there been anyone stationed at the entrance so far as McGarvey had been able to determine.

He crossed the gravel driveway, mounted the three steps to the porch and knocked on the front door. Without waiting for Rencke to answer it, he let himself in.

The house was very still. The odors of Rencke's cats mingled in the air with the odors of electronics equipment. But nothing moved. It was as if the place had been abandoned.

He'd brought a bag of Twinkies for Rencke. Laying them on the hall table, he took out his Walther, eased the safety catch on the off position, and moved silently to the archway into the living room.

Nothing seemed out of place except that only one computer monitor seemed to be working. Everything else had apparently been shut off. The one screen that was lit showed nothing but the color lavender.

Turning back into the stairhall, McGarvey stopped and cocked an ear to listen. Still there were no sounds from anywhere in the house.

It was possible that Rencke's computer hacking had been detected and he'd been arrested, but McGarvey doubted it.

"Otto?" he called out.

There was no answer. He went to the foot of the stairs and stopped again to listen. Had there been a movement on the second floor?

"It's me. It's Mac."

A toilet flushed, and Rencke, still wearing the same clothes from last night, appeared at the head of the stairs.

"Did you bring my Twinkies?" He asked, yawning as he came down.

McGarvey smiled and nodded. The man was incredible. "I brought them," he said, putting away his gun. "The house was quiet, I thought something was wrong."

"What were you intending on doing, shooting my cats?" Rencke asked. "They're outside. Now, my Twinkies, I'm starving."

McGarvey gave Rencke the bag and followed him back to the kitchen. Unwashed dishes were piled in the sink, and a pot of something had been allowed to cook down to a charred mass on the stove. The burner had been turned off, but the pan had been left as is. Empty cat food cans littered the floor, and in a back hallway, several litter boxes were full to overflowing.

Rencke got a carton of milk from the refrigerator. "Did you see it?"

"What?"

"My beautiful lavender. Or are you color-blind?"

"I saw it," McGarvey said. "Did you get in?"

"Just like raping a willing virgin," Rencke said, brushing past McGarvey and heading back to the front of the house. "With ease. With ease."

"What did you find out?" McGarvey asked, following him.

Rencke plunked down in front of the lavender terminal. "It's a scary world out there, Mac. And it's getting scarier, if you know what I mean."

He opened a package of Twinkies, ate them both and then drank nearly half the milk, some of it spilling down his front. No crumbs or milk, however, got anywhere near the equipment.

"Some Company hotshot evidently found my rear-entry program and replaced it with a fairly sophisticated system of interlocks. They're finally starting to use their heads over there. A day late and in this case a dollar short, but they're thinking." Rencke drank some more milk. "I don't think there are more than three people in the world besides me who could have gotten in like I did."

"Were you detected?"

"No," Rencke said. "At least I don't think so. But this is hot stuff,

Mac. I mean short of Russian tanks rolling down Pennsylvania Avenue, the hottest."

"Did you make printouts?"

Rencke was eating another Twinkie. He nodded. "But when I was done I shredded the lot," he said, his mouth full. "I didn't want that kind of shit lying around here. I'd rather have a hundred ks of blow with a sign on it on my front porch."

McGarvey had pulled up a chair. "Tell me what you found out."

"First I want something from you."

"Name it."

"You said Karl Boorsch was the rocket man at Orly last week. What were you doing there? What was your relationship with him and this STASI group?"

McGarvey told Rencke everything, including his history with Marta and the Swiss Federal Police, Colonel Marquand's information, and about the pair who'd showed up at Kathleen's house this morning.

"You're certain they were Company muscle?" Rencke asked.

"It was a Company car. I have no reason at this point to suspect they were anything but Murphy's people."

"You would have been leaving your ex in a hell of a jam otherwise," Rencke said thoughtfully.

McGarvey had had the same thought.

"You weren't followed here? By anyone?"

"No."

Rencke looked at the lavender screen. "They're busy over there this morning, so it's too dangerous to get back in. If you want to wait until tonight, I'll show you what I came up with. But if you're in a hurry—and I think you should be in one hell of a hurry—you'll have to rely on my memory as well as my veracity."

"I trust you, or else I wouldn't have come here in the first place," McGarvey said.

"What are your intentions? You said you'd meet with Murphy."

"It might depend on what you've come up with. Marta was a good friend."

Rencke was silent for a long moment or two. McGarvey thought he could hear the cats mewing at the door.

"I dipped into your file while I was at it," Rencke said. "You've been up against the best, and survived, though not without injury. A couple of times you almost bought it."

McGarvey said nothing.

"This one is bigger, or at least I think it could be. Maybe more important. But you'd be up against a highly trained and well-motivated group. Not just one Russian hitman."

"Then there is a group of ex-STASI field officers?"

"They're called K-1, but what the significance of that is, or even if it's true, isn't clear. You have to remember that all I'm giving you is what came out of CIA archives, and out of one Operations file. Any of that could be in error. You know the drill."

"Do you know where they're headquartered?"

"There've been rumors that they went to ground somewhere in the south of France. Provence. Maybe even Monaco. But no one down there is talking, even to the SDECE."

"If the Action Service involves itself that might change. Anything on the leadership?"

"There were about three dozen names on the possibles list, which I think is nothing more than a list of STASI goons still missing. Boorsch was on the list, and so was General Ernst Spranger."

"The butcher of the Horst Wessel," McGarvey said. He'd been number three in the STASI, in charge of Department Viktor, modeled after the KGB's assassination, kidnapping and sabotage section. His intelligence was outdone only by his ruthlessness.

"You know the name?"

McGarvey nodded. "If he's on the loose he'll be the one in charge. And in fact it was probably Spranger who formed the group. But what about their finances? They couldn't have gotten much out of East Germany. There wasn't much there to get at the end."

"We'll come back to that. First, do you know why Boorsch shot that airliner out of the sky?"

"It had to do with a couple of CIA case officers aboard. But the Paris COS wouldn't tell me a thing."

"Don Cladstrup and Bob Roningen," Rencke said. "They were on their way to Lausanne with a Swiss national by the name of Jean-Luc DuVerlie. Do any of those names tickle your funnybone?"

"Roningen was a weapons expert at the Farm, I think," McGarvey replied. "But who was DuVerlie?"

"An engineer with the Swiss firm of ModTec."

There was something in Rencke's eyes. Something, suddenly, in his voice. McGarvey sat forward.

"What is it, Otto?"

"Do you know what ModTec is into? Among other things."

"No."

"In order to construct a nuclear weapon these days you only need three high-tech elements. The rest of the components are of the hardware store variety. You need a critical mass of weapons-grade fuel—plutonium or enriched uranium, for instance. You need an initiator, which is nothing more than a tiny source of high energy particles to get the chain reaction going. Sort of like the lighted match tossed into a pile of firewood. And you need a number of electronic triggering devices to ignite the dynamite or whatever other explosive you use to force the plutonium together. ModTec builds the triggers, and DuVerlie was one of the trigger engineers."

"Spranger's group went after the triggers, is that what you're telling me?"

"Evidently. Which our Deputy Director of Intelligence Tommy

Doyle believes is only the tip of the iceberg. It's his theory that K-1 is after the whole enchilada. A working nuclear weapon . . . or the parts to build one."

"Did they get the triggers?"

"Unknown."

"How about the other components . . . the initiator and the fuel?"

"Unknown."

"What else?"

"There were two new entries in the file, generated in the Paris Station. Tom Lynch was the signatory, and his source was your Action Service Colonel Marquand."

"About finances. Marquand told me that the SDECE believed the STASI group maintained bank accounts in at least two Swiss cities, Bern and Zurich."

Rencke nodded. "The currency paid into at least one of those accounts was in yen."

"Japan?" McGarvey said, stunned.

"The source was unknown, but the currency was Japanese. Makes for some interesting speculation, doesn't it."

"Jesus, I guess," McGarvey said sitting back. "What else?"

"That's it except for one little item concerning you. Seems as if you knew Karl Boorsch."

McGarvey nodded. "We had a run-in a few years ago."

"Did you recognize him at the airport?"

"Yes."

"But you didn't report it. That may have generated some suspicion. You have some enemies at Langley, among them the Company's general counsel."

"Ryan."

"Right," Rencke said. "Listen, Mac, I may be reading between the lines, but I think they might be on a witch-hunt out there, and you may be one of their primary targets."

"I can take care of myself. But I want you to destroy your enter and search program. If someone gets wind of the fact that you've been . . ."

"Dallying in the valley they'll put me in jail and throw away the key." Rencke smiled. "Before they did that I'd unleash Ralph."

"Ralph?"

"He's a super-virus. Wouldn't be a computer program or memory load in the entire defense-intelligence community left intact. And I don't even need my computer to activate it. I only need access to a telephone." Rencke was grinning maliciously. "They won't fuck with me and get away with it."

It was after one in the afternoon when McGarvey showed up at the main gate to the CIA's headquarters at Langley. He'd rented a car from Hertz, and he waited behind the wheel while one of the civilian contract guards notified Phil Carrara that he had a guest. The reaction was almost immediate.

The guard came back out, a tense expression on his face. "Do you have any identification, Mr. McGarvey?"

McGarvey handed out his passport, and the guard took it back inside. Two other guards came out, but they remained across the road, watching him.

A half minute later the first guard came out and returned McGarvey's passport, as well as a visitor's pass for the car and a plastic lapel pass.

"Drive straight up under the entry canopy, sir. Mr. Carrara is coming down."

"Thanks," McGarvey said, and he drove the quarter mile up through the woods and out into the broad clearing where the headquarters building stood.

It'd been a while since he'd been here last, and the old wounds, both mental as well as physical, gave him a twinge. He'd given a lot of himself to this place, or to its ideal, yet he never had been able to clearly answer his own question: Why?

In the old days he'd convinced himself that it was a matter of honor, but in the last days he'd come to realize that he had no real idea what that word meant.

Carrara was waiting at the main entrance when McGarvey parked his car in the visitors spot. "Do you pull this crap just to thumb your nose at the establishment?" the DDO asked angrily.

McGarvey had to smile. "Somebody has to do it, Phil. Otherwise you people would begin to take yourselves too seriously."

22

McGarvey had to sign in at the main desk and be searched with a metal detector before he was allowed to go up on the elevator with Carrara. He'd disassembled his Walther and hidden it among his toiletries back at the hotel. He didn't think the pistol would be confiscated today, but he hadn't wanted to take any chances. He figured he'd be needing it soon.

"Your ex-wife is upset with us, and you," Carrara said on the way up.

"Can you blame her? It was a dumb move, sending your people out there like that."

Carrara looked at him. "Were you so sure that they were ours?"

"The only people in the world who wear plaid sport coats and have short haircuts are your Technical Services legmen. And maybe the odd used-car salesman."

"Tom Lynch said he was quite explicit when he passed the general's orders along to you."

"I'm not on the payroll, Phil. I don't take orders from Murphy. Besides, I had a few things to do in Europe first. And I did come here under my own power."

"Where'd you go in such a hurry this morning?"

McGarvey ignored the question, and moments later the elevator opened on the seventh floor. McGarvey had to sign in again with security people, and this time he was subjected to a hands-on search as well as a metal detector walk-through. Murphy's personal body-guard waited in the outer office, and he carefully scrutinized both McGarvey and Carrara when they were passed through by the general's secretary.

Murphy's office was huge, and very well appointed, with a large desk, bookcases, a leather couch and chairs, and a bank of television monitors and communications equipment. Large windows looked out over the beautiful rolling hills to the south.

Lawrence Danielle and Tom Doyle were seated across from Murphy, who was talking to someone on the phone. When Carrara came in with McGarvey he hung up.

"Welcome home," he said.

"Thank you, General, but I don't know yet if it's good to be back. Or, how long I'll be here."

"There are a few things I'd like to discuss with you, and then we'll offer you another assignment. If you're willing, and if you're up to it."

"I thought as much," McGarvey said.

Murphy motioned him and Carrara to take seats and he picked up his telephone and buzzed his secretary. "Ask Howard to step in for a moment, would you?" He hung up.

"I'm sorry about your two people aboard one-four-five," Mc-Garvey said.

Murphy nodded. "I understand your friend from Switzerland was also aboard. Quite an unhappy coincidence."

"Just that. Nothing more."

"Yes," Murphy said. "We'll see."

Howard Ryan, the Company's general counsel, came in and handed a thin file folder to Murphy. He avoided looking at McGarvey for the moment. Their animosity toward each other went back several years.

"Stick around, Howard. We might need a point of international law," Murphy said. He extracted a printed form from the file folder and handed it across to McGarvey. It was a memo outlining the National Secrets Act and the penalties for divulging classified material to anyone not authorized. "Sign that and we can get started."

McGarvey laid the memo back on Murphy's desk. "If I decide to take the assignment, I'll sign it."

"You'll sign it now, or we'll have you in jail," Ryan blurted.

McGarvey lanquidly turned to him. "On what charge, counselor?"

"Complicity in the murder of one hundred fifty-one crew and passengers aboard the Airbus, and a half-dozen assorted others on the ground."

This was a setup, of course, to try to get him to inadvertently admit something. Murphy and the others were not interfering for the moment. It had always been the same. He'd been a pariah here since Santiago, yet he'd been recalled time after time to help out. They hated themselves for their dependence on him, and consequently they despised and mistrusted him.

"How do you figure that?"

"You knew that we had people aboard that flight, and you knew that an ex-STASI officer by the name of Karl Boorsch was at the airport—you can't deny that you were following him for one reason or another. And yet although you had every opportunity to give the warning, you failed to do so. Makes you a party to an act of terrorism."

"I see," McGarvey said.

"Well?" Ryan demanded.

"I deny the charge, although I admit I thought I recognized Boorsch, but only after I'd cornered him in the VIP lounge."

Ryan started to protest, but Murphy held him off. "Why didn't you tell Tom Lynch about Boorsch? It was important."

"Because I wasn't sure."

"That you recognized him?" Ryan asked.

"I wasn't sure about Tom Lynch or the entire Paris station, which has had problems ever since our embassy was destroyed last winter."

"You were going to tell us about him this morning?" Murphy asked dryly.

"Yes," McGarvey said. "As well as my talk with Phillipe Marquand. You're familiar with that name?"

Murphy nodded.

"And the real reason you went first to Switzerland?" Carrara asked.

"That too," McGarvey said. "Marquand told me that the STASI had formed a freelance group with bank accounts in Zurich and Bern. Boorsch was a member of the organization, and Marquand hoped that if I showed up in Switzerland the others might get nervous and come after me, exposing themselves."

"What happened?"

"Absolutely nothing. I only got as far as Lausanne before the Swiss Federal Police arrested me and kicked me out of the country."

Murphy and the others exchanged glances. "Howard?" the DCI asked the Agency counsel.

"What were you doing at Orly that morning?"

"Seeing an old friend off."

"How'd you know we had people aboard that flight?"

"I didn't, although I knew they were there at the airport. I spotted their car out front. I thought they might be following me again. It's happened before."

"And Boorsch?" Carrara asked.

"If you check my file downstairs you'll see that he and I had a couple of near-misses a few years back."

"Are you saying that Boorsch may have recognized you as well?" Doyle asked, speaking for the first time.

"Almost certainly."

"Which means it's possible that the others would know your face as well," the Deputy Director of Intelligence said.

"That was Marquand's thinking. The French, by the way, don't feel as if we're cooperating with them."

Murphy seemed to have made a decision. He turned again to the Agency's counsel. "Well?"

"Have him sign the memo before you proceed. But if you want my opinion, I say lock him up and throw away the key. He's a dangerously outmoded relic, and has been for some time. If we go ahead and use him again, we'll be just as guilty by association." Ryan got to this feet.

McGarvey looked up, made a gun out of his forefinger and thumb, pointed directly at the man and let the hammer fall.

Ryan shook his head, turned on his heel and left the DCI's office.

Taking a ball-point pen out of his jacket pocket, McGarvey signed the Secrets Act memo, then sat back in his chair. "I'm assuming you want me to go after this STASI organization, and you believe that I'll have a better chance than you of digging them out because they'll recognize me."

"Something like that," Murphy said. "Your starting point, of course, will be their bank accounts in Zurich and Bern." He turned to Carrara. "We'll have to get him back into the country. Do you foresee any problem?"

"I'll manage that on my own," McGarvey broke in. "If and when I need help I'll ask. But as soon as I get started I'll answer only to Phil Carrara. Personally."

Lawrence Danielle, who had sat silently through the entire discussion, suddenly looked to Murphy. "Do you think that's wise, Roland?"

"What's your point, McGarvey," Murphy asked.

"No point," McGarvey said. "It's just the way it's going to be."

"Do you think there is a leak among one of us?" Danielle asked in his soft voice. He was nearing retirement, and he looked and sounded tired, but he was still a power to be reckoned with.

"I don't know. But when my life is on the line I've learned to keep very close tabs on exactly who knows what I'm doing and how I'm going about it."

"Fair enough," Murphy said after a slight hesitation.

"But before I start, or even agree to take this assignment, General, you're going to have to answer a couple of my questions. If I think you're lying to me, or not telling me the entire truth, I'll back out."

Murphy nodded.

"Two of your people were aboard one-four-five. The STASI wanted them eliminated. Why? What were they involved with?"

"They were investigating the possibility that the East German group had targeted the Swiss firm of ModTec. One of their engineers, a man by the name of DuVerlie, claimed to have information about it. Phil will show you the file."

"What were the STASI going for?"

"ModTec designs and builds a number of components for nuclear weapons," Murphy said.

"The STASI may be after the technology, or perhaps even an entire bomb, is that what you're saying?"

"We don't know that yet," Danielle cautioned.

"But it's possible?" McGarvey insisted.

Murphy nodded. "Yes."

"Were they successful at ModTec? Did they get what they wanted?"

"We don't know," Carrara said. "DuVerlie never had a chance to tell us."

"Did you send someone else over there to find out?"

Carrara exchanged glances with Murphy before he answered. "Yes, we have a team investigating the company."

"What about Tokyo," McGarvey said, and the room suddenly went electric. He'd gotten their attention.

"What do you mean?" Murphy asked after a long moment.

"Marquand told me that payments into at least one of the STASI's Swiss bank accounts were in Japanese yen. Is there a connection? Have you gotten any indications from Tokyo Station that the Japanese might be interested in acquiring nuclear weapons technology?"

"God forbid," Danielle said. He was old enough to clearly remember Pearl Harbor and the days that had led up to it.

"Phil?" Murphy passed the question to Carrara.

"At this point there doesn't seem to be any connection between the Japanese and the STASI group, other than the possibility certain payments may have been made into a Swiss bank account in yen. But that currency is strong just now. Wherever they got that funding from, either on their own or through a second party, using yen may have been simply a matter of expediency."

They were lying, and it was so obvious from their faces and sudden change in attitudes that it was almost ludicrous. But he'd learned what he'd come to learn.

"I'll stay clear of ModTec for the moment, and concentrate on the bank accounts. They'll want to protect their money. But if your people find out something, anything at all, I'll expect to be told about it."

"Agreed," Murphy said.

"I'll spend a day or two here in Washington, working with Phil and going through what files you can give me."

"Whatever help we can provide you'll have. But you must

understand that you're not on anyone's payroll. If you run into real trouble, we'll do what we can, but you will be denied."

"It's never been any different, General," McGarvey said, getting to his feet. "Not even in the old days, when I actually was on the payroll."

23

Carrara was as helpful as he could be under the circumstances, but McGarvey believed that the man was working under constraints placed on him by Murphy, probably at Ryan's insistence.

They spent the afternoon together in operations territory on the third floor, going through the Agency's background information on the STASI. Ernst Spranger's name came up at the head of the list of ex-STASI officers whose whereabouts were presently unknown, as did the speculation that the group may have been based somewhere in the south of France.

The information was only useful to the extent that it verified Rencke's story. But Carrara was definitely holding back not only on the information about the STASI's bank accounts and possible connections with Japan, but about ModTec, and DuVerlie, the engineer who'd gone down aboard 145. The operational files in many cases had big gaps, especially on the time and contact sheets which should have outlined by time and date each contact made with DuVerlie or anyone else from the Swiss high-tech company.

Carrara offered no real explanation, nor did McGarvey question him too closely for the moment. Before he went back to Europe, however, he would have it out with the DDO. The last time McGarvey had worked with the man, Carrara had seemed open, and willing at least to try to help. This time he was definitely reticent.

It was six by the time McGarvey was ready to leave for the day. He figured there was little or nothing he could accomplish here for the moment.

"Where are you staying?" Carrara asked.

"Nearby," McGarvey said at the door from the DDO's office. "Don't have me followed, Phil. If I spot one of your legmen, the deal is off. Clear?"

Carrara nodded.

"And, Phil, if we're going to get anywhere at all, you'd better convince the general to take off the leash. Tomorrow I'm going to want some answers."

"What do you mean by that?" Carrara asked, his voice low.

"You understand," McGarvey said. "It'll be my ass hanging out in the wind. I want to know the real situation."

"You have it."

McGarvey shook his head. "The next time you try to doctor your field officers' contact sheets you'd better think about filling in the blanks."

Carrara smiled wanly. He sat back. "You don't trust anybody, do you?"

"In the old days I did."

"No one to unburden your soul to now? No one to share your troubles with? No one to help out when you're stuck?"

"What's your point, Phil? Am I to kiss and make up with that pissant attorney of Murphy's? Or let bygones be bygones with Danielle, who, if you'll look in the history books, was lead man on the headhunters team that kicked me out? Is that what you're angling for?"

"Might not hurt."

"It might get me killed."

Carrara just looked at McGarvey for a long moment. "I guess you've had your share . . ."

"Yes, I have," McGarvey interrupted, not sure exactly what the DDO was going to say, but not wanting to hear it anyway. "Talk it over with the general, and I'll be back tomorrow."

"Take care of yourself."

"I'll try," McGarvey said, and he left.

After-work traffic was still heavy by the time McGarvey signed out, turned in his visitor's passes, and drove off. But most of it was coming out of the city so he made good time despite doubling back twice to insure that he wasn't being followed. Carrara might show some restraint, but he didn't think Ryan would.

By 7:30 he had parked his car in a ramp three blocks from his hotel, had gone up to his room where he reassembled his pistol, took a shower and changed clothes, and was again out on the streets.

Any physical contact with Rencke was out of the question for the moment. Nobody's tradecraft was good enough to be one hundred percent sure of spotting a sophisticated surveillance operation.

If Ryan or Murphy, or whoever, wanted him badly enough they had the capabilities and the resources to tail him without his awareness: High-flying spotter aircraft with backup ground crews was one way in which it could be done.

Well clear of the hotel McGarvey called Rencke's number from a pay phone at a service station. He still needed the man's help.

The number was answered on the second ring. "At the tone leave your name, or come up on the bulletin board, I'm monitoring." The answering machine beeped.

"Is your line clear?" McGarey asked.

"Is the Pope Catholic?" Rencke answered, laughing. "You're in the file out there already, but only by number. They want to keep your involvement pretty much on the Q-T. Did you talk to Murphy's raiders?"

"I just got back, but I'm going to stay clear of you for a moment."

"Good idea. What's up?"

"They want me to go after K-1, but the files they showed me were filled with holes. Which means they're holding something back."

"Typical."

"But there's no reason for it," McGarvey said. "At least none I can see. I want you to get back into Operations and find out all you can about ModTec, and DuVerlie. There's something going on over there that has the Agency walking on eggshells."

"I'm in right now," Rencke said. "Could be they're trying to hide something, though I'm getting no sense of what yet. But they've yanked a lot of their line numbers which is very atypical."

"All right, keep on it," McGarvey said. "But watch yourself."

"I've always got Ralph in reserve. Not to worry."

"One other thing. Take a look at Tokyo Station's operations. When I asked Murphy about a possible Japanese connection with the STASI because of the yen payments into their accounts, he damned near swallowed his tongue. They all did."

"What do you want specifically?"

"I don't know," McGarvey said. "But it's my guess that something's going on over there that's got them worried."

"So, I'll go shopping."

"I'll talk to you in the morning. But like I said, watch yourself."

"I'm out of Twinkies."

"I don't think it's such a good idea for me to come over there now."

"Send them by cab," Rencke said, and he hung up.

The service station McGarvey had phoned from sold bread and milk and other convenience store items. He bought out their stock of Twinkies, and a couple of blocks from the ramp where his car was parked he hailed a taxi.

"I want you to deliver this package to the caretaker's house in

Holy Rood," McGarvey said. He gave the driver the exact location and a twenty dollar bill.

"Twinkies?" the cabbie said. "This person weird or something?"

"Or something," McGarvey said. "But friendly."

When the cab was gone, McGarvey retrieved his car from the ramp and headed back up to Chevy Chase. Kathleen would be intransigent after what had happened this morning, but he felt they both deserved another try. If for no other reason than their daughter Elizabeth, who'd been beside herself with joy when she'd learned that her parents might be getting back together. Liz was nineteen now, but that didn't stop her need for nurturing.

The sun had set but it was still dusk when he parked his car on the street in front of Kathleen's house. Something was going on at the country club. Cars were arriving in a steady stream. It struck him just then that this was Kathleen's life, but that it never could be his. Black tie dinners and receptions were tolerable once in a while, but not as a steady diet.

He almost got back in his car and drove off, but he wanted to talk to her. At least to apologize for this morning.

It took her a long time to answer the door, and when she finally did she was dressed in a thick terry cloth robe, a towel around her hair. She'd just stepped out of the shower.

"You," she said, but she made no move to close the door.

"Did you get your car back?"

"Yes. The police were here this afternoon. There is a warrant for your arrest. Car theft."

McGarvey shrugged. "I came to apologize for this morning. It shouldn't have happened."

"What was that, Kirk? Your coming here, or the two Neanderthals who came to arrest you?"

She was beautiful, McGarvey thought, looking at her face and long, delicate neck. Even more so now than twenty years ago when they'd first met. In those days they couldn't keep their hands off each other. They made love in his apartment and in her apartment, in hotel rooms, in his car, in the woods, and on the beaches around the Chesapeake Bay. It had been glorious those first two years.

"I'm sorry," he said, and he started to turn away.

"Two against one, and they didn't have a chance," she said, her voice softening. "Are you in any danger?"

"No."

"You wouldn't tell me if you were, would you," she asked rhetorically. "Not you. Ever the loner. Ever the stalwart soldier." Tears formed in her eyes. "But how about the stalwart husband? The stalwart provider? Where the hell were you during our marriage?"

"Doing my job . . ."

"What about me?" she cried. "What about my needs? Didn't you know how much I wanted you, needed you then?" She shook her head. "Hell, even now . . ." She turned away and took a few steps back into the dark stair hall.

McGarvey came after her, and touched her shoulder. "Katy?"

"What do you want here?"

"I wanted us to try to get back together."

"It won't work," she said. "It's impossible."

"Yes," McGarvey replied. "But I'm glad we at least tried for Elizabeth's sake."

"My sake too," she said, turning suddenly and coming into his arms. "I wanted to try too."

"I know," McGarvey said. It felt awkward holding her in his arms. Unnatural somehow. Wrong.

They remained like that for several long seconds, until she pulled away. She half-smiled up at him, the gesture wistful.

"The next time you hold a woman in your arms, Kirk, take off your gun first," she said. "It dampens the spirit."

24

Spranger was shown upstairs to the KGB's *referentura* section of the Russian Embassy in Rome. His escort was a young, attractive blonde woman, who said her name was Tatiana. She was from Leningrad, and her desire was someday to be stationed at the embassy in Washington.

"Comrade Radvonska is looking forward to seeing you again," she said, smiling. They spoke in German.

"I appreciate him taking time from his busy schedule," Spranger replied graciously. "Will he be long?"

"I don't believe so," the young woman said.

They entered a small conference room that could accommodate about ten people around a marble-topped table. Frescoes covered two plaster walls. Windows in the third opened down on a pleasant pocket piazza, deserted at this time of the evening. It was after midnight.

"Is he in the embassy now?"

"Yes, he is. As a matter of fact he is having supper with his family and some friends. He expressed his regrets in not inviting you to join them, but considering the unexpectedness of your arrival . . ."

"I quite understand," Spranger said. "If he will not be long, I'll wait. Otherwise I could return in the morning."

"Unfortunately, Comrade Radvonska leaves Rome first thing in the morning."

"Reassignment?"

"*Nein,*" Tatiana said. "May I offer you some refreshment? Vodka, schnapps, cognac?"

He was being put off, shown his place, because he no longer represented an agency sponsored by a legitimate government. But Radvonska, who until two years ago was the KGB *rezident* in East Berlin, had agreed to see him because in this business old alliances died hard. There was no telling when old friends might be needed again. And considering the trouble the former Soviet Union was in at the moment, friends were at a premium.

"No," Spranger replied. "This is not a social visit. And I too am a busy man." He glanced toward the door. "Please tell Comrade Radvonska not to concern himself about me. I shall find an alternative source for the information I'm seeking."

"I'm sure that will not be necessary. His engagement this evening is a legitimate one."

"And so are my needs."

The young woman's smile tightened. "If you will give me just a moment, sir, I will see that Comrade Radvonska is given your message."

"Do that."

Tatiana left the conference room and when she was gone Spranger went over to the window. A fine mesh screen covered the opening, and he could see where a wire was connected to it in one corner. The lights overhead were fluorescent, there was no telephone, and the only door in or out of the room was thickly padded. The methods were old-fashioned, but the room was for the most part surveillance proof.

The young woman returned five minutes later with an angry Yegenni Radvonska. The *rezident* was a barrel-chested man with thick, jet black hair. He was dressed in a warmup suit, CCCP stenciled on the left breast.

"Ernst," he said, stiffly embracing Spranger. "It's been too long since we last worked together."

"We're available any time you need us, Yegenni Sergeevich," Spranger said. "You know this."

"Yes, of course." Radvonska motioned him to take a seat, and he and Tatiana sat across from him.

Spranger looked pointedly at her.

"Tatiana is my trusted and most valuable assistant," the KGB chief of station said. "You may speak freely."

"I need use of KGB archives," Spranger began. "My people and I are working on a . . . delicate project, and something has come up for which I must have some information that only you can provide."

"Yes, and who is your client in this project?"

"I can't say. But I give you my personal assurances that my

client's aims are in no way at cross purposes with the policies or well being of Russia."

Radvonska studied him for a moment. "I will hold you to that assurance at a later date, Ernst. Please proceed."

"My group was involved in the July Second destruction of the Swissair flight from Orly Field, Paris."

Tatiana's complexion paled slightly, but Radvonska showed no reaction other than mild curiosity.

"One of my people was killed by French police, but only after he'd been cornered by a man we took to be an outsider. Well-built, tall, dark hair, wearing a British-cut tweed sport coat. At the time we suspected he might have been either a British or an American police officer, or even an intelligence service officer."

"Something you have subsequently learned has changed that opinion?"

"We now have reason to believe that he is a civilian. A man with whom we have done contract work in the past monitored a recent conversation in a Paris park between Thomas Lynch, who is the CIA chief of Paris station, and Phillipe Marquand, who is a high ranking officer in the SDECE's Action Service."

Spranger took a copy of an amended version of the transcript out of his jacket pocket and handed it across the table. He'd taken out Marquand's references to the Japanese yen payments into their Bern account.

"This came to us less than twenty-four hours ago. There was a delay in getting it out of Paris . . ." Spranger stopped.

Radvonska had looked up from the transcript, a knowing smile on his face, his eyes bright. He almost licked his lips. "McGarvey," he said.

"Yes, that was what Marquand called him. Do you know this name?"

Radvonska focused on Spranger. "Yes, my friend, and so should you. In fact I am very surprised that this man hasn't already killed you and destroyed your organization."

"What are you talking about?" Spranger demanded.

"Do the names General Valentin Baranov and Colonel Arkady Kurshin mean anything to you?"

"They were legends in their own time. But . . ." Again Spranger stopped in mid-sentence. "He killed them. It was McGarvey?"

Radvonska nodded. "Kirk Cullough McGarvey. As I said, if he is involved and was inside Switzerland, you may count yourself a very lucky man to be alive. But if he has gone to Washington to accept the assignment from the CIA, then your luck may not have very long to run."

"One man," Spranger mused.

"Yes, one man, Ernst."

Spranger looked up. "Then my people will kill him. Immediately."

Radvonska placed a forefinger on the side of his nose. "Do not become so overconfident. Under the present situation in Moscow the KGB will not be able to offer you much help. But some Russians have very long memories. I will supply you with the information you need."

"Give me photographs so that he can be clearly identified, and tell me about his haunts in Washington, and I will take care of the rest."

"A word of caution before you begin, Ernst. Unless McGarvey has involved himself directly in your operation, stay away from him."

"Did you know him? Personally?"

"I was an aide to General Baranov. I saw what McGarvey did to Arady Kurshin the first time they met."

"Then you have a personal interest."

"Yes, I do. And you must listen to me. If you are going to go up against him, you better stack the deck heavily in your favor. Back him into a corner. Take away his will to fight. Hurt him, even cripple him. But until those things are achieved, be very careful, because he'll not hesitate to kill you first."

"I'd go one-on-one with him," Spranger said. "There isn't a man on this earth I fear."

"You would lose," Radvonska said, and the simple directness of his statement stopped Spranger cold.

Tatiana was watching him, a very faint smile on her lips. Spranger had the urge to reach across the table and slap it from her arrogant face.

"Then I will back him into a corner first, as you say."

"Yes, and I will help you," Radvonska said.

"How?"

"By telling you about his ex-wife in Washington, but more importantly about Elizabeth, his daughter, who is presently in residence at a private school outside of Bern, Switzerland."

"Why haven't you gone after him?"

"We don't do things like that anymore," Radvonska said. "But you do."

"Yes, I do," Spranger said, and he couldn't keep the smile from his face.

25

"The question comes back to exactly what he was working on that got him killed," Bill Neustadt, head of the CIA's forensics team in Tokyo, told Ed Mowry. "It's been more than three days and still we don't have the answer."

"It's frustrating, Christ, don't I know it," Mowry said. "I was his assistant COS and he didn't say a word to me."

By contrast to Neustadt and most of the others Langley had sent over to help with the investigation, Mowry was a short, undistinguished man in his late forties. With a paunch, a receding hairline and a red, bulbous nose he was anything but athletic-looking. But he was a competent administrator and a good field agent in the industrial and economic espionage arena, which Japan had become.

"No contact sheet, no references in any file, no note on his desk calendar, nothing in his apartment, no mention to anybody why he was going to the Roppongi Prince Hotel that night, not even to his wife, and yet he was wearing a wire."

Mowry and Neustadt were meeting in the embassy's screened room in the section of Tokyo called Minato-ku. The hotel where Jim Shirley had been murdered was barely a half-dozen blocks to the west. It was after eight Tuesday morning, and none of them had gotten much sleep since Friday.

"Unfortunately the recording equipment he had taped to his

chest was completely destroyed," Neustadt continued. "In the meantime the Tokyo Metropolitan Police are starting to ask some tough questions. For instance: Witnesses say that Shirley met with a man at the hotel bar. A Westerner. The Dunée imposter?"

"Unknown."

"For instance: Were we aware that Shirley was heavily invested on the margin in the Tokyo Stock Market?"

"We've been over this a dozen times, Bill. This has taken me completely by surprise. All of it."

"I'm getting the impression that he was making ready to jump ship. Quit the Company and settle in here for the duration."

"It certainly looks like it," Mowry said glumly. "His wife Doris apparently has no plans to return to the States."

They were alone in the conference room. Neustadt leaned forward. "So tell me, Ed, do you think he was doing a little freelance work on the side? Something that may have backfired on him?"

Mowry had asked himself that same question a dozen times over the past seventy-two hours. "If you had suggested such a thing to me last week, I would have punched you in the nose."

Neustadt sat back and shook his head. "Beats me what I'm going to write in my report."

The telephone rang and Mowry picked it up. It was his secretary just down the hall. "Sorry to disturb you, Mr. Mowry, but when you get a chance there's someone in your office who wishes to speak with you. She says it's urgent."

"Who is it?"

"Yaeko Hataya. She's a USIA translator from downstairs."

"I'm going to be tied up all day. Have Tom or one of the others talk to her."

"Sir, she says it's about Mr. Shirley."

Mowry glanced at Neustadt, who was reading one of the files. "Be right there," he said, and he hung up. There'd been rumors that Shirley had had a mistress. So far she'd not come forward, and no one knew who she was.

Neustadt looked up. "Something?"

"One of my translators is getting excited. I've got to go hold her hand for a minute or two."

"Why don't you go over to the safehouse and get some rest. You look like I feel . . . like shit. Nothing's going to happen until Langley wakes up anyway."

"I guess I will," Mowry said, getting up.

"The apartment is clean," Neustadt said. "But use your own driver. I'll have my people right behind you."

"Will they stick around?"

"Probably. We'll see."

"I'll be glad when this is over," Mowry said, and he left the conference room.

"I put her inside," his secretary, Amanda Richardson, said. "Poor kid is terrified."

"I'll talk to her. In the meantime get my car and driver around front. I'm getting out of here for a few hours."

"Yes, sir."

The young woman was seated in front of his desk when he came in. Her hands were folded primly in her lap. She looked vaguely familiar to Mowry, who thought he might have seen her around the embassy. If she'd been Shirley's mistress, he'd had good taste.

"My secretary tells me that you know something about Jim Shirley."

"I was there when he was killed," Kelley Fuller said in a small voice.

Mowry had gone around behind his desk, and was about to sit down. He stopped. "You were there, at the Roppongi?" he asked, incredulously.

"In front, on the path behind the trees. I saw everything. It was horrible."

"Why did you wait to come forward?" Mowry demanded. He reached for the phone, but she half rose out of her chair.

"No," she cried. "You mustn't tell anyone. Not now! Not yet!"

"The investigators are here from Washington. They have to be told."

"Especially not them," Kelley said. "Jim was just as afraid of Washington as he was of the people here in Tokyo."

"What people? What are you talking about?"

"Jim called it the chip wars. There was money, so much it was hard to imagine. Billions."

"Of yen?"

She shook her head. "Dollars. In gold and diamonds. Jim said that so much wealth had corrupted everyone who'd come near it."

"Was Jim investigating this group?"

"Yes," Kelley said. "He was going to accept some of their money. But he had to prove that he believed in them. It had something to do with the Tokyo exchange. He would get information, and then he would buy some stock. I don't understand it all."

"Then why was he killed?" Mowry asked, barely able to believe what he was hearing, and yet instinctively feeling it was true.

"I don't know. But he was worried that someone in Washington had found out about what he was doing. Don't you see, Mr. Mowry, that nobody's to be trusted? Nobody?"

Their investigation into Shirley's assassination was getting nowhere. The Station had all but closed shop. Nothing of value was coming in or going out, and there was no telling how long the situation would last. The Japanese authorities were enraged, and Langley was hamstrung.

"Where are you staying?" Mowry asked, making his decision.

Kelley looked up and shook her head. Tears were sliding down her cheeks. "I ran away to the country Friday night, and I just got back now." She sat forward. "I can't go back to my apartment. Not now. Someone . . . might be watching."

"Were you working with Jim?" Mowry asked.

"Yes. He and I were . . . friends."

"Will you work for me? Will you help me find out who killed him? Together we can stop them."

She shook her head again. "I'm frightened. I don't know what to do."

She looked very fragile. Totally at wit's end. "I'm sorry, Miss Hataya, but we'll have to go through normal channels with our investigation in that case."

"No, please!"

"What is it?"

Kelley was wringing her hands. "I need a place to stay that's safe. That no one knows about."

"If I provided you an apartment like that, would you help me?"

"Yes."

Tokyo Station maintained two safehouses within the city. One, near the Ginza shopping district, was an open secret, but expenses for the other were buried in one of the embassy's housekeeping accounts. Only a few key station personnel even knew the place existed. Ironically it was located less than a hundred yards from the Tokyo Metropolitan Police Headquarters on Sakurada-dori Avenue and within sight of the Imperial Palace.

"We'll go there now," Mowry said, rising. "And you'll tell me everything you know. Everything."

Shizuko Igarshi was parked across the street from the U.S. embassy when Edward Mowry came out with a young Japanese woman, and they both got into the back of a waiting Lincoln Town Car.

The woman was somewhat unexpected, but then it was very common for Occidental men away from home to have young mistresses.

Igarshi kick-started his Honda 250 as the gunmetal gray Lincoln pulled smoothly away from the curb. He waited, and moments later a blue Toyota with two Americans inside pulled out of its parking spot, shot across the road, and fell in behind the Lincoln. It was as he had been told to expect. Mowry would be protected.

But who was the girl?

Igarshi waited for a break in the traffic and headed after them, keeping a couple of cars behind the Toyota.

The girl was probably not important, but he'd been taught to keep an open mind, especially when it came to Americans, and those around them. "They are a crude, bellicose and unpredictable people," he'd been warned. It was true.

Mowry's driver, a Japanese contract employee, knew the city well, and in less than ten minutes he pulled up in front of a sprawling three-story apartment building near the Imperial Palace's broad Sakurada Moat.

The Toyota made a sudden U-turn and parked directly across the street, leaving Igarshi no other choice but to continue beyond.

Mowry had already gotten out of the car, and the girl was just climbing out at that moment. Her eyes locked with Igarshi's for an instant, and then he was past.

Around the corner, thirty yards away, he hurriedly parked his motorcycle and rushed back to where he could see the front entrance of the apartment building. Mowry and the girl were going inside, and the Lincoln was leaving. But the Toyota remained.

Igarshi pulled off the paper air filter that covered his face, and wiped his mouth. For just that split second he thought he'd seen a hint of recognition on the girl's face. But that was not likely.

Killing Mowry, he thought, would be even more interesting than the first one, because this time they would have to take out the two Americans in the Toyota, as well as the girl.

26

McGarvey called Rencke's number from a pay phone downtown near the White House a few minutes before eight in the morning. He'd expected it to ring a long time, because Rencke would be in bed asleep by now. But it was answered immediately.

"Yes!"

"It's me," McGarvey said. Rencke had sounded breathless.

"Listen, Mac. All hell is breaking loose. I mean the shit has really happened. So it's up to you, but I say run and don't look back. The bastards want you. And listen, if you want my guess, I'd say it has something to do with Tokyo. They're killing people out there."

"Is your line still clear?"

"They're killing people out there, aren't you listening?"

"Is your line clear?" McGarvey repeated the question slowly. He could envision Rencke bouncing off the walls.

"Yes, yes! Clear, clear! But I don't know for how long."

"Calm down, Otto, and tell me what's going on. Did you pick something off the computer?"

"Hoo, boy, you betcha I did. The jackpot. On Friday, Tokyo time, which makes it . . . I don't know, Thursday or Saturday or something here, the friggin' chief of Tokyo Station was assassinated. Everybody went bananas over there and over here and everywhere. They red-lighted the thing."

"Who killed him?"

"Nobody knows. The Japs, apparently. Two of them in masks and hardhats. We got the masks and one of the hats at Yokosuka doing a DNA search. But now it looks as if the assistant chief of station has been targeted. Operations has evidently fielded a blind asset who got cold feet, or something."

"Is anyone making a connection between Tokyo and K-1?" McGarvey asked.

"If they are, they're not logging it in operational files. But the situation has definitely got their attention. Nuclear triggers from the Swiss. K-1's Swiss bank account loaded with yen. It's got to make somebody wonder. Operations has nixed your Swiss trip. It's already in housekeeping. I'd say, run."

"I can't. I'm already in too deep."

"Aren't we all," Rencke said.

"I'm going to need more help from you, Otto. If you're willing to stick with it."

"Tall orders or short orders?"

"Very tall."

"May have to go to pink," Rencke said, but McGarvey didn't catch the meaning.

"I need to find out two things. First if there have been any incidents involving the theft of fissionable material, enough to make a bomb, or the theft of initiators. Anywhere in the world."

"At any given time there's a half ton or more of plutonium missing. And it only takes seventy pounds or so to make a big bang. But you want to know if any of these incidents have any ties, however remote, with K-1, or especially with the Japanese. Right?"

"Right," McGarvey said. "And secondly . . . I don't know how you're even going to get started on this one, but, assuming that the Japanese are interested in getting their hands on nuclear weapons technology, or better yet the actual item, and assuming that the Japanese government itself is not involved, I want to know what Japanese interest group, military faction, or even private concern or corporation, would have the most to gain from such a project."

"We're talking big bucks. Major yen."

"That could be a start. Whoever it is would have to have the expertise to make contact with Spranger and his group. Maybe someone with East German ties."

"Or from the War," Rencke suggested. "Germany and Japan were allies."

"Yes," McGarvey said. "See what you can do."

"Okay. And thanks for the Twinkies."

One of Carrara's people met McGarvey downstairs and escorted him up to Operations on the third floor. There was a buzz of activity, and everyone seemed more animated than usual; on edge, in a hurry.

The DDO was just emerging from the briefing auditorium and he led McGarvey the rest of the way into his office. "We're putting

Switzerland on the back burner for the moment. We'll let our assets already in place handle it. The general wants to know if you're interested in taking on an assignment in Japan."

"I don't know. I'll have to talk to him, and then think it over."

"No time," Carrara said. "I've got a private jet standing by at Andrews for you. It'll get you to Tokyo via Seattle and then the Aleutians first thing this morning . . . Tokyo time. You can catch up on your reading on the way over."

"Does this have any connection with the STASI group? I asked about the Japanese connection yesterday."

"Frankly I don't know, Kirk. And that's the truth. I just hope to God it doesn't have a connection. The Japanese and nuclear weapons is a thought I'd rather not dwell on."

McGarvey held off for a long moment. Carrara was agitated. He wanted the man to focus his attention on what was being said.

"I'll probably take your assignment, Phil, but of course I'll need to know what's expected of me, and I still want to know what you were holding back yesterday."

Carrara looked at him bleakly, as if he were a man who knew he'd just been backed into a corner. "The two things may be mutually exclusive."

McGarvey said nothing.

The DDO started to reach for the phone, but then stayed his hand. "Which do you want first?"

"Orly."

Carrara nodded, as if he'd known that subject would be first. "DuVerlie was a snitch. He was going to show us where a fellow ModTec engineer was buried so that we would believe the fantastic story he was trying to sell us. He wanted a lot of money. I mean a *lot* of money."

"We're still talking about nuclear switches?"

"Yes," Carrara said. "The STASI group, which we're calling K-1, had approached another ModTec engineer with an offer to buy the switches. When the engineer held out for more money they killed him and hid his body. But DuVerlie found out about it, and figured he would be safer dealing with us than them, and probably make just as much money in the bargain."

"You knew about this K-1 group before DuVerlie approached you?"

"Yes," Carrara answered. "And we'd picked up rumors that one-four-five would be shot down."

"Because of DuVerlie?"

"We didn't know that."

"But you made the connection."

"Yes."

"But did nothing," McGarvey said, his stomach knotting up. "You didn't warn Swissair. Hell, you didn't even hold your own people from taking the flight."

"We warned Interpol that there might be trouble on an international flight out of France."

McGarvey could no longer sit down. He got to his feet. "That was fucking big of you. The public be damned."

"I don't set policy, McGarvey."

"Who does?"

Carrara looked away.

"You sonsofbitches ignored it all, and because of it more than a hundred fifty innocent people are dead." McGarvey went to the window and looked outside at the beautiful day. "There were other considerations, weren't there? Sources that would have been revealed if you'd warned the public." He turned back. "Christ, to what end, Phil? Tell me, have you or I or the entire CIA made even the slightest difference on how events have turned out over the past fifty years?"

Carrara looked up at him. "I have to believe we have, McGarvey. Else why do we do our jobs?"

The conviction that his entire life had been nothing but an exercise in futility suddenly welled up in McGarvey's breast. "Christ," he said softly, Mati's face rising up in his mind's eye. It took everything within his control not to turn on Carrara.

"Jim Shirley, our chief of station in Tokyo, was murdered on Friday by two as yet unidentified Japanese," the DDO said. "We learned overnight that Ed Mowry, our acting chief of station, may be next on their list."

McGarvey was listening with one part of his mind, while with another he was still thinking about Marta. Her mistake had been falling in love with him. It had cost her her life.

"Shirley had apparently been conducting a series of meetings with a man by the name of Armand Dunée, who supposedly was a spy for a Belgian bank operating in Tokyo. But he was an imposter.

In the beginning, in Lausanne, Mati had been a diversion. His real work had been the bookstore and his research on the French writer-philosopher Voltaire. But he'd been deluding her and everyone else, including himself. Once a spy, always a spy. Hadn't he heard that line somewhere?

"We have a blind source there who may have spotted one of Shirley's assassins following Mowry."

Mati had wanted him to give it up, as did Kathleen. But neither of them understood the thing inside of him that was his driving force. His sister had come close a number of years ago when she'd pleaded with him not to sell their parents' ranch in western Kansas after they had died. She'd inherited the cash and securities, but he had been given the land. "There's nothing wrong with being tied to the land," she'd argued. "A piece of ground cannot be tainted. Not that way."

But he'd disagreed, and had sold his parents' property without going back to see it. Daughters are not guilty of the sins of their fathers, he'd told another of his women. But what about the sons?

"We have a team in Tokyo, but no doubt they've been spotted. You might have a better chance of not only protecting Mowry, but finding out who wants to kill him and why."

McGarvey turned around. "Have you warned him?"

"He's been told that he may be a target. I sent over some help from Technical Services. But you've got to understand that we're limited in what we can overtly do just now. The Japanese authorities are very touchy."

"Have you told him about your blind source?"

Carrara looked uncomfortable. "Of course not."

"So Mowry doesn't specifically know that he's being tailed?"

"No."

"How about the Technical Services team?"

"We're keeping the need-to-know list to a minimum."

McGarvey shook his head. "What the hell is going on, Phil? The Company never did this sort of thing before."

"The world has changed," Carrara replied tightly.

"And that's it? The world has changed?"

Carrara said nothing.

"What's going on in Tokyo? Why was your chief of station killed, and why the blind asset?"

"I'm sending a briefing book with you so that you can familiarize yourself on the flight over. But in broad strokes we were asked to investigate the possibility that a Japanese corporation, or consortium of corporations, were going to institute an all-out technological-economic war on us. Specifically in the military-aerospace electronics field. First they would mount an espionage operation against U.S. companies doing research and development in order to find out to what point we'd taken the technology. And then they would simply better it."

"To what end?"

"Economic blackmail. Either we buy their new developments or they'd sell them on the world market."

"Shirley was killed because he was on to them?"

"It may not be that simple, Kirk. It may be that Shirley was involved in kickbacks. We're just not sure. But what's at stake here amounts to billions of dollars."

"Maybe they're after improvements in nuclear technology as well."

"ModTec is not the only manufacturer of those switches, nor are they the best."

"Assuming Shirley got caught in the middle, why target Mowry?" McGarvey asked.

"I don't know. Perhaps he was involved as well, or they think he was. Either way we'd like you to find out."

"What about your blind asset?"

Carrara handed McGarvey a photograph of Kelley Fuller. "She

works as an interpreter for the USIA at our embassy under the name Yaeko Hataya. She was Jim Shirley's lover."

"Shit," McGarvey mumbled half under his breath as he studied the photograph. She was a good-looking woman.

"You're going to have to stay out of the way of the Tokyo police. Needless to say they won't be sympathetic."

"Do you think the government is involved?"

"I don't know. I hope not, but I don't know."

"What's the girl's situation? How will we make contact?"

"Mowry has put her up in one of our safehouses. Once you're settled in Tokyo she'll get word to your hotel. She knows you're coming."

"But Mowry knows nothing about this?"

"That's right."

McGarvey had to shake his head. "When do I leave?"

"Immediately," Carrara said.

27

It was dawn. Igarshi parked the blue and white police van at the end of the block from the apartment building on Sakurada-dori Avenue, and watched the activity on the street for a few moments. Already traffic was getting heavy. In another hour the area would be a madhouse, and therefore anonymous.

He studied the apartment building through binoculars. The shutters on the second-story windows were still tightly closed and there was no sign of activity yet. But Mowry would be showing up sometime this morning. He wouldn't be able to leave his whore for long. At least in that aspect all Americans were alike.

A uniformed police officer came up the street on foot from the direction of the Imperial Palace. Igarshi started the van's engine. He did not want to be caught here.

"What's wrong?" Kozo Idemitsu asked from the back.

"A policeman is heading toward us."

"Ido?"

"I think so, but I'm not sure," Igarshi said. He raised the binoculars and studied the approaching figure. At first he couldn't quite tell, but then the cop raised his head, and Igarshi had him. "It's Ido."

"Something must have gone wrong. Contact Tanaka again and see if there has been any change."

As of ten minutes ago their observers near the American

embassy in Minato-ku had reported that Mowry was still inside. There was little likelihood that he could have gotten out without being spotted, but if he was on his way now it could make things difficult.

Igarshi picked up the bulky secure walkie-talkie lying on the seat next to him, and keyed the READY TO TALK button.

"Tiger, this is lion," he said. "Has hummingbird departed yet? We may have a developing situation."

He pressed the TRANSMIT button, and his digitally-recorded words were encrypted, compressed into a one-microsecond burst, and sent out.

"Stand by, lion. It looks as if his people have just pulled up out front."

"Any sign of hummingbird?"

"Not yet. Are you in position?"

"Yes, but Ido has broken his cover and is approaching us."

"See what the idiot wants, then get rid of him."

"Stand by," Igarshi radioed. Ido Meiji was the *koban* police officer assigned to this neighborhood. He was supposed to have provided them with a diversion if they ran into trouble. Later he would give his superiors false descriptions of the assailants he'd so bravely tried to stop. But his story wouldn't hold up if someone remembered seeing him talking with the officers in the van.

Igarshi rolled down his window as the cop stopped to check the locked security shutter in front of a shop. He turned and came over to the van.

"I thought it was important for you to know that the woman left the apartment early this morning," Ido Meiji said breathlessly.

"Are you sure?" Igarshi asked.

"Yes, of course. I watched the entire thing. She went around the corner to the telephone box and made a call of twenty-seven seconds duration, and then returned to the apartment."

"She's back now?"

"Yes. But maybe she suspects something. Perhaps she telephoned a warning."

"Return to your position," Igarshi ordered, making his decision. Mowry was the prime target. They couldn't let anything get in the way.

"You mean to continue?"

"Yes. Now, go."

The cop half bowed, then turned and walked off. Igarshi snatched the walkie-talkie and hit the READY TO TALK button.

"Tiger, this is lion. Ladybird left the apartment this morning and made a brief telephone call to an unknown party."

"Never mind that," Tanaka radioed. "Hummingbird is getting into his car now. We'll be on our way in under a minute."

"The woman may have seen something. She might have warned him."

"In that case she would have remained inside the apartment and used that telephone," Tanaka shouted. "Remain at your position. I'll advise you of any change in plans."

"Roger," Igarshi said, and he tossed the walkie-talkie aside in disgust. They were dealing with a deadly business here. There was no room for mistakes, and even less room for blindness.

"This won't be so good if the girl warned somebody," Idemitsu said.

"Don't be a fool," Igarshi countered impatiently. "What does it matter?"

"You said yourself that she got a good look at you."

"I was mistaken."

"How can you say that?"

"Are you ready back there?" Igarshi shouted.

"Yes," Idemitsu said after a moment. "I am ready now."

"Then nothing has changed."

"Yes, I understand."

"She's just an empty-headed whore. After today she will be dead."

Kelley Fuller watched the street through the slats in the bamboo shutters that covered the window in the tiny living room. The cop had crossed the street from the police van and was heading past the apartment back to the corner. It was the same *koban* cop who'd followed her to the telephone, she was certain of it.

Which meant what? she asked herself, trying to think it out. That the Tokyo Police had mounted a surveillance operation on her? Or more likely on the apartment?

Phil Carrara had warned her that the Japanese authorities were extremely agitated over Shirley's assassination. It wasn't so much the brutal nature of the killing that was disturbing them as it was the fact he'd been CIA. The Soviet Union, Communist China and North Korea were just across the narrow Sea of Japan. No one wanted a new battle in the old Cold War to erupt here with those enemies so close at hand.

If Mowry were being identified as CIA—which was entirely possible given the present apparent state of security at the embassy— then his coming here to a secret apartment would raise some embarrassing questions.

It would also mean that her effectiveness would be at an end. They might never find Shirley's killers, or their real reason for targeting the CIA, beyond the public speculation that the incident had been an act of anti-American terrorism.

Again the ghastly picture of his body on fire rose up in her head and she closed her eyes.

A bullet in the head would have been one thing. But the way Shirley had been murdered had been a message. A strong message. But from whom?

From the man on the motorcycle who'd followed them here? His eyes had been hauntingly familiar to her. And she'd felt in her heart that he'd been one of the two in front of the Roppongi Prince that night.

"Help me," she said softly. She didn't know what to do.

The man Carrara had sent from Washington had touched down at Narita Airport earlier this morning. By now he'd be in place at the ANA Hotel Tokyo near the embassy. He would have to be warned, as would Mowry. But then what?

Mowry had no real idea what he was up against. None of them did.

From her vantage point she could just make out a figure behind the wheel of the van, but little else. It was obvious they were waiting for something, or somebody.

She picked up the phone and dialed the embassy's number. When the operator answered she asked for Mowry's extension. his secretary came on.

"Three five eight."

"Please, may I speak with Mowry-san. This is Yaeko Hataya."

"I'm sorry Miss Hataya, but Mr. Mowry is not here."

"I see," Kelley said. "Can you tell me, is he in the embassy, or has he left?"

"He's gone," Mowry's secretary said.

"I see. Thank you," Kelley said. She broke the connection and called the ANA Hotel Tokyo. "Please connect me with the room of Mr. Kirk McGarvey. He is a registered guest of yours who was due this morning."

"I'm sorry, madame, but Mr. McGarvey has not yet arrived," the hotel operator said after a moment. "Would you care to leave a message?"

"No. That will not be necessary."

Kelley hung up and looked out the window again. The police van was still in place. Mowry was undoubtedly on his way here, which didn't give her much time. But the only thing she could do now would be lead the police away from the apartment. Everything could be sorted out later.

28

The taxi dropped McGarvey off in front of the Imperial Palace's Outer Garden East Gate, the morning coming alive with traffic. Already the first of the joggers were starting their three-mile runs around the palace. Everyone ran the course counterclockwise. It was tradition, on which the Japanese were very big.

Although he'd gotten plenty of rest on the long flight over the Pacific, his body clock was still telling him that it should be the middle of the evening, not first thing in the morning. He'd taken a shuttle bus from the airport to catch the train into Tokyo's Keisei-Ueno Station, and from there a cab to his hotel where he dropped off his bag with the bellman.

His gun had come through customs in a diplomatic pouch, the package returned to him on the other side of the barrier. The weapon was a comfortable weight at the small of his back, though if the local authorities discovered he was armed, he would face immediate arrest and deportation.

He crossed the moat and entered the relative peace of the garden. There were so many people packed in such close quarters in Tokyo that parks and gardens were places revered almost at a religious level.

Reading between the lines of Carrara's report, McGarvey had come to the conclusion that Jim Shirley had been the only effective field officer here, but that even he had been suspect in the end.

Mowry was an administrator and Kelley Fuller, A.K.A., Yaeko Hataya was starting to fall apart, which left a very big and dangerous blind spot when it came to Japan. He couldn't help compare the situation to the days before Pearl Harbor, when there'd been another serious lapse in hard intelligence on what the Japanese were up to.

Rightly or wrongly there was a growing paranoia about exactly just where the Japanese were headed these days. As Carrara pointed out, it wasn't so much that they seemed to want to buy everything they could get their hands on in the States—the British owned nearly twice as much property in the U.S. as the Japanese did. But it was *what* the Japanese were buying, and how they were going about it.

Owning a building in midtown Manhattan was one thing, but buying out a major communications industry, including a movie production company and a major book publisher, was another. As was a rumored move to buy out a major U.S. aircraft company. In each case the Japanese promised not to make any changes in company policy. That, of course, was forgotten the moment the ink was dry on the contracts.

"We can't afford anti-Japanese sentiment, but neither can we afford a Japanese buyout of what's vital to this country," Carrara said.

Finding out who was behind the assassination of Shirley, and how that connected to Carrara's sweeping generalizations was a tall, if not an impossible order. One which McGarvey had his doubts about being able to fulfill. And there was still the nagging suspicion at the back of his mind that somehow the Japanese were connected with Spranger and his group of ex-STASI officers.

At the south end of the gardens the ornate Sakuradamon Gate crossed another moat to the end of Sakurada-dori Avenue. A couple dozen joggers were warming up in the courtyard between the portals of the gate. McGarvey stopped just inside the garden.

On the corner was the Tokyo Metropolitan Police Building, and across the street was the Ministry of Justice housed in a nondescript old brown brick building. This area was the heart of the Japanese government. Within a few blocks were the Ministries of Foreign Affairs, Education, International Trade and Industry.

The CIA's safehouse was in a building used by foreigners doing business with the government. Activities unusual for any other part of Tokyo were common here and raised few suspicions.

"So far Mowry hasn't officially told anyone that he's stashed Kelley over there," Carrara had said.

"Which means he's got something to hide."

Carrara shrugged. "The Station leaks, and he doesn't want to end up like Shirley."

"What'd the girl tell him?"

"That she saw Jim Shirley's murder and that she's frightened she'll be next."

"But he hasn't told any of that to your Technical Services team?"

"No, but they're keeping an eye on him twenty-four hours a day. They know he's got a girl there, but they don't know who she is."

"And you haven't clarified the situation."

Carrara shook his head.

"You really are a bastard after all," McGarvey said, but the DDO hadn't responded.

It was the business, McGarvey thought, watching the street. When government policies became the primary consideration, people became expendable. It had happened to him, only he'd been tough enough—and lucky enough—to survive. So far.

Already the first of the clerks and bureaucrats were heading to work, and traffic was beginning to pick up. In another hour or less all of Tokyo would become a congested mass of humanity on the move. Half hour taxi rides would take two hours or more. Buses and trains would be packed to overflowing. The city streets would become anonymous for the field officer as well as for the killer and his victim.

Crossing Harumi-dori Avenue with the light, McGarvey headed past the Police Headquarters keeping his eyes and ears open, trying to absorb what was the norm for this area; looking for the routine, the ordinary, the usual ebb and flow so that he could pick out the odd, out of place person or vehicle.

In Europe he understood what he saw. Here, though, it was different: The people, the scenery, even the flavor and odors on the air were odd by Western standards.

"Between you and the girl you can keep an eye on Mowry," Carrara had said. "If they do make a try on him, you'll get your lead."

"Short of that?"

"Keep your eyes open," Carrara said. "Something will come up. With you it always does."

The safehouse was in the block beyond the Police Headquarters. Some shops were beginning to open, and traffic, especially pedestrian, was getting heavy.

At the near corner a uniformed police officer was speaking on a telephone at a police callbox outside a tiny cubicle. At the far end of the block a blue and white police van was parked on the opposite side of the street.

As McGarvey passed, the cop at the callbox glanced up at him, but then turned away.

Something was happening here. Or was about to happen. That much he could pick out.

Then he spotted her. Kelley Fuller had just emerged from a building in the middle of the block and was heading directly toward him. She was thirty yards distant, but he had no trouble recognizing her from the photographs Carrara had included in the briefing package.

Nor was there any doubt from the way she was moving that she was in trouble. Immediate trouble.

Igarshi could hardly believe his eyes. It was Mowry's whore. She was on the move. Now! Of all times! She must have seen something and warned the American. She'd probably spotted Ido. The bastard!

He grabbed the walkie-talkie, pushed the READY TO TALK button and screamed into the microphone. "Tiger, this is lion. The woman just left the apartment. She's getting away!"

He hit the TRANSMIT button and a moment later, Tanaka came back.

"Never mind her for now. We're just around the corner from you. Get ready."

"We can't let her escape," Igarshi shouted.

"Stand by. We're coming."

Igarshi tossed the walkie-talkie aside, and started the van's engine, as Mowry's chauffeured Lincoln appeared in his rearview mirror, the opposite direction from where he'd expected it.

Ten feet from McGarvey, Kelley glanced over her shoulder, back the way she had come, and she pulled up short, almost stumbling over her own feet.

A big American car had just turned the corner at the end of the block and was barreling up the street. A light blue Toyota with two men inside was directly behind it.

The woman started back, but McGarvey caught up with her in two steps and grabbed her arm.

Something was starting to go down. The blue and white police van was pulling away from the curb, and a red Mercedes was squealing tires coming around the corner.

Kelley tried to yank her arm free, but McGarvey forcefully pulled her off to the side. "Miss Hataya, it's me. Kirk McGarvey!"

For a split second Kelley's face was screwed up in a grimace of terror and the raw animal reaction to being cornered. She looked back over her shoulder, wildly thrashing her free arm in an effort to escape as the Lincoln made a sudden U-turn and stopped in front of the apartment building.

"We have to warn him," she cried.

The blue Toyota pulled over to the curb across the street, the police van and Mercedes right behind it.

"We're not going up against the Tokyo Police," McGarvey said, hauling her into the shelter of a small used-book stall.

"Something is wrong, I tell you."

"Wait," McGarvey said forcefully. Something *was* wrong here, but he didn't know what it was. No matter how agitated the Japanese authorities were because of the incident involving the CIA, arresting an American diplomatic officer was an extreme move.

The *koban* cop from the corner came past in a run, his pistol drawn, as the police van pulled up opposite Mowry's limousine. The acting chief of station got out of the car, and turned to see what was happening.

The red Mercedes stopped alongside the Toyota, and for several beats it seemed as if nothing would happen. Traffic flowed around the two stopped vehicles, but everything else seemed to be in stasis. Like a time bomb ready to go off.

A uniformed cop jumped out of the back of the van and hurried around the big American car. He carried what appeared to be a large fire extinguisher, but he was holding it as if he were about ready to put out a fire.

Or start one! The chilling thought suddenly flashed into Mc-Garvey's head. They weren't cops!

"Get down," he shouted, pushing Kelley farther back into the book stall.

The driver's side window in the blue Toyota suddenly burst into a million pieces, blood spraying the inside of the windshield as one of the men in the Mercedes opened fire with what sounded like a silenced Uzi . . . the clatter of the expended shell casings louder than the actual shots.

McGarvey yanked out his pistol as he sprinted forward, switch-ing the safety to the off position.

Mowry reared back, inadvertantly placing himself between the koban cop and the cop with the fire extinguisher, leaving McGarvey no shot.

"Get back, get back!" McGarvey shouted, knowing that he was already too late.

The cop from the van raised the fire extinguisher, and a geyser of flame twenty-five feet long gushed from the horn-shaped nozzle, completely engulfing Mowry, as well as the koban cop behind him.

McGarvey spun on his heel and darted behind a parked taxi, the heat from the flame thrower so intense even at a distance of fifty feet that it made his eyes water and singed the hair on his head.

Mowry and the koban cop were both screaming inhumanly as they did a macabre little jig, almost as if they were marionette puppets on strings.

The air was filled with the stench of gasoline and burning flesh. Traffic was coming to a screeching halt, people were falling back, running away, screaming in terror.

The Lincoln started to pull away from its parking place, but got only five feet before its windshield disintegrated in a hail of auto-matic gunfire from the driver's side of the police van.

A second burst of flame from the bogus fire extinguisher completely engulfed Mowry and the koban cop again as McGarvey popped up and fired three shots in rapid succession.

The column of flames suddenly veered wildly left, splashing the fronts of the buildings across the sidewalk as Mowry's assassin staggered backward.

McGarvey snapped off a fourth and fifth shot, the last hitting the flamethrower's fuel tank which erupted in a huge fireball, instantly killing the man.

The police van burst into flames, and the driver, also dressed in a police uniform, jumped out, firing his Uzi toward McGarvey, forcing him down behind the taxi, glass and bits of bullet fragments raining down on his head.

Mowry and the *koban* cop had stopped screaming. They were mercifully dead. But in the near distance McGarvey could suddenly hear the sounds of sirens. Probably behind the police headquarters in the last block.

He popped up again and fired two shots at the cop who was scrambling into the back seat of the already moving Mercedes. Then a third. The fourth time he pulled the trigger the hammer fell on an empty chamber.

The answering automatic weapons fire raked the taxi McGarvey was crouched behind, almost completely destroying it.

He ejected the spent clip from his Walther PPK, slapped home a fresh one, relevered the ejection slide and jumped up as the Mercedes accelerated down the street.

He managed to get off two shots before the risk of hitting an innocent bystander became too great. Then he turned, looked toward the still-burning remains of Mowry and the cop, holstered his pistol and hurried back to Kelley Fuller, who was shaking with fear and rage. The sirens were very close now.

"We have to get out of here," he told her. "But you're going to have to act normal."

"What?" she cried incredulously, but she didn't resist as McGarvey took her arm and led her away, back toward the Imperial Palace gardens, past the Police Headquarters building.

29

"Who the hell was that bastard?" Tanaka demanded. He was an expert driver and he knew Tokyo very well. He'd gotten them clear before the police arrived.

"I don't know," Igarshi shouted wildly. "He came out of nowhere. Kozo didn't have a chance."

"We have to find out. He's with the girl, and she may know too much."

"We have to kill them," Heidinora Daishi said from the front seat. "They're witnesses." He'd killed Mowry's two bodyguards in the Toyota.

"I agree," Tanaka said. He glanced in the rearview mirror at Igarshi who was changing out of the police uniform. "Are you injured?"

"Just a scratch on my leg. But it was close."

"Did you see where they were headed?" Heidinora asked. He was a bulldog of a man, with a short, thick torso and massive arms. He was a ruthless, efficient killer.

"The Imperial Palace," Tanaka replied through clenched teeth. "We'll go there now and finish the job."

"We'd better," Igarshi muttered. "I for one don't want to go back empty-handed. But we have no flamethrower."

"It doesn't matter. We'll enter the garden from three different directions to cut off any possible escape. The moment we spot them we shoot."

"What about the car?"

"We'll leave it," Tanaka said, hauling the big car around the corner onto Hibaya-dori Avenue. He pulled up in front of the east gate into the Imperial Palace's Outer Garden. "Take this entrance," he told Heidinora. "Igarshi and I will come from the south side and drive them toward you."

"Very well," Heidinora growled, and he got out of the car and entered the garden.

Police units seemed to be converging from all over the city on the scene of the killings. Violent crime was relatively unknown in Tokyo, and when it occurred the police were quick to respond. McGarvey led a shaken Kelley Fuller across Harumi-dori Avenue into the Imperial Palace's Outer Garden. Most of the joggers were already gone on their circuit of the palace grounds, but a few stood at the outer portal looking to where black smoke rose into the morning sky.

"They weren't the police," Kelley said.

"You're right, but there's nothing we can do about it for the moment," McGarvey said. He pulled up short just within the garden and studied the approaches behind them. The Mercedes would be back. Today's attack had been well planned and coordinated. Whoever they were, they would not want to leave any loose ends dangling.

"I tried to warn Mowry, but his secretary told me that he'd already left. And your hotel said you hadn't checked in yet."

"Where were you going?"

"I was trying to lead them away. But God, I didn't know this would happen." She was distraught, and clearly on the verge of breaking down.

"All right, listen to me. They saw which way we headed, and they're probably going to come back for us. Have you got someplace to go? Someplace where you can hide at least for the rest of the morning?"

"I had an apartment, but I'm not going there now," she said. "Maybe the embassy."

"No," McGarvey said. "The moment the authorities found out you were there they'd demand that you be turned over to them. You're a material witness to at least one killing."

"So are you," she said.

"That's right. But so long as we make no contact with the embassy the police won't know who we are."

"That's just great," Kelley said bleakly. "If we run for safety the Japanese police will take us. If we stay on the streets, the maniacs who killed Shirley and Mowry will have us."

"I want you to go over to my hotel and wait for me in the coffee shop, or the lobby. Anyplace that's public, where there are a lot of people."

Kelley's eyes widened. "What are you talking about? You mean right now?"

"Yes. Take a cab."

"What about you . . . ?" She looked closely at him. "You're going to wait here for them?"

"One of them is already dead, and I may have wounded the second. Which leaves two more, possibly three. I'd like to even the odds a bit, and then have a little chat with whoever is left."

"You're crazy."

"So I've been told."

"You saw what they did to Mowry. God, they did the same thing to Shirley."

The red Mercedes slid to a halt a hundred feet away on Harumi-dori Avenue. McGarvey spotted it out of the corner of his eye and pulled Kelley back out of sight behind the gate as a slightly built man got out of the back and started up the broad pedestrian walkway. He was limping. The car left immediately, but not before McGarvey saw that the driver was now the sole occupant.

"He's the one from the van," Kelley said. "At least I think so. But he was wearing a uniform then."

"It's the same one," McGarvey said. "But one of them is missing. He's probably somewhere behind us, and this one means to drive us into him."

Kelley looked wildly from the approaching figure, back down the tree-lined concourse that led into the garden. Already the park was beginning to fill up. "We have no idea what he looks like."

McGarvey had gotten a vague impression of a bulky man in the front passenger seat, but he had not gotten a clear look. "No, but he shouldn't be so hard to spot once this one tells me what he looks like."

The driver of the Mercedes would probably abandon the car and come in from the west, boxing them in, leaving them only one direction to run. The killers were taking a big risk of being spotted by the police, which meant they considered McGarvey and Kelley very important.

"We can let him pass and duck out behind him," Kelley said.

The police imposter was less than fifty feet away, his right hand stuffed into the light brown jacket he wore now. Passerby didn't look directly at him; the Japanese were too polite to stare. But it was clear that his presence, blood on one leg of his trousers, was causing a stir. It would be only a matter of a few minutes before the alarm was sounded and the police showed up.

"As soon as he comes through I want you to do just that," McGarvey said. "Grab a cab and get out of here."

"I don't want to leave you here like this, not with three-to-one odds," she argued, and McGarvey looked at her with a new respect. She was frightened half out of her mind, but she was willing to stay and help.

"Are you armed?"

"No."

"Then go to the hotel and wait for me there."

The killer was nearing the gate, and McGarvey pulled Kelley farther back behind the portal, so that they were completely hidden for the moment.

"What if you don't show up?" she whispered urgently.

McGarvey took out his pistol and switched the safety off. This was the last of the ammunition he had with him. But he was going to avoid at all costs any kind of a shootout here in a public park.

"If I'm not back by noon, make contact with Phil Carrara, he'll know what to do," McGarvey said. "Now get ready to go."

"This is stupid," she whispered in desperation.

"You can say that again," McGarvey agreed.

The man came through the gate, and as soon as he was past, McGarvey stepped out from around the portal and fell in behind him. Kelley darted around the corner and out the gate.

"I don't want to kill you, but I will unless you do exactly as I say," McGarvey said in a conversational tone.

Igarshi practically jumped out of his skin. His step faltered and he started to withdraw his hand from his pocket.

"I killed your friend back there, I won't hesitate to put a bullet in your spine," McGarvey warned.

"Who are you? What do you want here?" Igarshi demanded, his English very bad but understandable.

"My questions," McGarvey said. "But first I want to know who hired you to kill Shirley and Mowry . . ."

Igarshi was incredibly fast. With his right elbow he knocked McGarvey's gun hand aside, and then spun around, smashing three well-aimed blows into McGarvey's chest and throat within the space of barely one second.

On instinct alone, McGarvey was just able to fall back, sidestepping the killer's next blows, and smash the butt of his pistol into the back of the man's neck. Igarshi went down with a grunt.

Several people stopped and turned to see what the commotion was all about, and McGarvey stepped back, bringing up his gun as the Mercedes driver came down the broad path on the left in a dead run.

Tanaka fired three shots, one of them hitting a bystander, one smacking into a tree and the third plucking at McGarvey's sleeve.

McGarvey turned sideways to present less of himself as a target, and squeezed off two measured shots, both hitting the oncoming Japanese in the chest, driving him to his knees and then down.

A woman was screaming and another woman was down on her knees beside the bystander who'd been shot, wailing and wringing her hands.

McGarvey hauled the dazed Igarshi over on his back. "Who hired you to kill Shirley and Mowry?" he demanded. There wasn't much time. Already in the distance there were more sirens.

Igarshi snarled something in Japanese and lunged upward, grabbing the barrel of McGarvey's pistol. The gun discharged, the bullet entering the man's forehead, his head bouncing off the gravel path and his eyes filling with blood.

He'd committed suicide!

McGarvey recoiled and then looked up as a heavyset man built like a Sherman tank came charging down the main concourse. He looked like a wild animal.

Stepping back, McGarvey brought up his pistol in both hands and crouched in the shooter's stance. Heidinora stopped in his tracks ten feet away. He was unarmed, an expression of pure hatred on his round, rough-featured face. The sirens were much closer now, and it was clear that he heard them.

"I don't want to kill you, but I will not leave Tokyo until I have answers," McGarvey said.

Heidinora backed up, his hands spread in a gesture of peace.

"Remember my face," McGarvey said, lowering his pistol. "I'll want answers to my questions."

Heidinora nodded once, then turned on his heel and walked off. Holstering his pistol, McGarvey turned in the opposite direction and headed out the gate to Harumi-dori Avenue.

BOOK THREE

30

A gentle sea breeze ruffled the potted flowers on the veranda of the villa that overlooked the Principality of Monaco and the azure Mediterranean. Surrounded by fragrant eucalyptus trees, the expansive, low, stuccoed house was enclosed within a tall concrete fence topped with glass shards. Doberman pinschers patrolled the grounds at night, and along with a sophisticated system of extremely low-light-capable closed-circuit television monitors, the Villa Ambrosia was a relatively secure fortress without being ostentatiously so.

Ernst Spranger, dressed in sandals, white slacks and a bright yellow short-sleeved Izod, came out to the veranda to greet his guest who'd just been announced. The short, slightly built man stood at the low rail, looking at a half-dozen sailboats in the distance. It was just eight in the morning, and Spranger was in a pensive mood in part because of the events, or lack of events, over the past few days, and in part because of this man's unexpected presence.

"Your coming here today may cause us a problem, unless you took care not to be seen," Spranger said.

The Japanese man turned around and smiled. "You should not

worry about such inconsequential details when there are so many other things to be concerned about, Herr Spranger."

Spranger crossed the veranda and shook hands with the man. "Nonetheless, Mr. Endo, I trust you took the proper precautions."

"Naturally."

"You understand that we have other clients who must also be protected."

The expression in Endo's eyes was unfathomable, but he did not stop smiling. "My message will be brief, but let us sit down together as friends, still."

Liese was watching and listening from a room in the rear that contained the villa's security equipment. Later they would go over the tape together to make sure neither of them had missed anything.

The Italian houseboy served them tea when they were settled and after he withdrew, Endo pushed his cup aside and sat forward.

"Tell me what progress you have made concerning Mr. McGarvey. It is still our wish to stop the man."

"We have temporarily lost direct track of him in Washington. My people there think he may have left the area, but at this point we're still not certain. In any event, it's not our intention to confront him directly . . . and certainly not on his home ground."

"Your intentions are . . . ?"

"To lure him back to Europe, of course, where we will set up a killing zone of our own choosing."

"When and where will this be accomplished?"

"The when is very soon, but to answer your question about where is more complicated. We have reliable intelligence that McGarvey may be an extraordinary man who might not be so easily cornered and killed. First he must be given an incentive to do what we wish, and then he must be softened up. But the odds are with us. We'll stack them that way."

"Are you afraid of this man?"

Spranger bridled at the question. "Of course not."

Endo shook his head. "You should be, Herr Spranger."

"What do you mean?"

"Mr. McGarvey is presently in Tokyo, where he gunned down three of our people in cold blood. And in broad daylight, I might add, with all of the odds, as you say, stacked against him. Now the police are investigating us as well as the Americans. It is an intolerable situation. One which we have paid your organization a great deal of money to prevent."

The news was stunning. Spranger needed time to think. "Has he gone back to work for the CIA?"

"The fact that he was so recently in Washington makes that a distinct possibility. As does the fact that he was seen with a woman who has been identified as the mistress of two CIA officers."

"Who are these men?"

"The chief of station and his assistant," Endo said. "We eliminated both of them."

"*Verdammt*," Spranger swore. "Is the CIA investigating your operation?"

"That is no concern of yours, Herr Spranger. This man must be made to leave Tokyo. Immediately."

"If you're being investigated by the CIA, if they are making the connection between you and what happened in Paris, then our entire contract is in grave jeopardy."

"The connection has not been made as yet. But time is of the essence. You must lure McGarvey out of Japan immediately."

"It may take some time," Spranger said, his thoughts racing. "There are certain details still to be worked out."

"Work them out," Endo said, standing. "You have twenty-four hours in which to do it."

Spranger looked up. "Or else?"

"We will cancel our contract with you, and demand an immediate repayment of all monies we've paid to date."

"Don't threaten me," Spranger warned.

"Our reach is much longer than you would think," the Japanese said. "Do this for us and you will be a wealthy man. Fail and you will die."

Endo turned and left the veranda. His car and driver had waited in front for him.

Liese, wearing a stunningly revealing string bikini, came out of the house a moment later, and sat down across from Spranger. She was smiling.

"Why the hell did the bastard go to Tokyo?" Spranger asked. "What the hell is he playing at now?"

"It doesn't matter," Liese said.

Spranger focused on her. "What are you talking about?"

"The news from Bern," she said sweetly. "It has finally come."

"I see," Spranger said, grinning. It was as if a giant weight had been taken off his shoulders.

31

Traffic on the Washington Memorial Parkway was heavy, though most of it was headed toward the city, and not north, along the river. Already the morning was hot, humid and hazy, and only when the Mercedes convertible turned off the main highway up the Bureau of Public Roads' treelined entry road, was there any relief.

"I'm here to speak with Phil Carrara," Kathleen McGarvey told the gate guard. "I didn't make an appointment, but if you'll just tell him who it is, he'll see me."

"Yes, ma'am," the guard said, and went back into the glass-fronted hut.

During the few minutes it took him, there was a steady stream of traffic into the CIA Headquarters. Most spies, Katheleen reflected, were nine-to-fivers like the rest of official Washington. She'd had the misfortune of picking one who wasn't.

"Someone will meet you in the lobby, Mrs. McGarvey," the guard said, giving her her visitor's passes. "Just to the right after the clearing."

"I know the way," Kathleen said, and she drove up the hill. It'd been years since her one visit here, and she'd vowed then never to come back. Now she was frightened. The same old fear as in the early days. This time it was the call.

She signed in with the guards in the lobby, and after her purse was searched, a young man who said his name was Chilton escorted her up to the DDO's office on the third floor.

Carrara was waiting for her at the door to the office. "This is certainly a surprise, Mrs. McGarvey."

"Not a pleasant one, I'm sure," Kathleen said, preceding him into his office and taking a seat in front of his desk. She wore a crisply tailored off-white linen suit, and a pastel green blouse with matching shoes and broad-brimmed hat.

"The Agency regrets the intrusion of your house the other day," Carrara said going around behind his desk. "But if there's anything I can do personally . . ."

"I want to know where Kirk has gone off to this time," she said.

"I'm sorry, Mrs. McGarvey but I don't know anything . . ."

"Short of that I want to get a message to him." She crossed her legs. "I won't leave here until I get what I've come for. And if need be, I'll speak with the general."

"I don't know if that will be possible, this morning," he replied, and for the first time Kathleen noticed that something was wrong. It looked as if he hadn't slept or shaved in a week. His complexion was pale, and his eyes bloodshot.

"I'll wait right here if I have to," she said. "Kirk is on another assignment for you, and I must get word to him."

"He told you that, Mrs. McGarvey?" Carrara asked sharply.

"Not in so many words. But I know him. One day he is here, and the next day, after your people show up at my front door, he disappears. I merely put two and two together."

"I'm sorry," Carrara said tiredly. "I don't know where he is. And even if I did I could not tell you. I'll have you escorted back downstairs to your car."

"You're lying! You're hiding something. And believe me, I mean to have it out today. I won't take no for an answer."

Carrara stared at her for a long moment or two. "What's so important that you need to get a message to him at this moment? Can't it wait?"

"I'd rather not say."

Carrara shrugged. "We won't deliver secret messages, Mrs. McGarvey."

"That's ludicrous coming from a man like you in a place like this."

"Nevertheless."

"The last time we saw each other I kicked him out of my house. I want to tell him that I was . . . wrong. That I'm sorry."

Carrara said nothing. It was obvious he didn't believe her.

"If he gets killed it'll be too late," she said, raising her voice.

"I repeat, Mrs. McGarvey, what makes you believe that your husband is working for us?"

Kathleen looked away. It was probably a mistake coming here like this. Something important was apparently going on. Something that was worrying the Deputy Director of Operations. And whatever that was, it had to be big. But now that she was here, now that she had come this far, she was determined to see it through. She owed that much to Kirk, and to herself.

"Are you going to allow me to get a message to him?" she asked, looking back.

"Not without more information. I'm sorry, but no."

"Then I want to speak with General Murphy."

"The Director is not available today."

"I don't believe you," Kathleen said. "If need be I'll march directly over to the Hill and raise such a stink with the Joint Intelligence Committee, several members of which are regulars at my home, that all of Washington will hear about it."

Carrara sighed. "Very well," he said, and he picked up his phone. "Ask the director if I may bring Mrs. McGarvey upstairs this morning to have a word with him."

The Asia Center of Japan Hotel was near the center of Tokyo and barely fifteen minutes on foot from the Roppongi District and the American Embassy. McGarvey stood at the window of their tiny third-floor room, watching the late night traffic below on the street as he waited for his call to the States to go through.

He'd picked up Kelly Fuller in the lobby of the ANA Tokyo Hotel, and then checked in there to leave a track. Later they'd come over to this smaller and far less conspicuous hotel that she had assured him catered to foreigners. No one would notice him here, nor had he been required to show his passport or any identification when he'd registered under the German workname Rolf Eiger.

For the time being at least he figured that he and Kelly would be safe here. Sooner or later he was going to have to get word to Carrara about what happened. But first he wanted to make sure that their backs were covered.

"Anything?" she asked, coming out of the postage-stamp bathroom.

He turned away from the window and shook his head. "I think we'll be all right here for a day or so. But we'll have to keep on the move, or find a better place."

"Until when?"

"Until I finish what I was sent here to do."

"Which is?" she asked, her voice brittle.

"Find out who killed Shirley, and Mowry, and why," McGarvey answered. "If you want out, I can arrange it."

She looked at him, a wistful set to her mouth, but then she turned away. "I'll stay. Besides, there's no place I could go where they wouldn't find me eventually now that they know my face."

The telephone on the bedstand rang, and McGarvey answered it. "Yes?"

"I have your party," the operator said, and the connection was made.

"Otto, have you made any progress yet?" McGarvey asked. It was 9:00 in the morning, Washington time.

"I tried to find you. But no one knows were you are, or they're not admitting it," Rencke said. "This is getting really weird."

McGarvey's gut tightened. "Who'd you call?" he asked, keeping his voice normal.

"Not actually call, except for your ex. But you're on the computer across the river."

"Listen to me now. I don't want you trying to make any personal contacts. I want you to wait for me to call you. No matter how important it is. Do you understand?"

"Oh, sure, but listen up, *compadre*, the people over there are definitely looking for you. And worse than that they're beginning to suspect a mouse in the pantry."

"Meaning you?"

"Bingo. But I've got a few more tricks up my sleeve if you want me to go for broke."

"Have you found anything so far?"

"Only in the negative sense. It's definitely not the government. Nor is there any . . . material missing from their power plants, if you catch my drift. So whoever is going for the bacon isn't picking it up at home."

"I need the help, but it's up to you," McGarvey said carefully. "You know what's happened already. Including the latest?"

"It may take a little while, but I'll stick with it. I hate getting pushed around, you know. And besides, I'm out of Twinkies again."

"I'll buy you a carload."

"I'll hold you to it."

McGarvey got the stateside operator back, and had her place a call to Kathleen's number. But there was no answer, and hanging up he tried to put her out of his mind. Rencke had called her. She'd told him nothing, because she knew nothing. And that was the end of it. He hoped.

32

Roland Murphy got up and came around from behind his desk as Kathleen McGarvey entered his big office with Phil Carrara. Another, prim-looking man, who'd been seated on a leather couch across the room, languidly got to his feet at the same time. He was scowling.

"Kathleen, what an unexpected pleasure," the DCI said.

"It's good of you to see me on such short notice, General," she said. They shook hands.

"Have you met our General Counsel, Howard Ryan?"

"No," Kathleen said, exchanging glances with the man. "I won't take up much of your time this morning. I simply need a little of your help, and I'll be off."

The DCI motioned for her to take a seat, and when she was settled he went back to his own chair behind his desk. Carrara remained standing by the door, and Ryan perched on the arm of the couch. For a moment it felt to Kathleen as if she were in for an inquisition. But then her reception was nothing less than she'd expected.

"I'm assuming that your visit to us this morning has something to do with your ex-husband," Murphy said.

"Mrs. McGarvey is of the opinion that Kirk is working for us," Carrara said.

"What makes you think so?" Murphy asked. "Did Kirk tell you that himself? Did he tell you that he'd taken on an assignment for us?"

"He didn't have to. I know him well enough to know when he is off in the bush."

"Apparently you don't know him well enough to keep him," Ryan said.

Kathleen shot him a dirty look, and she started to say something, but changed her mind. She'd heard about him. They called him the "toy spy."

"Let's assume for the moment that he is on assignment for us," the DCI said. "You understand that we could not confirm or deny it, let alone tell you where he was. You do know that."

Kathleen nodded. She'd gotten at least part of what she'd come for, and it didn't make her happy. "I want you to get a message to him."

"That might not be possible, Kathleen."

"Tell him to come home. Immediately. His family needs him."

"Just what's that supposed to mean . . ." Ryan said, but Murphy cut him off.

"Even if he was working for us, would you expect me to pass such a message to him?" Murphy asked.

"Yes," Kathleen said. "And in exactly those words. Shall I repeat them?"

Murphy stared at her for a long second, but then shook his head. "It's not necessary."

"Well?" she asked.

"I'll do what I can. But let me ask you something. Do you believe that you are in some danger?"

Kathleen was startled. It was exactly what she believed because of the warning she'd received, but hearing it here was disquieting. "Am I in some danger, General?" she asked, keeping her true feelings out of her voice.

"No," Murphy said. "No more than any of us are who live in Washington."

"Somehow that's no comfort," Kathleen said rising. "See that Kirk gets that message."

"I'll do what I can," Murphy said.

"That was some cryptic message," Murphy said when Carrara returned from escorting Kathleen downstairs. "Any thoughts on it, Phil?"

"Well, besides his ex-wife, he's got a daughter attending school in Switzerland, and a sister, her husband and a couple of kids out west somewhere. Utah, I think. Mother and father are dead. And so far as I know there's no one else."

"What'd she say to you on the way downstairs?" Ryan asked.

"Nothing. Not a word."

"What about this daughter in Switzerland?" Murphy asked. "Could there be any connection between her and Lausanne? Do you think Spranger's people might go after her?"

Carrara shook his head. "There's no reason for them to believe at this moment that McGarvey is investigating them. And of course after what's happened in Tokyo, he might have his hands full over there for the foreseeable future."

"Any word from him yet?"

"Nothing," Carrara said. "But what about his ex-wife's request? We're not going to send that sort of a message to him, are we?"

"Of course not," the DCI replied. "But what was the hidden message?"

"Maybe there wasn't one. From what I understand McGarvey was on his way here in any event to try to get back together with her."

Ryan sniggered.

"You believe she wants him back?"

"It may be nothing more than that."

"Why did she come out here then?" Murphy asked.

"She's a bright woman, General. We showed up at her house looking for Kirk, and he suddenly disappears. We either arrested him, or sent him off on assignment. She's seen the precedents."

"Have her followed," Ryan suggested.

"I don't think that's such a good idea," Carrara said. "As I say, she's an intelligent woman. If she were to get wind that we were watching her, she could raise a stink. She knows half of Washington."

"For the moment I'm going to go along with Phil," Murphy said. "But I think I'll have the Bureau put a tap on her telephone. Just for the next few days or so. If she makes any kind of a move, we'll step in."

"We shouldn't have any problems with that," Ryan said. "I can make a decent case of the request, considering what McGarvey is doing. Might take twenty-four hours though."

"See to it, Howard. But I want to come back to my original question. Her message was cryptic. Does she know something? Did Kirk tell her some of his little secrets? Or is it possible after all that someone has gotten to her?"

"Do you mean the East Germans?" Carrara asked.

"Or the Japanese."

"It's possible."

"A soft kidnapping," Murphy said. "Get a message to your husband, Mrs. McGarvey. Tell him to back off or we'll come after you."

"As I say, General, it's possible," Carrara answered.

"I'm not asking that, Phil. Anything is possible. What I am asking you, is it probable?"

Carrara shook his head. "I don't think so."

"Why?"

"She would have screamed bloody murder."

Murphy looked away. "Maybe she did, and we didn't listen."

33

Elizabeth McGarvey emerged from the Bern Design Polytechnic's Residence Hall Picasso a few minutes after five in the afternoon and unlocked her twelve-speed mountain bike from its rack. The lake air was pleasantly cool and fresh on her bare arms.

At nineteen, Elizabeth was a slender, long-legged young woman with what a former boyfriend had called an "interesting" face of pleasant angles, high cheekbones, a delicately formed nose, a full, almost pouty lower lip and large, brilliantly green eyes that looked at the world with keen intelligence and a hint of amusement. She had her mother's beauty, and her father's spirit. A devastating combination of which she was inwardly proud.

In high school in the States she had done poorly, partly because she was bored, and partly because she'd come from a broken home. When her father had showed up last year, and her mother had not rejected him out of hand, she had blossomed. Life had become important. There was so much to be learned in the world; so much to be grasped, so much to see and do and be, that at times she could barely control her enthusiasms.

She was learning design, everything from fine arts to ergonomics, here outside of Bern near Lac de Neuchâtel, and loving every second of it.

"Going into town again?" someone asked behind her.

She turned around as Armand Armonde, one of her fine arts

instructors, came up. He'd had a thing for her since January when she'd started in his oil and acrylics class.

"Get your bicycle and join me," she said. "It's barely five klicks."

"I'd prefer to drive, *ma cherie*. May I give you a lift?"

"I need the exercise. But you can buy me a cognac at the Hansa Haus."

Armonde was a devastatingly good-looking Parisian, who at thirty still hadn't lost his boyish charm. "And then what?" he asked, pleasantly.

Elizabeth grinned. "I go to the boutique to buy a pair of nylons, then get back on my bicycle and return here. I have a ton of homework, remember?"

"Better yet, we could have dinner together, and afterward return to my studio where I would help you with your work."

"My daddy taught me never to mix pleasure with business, especially if your business is important to you. My studies are."

"A wise man?"

"The wisest," she said. All her life she'd made up quotes which she attributed to her father whenever she figured the situation warranted it. After so many years she'd come to believe them.

"But then you cannot continue your studies, as you have been, twelve months of the year. Sooner or later you will take a holiday and I will be there."

"I might take you up on it," Elizabeth said. "In the meantime, a simple cognac?"

Armonde nodded. "Of course."

"See you in town then," she said, mounting her bike, and she took off down the hill, her long hair streaming behind her in the wind.

Past the tall iron gates guarding the school property, the narrow driveway ran down to a macadam country lane into the small town of Estavayer-le-lac. Now, in the summer, the town was busy with tourists, but in the winter the entire countryside became almost monastic. The changes in season and population suited Elizabeth. In the past few years she'd lived with her mother's constant striving for recognition, which in Washington meant a steady stream of cocktail parties and dinners, with hardly a normal evening. If her mother was home, the house was filled with guests. If the house was quiet, her mother was gone.

Elizabeth craved normalcy, craved routine. And, she supposed, she craved acceptance. Most of all by her father.

The route into town was mostly downhill, though the grade wasn't very steep so that the ride back wasn't difficult. She often made the short trip in the afternoons after classes, and sometimes on weekends if the weather was nice, to see the town and the lake, but mostly for the solitude. This time alone gave her a chance to think about herself, about her future, and about her mother and father. Even if they did get together again, she was starting to believe that it would never stick.

Her mother had been reasonably open and honest about the relationship she'd had with her husband; her fears and her complaints, and his frequent absences, and apparent indifference. And although he said he was coming back from Europe, and her mother said that she would forgo the social scene, Elizabeth didn't think that either of them could change their lives so radically.

Which left her a little sad, though she was determined that if her childhood relationship with her father was lost forever, she would make every effort to make sure she had an adult relationship with him.

So far as she could figure, her mother had been, and continued to be, too weak a person to be married to such a man as Kirk McGarvey. Elizabeth decided that she would be different. She did not want a stranger for a father.

Closer into town traffic increased and Elizabeth rode all the way to the right, nearly off the road, so that cars and trucks would have an easier time getting past her.

About a mile out, she glanced over her shoulder. A dark Mercedes sedan was hanging back just a few yards behind her, the driver and another man staring intently at her.

She slowed down and waved them on, but after a few seconds when they didn't pass she looked back again. They had slowed down, and it appeared as if they had no intention of passing her.

"Idiots," she mumbled, pulling off the paved surface and stopping. She half dismounted and looked back. The Mercedes stopped ten yards behind her.

For a moment she didn't know what to make of it, but then Armonde's gray Fiat appeared at the crest of the hill, followed by another car and a delivery van.

The passenger in the Mercedes started to get out when the driver looked in the rearview mirror and apparently said something, because the passenger looked back up the highway.

He immediately got back in the car, and the Mercedes pulled away, spitting gravel from its rear tires as it accelerated.

As it passed Elizabeth, the passenger looked out his window, a grim, almost hateful expression on his broad, pale-complected face. The look had been so intense it made her shudder, and she watched as the car disappeared around a bend in the road.

The plates were French, a big oval F decal on the trunk lid.

Armonde beeped and waved as he passed, and when the car and van behind him had also passed, she got back on her bike and continued into town, the brief incident more puzzling to her than troubling.

34

"What was that all about on the road?" Armonde asked when he and Elizabeth were settled at the Hansa Haus.

"With the Mercedes?" she asked. "I don't know. Some crazy tourists who liked my behind, probably. They were French." She idly fingered the half-carat diamond necklace her father had given her last year.

Armonde smiled. He had the Gallic reserve and was amused by Elizabeth's directness. "And a wonderful *derrière* it is. But I thought it was someone you knew."

"No," Elizabeth said, preoccupied for the moment with her thoughts. Whoever it was in the car had definitely wanted to make contact with her for some reason. But what had been most puzzling about the incident was the expression on the man's face as the car passed her.

The small gasthaus had filled up with the usual after-work crowd as well as a few tourists, and the room had become smoke-filled and noisy. Suddenly Elizabeth no longer wanted to be there. She wanted peace and solitude. She wanted to return to the school.

She drank her cognac straight back, and waited for a bemused Armonde to finish his.

"Another?" he asked.

"No, but I'd like you to drive me back to the school."

"Now?"

"Yes," she said. "We can tie my bike on the roof of your car. If you don't mind."

"No, of course not. But what about your nylons?"

She glanced toward the door. She was starting to feel claustrophobic. The last time that had happened to her was when she was little, in Washington, and there'd been a clothes dryer fire in the laundry room. Everyone said she'd probably smelled the smoke, but she'd known differently. She'd *sensed* danger. Like ESP, she'd tried to explain, but no one would listen.

"I don't need them," she said, getting up.

"Is something wrong, Elizabeth?" Armonde asked, rising.

"No. I just want to go. Now."

"As you wish," he said. He laid some money for their drinks on the table and, outside, helped Elizabeth heft her bike up on top of the small car. He got some twine from the trunk and tied the bike in place.

"Is it about that car?" Armonde asked as they headed through town, the big lake at their back.

Elizabeth looked at him, not understanding for a moment what he was asking her. She'd been thinking about Washington and her mother, and especially about her father. She knew, in a vague sense, what he did for a living. It involved the CIA. But she'd never been told the whole story. For some reason her lack of knowledge bothered her just now.

"The Mercedes?" Armonde prompted, and Elizabeth shook herself out of her thoughts.

"No," she said. "The smoke and the noise just got to me, that's all. It gave me a terrible headache."

"Standard American," Armonde said ruefully.

"What?"

"The standard American feminine excuse."

She smiled and touched his arm. "No, honestly, I do have a terrible headache, but it doesn't have a thing to do with you."

"Really?"

She nodded. "Really. Even if I didn't have a headache, I wouldn't have dinner with you tonight."

Kathleen McGarvey's plane from London's Gatwick touched down at Bern's small airport just after 6:30 P.M., and she got lucky with the last rental car from the small Hertz office. A helpful clerk showed her on a map how to get down to the Design Polytechnic, which was about twenty-five miles to the southwest. She was on the highway by seven.

Kirk's great desire had been for them to live in Europe. But from the start it had been an idea she'd resisted, though exactly why she'd never really been able to answer. Coming here to see her daughter gave her a strange intimation of what their life together could have been like.

Neat. Driving through the outskirts of Bern, and then southwest on the highway, the word kept coming up in her mind. The towns she passed through, and the countryside in between, seemed to be freshly swept. Scrubbed. Groomed. The entire country, or what she was seeing of it, seemed to be a cross between Disneyland and a carefully tended park. Clean. Almost, but not quite, sterile.

For five years Kirk lived in Lausanne, not too far to the south. On the way across the Atlantic this morning aboard the BOAC Concorde SST, she had toyed with the idea of taking Elizabeth with her to visit the city. But it was a foolish notion. That life, the missed opportunities, was dead and gone. There was no use in dredging it up. She wanted only to pick up her daughter, explain the situation to her as best she could and then take her back to Washington to relative safety.

There was little doubt in her mind that the general had ordered someone to watch her. But she had not been interfered with so far. Which either meant she'd been too fast for them, or that their orders were to watch but not touch. In any event she wanted to be back in Washington by tomorrow afternoon where she could be certain they were keeping an eye on her and Elizabeth. As soon as Kirk surfaced again and gave them the all clear, Elizabeth could return to school.

She passed through the small town of Avenches a little before eight, and a few miles farther took the Estavayer-le-lac road. Just past the even smaller village of Payerne, a driveway was marked with a sign for the school and she turned off the paved highway, a little thrill of anticipation fluttering in her stomach. It had been months since she'd last seen Elizabeth, and she wanted to hear all the news.

Elizabeth stood at the window of her dormitory room watching the early evening. There'd been no traffic except for the blue Ford Taurus that had come up the driveway about ten minutes ago. It had been too far away to see who'd been driving, but there were visitors every day.

"Instead of moping around here, why didn't you have dinner with him?" her roommate, Toni Killmer, asked from the open door to the bathroom. She'd been washing nylons and panties.

"I didn't want to spend the evening fighting him off," Elizabeth said, turning around.

Toni's parents were wealthy New Yorkers. Like Elizabeth she was studying design, but unlike Elizabeth she was here because she'd been kicked out of three other schools, and no one else would have her. She and Elizabeth had become fast friends.

"Why fight? The man is an absolute hunk."

Elizabeth laughed. "Do you want him?"

"Fuckin' A."

Elizabeth had to laugh again. "Toni, you are definitely crude."

"Not crude, sweety, just h-o-r-n-y," Toni said, and someone knocked on the door. "Him?" she mouthed the word. "*Entrez*," she called.

Kathleen came in, her linen traveling suit lightly crumpled, but her makeup and hair perfect. "I've had a terrible time finding you."

"My God, mother. What are you doing here?"

Kathleen smiled tightly and glanced at Toni, who stood in her bra and panties at the bathroom door. "I've popped over to take you to dinner. You haven't eaten yet, have you, dear?"

"No. But I mean, is something wrong?"

"Of course not. Can't a mother come visit her daughter at school?"

"Yes, but . . ."

"Get dressed now, Elizabeth, and we'll find a place to eat. I think I passed a nice-looking restaurant a few miles back."

Elizabeth tried to read something from the expression in her mother's eyes, and from her voice. Something was wrong, she was reasonably sure of that. But to what extent there was trouble, it was almost impossible to tell.

"Mother, I'd like you to meet my roommate, Toni Killmer."

"Mrs. McGarvey," Toni said pleasantly.

"Of the New York Killmers?"

"Yes, ma'am."

"I know your mother. Lovely lady." Kathleen turned back to her daughter. "Well, get dressed, dear."

"May I invite Toni along?" Elizabeth asked.

Kathleen's expression became apologetic. "No, I'm sorry, dear, but I have something . . . well, something private to discuss with you. You understand."

"Yes, mother," Elizabeth replied, and she *did* understand. Something was definitely wrong.

35

It took Ernst Spranger a full five minutes to work his way in the near-darkness up through the woods from the road to a position where he could see the Design Polytechnic's main administration building, and beyond it the Picasso Residence Hall. Nothing moved below, but there were lights in most windows; late classes in some of the buildings, and students settling down to their studies in others.

He keyed the burst walkie-talkie. "I'm in position. Everything looks quiet from here." He hit the TRANSMIT button.

A moment later Liese came back. "We're starting up the driveway."

Spranger wore a black jumpsuit which made him practically invisible. He would guard the west flank of the school property, while Bruno Lessing, who'd taken up position on the other side of the long driveway, would guard the east flank.

"Are you ready, Bruno?" he radioed.

"All set here." Lessing's voice came softly from the walkie-talkie speaker.

"Peter?" Spranger radioed.

"ETA at our rendezvous point in about ten minutes," a third voice answered.

"Stand by," Spranger acknowledged, and he raised his binoculars as Otto Scherchen and Liese, driving a four-door blue Peugeot sedan, appeared below, passing the administration building and parking at the side of the Picasso Residence Hall. They were posing as Swiss Federal Police Officers. Scherchen would remain in the car as a backup in case of trouble, while Liese went inside to talk to the girl.

Radvonska's warning in Rome that McGarvey was something special had been very specific. "If you can trust the man to do anything, trust him always to do the unexpected," the KGB *rezident* had warned.

"With him it's not likely you would get a second chance. For instance: It might even be possible that he's assigned someone to watch his daughter. Be careful that you do not walk into a trap."

Herr and Frau Schey, posing as the parents of a prospective student, had come to the school and had a long chat with the dean of admissions. Afterwards they'd been taken on a tour of the campus, including the Picasso Residence Hall.

They had actually been inside Elizabeth McGarvey's room, and they had tramped all over the campus, even having tea with the faculty afterwards. They had returned with detailed sketches of everything.

"The only sign we saw that anyone was paying special attention to the girl was a young man identified for us as one of the staff. An instructor by the name of Armand Armonde."

"Do you think it's possible he's on staff as a cover for a job as bodyguard to the girl?" Spranger had asked.

The Scheys exchanged glances. "I would say no," Dieter Schey said. "But anything is possible."

Liese climbed out of the car, straightened the skirt of her conservatively cut blue suit, and entered the building without looking back.

"She's inside, everybody stay alert," Spranger radioed.

"Just over seven minutes to rendezvous," Dürenmatt came back. He was at the wheel of a semi tractor-trailer rig, northbound on the Bern-Lausanne highway. The rendezvous point was a turn-around just north of the intersection with the Estavayer-le-lac road.

The timing was tight, but so far everything was going exactly according to schedule.

Spranger tightened his grip on the binoculars as he studied the side and back of the residence hall, and the area between it and the administration building.

If there was to be any trouble it would happen in the next minute or so. If the girl put up a fight, and Liese had to use force to subdue her, and that action was witnessed by someone who decided to interfere the entire operation could fall apart.

"What do you want me to do in that case?" Liese had asked him.

Spranger shrugged. "She will have seen your face," he said. "If it comes to that you will have no other choice but to kill her and anyone else who could recognize you."

Liese grinned, the expression feral. "Mr. Endo would not be happy."

"Perhaps, but it would probably lure McGarvey out of Japan just the same."

The dormitory corridor smelled of a combination of liquor, cigarette smoke, and a dozen too-strong colognes and aftershave lotions. Liese hesitated in a stairwell, testing the air and listening to the distant but pervasive hum of conversations, radios and stereos and television sets, of clacking typewriters and hair dryers and electric shavers.

Like Dresden, she had the fleeting thought. But not so much like her college days when she'd transferred to Moscow University.

The sounds and smells were normal here. Nothing bad was happening, and no one expected anything bad to happen.

If it came to a kill, she told herself starting upstairs, it would be easy. No one would interfere.

At the third-floor landing she felt in her shoulder bag for her silenced Bernadelli .32 caliber automatic, checking to make sure that the safety catch was in the on position as she looked through the window into the corridor.

A young man, a towel around his neck, was leaning against an open doorway talking to someone in one of the rooms. At the far end of the corridor two girls dressed in shorts and T-shirts, their legs well-tanned, were engaged in conversation. Just across from them, two women, one of them older, both of them dressed for the street, came out of one of the rooms and started up the corridor.

For an instant Liese disregarded them. But then she realized with a start that one of the women was Elizabeth McGarvey, and she stepped back.

They were obviously going out. Dinner perhaps, or a show in town. They definitely were not dressed for campus.

She checked the window again. They were barely five yards away, Elizabeth talking, saying something to the older woman.

Liese turned and hurried halfway down to the second-floor landing, then turned and calmly started back up, as the third-floor door opened and the two women entered the stairwell.

They started down, moving over so that they could pass, when Liese stopped short.

"Are you Elizabeth McGarvey?" she asked, feigning surprise.

Elizabeth and Kathleen stopped, a wary look on Kathleen's face.

"Yes, I am," Elizabeth said.

Liese dug in her shoulder bag and brought out her blue leather identification booklet. She flipped it open and held it up so that both women could see her picture ID and gold shield. "My name is Liese Egk. Federal Police. I've been sent from Bern to fetch you."

Elizabeth was instantly concerned. "What is it? What's happened?"

"It's about your father," Liese said, watching the older woman. There was something familiar about her. Something from a file folder. From photographs. "I'm afraid there's been an accident."

"Oh, my God," Kathleen said. "Is Kirk here, in Switzerland?"

Suddenly Liese had it, and she could hardly hold back a broad grin. "I'm sorry, madam, but this is a personal matter."

"You don't understand," Elizabeth said. "She's my mother. Now what has happened? God, tell us."

Armonde was just coming across the driveway from the Fine Arts Building as the Peugeot headed down to the driveway. Elizabeth looked out at him, and he half-raised his hand, startled, as they passed.

"Is it serious?" Kathleen was asking the policewoman and her driver. "Has he been injured?"

Liese glanced back. "I'm sorry, Mrs. McGarvey, but I don't have any further information. I was simply ordered to pick up your daughter."

"Then someone must be trying to reach me in Washington."

"I wouldn't know, ma'am."

Elizabeth was having a hard time keeping her thoughts straight. She kept envisioning her father lying on the floor or on the ground somewhere, blood pouring from the back of his head. She had the distinct feeling that she was seeing him moments before his death. Something very dreadful had happened, and she felt so terribly helpless, ineffective, useless.

At the end of the driveway, they turned left toward the Bern-Lausanne highway, and their taciturn driver sped up, the night suddenly and ominously dark.

"What about my car?" Kathleen asked. "It's a rental from the Bern airport."

"We'll have someone pick it up, ma'am," Liese said.

"My luggage is in the trunk."

"Yes, ma'am, we'll take care of that as well."

Last year when he'd come home briefly, Elizabeth had thought he'd looked tired. Completely worn out, and above all lonely . . . alone.

"Where exactly is it we're going?" Kathleen asked. "Police Head-quarters in Bern? A hospital? The American consulate?"

Liese didn't answer, and Elizabeth looked up out of her thoughts, then looked at her mother who was clearly becoming alarmed.

"May I see your identification again?" Kathleen asked.

Liese reached for something on the seat next to her, and when she turned around she was holding a gun in her hand. She cocked the hammer. "No more questions."

"You're kidnapping us," Kathleen said. "My, God, you're actually kidnapping us."

"Yes, we are."

"Then my father hasn't been hurt?" Elizabeth asked, relief suddenly washing over her.

"Not yet," Liese said. "But you'll be there when it happens." She laughed.

Elizabeth grinned. "I'll be there, all right," she said. "But you've got to know that you fucked up this time."

Liese looked at her, surprised. "Yes?"

"Yes," Elizabeth said confidently. "My father is going to tear you a new asshole."

36

It was only two-thirty in the afternoon, but Carrara had been going steadily for the past four days and he was seriously considering throwing in the towel and going home for some much-needed rest. There'd been nothing out of Tokyo since yesterday. McGarvey and Kelley had simply disappeared, and Tokyo Station was completely closed down.

His secretary buzzed him. "Sargent Anders from Technical Services is here. He says it's urgent."

"All right, I'll see him."

Moments later the Technical Services director came in. He seemed out of breath, and extremely agitated. "We've just got a break in this operation, but you're not going to like it."

Carrara motioned for him to take a chair. "Are you talking about Tokyo?"

"Yes, and Switzerland."

Something clutched at Carrara's gut. "You've made a bridge?"

"The Golden Gate," Anders said, his eyes shining. "Have we had any word from McGarvey or Kelley Fuller?"

"Nothing yet. But what have you got?"

"Remember the encrypted burst-transmission walkie-talkie the French found at Orly? The one Boorsch had used?"

Carrara nodded. "Have we got an ID on the manufacturer?"

"Depending on your point of view something even better. A

duplicate was found by the Tokyo Police in a red Mercedes parked near the Imperial Palace Outer Gardens."

"The red Mercedes from the attack on Mowry?"

Anders nodded. "And a third duplicate, charred but recognizable, was found in the burned-out remains of the bogus Tokyo Police van in front of the safehouse."

The implications were overwhelming. Carrara sat back wearily in his chair and closed his eyes for a moment. If the Japanese were supplying Spranger's group of ex-STASI thugs with advanced communications equipment, and if K-1 were after nuclear weapons technology, what was there to look forward to?

"A DNA trace from what we found in the truck used in Shirley's assassination matched with one of the bodies in the Outer Gardens. Same people killed Shirley and Mowry and my two people over there."

"And presumably it was the same people who shot down the Airbus . . . or ordered it destroyed."

"Yes, sir," Anders said. "It looks like the Japanese are in this up to their ears."

"It's not the government."

Anders shrugged. "That's not for me to say. But whoever it is—a political or military faction, a corporation or an individual—they've got big bucks. This sort of thing doesn't come cheap."

"Nor does capitalizing on the technology Spranger and his people are stealing for them."

"I'm not sure it's that complicated," the Technical Services director said. He took off his glasses and polished the lenses with his handkerchief.

"What do you mean?"

"We don't know yet if that's what K-1 was after in Switzerland."

"The triggers . . ." Carrara objected, but Anders held him off.

"Excuse me, sir, but the impression I get is that they weren't necessarily after the technology so much as they were trying to buy the specific item. They wanted the actual working triggers. The devices themselves."

"Same thing."

"I don't think so. If they were after the technology as such, then I would tend to believe that the Japanese, or someone in Japan, wanted to learn how to build nuclear weapons."

"The Japanese are developing a credible rocket program. They'd have the delivery system."

"Nasty thought, isn't it?" Anders said. "But if someone over there was simply interested in purchasing the triggers and an initiator and seventy or eighty pounds of plutonium, then I'd say their aim was to build an actual weapon."

Carrara sat back. "Terrorists."

"They didn't hesitate to shoot down that Airbus loaded with innocent people," Anders said.

"No. The question is, how far along are they? How close have they come to gathering everything they need to make such a device?"

"And once they've got the bomb, what's the target?"

"The answers are in Tokyo," Carrara said, picking up his telephone. "I don't care what it takes, Sargent, but we must find McGarvey. Immediately."

"I've got an idea on that score as well," Anders said.

"Just a minute," Carrara said to his secretary on the phone, and he put his hand over the mouthpiece. "Go on."

"We think someone is hacking in our computers. And considering the nature of the files the intruder has been trying to pry open, we think the hacker may be working for McGarvey." Ander smiled ruefully. "The son of a bitch has got friends everywhere."

Carrara nodded. "You think we can get a message to McGarvey via this intruder?"

"It's worth a try."

"Do it," Carrara said, and he removed his hand from the telephone mouthpiece. "Tell the general I want to see him immediately." He smiled grimly. "No, *tell* him."

To the east the sky seemed to be getting brighter with the false dawn as McGarvey sat smoking a cigarette by the window. Behind him, Kelley Fuller rolled over on her tatami mat and sighed. They'd both spent another restless night.

It was the confinement, he thought. But just now Tokyo was a dangerous city for them. Until Rencke could supply him with a name they could only stumble around in the dark. Sooner or later they would end up like Shirley and Mowry. There'd be no defense against such an attack.

"What is it?" Kelley asked softly from the darkness.

"I'm waiting for my call to go through."

"To your friend?"

"Yes. Can't you sleep?" McGarvey turned from the window. Kelley was sitting up. She wore one of his shirts as a nightgown. It was very big on her, and made her look even smaller and more vulnerable than she was.

"How long must we wait?" she asked.

"Until we get some answers . . ."

"Which could be never!"

"There are a lot of powerful people working on this," McGarvey said patiently. They'd gone over this several times already. "Sooner or later at least some of the answers will be forced. It's inevitable."

"In the meantime we hide and do absolutely nothing. I'm going crazy."

"If you want to go home I'll arrange it for you," McGarvey said. When the time came he would need her as a guide through Tokyo's labyrinths. But if she folded she would be less than useless.

"You didn't see him on fire in front of the Roppongi Prince," she said softly. "You didn't hear his screams, his pleas for someone to help him." She hesitated. "You didn't . . . smell the odor of burning flesh."

The telephone rang, and McGarvey stubbed out his cigarette and picked it up. "Yes?"

"I have your party on the line, sir," the operator said.

"Thank you," he said. "It's me, anything new?"

"Let me tell you, I'm either going to have to get out soon or I'll be forced into setting Ralph loose on them."

"Are they on to you?"

"Looks that way. Are you keeping your socks dry?"

"Trying to," McGarvey said. "Have you anything for me? A name?"

"No names yet, but apparently you're in the right place. Seems like the local cops found a pair of highly unusual and very sophisticated communications devices that match the one the cops at Orly came up with."

"Are the Japanese authorities cooperating with us now?"

"I'm not clear on that point, but hang on to your suspenders. Looks like Phil or somebody over there has put out a call for you. They want, in a most urgent manner, for you to make immediate contact."

"Put out the call how?"

"Well, that's just it, you see. They know that someone is dallying in their valley, and the smart buggers figure it's your doing. Get a message to the intruder and ergo, the message is got to you."

A Tokyo police van passed on the street below and disappeared around the corner at the end of the block.

"They're making the connection across the river," Rencke was saying. "And it's got them shakin' in their boots."

"But it's not the government over here?"

"I'm getting no indications. But whoever it is has got to be a well-heeled dude. And just now there's oodles if not googols of them."

Another police van pulled up at the end of the block. "Hold on a second," he told Rencke, and he motioned for Kelley to get up. "Get dressed, we're leaving," he whispered urgently, and he turned back to the phone.

"Mac?" Rencke asked. "Is everything okay?"

"No," McGarvey said. "But listen, you may be going about this from the wrong direction. Granted it may have to be a wealthy Japanese, but it's more than that. We're looking for a wealthy man or group, who would have a motive to assemble the parts for such a device."

Rencke sucked his breath. "Revenge," he said.

"I'll call you soon," McGarvey said, and he hung up.

The first police van returned and stopped at the opposite end of the street. Two police cars passed it and slowly approached the hotel.

"It's the police," McGarvey said to Kelley, who was hurriedly dressing in slacks and a sweatshirt.

"They're looking for us," she said.

McGarvey slipped on his shoes and threw his things into his overnight bag. Under no circumstances did he want to get into a gun battle with the legitimate police. But there was no way of telling for certain who was legitimate and who wasn't until after the fact.

A minute later he and Kelley stepped out into the narrow corridor. Their room was on the fourth floor, and already they could hear some sort of a commotion going on in the lobby.

"We'll go out the back, so long as they haven't blocked the alley," McGarvey said as he led the way to the fire escape he'd discovered a half hour after they'd checked in.

Nothing moved below in the dark, crowded alley. During the day the narrow, winding pathway was crammed with tiny shops, stalls and vendors selling everything from American video tapes to bolts of silk, electronic games, potency potions and powders, live eels and traditional kimonos. At this hour, the permanent shops were tightly shuttered, and the vendors had taken their stalls away.

They reached the alley, and hurried off into the darker shadows as four uniformed police officers showed up from the opposite way and rushed to the back of the hotel.

Well clear of the hotel, they ducked into a subway station and took the escalator down. The first trickle of workers on the way to their jobs was beginning. Within an hour the city's entire mass transit system would be mobbed.

"Did your friend come up with something yet?" Kelley asked on the way down.

"He's close. We're going to need to stay hidden for a little while longer, though. Is there someplace?"

Kelley looked up at him, the expression in her eyes hard to read. She was frightened, that was reasonably clear, but she was also determined. He had no idea what motivated her.

"The trouble is that you're a foreigner. You stick out."

"There must be tens of thousands of Westerners in Tokyo at any given moment."

"The police are very efficient."

"Then we'll have to get out of the city for a day or so."

Kelley was shaking her head. "It's not necessary," she said. "We will go into Shinjuku's Kabukicho."

"What is that?"

"A district of the city where anything might happen, for a price."

"Is there a place there we can hide?"

"Yes," Kelley replied, smiling faintly. "Several places where no questions will be asked of anyone, providing the money lasts." She smiled again. "They are called 'love hotels.' You will see."

37

Elizabeth McGarvey held her mother's hands in hers. There was some traffic on the road, and she knew that there would be even more on the main highway tonight. If she could only signal a passing car or truck, indicate that they were in serious trouble, there might be a chance that the real police would be notified in time. From what she'd seen during her one year here, the Swiss were an extremely efficient people.

But the woman continued to hold the pistol on them, and Elizabeth had little doubt she would use it if need be. There was something dead and cold in her eyes and in the set of her mouth. She was certainly beautiful, in a European way, but she seemed distant, and totally devoid of normal human feeling.

Armand had been clearly surprised to see her leaving the campus after what she'd told him earlier. Providing he didn't go back to his studio to sulk, he might be talking to Toni this very moment. He'd learn about Elizabeth's mother showing up, and about some kind of trouble at home, which would seem logical to him until he found the rental car where her mother had parked. He was intelligent. He would put two and two together, realize that Elizabeth was in trouble, and would call for the police.

But why should he? There was absolutely no reason for him to sound the alarm. He'd worry about turning out the fool, as would anyone in the same situation.

The driver had glanced in the rearview mirror several times in the last minute or so. He did it again.

"*Somebody is following us,*" he said in German.

German and French were Elizabeth's two languages. Her mother said she inherited the ability from her father. But this didn't sound Swiss-German. It sounded to Elizabeth more guttural, more like Plattedeutsch from the Rheinland.

"*There is traffic behind us,*" Liese replied.

"Yes, but this one has passed at least two cars to get behind us, and now he is maintaining his position."

"The little one directly behind us?"

"Yes."

Elizabeth started to turn around, but Liese sharply nudged her cheek with the gun barrel. "Eyes straight ahead!"

"Stay away from me, bitch."

"If need be I will kill you here and now," Liese said.

"I don't think so. Not if you want to lure my father here."

Liese was unimpressed. "You're correct. Perhaps I will merely break all your fingers. Or maybe bruise your cute little tits. Or you might still be a virgin. That can be fixed."

Elizabeth was shaking with fear and rage. She started to shout something, but her mother held her back.

"Let's just do as they say, Liz. Your father will handle it when the time comes."

Elizabeth turned to look at her mother in surprise.

"That's right dear, it won't be long now."

With her free hand Liese picked up a complicated-looking walkie-talkie and pressed a button. "Ernst, looks as if we've got a tail," she said, and she pushed another button.

"Right. It's a gray Fiat, from the school, I think. He passed me, but I'm coming up on him now."

It was Armand's Fiat, Elizabeth thought. It had to be! But what did he expect to accomplish by following them? He was a beautiful fool.

"What do you want to do about it?" Liese radioed.

"Stand by," the voice came from the speaker. "Peter, are you copying?"

"Right. I'm about two minutes from the rendezvous. Shall I abort?"

"Negative. Proceed as planned. Liese, have you got your situation under control?"

"Yes."

"Then proceed to the rendezvous. Bruno and I will take care of our uninvited guest."

"What?" Elizabeth asked incredulously. "He's got nothing to do with this. He doesn't even know about my father."

"You know who is back there?" Liese asked. "Is it Armonde?"

Elizabeth was shocked. How had they known? Who were these people? "I don't know."

"Your father hired him to watch over you, did you know that? Is he your lover? I'm told that he's quite good looking. Tell me, how is he in bed?"

Elizabeth closed her eyes tightly, and for the first time in a very long while, she was drawing some comfort from her mother's touch. This wasn't happening. It was a nightmare. Yet it was real.

They merged with northbound traffic on the Bern-Lausanne Highway. A big semi truck marked Pirokki Shipping, Ltd., was directly in front of them. Almost immediately the driver signaled he was turning right, and the truck began to brake.

Liese keyed the walkie-talkie. "We're directly behind you, Peter."

"I see you."

"Ernst?"

"We're approaching the intersection. Don't wait for us. Just do it."

"We're turning off now," Liese radioed and she put down the walkie-talkie.

The big truck turned onto a gravel driveway that looped through the woods for a hundred yards before leading back up to the highway. It was used as a rest stop as well as a turnaround. One other semi was parked off to the side, but the cab was dark, the driver either asleep in the back, or gone.

The Pirokki Shipping truck pulled up and shut off its head-lights, leaving only its parking lights illuminated.

"We're getting out of the car here," Liese said as they pulled up behind the Pirokki truck. The driver shut off the Peugeot's lights and engine, and got out of the car. He opened the rear door on Kathleen's side.

"Out, *schnell*," he said, his voice low and rasping.

Kathleen and Elizabeth climbed out of the car, and Liese, the pistol still in hand and the bulky walkie-talkie slung over her shoulder by its strap, hurried around the back to them.

"Let's go," she said motioning toward the truck.

Their driver opened a side door in the truck, pushed some boxes aside, and then waved them on.

Kathleen was the first, and he started to help her up, when she balked and tried to pull back. "It's dark."

He grabbed her arm and half-pulled half-shoved her up through the opening into the pitch-black interior.

Armonde's little Fiat came up the driveway, its headlights illuminating the scene, and slid to a halt. A second later a dark Mercedes pulled in behind it, and two men jumped out before Armonde could do a thing.

The Fiat's door started to come open as one of the men reached the car, and he raised his right hand.

"Armand," Elizabeth cried at the same moment three silenced shots were fired into the Fiat.

Scherchen grabbed Elizabeth's arm and shoved her up inside the truck and slammed the door, locking it behind her.

38

Clouds had rolled in and it had begun to drizzle when the blue and white Swiss Regional Police car pulled off the highway just north of the road to Estavayer-le-lac. Rain glistened on the leaves, and puddled on the gravel driveway into the truck turnaround.

As part of their routine patrol they usually checked this place once or twice on a shift. This was their first sweep for the evening.

"Looks like headlights," Adler Böll said as they came slowly around the curve. "There," he said.

His partner, Thoma Grillparzer, rolled down the window on the passenger side, switched on the spotlight, and shined it toward the gray Fiat sedan. Immediately they could see that something was wrong, and Böll stopped five yards away.

The driver's window was shattered, and what looked like a great deal of blood had splashed up against the inside of the windscreen and the passenger side window.

Böll snatched the communications radio handset, and keyed the push-to-talk switch. "Central Control, this is unit one-seven-green."

"One-seven-green, roger."

"We have a possible homicide scene, request immediate backup."

"Rolling. Say location."

Grillparzer got out of the car and drew his service revolver.

"Hold on and I'll cover you," Böll said, and he quickly radioed their location and the exact situation as they knew it at that moment. The only other vehicle in the rest area was a sixteen-wheel truck parked and dark fifty yards away.

Böll got out of the patrol car, and drew his revolver. He remained in a protected position behind the car as his partner approached the Fiat still brightly illuminated by the spotlight.

"One man down in the front seat," Grillparzer shouted back. "There's a lot of blood. Looks like one or more head wounds. Deep."

"Any movement?" Böll yelled.

"No," Grillparzer said. "Wait, wait! Mother of God, I think he's still alive."

Böll rushed across to the Fiat as his partner holstered his weapon and hurried around to the passenger side where he yanked open the door.

"Fingerprints . . ." Böll said, but the word died on his lips. The victim had been shot at least twice: Once in the forehead and once in the side of the head just above his left ear. He was slumped across the gearshift lever, his head and upper body resting on the passenger seat. His eyes were fluttering and he was trying to speak, but his voice was very weak.

Grillparzer looked up.

"Backup units are on the way," Böll said. "They'll be sending an ambulance."

Grillparzer took off his cap and leaned inside the small car. "We're police. An ambulance is coming. Can you hear me? Who did this to you?"

Böll suddenly recognized the man. He'd seen him often in Estavayer-le-lac. He was an instructor at the Design School. Armand something.

"A truck?" Grillparzer asked. "A white truck?"

Böll's eyes immediately went to the truck parked farther up the driveway. It was gray, not white.

"Elizabeth who?" Grillparzer asked. He looked up again. "There's been a kidnapping. Elizabeth someone. Whoever did it, shot him."

It was well after eleven by the time the crime scene was secured and Bern Chief Investigator Yvonne Coquillat came over to speak with Böll and Grillparzer. They were tall, atheletically built men, while she was short and slight. But she had a tough reputation. Both officers were respectful.

"We're nearly finished here," she said. "As soon as the evidence van leaves, you can return to your duties."

"Will you need our reports tonight?" Böll asked.

"In the morning will be soon enough," the chief investigator said. "Unless there's anything you might have remembered in the past hour?"

Grillparzer shook his head. "Anything on the white truck yet?"

"We've put out an APB, but so far as I've heard there's been no sign of it so far."

"What about Armonde?" Böll asked. He'd remembered the instructor's last name.

The chief investigator shook her head. "He died enroute to the hospital. The medics said his wounds were too massive. Sorry."

"Yes, madam," Böll said.

"Well, you can leave in a few minutes," the chief investigator said, and she started to turn away, but suddenly stopped dead. She turned back, her eyes narrowed. "What did you say?" she asked.

Böll was confused. He shook his head. "I'm sorry?"

"About the gunshot victim. You used his name."

"Yes."

"You know him?"

"Yes," Böll said, realizing he was in trouble. The evidence team had identified the dead man from his papers. He hadn't thought to tell anyone that he slightly knew the victim. "I believe he was an instructor at the design poly."

"Here?" she asked. "Just down the road?"

"Yes."

"Why in heaven's name didn't you say something?" the chief investigator demanded.

"I didn't think it was important that I personally knew him . . ."

"Where is your brain? He got himself killed by stumbling into the middle of an apparent kidnapping." She shook her head in exasperation. "I'm going down to the school. Get in your unit and follow me."

"Madam?" Böll asked.

"The man mentioned a woman's name. Elizabeth. Now that we know he was an instructor at the school, we might reasonably suppose that Elizabeth is a fellow instructor, or perhaps a student. In any case, we have a lead!"

It was three o'clock in the morning when the bedside telephone of Swiss Federal Police Supervisor Johann Meuller rang, dragging him out of a deep sleep.

His wife stirred beside him as he picked it up. "Yes?" he mumbled.

"Terribly sorry to bother you at such an hour, sir, but something has come in that I thought you would like to know about immediately."

It was Brent Wylie, Mueller's number two, a no-nonsense cop who had worked his way into the Federal Police by dint of brilliant and tireless effort. He'd never been given to making statements lightly.

Meuller switched on his table lamp and sat up, his sleepiness leaving him instantly. "Yes, what it is?"

"It's about Kirk McGarvey."

"Is he back?" Mueller asked angrily. Marta Fredricks had been like a daughter to him. He'd never forgiven McGarvey for making her fall in love, and his enmity had grown when she'd been killed in the crash of flight 145.

"Not yet, but he'll probably be coming."

"Don't be cryptic, Brent. What are you talking about?"

"Sorry, sir. You know that McGarvey's daughter, Elizabeth, currently attends the Bern Design Poly in Estavayer-le-lac?"

"Yes."

"Apparently she was kidnapped last night," Wylie said.

"*Gott in himmel,*" Mueller muttered. "By whom, someone trying to get to her father?"

"It's unknown at this point. But it's worse than that."

"It can't be."

"Evidently the girl's mother was visiting the school, and she was taken along with her daughter."

"McGarvey's ex-wife?"

"Yes, sir."

Meuller threw the covers aside and felt for his slippers as he talked. "I'll be there within the hour. Put a call through to Washington for four-thirty our time. I want to speak with the general."

"It'll be ten-thirty at night over there."

"I don't care. Next, call the French and find out if they have unearthed any leads on the flight one-four-five case, especially anything that might lead back to McGarvey. Ask the same of Interpol. Oh, and see if you can find out where McGarvey is at this moment. Then gather the latest reports on this . . . incident, and have them on my desk."

"Yes, sir," Wylie said.

Mueller hung up, and shuffling into the bathroom he was struck with the notion that he'd known something like this would happen ever since he'd learned that Elizabeth McGarvey had enrolled in a Swiss school. Death and destruction followed the girl's father wherever he went.

39

"When I was a child in Honolulu my grandfather told me stories about the western desert," Kelley Fuller said.

McGarvey was seated in a tub of extremely hot, scented water to his neck. He turned at the sound of her voice as she closed the rice paper door. He could hear traditional Japanese music playing elsewhere in the building.

"He said that he was sent there simply because he was of Japanese descent." She pinned her hair up, exposing her tiny ears and long, delicate neck. "He hated America until he died."

"I thought you were sleeping," McGarvey said. It was nearing noon, but in this place time seemed to have no meaning.

It was called the Sunny Days Western Ranch, and was housed in a nondescript but expansive two-story building off a crowded back street in the Shinjuku's Kabukicho District. On the first floor were the public baths, hostess rooms and kitchens, while the second floor was reserved for suites. They had rented a bedroom, sitting room and small bath.

The tariff was fabulously expensive, but the place was absolutely safe. No questions were asked or answered here. McGarvey had drawn an American Express card under a workname from his Channel Island account before he'd left Paris. A few eyebrows might be raised in Jersey when the bills started coming in, but they would be paid without hesitation and in secrecy.

"It was not possible to sleep. So I have come to wash your back, McGarvey-san," Kelley said. She wore a snow-white kimono which she opened and dropped to the floor. She was nude, her legs long and delicately formed, her belly nearly flat, her hips almost boyish, and her breasts small, the nipples large and very dark. She looked exotic.

"This isn't necessary."

"You will save my life, I believe. I wish to thank you now, while there is still time." She sat on a small stool and using a big natural sponge and a wooden bucket of warm soapy water, washed herself.

McGarvey watched her. "We may not find anything," he said. "In the end you may have to return home."

She glanced at him, her eyes round, almost as if she were a startled deer. "But your friend told you something this morning that troubled you." She shook her head. "You will not leave Tokyo until you have struck back."

"I need a name and a face before I can do anything."

"You will find what you are seeking," she said serenely. She rinsed herself with a bucket of clear water and a ladle, then joined McGarvey in the tub, kneeling on the bench behind him so that she could scrub his back with a rough towel.

"Perhaps not."

"It's terrible to live in fear. I have, all of my life, you know. Now, there is nothing to go back for."

"What about your parents?"

"My parents also hated America, and they taught this to me so that when I finished school I decided to work for the Central Intelligence Agency so that I could learn secrets which I could give to their enemies."

"Did you become a traitor?"

"No. In the end it was impossible."

"Why?"

"Because I saw that my grandfather and my parents were wrong."

McGarvey turned to her. She was crying silently, tears streaming down her cheeks. Slowly, carefully, as if she were a fragile, easily breakable objet d'art, he gathered her into his arms, and they began to make love.

"I understand," he said. And he did, because he'd also been afraid.

It was after midnight in Washington and McGarvey could hear the strain in Rencke's voice on the telephone. The man had probably worked around the clock since he'd been handed the problem.

"I may be on to something," Rencke said.

"Have you got a name for me yet?" McGarvey asked. He was calling from a private cubicle just off the manager's office on the first floor. He'd been assured that the phone was completely untraceable.

"I did what you suggested, looked for a motive. What we're talking about here, I figure, is a case of hate and contempt. I mean really massive. Combine that with the money to do something about it . . . we agree that this dude is well-heeled . . . well, there'd have to be some public notice."

"What do you mean?"

"Nobody would catch it for what it really was, I don't think. But look, if you're worth let's say a billion dollars, and you spend your life trying to screw Americans, something will come up."

McGarvey was beginning to see what Rencke was getting at, and it did make sense. "State might have something."

"Them and the Company's Intelligence Directorate's archives, and of course the Defense Intelligence Agency's files."

"You've been in their computers?"

"Of course. But the real paydirt came when I checked out the *New York Times'* files, with cross references in three newsmagazines and two television networks. I came up with a nifty little search program that sought out anti-Americanisms based on a weighted scale . . . one to a hundred. For instance: Making a flat-out public statement that a man hated America and would do everything within his power to bring it down, would be worth anywhere from seventy-five to a hundred points, depending on whether or not the man had control of enough money to buy and put to use one of the devices K-1 is going after. Do you follow my drift so far?"

"Go on," McGarvey said.

"I came up with beaucoup names. Seems as if there's a lot of dudes in the empire who've got varying degrees of hardons for us. So I had another brainstorm. Wait'll you hear this one. Just for the hell of it I added two other parameters to my search program. Number one: I figured that in order to pull this sort of a thing off our bad guy would have to be worth at least a hundred large. I mean a hundred million U.S. Agreed?"

Terrorism was fabulously expensive if it was to be successful. Many small countries couldn't afford it. A hundred million wasn't out of line. "Agreed."

"Hang on to your socks. Now come motives, and I came up with a few dillies. For instance: How about former prisoners of war? How about Japs whose businesses had failed because of U.S. policies?" Rencke giggled. "Or the grand-dilly of them all. How about dudes who lost families or loved ones in Hiroshima or Nagasaki?"

McGarvey was speechless for a moment or two. Christ, it fit. A man whose family had been destroyed by an American atomic bomb, and who'd later made his fortune, could be thinking of revenge. But there'd have to be more.

"Have you come up with a name yet?"

"No," Rencke admitted. "But I've come up with a half-dozen candidates whose birthplaces, and whose backgrounds during that period of history are unclear. I'm working on that."

"I want you to throw in one other consideration," McGarvey said. "I don't think simple revenge would be enough. Whoever this person is, he is rich. In order to get there he has to be smart; shrewd, at the very least, perhaps even brilliant."

"Which means he'd have to have another motive. He'd have something to gain by using his little toy."

"Exactly."

"If I can't buy the Rockefeller Center, I'll nuke it," Rencke said.

"Something like that."

"I'll get on it," Rencke said, and already McGarvey could hear the faraway note in the man's voice which meant most of his mind was elsewhere; working on the problem at hand.

"I'll call later," McGarvey said.

"Oh, wait," Rencke came back. "I almost forgot. Your name has come up again across the river. They want to make contact with you in a worst way. It has something to do with your daughter and ex, I think."

"What about them?"

"I don't know," Rencke said distantly, and the connection was broken.

McGarvey's call to Carrara's home was automatically routed to his office at Langley. The DDO sounded harried, even worried, but not at all surprised.

"Who have you got hacking for you?" Carrara asked. "My records people are having fits."

"What about Kathleen and my daughter?" McGarvey asked, ignoring the question. "Has something happened to them?"

"They've been kidnapped."

The air left the room. "By whom?"

"We don't know yet. Evidently your ex-wife was visiting the school outside of Bern, and both of them were taken just a few hours ago. The general got the call personally from the Swiss Federal Police."

"K-1?" McGarvey asked, dreading the answer he knew he was going to hear.

"We think so. It has all the earmarks of a Spranger operation. An instructor from the school evidently got in the middle of it and was shot three times in the head."

"Any leads?"

"They may have been taken across the Swiss border into France. The Sûreté may have a lead."

"Call Marquand," McGarvey said. He was sick at his stomach.

"Already have. He'll meet you in Paris."

40

At Roland Murphy's suggestion the President had called his National Security Adviser Daniel Milligan and Secretary of State John Cronin to the Oval office for an 8 A.M. meeting. It was a few minutes after that hour and the three men were looking at the DCI, grim expressions on their faces.

"Let me get this absolutely clear, Roland," the President said. "What you're saying is that some group, or perhaps some individual in Japan is being linked to the STASI organization's effort to steal the components of a nuclear bomb?"

"Yes, sir. Our best evidence seems to be pointing in that direction."

"But it's not the government," Secretary of State Cronin asked. "You're sure of that?"

"We're not sure of it, John, but we don't think it's likely. There've been no indications whatsoever out of Tokyo."

"Nor was there before Pearl Harbor," Cronin grumbled.

"That's not true," Murphy said. "We had plenty of warnings before Pearl, but they were ignored." Murphy turned back to the President. "The government or the military wouldn't simply be after the parts, they'd be after the technology itself. A technology, I might add, that their own scientists could come up with."

"I'm inclined to agree," the President said. He turned to his National Security Adviser. "Dan?"

"I tend to agree with Roland, as well. The Japanese government has no need to become a nuclear power. Hell, they lost the war but they're sure winning the peace. They're outshooting us with their currency, their technology, and before long maybe even their GNP. Why risk world censure by joining the nuclear club? They'd have nearly everything to lose, and almost nothing to gain. Nuclear weapons, at least so far as governments go, have become almost useless."

"But not in the hands of a terrorist," Murphy said.

"No," Milligan said. "And we all knew it would happen sooner or later. What are the latest estimates of how much weapons-grade plutonium is missing each year? Enough to make a dozen effective bombs?"

"More," Murphy said. "But this is the first time we've detected a concentrated effort to come up with all the components."

"Except for Libya's attempts a few years back," Cronin said. "And more recently, Iraq's."

"I'm not talking about governments now, John. I'm talking about individuals."

"This sort of thing would take a lot of money, wouldn't it?" the President asked.

"In the tens of millions of dollars at the very least," Murphy said.

"Which narrows down the field, somewhat, especially if we're limiting ourselves to the Japanese."

"There are a lot of rich people in Japan at this moment in history. My people are working on ways to narrow down the list, but it's going to take time. We don't even have a motive yet. In the meantime the Agency's operations in Japan are all but shut down."

"I'm sending John to Tokyo in a few days. He'll speak with Prime Minister Kunihiro, but there's no guarantee anything positive for us will come of it. Eight murders in a few days time in Tokyo, five of them Americans, has got everyone on edge." The President sat back, his chin resting on a bridge of his thumb, forefinger and middle finger. "It was my understanding, Roland, that you had sent some additional people over there . . . someone not directly connected with our embassy."

Murphy nodded. "We have even more trouble on that score, Mr. President. You may recall the name Kirk McGarvey."

"He was involved in stopping the people who kidnapped that submarine of ours in the Mediterranean a few years back."

"Yes, sir. And he was responsible for getting that shipment of gold through to Iran."

"Yes. That was one of the reasons the Iranians cooperated with us when we kicked Saddam Hussein out of Kuwait. If McGarvey's involved now, the scale has been tipped to our side."

"It's very likely the STASI group has had the same thought," Murphy said. "They may have found out he was involved and done something about it."

No one said a thing.

"McGarvey is divorced. His ex-wife lives here in Washington. She came to see us yesterday morning. Somehow she figured out that McGarvey was working for us, and she wanted to get a message to him."

"What message?" the President asked.

"It was nothing important. At least we didn't think so. Before we could react, she disappeared from the Washington area. McGarvey has a nineteen-year-old daughter attending a school of design outside of Bern. His ex-wife showed up there last night, and she and her daughter were kidnapped by a person or persons unknown."

"The STASI organization?"

"It's possible. The Swiss, and now the French, are helping us. They may have a lead."

"Has McGarvey been told?"

"Yes, Mr. President. He's on his way to Europe at this moment."

"If the STASI kidnapped them, was it to lure McGarvey out of Japan?"

"Yes, sir."

"Into a trap?"

Murphy nodded. "We're doing everything we can to help him."

"Indeed," the President said. "Because I want to make something else very clear to you, General. McGarvey has been of great service to this country."

"Yes, sir."

"And now, we owe him."

41

The weather in Paris was overcast and rainy when the Japan Airlines 747 touched down at Charles de Gaulle Airport. It was a little before three in the afternoon but the day was dark and chilly, which served to deepen McGarvey's already bleak mood. He'd had little else to do during the long flight from Tokyo via Calcutta but worry.

Carrara had not suggested he drop everything in Japan, but his not-so-subtle between the lines message had been quite clear. Spranger had taken Kathleen and Elizabeth to lure McGarvey to Europe where they meant to kill him. Everyone wanted him to take the challenge.

In the old days, the field officer's family was inviolate. That wasn't the case any longer. What few restraints men like Spranger had worked under were no longer in place. Nothing was sacred. The stakes in the Cold War had been high, but they were even higher now in the invisible war. Ten years ago the fight had been over ideologies. These days it was over money. What little honor there'd been was totally gone.

It was their game. They had made the rules. And if that's the way they wanted it, he would play it out this time . . . no holds barred.

A tall, lanky man with thick eyebrows over a hawkish nose was waiting for him at the arrivals gate. "Name's Robert Littel. You got any other baggage?" He spoke with a Texas twang.

"Who told you I'd be on this flight?" McGarvey asked. This wasn't beyond Spranger.

"Nobody. Phil Carrara just said you were coming and we were supposed to watch for you. Now, if you'll shake a leg we'll get you out of here and down to the chopper."

"Have you got something?"

"Yeah, but I'll tell you all about it on the run. We don't have much time if we're going to make the show."

McGarvey fell in step beside the taller man as they walked past the passport control booths without challenge and then through customs and downstairs.

"Is Marquand here?" McGarvey asked.

"He's in charge down in Grenoble. But he sent René Belleau, his number two. A little prick, but I think he'd be one tough sonofabitch backed into a corner."

On the ground level, before they went through the steel door, McGarvey grabbed Littel by the arm and stopped him. "What's going on in Grenoble?"

Littel started to challenge McGarvey but then thought better of it. "How much did Carrara tell you?"

"That someone kidnapped my ex-wife and daughter, and that the French had a lead."

"Apparently they were taken from the school and loaded aboard a white truck. A semi. It was seen crossing the frontier at Jougne, above Lausanne. This morning it was located in a barn at the end of a road that leads up to a mountain chalet about six miles north of Grenoble."

"Any sign of them or the kidnappers?"

"At last word, no. The Action Service has got the place surrounded, but they're waiting until nightfall to move in."

"Who owns the chalet?"

"It belongs to a property management company in Grenoble. Three days ago it was leased to a couple by the name of Schey. Two days ago the same couple visited the Design Poly outside Bern, evidently to look the place over."

It was too pat. If this was Stranger's doing, he'd left too many clues on the trail. He'd practically advertised his whereabouts. Why?

The clues were lures, of course, meant for McGarvey. But they wouldn't have allowed themselves to be cornered so easily. Something else was happening. Something . . .

"The chopper is waiting, Mr. McGarvey," Littel prompted after a few moments.

"Right," McGarvey said looking up out of his thoughts. But he was troubled.

Belleau was waiting impatiently for them aboard the idling Dassault SF-17 transport helicopter, and even before they had strapped in, the sleek machine was lifting off the pad and accelerating south as it climbed at a sickening rate.

The chopper was a stripped-down version of the transport helicopter, with larger engines for greater speed and extra fuel capacity for greater range. The noise level in the main cabin was so great that any sort of a normal conversation was difficult.

The compactly built, deadly looking Frenchman motioned for McGarvey to don one of the headsets and plug it in.

"What were you doing in Tokyo, Monsieur McGarvey?" Belleau's voice came through the earphones.

"I was on vacation. Can we establish communications with Colonel Marquand from here?"

"I asked you a question," the Action Service officer said, his eyes narrow.

"I answered it."

"You are on French soil now, you *salopard*, and you'll do as you're told."

"*Don't fuck with me you little cocksucker, or I'll throw you out of this helicopter at altitude,*" McGarvey said in his best gutter French.

Belleau's eyes widened in surprise, and a faint flush came to his cheeks. "Phillipe told me that you were quite the specimen." He smiled ruefully. "For now I will simply assume that you were seeking a connection between the Japanese and these East German bastards."

"There is a connection," McGarvey said, relenting a little. "But to this point that's the only thing I'm certain of."

Belleau nodded, and he glanced at Littel, who was listening on another headset. "Do you believe that your wife and daughter were kidnapped to force an end to your investigation in Tokyo?"

"It's possible."

"Then you must have been getting close to something or someone."

McGarvey took off his headset and leaned closer to the Frenchman who did the same, effectively blocking Littel out of their conversation for just a moment.

"If you help me in this matter, if you do not interfere, I promise to share with you whatever information I come up with later."

Belleau looked into his eyes for a long moment, but then nodded, and they both sat back and put on the headsets. Littel was clearly upset.

"What was that all about?" he demanded.

McGarvey ignored him. "Can we make contact with Colonel Marquand from here?"

"Yes, but it is inadvisable. It's possible that the kidnappers are monitoring our frequencies."

"You're probably right," McGarvey said. "Did you bring a map of the area? I'd like to see what we're facing."

"Yes," Belleau said. He took a large-scale map from his briefcase and spread it out on a small fold-down table and switched on a gooseneck spot lamp.

McGarvey leaned forward so he could see better. The map's area of detail included the town of Grenoble and about five or ten miles in each direction.

Belleau pointed with a pencil to a spot north of the city, along highway D912, which was indicated as a secondary road and scenic route through the mountains.

"The base of the driveway is at slightly more than sixteen hundred meters," Belleau said. "Here, just below the Col de Porte pass at eighteen hundred sixty-seven meters."

"The barn is where?"

"Just off the highway, and the chalet is one kilometer farther up the driveway, at an elevation of one hundred-fifty meters above the barn."

"It's a very steep driveway," Littel said.

"No other way in or out?" McGarvey asked.

"Not by car or truck," Belleau said.

"How about with a four-wheel drive, like a jeep?"

"Not possible. This area is all very rugged. One would need to be a mountaineer to move off the road."

"Helicopter?"

"The wind currents in the mountains are formidable."

McGarvey sat back. "Of course there's no guarantee they're still there."

Belleau shook his head. "If they are, however, then they are cornered."

"I think it's unlikely they're still there," McGarvey said, reaching for his overnight bag. He took out his toiletries kit and removed the components of his Walther PPK as Belleau and Littel carefully watched.

"But you're going in armed, just in case," Littel said.

"I hope they are there," McGarvey said, looking up. Both Littel and Belleau shivered.

42

The Action Service helicopter touched down on the police barracks parade ground on the western outskirts of Grenoble, the city's modern skyscrapers rising against the mountain backdrop. The wind was gusty but the weather was much clearer here than in Paris. And much colder.

Marquand was waiting for them aboard an Italian touring coach marked Lake Geneva. Its windows were mirrored so that from the outside nothing could be seen of the interior. He and McGarvey shook hands.

"You've arrived just in time, Monsieur," the short, heavily built colonel said. "We were just about to leave."

"Has the situation up there changed in the past few hours?" McGarvey asked. It was obvious Marquand knew Littel, so there'd been no need for introductions.

"At five o'clock a package was delivered to the front door of the chalet where it remains." Marquand looked at his wristwatch. "That was nearly two hours ago. It was addressed to a D. Schey . . . we're assuming for the moment that the D stands for Dieter . . . from the Georges Cinq Hotel in Paris."

"Was there a name?"

"It was a little joke. The sender was marked as E. Spranger."

"You checked with the hotel?"

"Naturally. And with the delivery service. Of course Spranger is not at the hotel, and so far as the delivery service clerk in Paris can recall the package was dropped off at their office by a middle-aged, matronly looking woman, who paid in cash."

"How much does it weigh?"

Littel and Belleau looked puzzled, but Marquand understood. "It was heavy. Slightly more than ten kilos."

"Then I would hope that you have instructed your people to treat that package with extreme respect."

"Yes," Marquand said. "It would seem now that the chalet is deserted."

"But we cannot be one hundred percent sure," McGarvey said, thinking of something else. "We'll have to find out."

Marquand looked sharply at him. "What is it?"

"You were right in the beginning, there is a Japanese connection. I've just come from Tokyo where our chief of station and his assistant have both been assassinated."

"Mr. McGarvey, may I have a word with you outside?" Littel interrupted.

"No," McGarvey said. "A pair of walkie-talkies like the one found at Orly were used in Tokyo."

"Are the Japanese authorities working with you?"

"No one knows I was there except, apparently, for Spranger and whoever he's working for."

"But why?" Marquand asked. "What the hell do they want?"

"McGarvey," Littel cautioned.

"I don't know yet," McGarvey lied. "But obviously I was getting close, or else Spranger wouldn't have tried this move."

"I think you're lying now," the Action Service colonel said, but then his expression softened. "You understand that the outcome of this . . . situation, might not be very pleasant for you."

"They're not dead," McGarvey said flatly.

"In cases like these . . ."

"They're not dead," McGarvey repeated, looking into Marquand's eyes. "Spranger means to trade with me."

"For what?" Littel asked.

"My life for theirs."

"Then why the package bomb, that doesn't make any sense."

"It's there to let us know they're serious," McGarvey said. "If it kills me, so much the better."

"The bastards," Marquand said, tight-jawed. "We would have walked right into the middle of it."

"Spranger's one of the best."

"Yes. And well-funded. Buy why the Japanese?"

"When I find out, I'll let you know."

"Do that," Marquand said. "In the meantime, they will have left something up there for you to find. Some clue as to their whereabouts."

"Maybe not," McGarvey answered. "They've lured me away from Tokyo. Maybe there'll be nothing up there."

"Except death," Belleau said grimly.

A half-dozen of Colonel Marquand's Action Service operators came along on the bus, which passed the entrance to the Chalet's driveway shortly after dark, and pulled off the highway onto a scenic overlook area at the crest of the Col de Porte pass. Their driver switched off the coach's lights just as they crested the hill so that from below it might seem as if the bus had simply disappeared from view as the road started down the other side.

One of the men immediately opened a window, and set up a light-intensifying scope on a tripod. He trained it on the chalet about a mile below them.

"Anything?" Marquand asked.

On the way up they'd all changed into dark jumpsuits, and had blackened any exposed skin.

"There is a very dim light in the upstairs corridor," the scope operator said softly without looking up. "Stationary. Maybe a night light. No movement."

"Outside?" Marquand asked.

The others had left the bus and were opening the cargo bays, leaving Littel and McGarvey alone for a moment. The Texan pulled McGarvey aside.

"Look here, I don't know what you're up to, but my instructions were specific. You're not to breathe a word of your Tokyo operation to the French."

"Just what is it I'm doing in Tokyo?" McGarvey asked.

"I don't know . . ."

"You haven't been told my assignment?"

"No, sir. Just that you were coming to France and to provide you with whatever help I could, but to make damned sure you didn't say anything of importance to the Frogs."

McGarvey had to smile despite the situation. "How's your hand-to-hand combat skills?"

Littel was taken aback by the question. "Fair," he said.

"I'm told Marquand is an expert. I would assume his men are pretty good too. I don't think they'd like to hear you call them names."

Littel glanced over at Marquand and the scope operator. "I didn't mean anything."

"They're Frenchmen, or Corsicans, depending on what mood you catch them in. Do you understand?"

"I got you, but I still have my job to do."

McGarvey patted him on the arm. "I won't tell them anything they don't already know. But at the moment they're risking their lives to help rescue my family. I owe them, wouldn't you say?"

"Ah . . . yes, sir."

Marquand was checking his wristwatch again. "Six minutes," he said, looking up. "Time to go."

"Any movement in or around the chalet?" McGarvey asked, following the Action Service colonel off the bus.

"None," Marquand replied tersely.

His troops had taken eleven small motorbikes from the coach's cargo spaces, and started them all. The small engines were so highly muffled that almost nothing could be heard head on, and only a light purring noise from the rear.

"Ten of my people have been in position behind and to the east of the chalet since early this afternoon. In about five minutes they'll start moving in. In the meantime, we'll go down the mountain, secure the barn and the truck on one; proceed to and secure the front approaches to the house on two; neutralize the package, if need be, on three; and make entry through the windows and main door on four. Questions?"

There were none.

The Action Service troops were armed with stun grenades and silenced MAC 10s. Littel carried a .44 magnum, not silenced, of course, and McGarvey stayed with his Walther.

The troops were watching him as he took it out and checked the action. Marquand shook his head. "If it was anyone else but you, Monsieur, carrying such a toy, I would say he was a fool."

"It's an old friend."

Marquand smiled faintly. "So I'm told." He turned abruptly to his troops. "*Allons-y, mes copains.*"

They all mounted and peeled out onto the highway from behind the bus in pairs, the throttles wide open, the bikes hitting sixty miles per hour down the hill.

If there was to be trouble here, these men plus the force coming up from the rear would be more than enough to handle it. But racing down the hill McGarvey was certain of two things: That Kathleen and Elizabeth were not here, and that a message would be waiting for him and him alone.

Spranger's purpose was to lure McGarvey out of Tokyo, and then meet head-to-head but only at a time and place of the East German's choosing when the odds would definitely be against McGarvey.

The road flattened out for about twenty yards, a field of mountain grasses and flowers protected by a split rail fence to the right. A gravel driveway led past the field and up the side of a very steep hill to the chalet in the distance. A large stone barn with a sharply pitched shake roof sat just off the driveway about fifty yards from the road.

The mountainside was in complete darkness. Only Grenoble down in the valley was lit like phosphorescent points in a black sea.

Two of Marquand's force continued straight up the driveway to act as advance scouts on the chalet's front entrance, while the others quickly surrounded the barn.

On Marquand's signal one of them used a bolt cutter to remove the heavy padlock from the main doors, and hauled them open.

On signal, their MAC 10s sweeping from the center outward, two Action Service officers rushed into the barn.

For several long seconds there was absolute silence, until one of them came to the doorway. "Clear," he called softly.

"Hold up, I want to check out the truck before we proceed," McGarvey said.

Marquand motioned for his people to hold their positions, and he went with McGarvey into the barn where the large white semi-truck had been hidden. The markings on the side were for PIROKKI SHIPPING, LTD., ATHINAI.

"The truck was reported stolen from Amsterdam," Marquand said.

"Pirokki?"

"No such company."

The side door in the trailer was open. One of Marquand's troops shined a flashlight inside, but the trailer was empty except for a few pieces of cardboard.

"Nothing here," Marquand said, and McGarvey followed him out of the barn, glancing back for another look at the markings on the side of the truck.

At the top of the hill Marquand's other people were already in position at the rear and to the east of the chalet. He gave a signal and two of his people ran, dodging across the grassy area beside the driveway, and silently mounted a low entry area at the front door.

One of them held a narrow beam penlight on the package, while the other began to work on it, shielding it with his body to minimize the effects of a possible explosion to his partner.

A full ninety seconds later, he picked up the package and gingerly carried it well away from the chalet where he carefully laid it on the ground, then he turned and moved away from it, signaling the all clear.

"Do your people have a clear identification on the non-targets?" Littel asked.

The Action Service colonel glanced back at him, then McGarvey, and nodded. "But it will be for the best if you do not get ahead of me. My boys might mistake you for one of the perpetrators."

"All right."

Six of Marquand's men flattened themselves against the front of the house, two each on a pair of ground-floor windows and two with a small battering ram on the door. On the count of three they smashed in the door, busted out the window glass and made simultaneous entry, their MAC 10s up and ready to fire.

From the rear they could hear the sounds of breaking glass and splintering wood, and seconds later McGarvey and Marquand, acting as backup in case the situation inside became critical, raced up onto the stone entry area and took up positions on either side of the door.

On the count of three they rolled inside, spreading left and right, their weapons up.

"Red clear," someone shouted.

"*Vert, aussi*," someone upstairs responded.

Marquand held his position, motioning for McGarvey to do the same.

For several long seconds the chalet was deathly still, but then from somewhere at the back of the house, a third team leader shouted the all clear, and the lights came on.

"Looks as if you were correct," Marquand said, straightening up and switching his weapon's safety to the on position.

McGarvey did the same, and holstering his pistol, went into the expansive living room, the sloping ceiling open to a loft above, a natural stone chimney rising up from a massive fireplace in the middle of the room.

Littel entered the chalet, and moments later Marquand was issuing orders that the house and grounds be thoroughly searched.

The chalet was a typical rental unit, with the same sterility as a hotel room, and yet McGarvey had a sense that Kathleen and Elizabeth had been here, however briefly.

Spranger wouldn't have gone to this much trouble for nothing. The truck was here. It meant something. Greek, perhaps. Toward Greece.

But what else?

"Nobody home?" Littel asked, crossing the living room to the fireplace.

No one paid any attention to him. Marquand's men from front and back were swarming all over the house, from the root cellar to the attic crawl space above the servants' quarters off the kitchen.

There was no fire on the grate, but there had been, and Littel took a poker from the hearth rack and began idly poking through the ashes.

Marquand left the room and McGarvey was alone with his own thoughts for the moment. On first coming into the chalet he'd thought he smelled perfume. Faintly, but there. He tested the air again, but if anything the house now smelled neutral to him.

"McGarvey," Littel said softly.

Kathleen had always worn perfume, of course. But she'd been subtle about it. This had been different.

"McGarvey," Littel called, still softly, but more insistently.

McGarvey looked up. "What is it?"

"Take a look," the Texan said, motioning him over.

McGarvey joined him at the fireplace. Littel had found a diamond necklace in the ashes. It was Elizabeth's. McGarvey recognized the setting. It had been his mother's. The only personal thing he'd ever gotten from her, the only thing he'd ever had to remind him of the side of his mother that he'd always loved.

But the setting and the necklace itself, both 18-carat gold, were intact, which meant the necklace hadn't been subjected to any heat. Yet the diamond was black with burned creosote or pine tar.

"It's my daughter's," he told Littel, who nodded.

"I know. I saw it in a file photo. I recognized it right away. They were here."

McGarvey pocketed it as Marquand appeared at the balcony above. He looked up. "Have your men found anything yet?"

"Not yet," the Action Service colonel said. "You?"

"Nothing," McGarvey replied, conscious of Littel's eyes on him. "I don't think they were ever here."

43

A green and white private medevac ambulance pulled up on the quai beside the 208-foot Greek cargo ship *MV Thaxos* at two in the morning. A thick, oily fog that smelled of the sea, wet cordage, spilled bunker oil and raw sewage blanketed the low island city of Venice. The only sounds were machinery noises from the ship's generator, and somewhere in the distance a bell buoy.

"Turn off the lights," Spranger said from the back of the ambulance, and their driver Peter Dürenmatt switched them off, but left the engine running.

"There go the lights on the bridge," Liese said a few moments later. She'd ridden in front since the Italian border beyond the Col du Mont Cenis above Torino. All of them were dressed in white medical garb.

They hadn't been delayed at all. The French border people had simply waved them through, and the Italians had clucked sympathetically, with one eye checking the paperwork of the two Yugoslavian cancer patients, and with the other looking up Liese's short skirt.

"Okay, there's Bruno," Liese said. "They're coming down now."

"As soon as we're unloaded, get rid of the ambulance," Spranger told Dürenmatt. "We sail when you return."

"See that you wait. The French can't be far behind us, and I have no wish to remain here in Venice waiting for them."

"Just be quick about it," Spranger said.

Liese came back and helped him release the straps holding Kathleen and Elizabeth on their portable gurneys. They'd both been heavily sedated since shortly before they'd left the chalet, but that had been more than twenty hours ago, and Elizabeth was beginning to show signs that she was coming around.

They were dressed in hospital gowns, and the hair had been shaved from their heads, their scalps marked with surgical pen. The extra touch had been a wasted effort, because the border police had not asked to have a look at the patients.

"They'll be angry when they wake up and see what we've done," Liese said. "Especially the young one."

"It won't matter," Spranger replied. "They'll be dead in a couple of days in any event."

"Such a pity," Liese said, brushing her fingertips across the nipples of Elizabeth's breasts.

"Your appetites will be your undoing one day."

She looked up and smiled coyly. "But in the meantime . . ." She let it trail off.

The ambulance's rear door opened and Bruno Lessing was there with two crewmen from the ship. "Any trouble crossing the border?"

"No," Spranger said. "How about here?"

"We have our clearance papers, and the radar set is up to date. The captain assures me we can sail tonight."

"Good. As soon as they're aboard and Peter gets rid of this ambulance, we'll leave."

The *Thaxos'* crewmen lifted Kathleen and Elizabeth out of the ambulance and carried the unconscious women up the ladder aboard the ship. Liese went with them, while Spranger and Lessing went directly up to the bridge where the captain was waiting.

His name was Andreas Bozzaris, and he was a tough little Greek whose primary source of income was arms smuggling from the continent of Europe across to Africa. He'd done work in the past for the STASI, transporting people to and from the Black Sea.

He was nobody's fool, but he was fearless, and his loyalty went strictly to the highest bidder.

"Ernst. I thought by now that the Germans would have lined you up against the wall and shot you."

"Would you mourn my passing?"

The Greek laughed. "No, but my bank account would."

"Are we ready to sail?"

"We have been for the past twelve hours."

"Then make your final preparations, Captain. As soon as Peter comes aboard we'll leave."

"For Izmir?"

"Yes," Spranger said, smiling faintly. "For Izmir."

* * *

Elizabeth regained consciousness first, and as she awoke she sat up and swung her feet over the edge of the narrow cot. She felt groggy, her lips thick, her mouth and throat extremely dry.

She was in a small cabin, aboard what she immediately understood was a ship. They were moving, she could hear the engine noises, and feel the bows rising to meet the swells, and it was nighttime. She could see the blackness outside through the single porthole.

Her mother was huddled under a thin brown blanket on a cot against the opposite bulkhead. She was still out, but something was different about her. Something wrong, and as Elizabeth tried to work it out in her still drug-befuddled brain, she reached up and touched the top of her head, which she suddenly realized was cold.

She had no hair. She was bald. And so was her mother. The bastards had shaved them!

She shoved aside her blanket and got to her feet. She stood swaying for a moment, trying to keep her balance as a wave of nausea washed over her, trying to work out in her mind what was happening to them.

They'd been drugged back at the chalet, but not before she'd managed to hide her necklace in the fireplace. The Swiss or somebody would find it sooner or later, and she could only hope that her father would be notified, and that he would recognize the clue for what it was.

It was a long string of ifs, but they'd been lucky overhearing their kidnappers talking about their plans. It had been their only mistake so far.

She tottered across to the other bunk and checked her mother, who was unconscious but seemed only to be sleeping peacefully. Someone had drawn circles and arrows on her mother's scalp with a pen, making her look bizarre.

Again her hand went to her own scalp. It had been made to appear as if they were hospital patients. Probably to get them across a border without questions. They were no longer in France.

She went to the porthole and looked outside, but there was very little to see. Mostly darkness and fog, and perhaps a vague glow off in the indistinct distance.

Armand was dead. There was little doubt in her mind. Poor, silly Armand who'd wanted to have an affair with her. A Parisian whose gallantry had cost him his life.

Elizabeth heard the cabin door open and she turned as Liese Egk came in with a bottle of wine and two glasses.

44

A light drizzle fell from a deeply overcast sky as the Dassault helicopter touched down at Charles de Gaulle Airport. It was just dawn, and the terminal area had a deserted air, the lull before the day's international flights began arriving and departing.

McGarvey and Littel had ridden up with Marquand and Belleau. For most of the three-hour flight no one had said much. Elizabeth and Kathleen and their kidnappers had simply disappeared, leaving behind no trace.

The alert had gone out to every airport, train station and bus depot in the Grenoble area, as well as the border crossings in all of France. Word had also been sent to every police district to check every hotel, inn or any other place of lodging for the two women and their captors.

"It will take time," Marquand explained on the tarmac. Two cars were approaching, one of them from the U.S. Embassy at Littel's behest. "But if they have left France we will learn of it, or if they are still here we will find them."

"In the meantime?" McGarvey asked.

Marquand shrugged. "We wait, naturally. But what about you? Will you return to Tokyo now, or wait here?"

"They're still in Europe."

"Yes, and where is this?"

McGarey looked into the Action Service colonel's eyes. "I don't know yet, but I will find them."

"If they are in France, Monsieur, you will let me know before you do anything. Anything at all."

The embassy car pulled up and Littel opened the rear door. "Mr. McGarvey."

"I will insist on this," Marquand said.

McGarvey nodded. "If they are in France I'll call you." He and Marquand shook hands. "Thanks for your help, Colonel, but I think that Grenoble was just a diversion."

"You know where they are?"

"Not yet."

"You found something at the chalet. Something that has given you a clue as to their whereabouts. What was it?"

"They're not in France," McGarvey repeated. "The case is out of your jurisdiction."

"I could have you detained for withholding information," Marquand said in frustration.

Belleau stepped to one side, his right hand inside his jacket, ready for trouble.

"That wouldn't help anyone," McGarvey said, in a reasonable tone. He got into the car, and Littel scrambled in after him.

"I want to know," Marquand called after them. "I'm on your side, McGarvey."

"Get us out of here," Littel told their driver, and they headed off leaving the two Frenchmen standing beside the helicopter. "That was a slick move. You really told them. Christ, that Marquand is a son of a bitch . . ."

"Shut up," McGarvey said mildly, cutting Littel off in mid-sentence.

McGarvey reached into his jacket pocket and fingered Elizabeth's diamond necklace. The clasp was intact, and latched, which meant the necklace hadn't been taken from her forcefully. She had unsnapped the clasp, lifted it from her neck and relatched the clasp.

He turned that thought over in his head for a little while. She'd been out of sight of her kidnappers for a few moments. She knew something; she'd figured it out, or seen something, or overheard them talking . . . whatever. But she'd come up with a bit of information that she wanted to make sure only her father would understand. So she'd left her necklace.

What next? Alone, her necklace off, the clasp relatched, she'd tossed it into the cool fireplace.

Check that. First she'd blackened the stone with a bit of creosote or pine tar. She'd blackened the diamond. The move had been deliberate. She was telling him something.

McGarvey closed his eyes, the solution suddenly coming to him. But it was simple . . . too simple for mere chance. It was Spranger again, telling him something. The East German had left the clue, or had maneuvered Elizabeth into leaving it.

Either way, it was a sign post: Here I am. Catch me if you can.

45

"In forty minutes the Japanese Ambassador to the United States is going to walk through that door and start asking me a lot of tough questions," the President said. "And if he decides to hold a news conference either before our meeting, or afterward, the cat will be out of the bag."

It was Saturday noon. The President had called a number of people to the Oval office, among them his National Security Adviser Dan Milligan, Secretary of State John Cronin, his advisers for Far East Affairs Harvey Hook, and Domestic and International Finance Maxwell F. Peale, his Press Secretary Martin Hewler, and the DCI Roland Murphy.

"At least it's the weekend," Peale said. "The panic on Wall Street won't be so bad."

"If he holds it inside his embassy, there won't be much we can say or do," Hewler said. "But once he steps outside, we'll do the orchestration." Hewler was a big, shambling bear of a man with a direct and very honest view about everything and everyone. He was enormously popular among the press corps.

"Don't tell me somebody's watching him," Cronin said.

"I have a friend over at the *Post* who'll tip me off if Shirō makes a move."

"Won't this friend of yours take this request as a news story in itself?" Cronin pursued the issue.

"No," Hewler said simply.

Cronin turned back to the President. "Of course, none of this comes as a surprise. Prime Minister Kunihiro has shown that he's willing to go to almost any lengths to save face. He took a terrific battering over the Diet's failure to come up with what he thought was a fair amount of financial help to the Western Alliance for the war with Iraq. This now may be nothing more than a catalyst for him."

"He's clutching at straws," Harvey Hook, the Far East expert said. "But I have to agree with John. There is a new feeling of national unity in Japan that is increasingly causing overt moves, especially in the marketplace. We've talked about this before."

"Nobody has prevented them from investing here," Peale said. "But what Harvey is getting at are perceptions and the backlash they're causing."

"Get to the point," the President said harshly.

"The point is this, Mr. President," Hook said. "Rightly or wrongly there is a growing anti-Japan sentiment in this country. The Warsaw Pact has been dismantled. The Russian threat has faded with their internal problems. Quaddafi is quiet. Iran is behaving itself. We've settled the issue with Iraq. And China is being docile for the moment. So who will be our new enemies? The Japanese?"

Hook looked to the others, but no one said a thing.

"The Japanese have a monetary surplus, and the public perception is that they're buying up America, so let's restrict trade with them, and let's place severe restrictions on what they're able to purchase in this country. The fact of the matter, however, is that the British own twice as much property in the United States as the Japanese do. But, the Brits are our friends. And their eyes are round, their skin is white, and they speak the same language, better than we do—they don't make Ls out of their Rs—and they didn't attack Pearl Harbor."

"We were talking about the Japanese reaction," the President said.

"That's right, Mr. President. The Japanese are reacting to the anti-Japanese sentiment in the United States. It has become a point of honor to them during a time when their national psyche, if you want to call it that, is so confused that political faction differences in Tokyo have damn near erupted into all-out war."

"What you're saying is that we've brought this on ourselves," the President's National Security adviser put in.

"What I'm saying is that the Japanese have become the second richest country in the world . . . in terms of GNP, and they don't know what to do with their wealth. They feel that they've become a superpower, and yet they've outlawed any real military. They are the only people in the world to have suffered a nuclear attack in a war they began and lost. They had to endure the reorganization of their own government at the point of a gun. Their own children have rebelled against the old traditions of music and dress. They've developed an inferiority complex over their short stature relative to Westerners, and even the shape of their eyes. So much so that they spend hundreds of millions annually on cosmetic surgery. And yet they are beginning to develop feelings of superiority that they're having a terribly difficult time in reconciling with everything else."

"The whole damn country is psychotic? Is that what you're trying to tell us?" Milligan asked.

"Confused," Hook replied softly.

"With their clout, that makes them dangerous," Milligan said. "Thank God they haven't developed a big military, or become a nuclear power."

"In the middle of all that they've taken official notice that we're spying on them," the President said, turning to Murphy. "What do I tell Ambassador Shirō?"

"That we do spy on them," the DCI said heavily. "We have been since shortly after the war, and no president before you, other than Truman, has suggested otherwise."

"That's not what I'm asking, General," the President said, a dangerous edge to his voice.

"No, sir, I understand that. But the fact of the matter is that some person or group in Japan has hired an organization of East German mercenaries to steal the components for a nuclear weapon. We don't know if they've been successful yet, though we're reasonably sure that they've got at least one of the parts. Nor do we know what their eventual target might be, or the reason they might be doing such a thing."

"But we do know there have been killings," the President said.

"Yes."

"Which is exactly what Ambassador Shirō is coming here in a few minutes to ask me about. What do I tell him?"

"That two economic advisers to the U.S. Ambassador to Japan were murdered by a person or persons unknown, and for unknown reasons. And that in a wholly separate incident, an unknown Occidental, possibly an American, was involved in an altercation in the Imperial Palace's Outer Gardens in which one or more Japanese nationals were killed."

"He'll know that's a lie."

"Yes, Mr. President, he'll almost certainly know that."

"You're suggesting that I stonewall it."

"I don't think we have any other choice, Mr. President. Otherwise we definitely would be letting the cat out of the bag as you say." Murphy leaned forward to emphasize his point. "Involve the Japanese and we will be barred from continuing our investigation on their soil."

"A predecessor of mine ended up with egg on his face when he tried to deny that we were sending U-2 spy planes over the Soviet Union."

"Yes, sir, there are risks."

"In this case we're talking about spying on a friendly country."

"Yes, sir."

"And if, as it has been suggested this morning, the Japanese are confused, and they are trying to save face by using this incident as a catalyst, the financial implications could be enormous."

"It couldn't come at a worse time," Peale, the president's economic adviser, suggested.

"You can say that again, Maxwell," the President agreed. "I'm going to have to offer the man something. Some concession, some promise, something. Anything."

"Stall him," Murphy said.

"Why?" the President asked sharply.

"If we can offer the Japanese government the villain, especially a Japanese villain, with the promise that we'll keep it quiet, they'll find a way to save face. I can guarantee it."

"What are you talking about?" Cronin demanded, but the President held off his secretary of state.

"Just a minute, John."

"We may be on the verge of a breakthrough in Europe," Murphy said.

"McGarvey?"

"Yes, sir."

"Have we found his wife and daughter? Are their kidnappers in custody?"

"Not yet," Murphy said. "But we were correct in our assumption that the kidnapping was carried out to lure McGarvey from Japan, which of course clinches the connection between the Japanese and the STASI."

Murphy quickly told them everything that had happened in France, including the obscure clue of the necklace and blackened diamond that McGarvey's daughter had evidently left for him in the chalet outside of Grenoble.

"What does it mean?" Milligan asked.

"We're not quite sure . . . or I should say we *weren't* quite sure until McGarvey made his move. If he's heading where we think he's heading then we'll have it."

"Go on," the President said.

"As of a few hours ago he was in Athens, which surprised us because earlier in the day he'd spoken with my deputy director of operations on the telephone from Paris. When he was asked what his next move would be, he said he was going to wait there. Sooner or later the kidnappers would make contact with him, he said. And he did check into the Hotel Inter-Continental, but he slipped out almost immediately and flew from Orly to Greece."

"How do we know this?" Milligan asked.

"You may recall, the French found a sophisticated communications device used by the terrorists at Orly. The SDECE handed it

over to us, and one of my Paris Station people gave it to McGarvey.
The idea was for him to use it to intercept the kidnappers' transmissions, if and when he got close to them. But we modified the
device, adding what's called an EPIRB . . . an Emergency Position
Indicating Radio Beacon. It's a National Security Agency-designed
version of a civilian device. It transmits a continuous signal that's
picked up by our satellites from which we can pinpoint his location
to within a couple of yards or less."

"He's in Athens, you say?" the President asked. "What does that
tell you?"

"He was in Athens, Mr. President. But he didn't stay long. He
went south to Piraeus, which is Athens' seaport, from where he
evidently hired a boat."

"Where's he going?"

"It took my people all morning to come up with the answer,"
Murphy said. "McGarvey is heading to the Greek island of Santorini."

"Yes," Cronin said, seeing it before the others. "Santorini, the
island most Greeks think was part of the lost city-state of Atlantis."

"I don't understand," the President admitted.

"Neither did I," Murphy said. "But my people tell me that
Santorini was also famous for its black diamonds."

"Clever," the President said after a moment. "And you say that
McGarvey figured this out on his own?"

Murphy nodded. "Nobody ever denied that the man was bright."

"His daughter too, evidently," the President said. "What can we
do for him? Assuming that the kidnappers are holed up somewhere
on or near Santorini. It's a big island, filled with tourists this time of
the year, I would imagine."

"The advantage might be ours for once. If we're reading our
signals right, the kidnappers may not be on the island yet."

"Explain."

"The Italian customs people reported that a Swiss medevac
ambulance crossed their border last night above Torino. It was
carrying two cancer patients, identified as Yugoslavian nationals.
Women. The ambulance was found abandoned near the waterfront
in Venice this morning."

"They're going by sea the rest of the way."

"Only one ship sailed from the port of Venice this morning, and
she was the Greek freighter *Thaxos*, a vessel we've long suspected
was used by the STASI for contract work."

"It could be them."

"Yes, sir. We have a satellite shot several hours old showing the
Thaxos entering the Mediterranean past Brindisi. I'd like to intercept them before they land on Santorini."

"How?" the President asked.

"The Sixth Fleet is nearby. I'd like authorization to use a unit of
SEALS to board the *Thaxos*, without warning, under the assump-

tion that McGarvey's ex-wife and daughter are aboard, held by Spranger and his people.

"That's piracy," Cronin blurted.

The President ignored him. "There'll be casualties."

"Yes, sir. Almost certainly."

The President thought about it for a moment or two. "What about McGarvey?"

"He'll be on the island a few hours ahead of time. If something should go wrong, he'd act as backup."

"Unknowingly."

Murphy nodded. "Yes, sir. For the time being I would leave him out of the operation."

"Not very fair."

"No, sir. But I believe that we have very high odds of success if we act now. Any move against Spranger once he got to the island could complicate our relations with the Greek government."

"Do it," the President said. "But keep me informed, General."

"Will do, Mr. President. What about the Japanese?"

"I'll stall Ambassador Shirō this afternoon, but I'm going to have to have some results. And damned soon."

46

The weather system that had moved in over western Europe was sinking unexpectedly to the southeast, and U.S. Navy meteorologists were predicting thickly overcast skies and rain by midnight over the entire Aegean Sea.

Moving silently, almost as if phantoms in the deepening twilight, the *CVN Nimitz* and her abbreviated task force were on station fifty nautical miles south-southwest of the island of Crete. They had spent the better part of the past eight months sailing back and forth just off the coast of Lebanon, showing the American flag during the latest round of fighting in the ongoing civil war there. It was time to be rotated home and they'd been steaming for Gib when they'd been given their temporary mission orders.

Lieutenant Edwin Lipton stood hunched over a weather radarscope in operations with the Nimitz group's chief meteorologist Lieutenant Commander Brent Eastman, and the chief of Air Operations, Commander Louis Rheinholtz.

Lipton was a SEAL, a fact that would have been obvious to the most casual observer, even if he hadn't been dressed all in black. Physically he stood out. Although he was only of medium height, his body was in perfect athletic condition, and with the way he held himself like a boxer ready to spring it was clear that his reflex speeds, coordination and endurance were probably very good. The look in his eyes and the expression at the corners of his mouth were those of a man utterly and totally committed to the task at hand, and completely devoid of any nonsense whatsoever. He and the five men in his elite strike group were highly trained professionals in the highest sense of the word.

"What are the chances for a break in the weather?" he asked. "We're under a full moon tonight."

"Less than ten percent, Lieutenant," Eastman said. "In fact the cloud cover will begin moving in over the region within the next hour. In two hours moonlight will not be a significant factor at all. Your real problem is going to be the next satellite overpass. It'll be blind."

Lipton studied the screen for a moment longer, then turned and crossed to the chart table where their present position was electronically updated on a continuous realtime basis.

The last known position of the *Thaxos* was about sixty miles southeast of Piraeus. She'd made a shortcut through the Gulf of Corinth and the Corinth Canal.

"On that course and speed she'd make Santorini around oh-one-hundred hours," Commander Rheinholtz said. "Another five hours, if that's where she's heading, if she doesn't change her speed, and if she takes the best direct-line course through the islands. There's still a lot of sea out there between us and them."

"Yes, sir," Lipton said.

"We'd attract too much notice if we sent out patrols to find them. You do understand that."

"Yes, sir," Lipton nodded. He stabbed a blunt finger at a spot just north of the island. "We'll wait here. When she passes, we'll get aboard."

"You're betting they won't put in at either the old port of Thira of the new port of Athinos."

"I don't think so. They'd have to figure they might run into some trouble with the authorities. I'm told that these people are sharp, and I'll have to go with that until it's proved differently. But it's my guess they'll disembark five miles offshore and come in here, or here." He pointed to the island's only two beaches. Everywhere else tall cliffs plunged into the sea, making a landing next to impossible.

"What if you miss them?"

Lipton shrugged. "Then it would be out of our hands. My orders are that we are not to conduct any operation on Greek soil. But we won't miss them, sir."

Commander Rheinholtz studied the chart. "We'll put up a couple of LAMPS III choppers to give you a steady over-the-horizon radar coverage to the north, and we'll splash you down around midnight."

"Ay, ay, sir."

"These two women are VIPs, but there's no telling what condition they'll be in."

"My people are briefed."

"Very well, Lieutenant," Commander Rheinholtz said, and he

glanced over at the plotting board they were using for this operation. "Where is Brightstar at this moment?" he asked. Brightstar was McGarvey's operational codename.

"He's just approaching the port of Thira, sir," the plotting board rating replied.

"No telling what he'll do when he finds out the *Thaxos* hasn't docked yet," Rheinholtz said. "I'll be glad when this night is over."

"Yes, sir," Lipton said, and it was clear that he meant it.

The moon was blood red on the horizon as the aging 37-foot fishing boat *Dhodhóni* chugged into the dramatic harbor of Thira. Once the crater of a volcano, the cliffs rose a thousand feet out of the sea, and from across the water McGarvey could hear the sounds of music echoing off the rock faces.

"You are looking for somebody," the grizzled old captain said, his broad grin nearly toothless. He'd been drinking ouzo most of the way over, but he didn't appear to be drunk.

"Two ladies," McGarvey said.

"Ah, the ladies. Not from this island. So they have come by water."

There were several boats in the harbor, but nothing McGarvey thought Spranger would have used. Of course the East Germans could have landed at Athinos, if they had already arrived and if the black diamond had not been a false clue, or if he had not misinterpreted it.

"Who do I see about them?" McGarvey asked.

The old man's grin widened. "If you are a policeman it may be difficult, you see."

McGarvey shook his head. "I'm not a policeman."

"But there is a stench of . . . trouble on you."

McGarvey was certain the old man had been about to say death, instead of trouble. "This is important to me. One of the ladies is my daughter, and the other my ex-wife."

The captain nodded. "When you find them . . . ?"

"Someone may have brought them here."

"Then you will kill this someone?"

McGarvey stared at the old man, and after a long time he nodded. "Yes."

"I thought so," the captain said triumphantly. "In that case I will help you."

"You?"

The captain laughed out loud. "Yes, me. You didn't think that I was a Piraiévs pig, did you? I am Spyros Karamanlis from Santorini. This is my island. You will see."

47

The Japanese ambassador to the United States made his official call on the President and left. The President's Press Secretary Martin Hewler called Murphy with the news.

"The man is not happy, but he's agreed to wait."

"How long?" the DCI asked. It was a little after three in the afternoon, Washington time, and after nine in the evening in the Aegean Sea.

"Not very long, General. We're going to need some action on this soon. Like first thing in the morning. Better yet, this evening."

"With any luck we should have something within the next three or four hours."

"With any luck," Hewler said. "Which translates into: We've got our fingers crossed, and should a miracle happen, we'll pull it off."

"Do your job, Martin, and let us do ours," Murphy replied sharply.

"Do that, General. Just do that much, and we'll all come out smelling like roses."

Paul Shircliff stepped up to tier B of the Special Operations balcony and plugged his headset into Patsy Connor's console. Shircliff was early swing shift OD at the National Security Agency's headquarters at Fort Meade, Maryland.

Patsy was just entering data from the latest KH-15 pass over the

Mediterranean, picking out the EPIRB signal from McGarvey's transmitter and isolating it against an area overlay map.

"Bring up more detail," Shircliff said softly.

Without looking up, Patsy punched a series of buttons, which expanded the map view displayed on her terminal. In this instance the scale was such that the island of Santorini barely fit on the screen. A tiny but very bright cross with a series of identifiers to its right indicated the EPIRB's realtime position. At this scale the cross seemed to be located in the harbor area of the port of Thira.

"Expand," Shircliff said.

Patsy hit another series of buttons, and now the map scale expanded so that the port of Thira itself mostly filled the screen. "This is the last enhancement," she said.

The EPIRB was transmitting from a location near the harbor, but not on the water. It was definitely ashore.

"How long has he been at that location?" Shircliff asked.

"About an hour."

"No movement?"

"None. He's remained within a three-yard radius the entire time."

"It's possible he'd ditched the transmitter then," Shircliff said, reaching for the folder of Greek maps on top of the console.

"Could be a hotel, I was about to check it out," Patsy suggested. "The transmitter could be with his luggage."

Shircliff opened a large-scale map showing the port town in detail. It took him a few moments to orient the computer's perspective with the printed chart. "Looks like a waterfront taverna."

Patsy looked up. "What do you suppose he's doing there, sir?"

"I don't know," Shircliff said shaking his head. "I don't know anything about the man except that he's damned important."

"Yes, sir."

"Let me know the moment he makes a move," Shircliff said, replacing the chart folder but keeping the Thira map out. "I'll be at my console."

Clouds were already starting to roll in from the west as Lieutenant Lipton and his five men clambered aboard the SH-3D Sea King that would take them out to the intercept point one hundred miles to the north. The wind was rising and the smell of rain was heavy on the night air. The weather system was developing faster than the meteorologists had predicted, but so far as the SEALS were concerned the weather couldn't have been better.

"No moon, overcast skies and choppy seas. The *Thaxos* crew won't know what hit them until it's too late," Lipton told his number two, Ensign Frank Tyrell.

"If we don't miss them in the darkness."

"You worry too much."

Tyrell, who was a deceptively thin and mild-mannered man, grinned. "It's a bitch, but somebody's got to do it."

Lipton started to strap in as the helicopter's engines came to life and the main rotor began to turn, but a runner from Operations came across the deck to the open hatch and motioned for him.

"Stand by," Lipton shouted up to the pilots, and he scrambled over to the hatch.

"Commander Rheinholtz wanted you to have the latest on Brightstar, sir," the rating shouted over the noise.

"Is he on the island?"

"Yes, sir. Apparently he'd been holed up at a waterfront bar for the past couple of hours."

"What's he doing there?"

"Unknown, sir.

Lipton thought about it for a moment, then nodded. "Get word to us the moment he moves."

"Aye, aye, sir. And good hunting."

McGarvey sat across from a very well-dressed man by the name of Constantine Theotokis, whom Karamanlis had identified as his uncle. Theotokis was a member of the Greek Mafia, and Santorini was *his* island in almost every sense of the word.

During the couple of hours they'd been together at the crowded, smoky taverna, a constant stream of runners came to their corner table with messages for him which they whispered into his ear. Afterwards he'd send them off on other errands.

"These people you seek are almost certainly the very same ones who have done business here previously," Theotokis said. He fingered the black diamond stick pin in his tie. "Unfortunately they are not on the island at this moment."

"They will arrive by sea," McGarvey said.

"Of course they will."

"Soon. Probably this evening. Late."

Theotokis nodded sagely.

"Will they land here or at Athinos? Or, considering what they are bringing with them, is there another less conspicuous place for them to come ashore? Let's say in a dinghy?"

Again the Greek gangster nodded wisely. "They have taken a deconsecrated church in the north. It is on a cliff above the grottoes within site of Oía and the volcanic island of Akrá. The only good approach is by sea. Overland . . ." He spread his hands. "It is a very difficult track, not to be advised in the darkness."

"But one could wait with a small boat."

"Yes. Such boats are available. Of course one would need a guide, perhaps two. They would have to be . . . paid."

"I understand," McGarvey said. "They would have to be discreet men. And men of a certain talent."

Theotokis mentioned a price. It was high, but it would guarantee professionalism. Yet there was something bothersome about the arrangement. About Karamanlis and his uncle. About the entire setup.

48

The fishing vessel *Dhodhóni*, her lights off, bobbed in the gentle swells off the protected east coast of the island. A few miles away they could make out a few lights above the almost sheer cliffs that rose in some spots five hundred feet straight out of the sea. In all other directions was darkness, the blackness of the sky merging with the blackness of the water.

Theotokis had suggested Karamanlis' boat, and had sent along a younger, darker, even more ruggedly built Greek by the name of Evangolos Papagos as crew.

It was nearing one in the morning, and they had been waiting just offshore since before midnight. So far they'd seen nothing. The three of them were in the wheelhouse; Karamanlis standing at the helm, McGarvey with his back against the door, and Papagos insolently facing him from the corner.

"How will we know this boat of yours?" Karamanlis asked, scanning the pitch-black sea to the north. They'd seen only one other boat since Thira, a freighter well south and heading into the open Mediterranean.

"If, as your uncle said, there is a route to the old church from here, then they'll show up sooner or later."

"Maybe you are being tricked," Papagos rumbled, his voice deep. He was staring out to sea.

"She'll probably be running without lights," McGarvey continued. "At least until Spranger and the others get off."

Papagos looked up. "What is your quarrel with Ernst Spranger?"

"You know him?" McGarvey asked, tensing.

"He's an old friend." The Greek grinned broadly, showing nicotine-stained teeth.

"Not to worry," Karamanlis was quick to explain. "He and my uncle have had a falling out. If it is the East German you are hunting, then we will help you."

The entire thing was a setup, McGarvey understood at last. Spranger had been one step ahead of him the entire way. He'd taken Elizabeth and Kathleen to lure McGarvey out of Japan, and then had marked the trail all the way here. To what?

To a killing ground, of course. Somewhere on the island, in the end, if he survived that long.

He focused on the two Greeks again. "How do I know you're telling me the truth? Maybe you're working for Spranger. The Germans always had a way with you Greeks. A fatal attraction on your part."

Papagos's jaw tightened. "You will find out very soon," he said.

Karamanlis said something to him in Greek that McGarvey didn't catch.

"Out there," Papagos said in English. "Two points to starboard."

McGarvey didn't bother to look. "You knew it would be here." He reached into his pocket, his fingers curling around the grip of his pistol.

Papagos shrugged, his eyes going to McGarvey's gun hand. "It's why we came. You hired us to intercept them. Well, we have. They're just out there. Dark, as you predicted."

"They must already be on the island," Karamanlis said. "We must have missed them."

"We'll check the boat," McGarvey said.

Karamanlis started to protest, but Papagos cut him off. "Naturally. Maybe something went wrong, maybe they're still aboard."

Again Karamanlis said something to him in Greek, and Papagos stiffened, his entire attitude suddenly changing.

McGarvey took out his gun and pointed it at them, Karamanlis' eyes going nervously from the gun to the starboard windows.

"We'll go over there now," McGarvey said.

"Why is it you are pulling a gun on us?" Papagos asked. "Don't you have any trust?"

"It may be a trap over there, you know," Karamanlis said nervously.

"Yes, it might be." McGarvey cocked the hammer.

"Do as he says, Spyros," Papagos said, a cunning look coming into his eyes. "And be quick about it. Let's help Mr. McGarvey find what he's looking for."

* * *

The *Thaxos* showed no lights, nor was there any movement on her decks. She was drifting slowly to the southwest, and there was no way of telling how long she'd been left apparently abandoned, but her portside boarding ladder was down and one of her lifeboats was missing from its davits.

"She's been abandoned," Karamanlis said, as they bumped up against the boarding ladder. He put the engine in neutral.

"We'll go aboard and see," McGarvey said, motioning with the gun. He opened the door and backed out on deck. No sounds came from the bigger ship. No machinery noises. Nothing.

Karamanlis and Papagos followed him out of the wheelhouse, and he stepped aside so that they could tie a line to the bigger ship then precede him up the ladder.

The cargo vessel was set to blow, there was little doubt in McGarvey's mind about it. That was what Karamanlis had told Papagos. And that was why they were both nervous. But so long as they didn't jump ship there was a possibility some time remained.

He had to make sure that Kathleen and Elizabeth hadn't been left behind. It was the kind of monstrous joke that Spranger liked most.

On deck a man dressed in dungarees and a watch cap was crumpled in a heap half in and half out of a hatch. Blood had pooled behind his head. He'd obviously been shot to death.

"Spranger's work," McGarvey said. "The rest of the crew are probably dead as well."

"He's probably planted explosives," Karamanlis said.

"Then we'd better hurry," McGarvey said. "We'll start with the bridge."

"What are you looking for?" Papagos asked.

"I'll tell you when I find it. But we're going to check every space aboard this ship before we leave. So if you're worried about being blown out of the water, I suggest you get on with it."

Karamanlis and Papagos exchanged glances, and for a long moment neither of them moved, until suddenly Papagos ducked through the hatch and was gone.

McGarvey started after the man, but Karamanlis shoved him aside and darted for the rail.

"Stop," McGarvey shouted, regaining his balance, and he snapped off a shot striking the Greek in the left leg and sending him sprawling.

Papagos fired from somewhere inside the ship, the bullet ricocheting off the hatch. McGarvey reared back at the same time Karamanlis pulled out his pistol and fired. The shot smacked into the bulkhead inches from McGarvey's left shoulder, leaving him no other choice but to fire back, his shot catching the Greek in the head just below the right eye socket.

* * *

The six-man team of SEALS rode in one rubber raft powered by a highly muffled eighty horsepower outboard. The boat was big enough for them and the two hostages they hoped to free, but no larger. There were no plans to bring anyone else out alive.

They had made all possible speed from their position well to the north the moment they'd received radar vectors on the stationary object just off the eastern coast of the island, and an update on McGarvey's position showing him converging on the same target. But they'd badly guessed Spranger's plans, and the mad dash across had taken nearly thirty minutes.

"Definitely a muzzle flash," Ensign Tyrell said. "Small caliber."

"Do you see anyone on deck?" Lipton asked. They were still a half mile out, but Tyrell was studying the ship through a starlight scope which showed figures as ghostly images in all but a total absence of ambient light.

"There was a movement just behind the flash, but the decks are clear now." Tyrell looked up. "How the hell did he get here before us?"

"They said he was a sharp sonofabitch. And the man is well motivated."

"I'll say," Tyrell agreed. "But this isn't going to make our job easier."

"No," Lipton said, tight-lipped. "No it won't."

49

The cell in which they'd been placed was small and very cold. A tiny window in one wall was dark. Kathleen lay on one of the cots, still only semiconscious, but Elizabeth sat on the stone floor in the corner, her knees hugged to her chest. Her head was spinning from the aftermath of the drugs she'd been given since Grenoble, with the almost total lack of food or water, and with what the woman—Liese Egk—had done to her aboard the boat.

She shuddered, not so much because of the damp cold, but because of what had happened. She felt dirty and used; as if she had been forced to age a hundred years overnight.

Yet there was enough defiance in her that she could fantasize about what would happen to her captors once her father got here.

"Keep your head down, because I'll be coming in swinging," he would say.

She could see him dressed in black, darting silently down a dark corridor, moving like a deadly jungle animal that no one could resist.

He'd have to be warned about the woman. It was the only trap they could possibly set for him, and yet in her heart of hearts she knew that her father would see through Liese Egk. He would recognize the woman for what she was.

"I wasn't born yesterday. I've been around. I've seen a few things."

In the end the Germans would be dead, Armond's murder

avenged. And she could almost feel her father's strength flowing into her as he led her and her mother away. It would be morning. The sun would be brightly shining, warm on her shoulders and head.

Her mother said something, but her voice seemed muffled and indistinct, and for a moment Elizabeth was confused. In her fantasies only her father ever spoke.

She remembered her father from when she was a young girl, but lately she'd had a difficult time visualizing exactly how it had been. At times she wasn't certain if she was recalling genuine memories or her fantasies.

"Elizabeth," Kathleen said thickly.

Elizabeth looked up out of her thoughts. Her mother had rolled over. She was clutching the thin blanket up to her chin but she was still shivering. "Are you all right, mother?"

"What's happening? Where are we?"

"I don't know for sure," Elizabeth grunted, getting painfully to her feet. She had to stand for a few seconds, holding onto the stone wall for support lest she lose her balance and fall.

"My God, what happened to your head?" Kathleen asked in shock.

Elizabeth raised her fingers to her bald skull. Already a light stubble had begun to appear. "Your head is the same. They wanted us to look like hospital patients."

"But why?"

"So that they could take us across the border without question."

"We're not in Switzerland?" the older woman asked, panicking a little. She seemed very frail and weak.

"We're in Greece, I think," Elizabeth said. "The island of Santorini. Or at least I hope we are." She tottered over to the window.

It was pitch-black outside, and she couldn't make out a thing. Even the dim light from a tiny bulb in the ceiling overpowered her night vision.

"What's out there," her mother asked anxiously.

"I can't see yet," Elizabeth said. She climbed up on the edge of her cot so that she could reach the bulb, and gingerly unscrewed it, plunging the room into darkness.

"Elizabeth?" her mother cried.

"It's all right, mother. I just want to look outside. I'll put the light back on in a minute."

"But I can't see. I'm frightened, and I'm cold."

Elizabeth felt her way across to her mother's cot and sat down, taking her mother's hands in hers. She leaned in close and lowered her voice in case someone was standing on the other side of the wooden door listening to them.

"Father will be coming to rescue us very soon," she whispered.

Kathleen's grip tightened. "How do you know?"

"I left a clue for him back at the chalet. In the fireplace. I'm sure he's found it already and is on his way with help."

"What kind of clue? What do you mean?"

"Don't worry about it. Father will know what it means, and he'll come for us."

"But that's what they want. Elizabeth, what have you done?"

"What do you mean?" Elizabeth asked, a sudden sick feeling coming to her stomach.

"I came to bring you back to Washington. One of your father's friends warned me that he was in danger. That we all were in danger."

"Daddy's working for the CIA again. Is that it, mother?"

"I think so. These people want to trick him into coming here so they can kill him."

"He's too good for them."

"He's only one man, my darling. And there's too many of them. They're too well organized."

"But before, back in Switzerland, you said that he would come for us."

"I know, but I was wrong for wanting it."

Elizabeth pulled her hand away and got up. Her mother was a contradiction. First she was weak, a simpering idiot, and then she was suddenly strong. What was happening?

Elizabeth went to the window, tears beginning to well up in her eyes. It was the drugs and everything that had been done to them that made her confused. That made them both confused, and say things they didn't mean.

At first she wasn't able to make out a thing; just as amorphous blackness, a featureless nothing. But then she thought she was seeing a movement far below. A white, almost ghostly swirl that lasted for a second or more, but then was gone.

"Elizabeth?" her mother called, but she ignored her.

The white swirl came again, rushing inward, far below, until suddenly she understood that she was seeing waves breaking on the rocks. The room they were in was perched on the edge of a hill, or a sheer cliff that plunged down to the sea. They were in a castle of some sort. A medieval keep. Perhaps a Roman or Greek ruin.

She was about to turn away when a tiny flash of light directly below caught her eye, and she sucked her breath.

Someone was outside, just beneath her window. Father?

She searched with her fingers in the darkness for a latch, and finding one, fumbled it open, breaking two of her fingernails against the stonework.

The window opened inward, a rush of fresh air bringing the odor of the sea into the room. Standing on tiptoes she was just able to look out over the edge. Barely ten feet below her a man dressed in black dangled from a series of ropes. He was concentrating on doing something directly in front of him. It seemed as if he was stuffing something into a big crack in the stones.

She almost called to him, but something made her hold back. It wasn't her father. He was the wrong build, his hair the wrong color. Even in the darkness she could see that.

He switched on a small flashlight for just a second or two, shielding it from the sea, but not from Elizabeth's view, and kept it long enough for her to see what he was doing.

She pulled back into the room, her heart pounding. The man had been attaching wires to whatever it was he'd stuffed into the crack in the wall.

Wires leading to explosives that when they blew would send this entire side of the castle into the sea far below.

50

McGarvey stood just within the hatchway that Papagos had disappeared through, and held his breath as he listened for a sound, any sound. But the ship was dead. Nothing moved, not even a whisper of air.

This entire thing had been a setup from the moment he'd shown up in Piraeus looking for a boat to bring him out to Santorini. Spranger had anticipated his every move and had stayed at least one step ahead of him since France.

"Kathleen." he shouted. "Elizabeth?" He stepped to the opposite side of the corridor, flattening himself against the bulkhead in the darkness.

There was no answer. No cry, no pistol shot, no movement. Nothing. But Papagos could be anywhere. There were a thousand places aboard for him to hide in the darkness. A thousand ambushes.

The question was, were Kathleen and Elizabeth aboard now? Was it Spranger's intentions to let them go down with the ship, knowing that an enraged, out-of-control McGarvey would come after him? Or was this just another of the man's obstacles before the final confrontation?

Straight down the corridor, about midships, a stairway led up to the bridge deck. He was going to have to search the ship for them.

Now. Immediately. Which meant he was going to have to start taking chances.

Tightening his grip on his pistol, McGarvey darted down the corridor and took the stairs two at a time. At the top he halted for just a second.

A narrow landing led to an open hatch onto the bridge. No lights illuminated any of the instruments or gauges, and only a very dim light filtered in from outside. A figure of a man was lying on the deck. He was dead, there was little doubt of it. All the crew would be dead, and the hatches locked in the open position so that when the sand kickers blew out the ship's bottom she'd sink in a couple of minutes, attracting no attention from shore.

Something moved below, on the main deck. McGarvey turned and looked down the stairs, but he couldn't see a thing. He'd heard a noise, lightly, metal against metal, perhaps. But there was nothing now.

Papagos trying to get off the ship?

McGarvey started down the stairs, and halfway to the deck he dropped low so that he could see into the corridor. The figure of a bulky man was outlined against the open hatch, his back to McGarvey. Something outside, on deck or out on the water was apparently holding his interest.

He backed up and turned around as McGarvey came the rest of the way down, and he stopped short. It was Papagos. He held what looked like a Russian Makarov automatic loosely at his side, the muzzle pointed down.

"Your wife and daughter are not aboard," he said. He was clearly agitated. There was no insolence about him now.

"Who's out there?"

"I don't know. I thought I saw something."

"Is that why you didn't jump ship?"

"Did you bring someone with you?" Papagos asked, his eyes narrowing. He looked like a cornered rat getting ready to spring.

"I didn't bring anybody. It could be Spranger."

"He wouldn't come here now."

"This boat is going to blow up. When?"

"I don't know. I swear to God, I don't know."

"Where are my wife and daughter, if they're not aboard now?"

"On the island. In the monastery." Papagos nervously glanced over his shoulder.

"How do I know you're telling the truth?"

"You must believe me," Papagos pleaded. He came forward a step and McGarvey raised his pistol.

"Put your gun down."

"Kill me and you'll never see your wife and daughter again. He's crazy. He'll kill them first, and then he'll kill you. He means to do it. He's got the power, even more than Constantine does. But I can help you. I know what he's up to."

Something bumped against the hull on the portside of the ship. The *Dhodhóni*, or a distraction? McGarvey, still holding his gun on the Greek, stepped farther back into the darkness.

"What are you doing?" Papagos whispered urgently.

"Put your gun down, and you might come out of this alive," McGarvey whispered back. If it was Spranger's people out there coming back to the ship for some reason, Papagos would provide a brief delay. Possibly long enough for McGarvey to gain the advantage. It would also mean that this ship wasn't set to blow after all.

"Fuck you," Papagos snarled, and he spun on his heel, darting for the open hatch as a black-suited figure appeared on deck.

The Greek cried out and got off one shot that staggered the man in the hatchway, but did not knock him down. McGarvey figured he was wearing a bulletproof vest. Then three silenced shots were fired down the length of the thwartships corridor from the starboard side, slamming into Papagos' back and head. He fell forward on his face, dead.

A second later another black-suited figure rushed down the corridor and as he passed, McGarvey reached out and yanked the man back into the shadows, putting the muzzle of his Walther to the man's temple.

"*Tell your people to back off,*" McGarvey said in German. "*Or I will kill you now. Do it!*"

The man McGarvey was holding didn't move a muscle. He was obviously a well-disciplined professional.

"Mr. McGarvey," someone called in English from the darkness above on the stairs. "I am pointing my pistol at your head. I want you to release Frank, and step away from him."

"Who are you?"

"My name is Ed Lipton. I'm a U.S. Navy lieutenant. We're SEALS here to rescue your wife and daughter."

Spranger? the thought immediately occurred. McGarvey wouldn't put this past the man.

"How did you find me?" he called.

"The walkie-talkie you were given in Paris was modified to include an EPIRB. Do you know what this device is?"

"Yes," McGarvey said. "Who gave it to me?"

"Mr. Littel on Mr. Lynch's instructions," Lipton answered.

"What else have you been told about me?"

"That you're one tenacious son of a bitch," the man McGarvey was holding said. "My name is Tyrell, and if you don't mind I'd like to be set free. My back is killing me."

McGarvey moved the gun away from Tyrell's head, released his grip around the man's neck and stepped out into the middle of the corridor. He was covered from the hatches at both ends of the corridor, as well as from Lipton on the stairs.

"Any sign of your wife and daughter," Tyrell asked.

"No, but I didn't have the chance to look," McGarvey said. "I think this ship is about to blow."

"Then we'd better hurry," Lipton said, coming down the stairs. "Frank, take Bryan, Tony and Bob, and start with the bilges and engine room. Jules and McGarvey will come with me on this deck and above."

"Everything is set here," Dürenmatt said, laying the remote control detonator on the table.

Spranger had been looking out to sea in the direction he knew the *Thaxos* was lying, although in the darkness he could not actually see the ship. He turned.

"Very well. Who is watching the landing area?"

"Bruno."

"Take Walther and Otto with you and join him. Once the ship blows we'll watch with the starlight scopes."

"How long do you want to wait before we get out of here?" Dürenmatt asked. He was a very large bear of a man. His specialty with the STASI had been killing men with his bare hands, slowly and with great relish.

"However long it takes for Mr. McGarvey to come to us," Spranger said turning back to the open window.

"He's probably dead out there, or else he will be soon."

"I don't think so, Peter. No, I think Mr. McGarvey is more resourceful than that."

"We can stand off, and when he comes up here . . . if he comes up here . . . we can blow this place."

"No," Spranger said with finality. "I want to see his face when he knows he's lost."

"Insanity," Dürenmatt said, half under his breath.

Spranger looked at the man, his left eyebrow slightly arched, his lips pursed. "Peter," he said softly. "If you ever talk to me like that again, I shall have you nailed to a post and skinned alive. Is that clear?"

"*Jawohl, Herr General*," Dürenmatt said, chastised. Even he realized that he had gone too far. "I am sorry."

"See to your duties, then."

"Yes, sir," the bigger man said. He clicked his heels and left.

Liese came in from the adjacent room that had once been a small chapel. She had overheard everything, and she was smiling.

"What if he doesn't lose, Ernst?" she asked. "Perhaps he's coming here not only to free his women, but also to see the look on your face when you know that you've lost."

Spranger didn't bother rising to her bait.

After a moment or two she chuckled, the sound low and soft. "How long before the ship explodes?"

"Less than three minutes," Spranger said, and he glanced back at Liese headed for the door. "Where are you going?"

"I want to see the look on Elizabeth's face. She's more interesting to me."

"Stay away from them."

"No," Liese said flatly. "We're going to kill them in any event. Perhaps I'll do the mother now. I'd like to see the little girl's reaction."

A slight flush had come to Liese's cheeks.

"You're disgusting."

She laughed out loud. "Yes, I am, aren't I?"

51

"I count six dead so far," Lipton said coming out of the crew's dining area. "Every one of them has been shot in the back of the head at close range. This STASI outfit are a bunch of bastards."

McGarvey was at the end of the corridor at the stairwell which led to the lower decks and engine room. "There's at least one more on the bridge. I think you'd better get your people off this ship before it's too late."

"They know what they're doing," Lipton said crossing the corridor and poking his head into the galley.

"So does Spranger."

Chief Petty Officer Jules Joslow came around the corner. "All clear in the crews' quarters," he reported.

"Any sign of the hostages?" Lipton asked.

"Negative. If they were ever aboard they left no traces that I could see."

"They're on the island," McGarvey said, one ear cocked at the stairway.

"You get that from the one we neutralized?"

"He said they'd been taken to the monastery where Spranger's waiting for me to show up. I think he was telling the truth."

"Spranger has got to know that you came out here . . ." Lipton said, but then he realized that he and his men had probably walked into the middle of a trap that had been set for McGarvey. A trap that

McGarvey was expected to escape from. And for the first time Lipton began to get the feeling that he and his people might be out of their league here.

"Lieutenant," McGarvey prompted.

"Right," Lipton said. "I think it's time we get the hell out of here. There's no one left alive." He turned to Joslow. "Get our raft away from this ship. I'll pull Frank and the others out."

"Aye, aye, sir," Joslow said.

"Cut the fishing boat loose too," McGarvey said. "I'm going to need her."

Lipton hesitated for just an instant, but McGarvey disappeared down the stairwell. "Do it," he told Joslow, and he hurried after McGarvey, a sinking feeling in his stomach that somebody was about to get hurt.

It was pitch-black below. Lipton pulled out his flashlight and switched it on, just catching a glimpse of McGarvey's back rounding a corner on the stairs one deck below. The man was fifteen years older than the oldest SEAL on his team, but he was just as quick, if not quicker, than any of them.

Lipton followed him, nearly stumbling over another body at the foot of the stairs. Like the others this one too had been shot in the head at close range. He wore greasy coveralls. He'd probably been one of the engine room crew.

A flashlight beam bobbed from an open hatch aft at the end of a corridor. Lipton started back when a series of four quick explosions from somewhere below rocked the ship, sending him sprawling.

When he scrambled back to his feet the light he'd seen in the open hatch was gone, and he could hear water rushing into the ship. A lot of water!

"Mission red! Mission red!" he shouted the emergency recall signal as he headed in a dead run for the open hatch.

Already the *Thaxos* was beginning to list hard to port. It would only be a matter of minutes, perhaps less, before she rolled over. They'd all be trapped down here with little or no chance for survival.

Bryan Wasley and Tony Reid, soaked with seawater and diesel oil, clambered through the open hatch just as Lipton reached it.

"The bottom's gone," Wasley gasped. He was shook up, but neither of them appeared to be injured.

"Get out of here," Lipton ordered, shoving them aside.

"Frank is down there with McGarvey."

"What about Bob?" Lipton demanded.

"He just disappeared," Wasley answered.

"Go," Lipton shouted and he braced himself against the list and shined the beam of his flashlight down into the big engine room.

Water was pouring in from the port and starboard bulkheads and from somewhere aft. Whoever had placed the charges knew what they were doing. There was no possibility of saving the ship.

Frank Tyrell was hanging on the ladder about eight feet below the open hatch. Already the water had risen to the rung he was standing on, and it was coming up fast.

"Frank," Lipton shouted down to him over the waterfall roar.

Tyrell, who was covered in diesel fuel and engine oil, looked up. "Get away!" he hollered.

"Where's Bob?"

"He got caught on the way up. McGarvey has gone down for him."

"Christ," Lipton swore, and was starting to swing out onto the ladder when Tyrell shouted.

"Here! He's got him!"

Lipton shined his light on the water as McGarvey surfaced with a sputtering Bob Schade. Tyrell grabbed the man by the arm but Schade shook it off.

"I'm okay," he shouted, coughing. "Get the hell out of here. Go, go, go!"

Already the water was up to Tyrell's waist and rising even faster. The ship would go in less than a minute.

He scrambled up the ladder and at the top Lipton hauled him through the hatch. "Jules is off with the raft and the fishing vessel. Don't hang around."

"Aye, aye," Tyrell said, and he headed down the corridor for the stairwell.

A moment later Schade hauled himself up, and Lipton helped him through.

"Come on," Lipton shouted, but Schade turned back.

"Mr. McGarvey is coming," he answered, and McGarvey's bulky form appeared in the hatchway. Schade helped him the rest of the way up.

"Is that everybody?" McGarvey asked.

"Yes, sir," Schade said. He was a solidly built twenty-seven-year-old.

"Then what the hell are we waiting for? I don't want to go swimming down here again."

"Aye, aye, sir," Schade said, and Lipton led the way back up as the ship continued to list to port.

At the top, the angle of the list was so severe they couldn't make it to the high side to starboard. Instead they slid down the corridor and had to dive under the water in order to clear the hatch to the outside, and then swim another thirty yards or so to make sure they would be well clear of the ship's superstructure when she rolled.

Lipton broke the surface and turned back in time to see the ship roll completely over and immediately start down by the stern. McGarvey had already surfaced and he was watching the distant shoreline of the island, not the ship, although it was nearly impossible to see much of anything. The weather had completely closed in over the past few minutes and a light drizzle had begun to fall.

Tyrell and the others were treading water a dozen yards away, and Schade remained a few feet behind and to McGarvey's left.

Lipton swam over to them. "Let's go."

The *Dhodhóni* was a hundred yards off to the northeast, the rubber raft in tow, and she was beginning to swing around toward them.

"Just a second, sir," Schade answered. He too was watching the shoreline.

Lipton followed their gaze, but he couldn't make out much of anything, except that the island seemed to be a darker mass that rose up out of the near-blackness of the sea.

"There," McGarvey said softly. He studied the shoreline for another moment or two, then turned around.

"What is it?" Lipton asked. "I didn't see a thing."

"There was a light showing high up on one of the cliffs."

"So?"

"It went out," McGarvey said.

Lipton shook his head, not understanding, but then his attention was diverted back to the ship. The bows were rising very fast now, up out of the water. For a long second or two the *Thaxos* seemed to hang on her tail, until she slipped quietly beneath the sea, the waves and eddy currents washing past the men, bouncing them in the water.

For a very long time, it seemed, the night was absolutely still, until they began to hear the hiss of the falling rain and in the distance the faint burble of the *Dhodhóni's* engine turning over at idle speed as she headed toward them.

On McGarvey's insistence they kept the *Dhodhóni* between them and the island as they boarded her, which further puzzled Lipton. But for the moment he was willing to go along with almost anything. His respect was growing by leaps and bounds. He'd been told about McGarvey, but nothing he'd heard had prepared him for the actual man. Besides, they owed him.

"No lights," McGarvey whispered. "And keep out of sight."

"What are you talking about?" Lipton asked.

"Spranger's people on the island were waiting for the *Thaxos* to go down, and now they're watching us through starlight scopes."

"Shit," Lipton swore half under his breath. He should have seen it earlier. "The lights on the monastery went out so that they could use the night optics. It proved that they were watching."

"That's what I figure," McGarvey said. "But they couldn't have seen you or your people dressed the way you are, and so long as they don't spot a lot of movement aboard this boat they'll never suspect that you're here."

"But they'll know that someone survived. Why not the one we neutralized?"

"There were two of them," McGarvey said. "And by now they would have radioed their mission accomplished."

"So Spranger knows that you're alive."

McGarvey nodded.

Lipton and Tyrell exchanged glances. They, along with McGarvey and Schade, were huddled on the bridge, Joslow still at the wheel. The engine was at dead idle, and they were barely moving against the swells.

"It doesn't look as if we'll be able to do much for you in that case, Mr. McGarvey," Lipton said. "My orders specifically forbid me to engage in any action on Greek soil. We cannot go ashore. And considering what has already happened, and the fact the Spranger has set a trap for you, I would suggest you go no further. Washington can handle it diplomatically."

"It's my wife and daughter on that island, Lieutenant," McGarvey said mildly, but the expression on his face, in his eyes, made Lipton shiver involuntarily.

"I understand, but I won't be able to help you."

"Can you communicate with Washington via your ship? Or did you come in from a base on the mainland?"

"We're off the *Nimitz* group just southwest of Crete."

"Have they got a LAMPS III up for you?"

Again Lipton and Tyrell exchanged glances. The man knew a lot for someone no longer on the regular payroll. But then to survive as long as he had, McGarvey would have to have the knowledge.

"Yes, sir."

"Get a message to Langley that Spranger and K-1 are holding my wife and daughter on the island in the monastery . . . give them map coordinates if you would. Tell them I'm returning to the port of Thira, and from there overland to the monastery."

"Sir?" Schade asked, but Lipton motioned him off.

"What can we do?" Lipton asked.

"Stand by out here in case they try to make a run for it."

Lipton thought it out for a second or two. They'd have to stay on station probably until dawn. In the rain they would be wet and miserable. But he nodded.

"It's going to take me a couple hours to get ashore, and maybe that long to make it back to the monastery. In the meantime your people can give you updates on my position. I'll carry the walkie-talkie with me."

"As soon as you're in position we'll start looking for the fireworks."

"Something like that," McGarvey replied, smiling wryly.

"I'd like to come with you, sir," Schade said.

"Negative," Lipton said immediately.

"Sir, Mr. McGarvey will have big odds against him on the island. I'll leave my ID, and go as a civilian. I'll take full responsibility."

"Goddamnit, Bobby. I've got my orders."

"I'll go AWOL if necessary, sir."

"I'll do it alone," McGarvey cut him off. "It's my fight, not yours."

"You heard the man," Lipton said. He stuck out his hand and McGarvey took it. "Good luck."

"Thanks, Lieutenant, but I prefer to make my own."

52

The narrow stairway that led five hundred feet down to the stone dock from the monastery had been cut from the living rock late in the seventeenth century, and countless pairs of sandal-shod feet had worn grooves into the steps. It followed the inside of a huge crack in the cliff face that wasn't visible from the sea.

Dürenmatt and the other three men were huddled out of the rain just within a ten-yard-wide overhang. A starlight scope set up on a tripod was trained out to sea.

"Any sign of him yet?" Spranger asked when he reached the bottom.

The four men looked up, startled. They hadn't heard him coming. Nobody said a thing.

"How far off is he?" Spranger asked. He was excited now that he was about to come face-to-face with McGarvey.

"Something's gone wrong, General," Dürenmatt said worriedly.

"What are you talking about?"

"The *Thaxos* went down, but the fishing vessel is heading away from, not toward us."

"Impossible!"

"See for yourself, Herr General," Lessing said, stepping away from the starlight scope.

Spranger hesitated for a moment. He didn't want to believe what he was hearing. He couldn't believe it. McGarvey's ex-wife and daughter were here. The man knew they were here. He had to respond. He had to come here to rescue them.

"Nothing from the boat?" he asked.

"If Karamanlis and that other fool had been successful we would have heard from them by now," Dürenmatt said. He glanced out toward the dark horizon. "If that sonofabitch is going for help we'll be cornered here."

"The chopper is ready to fly."

"Pardon me, General, but if the CIA puts pressure on the Greek government we might be grounded."

Spranger forced himself to calm down. This had become too personal, he decided. McGarvey was not the dark man, he was nothing more than an ex-CIA field officer. A good one, an assassin, but just another man for all of it. An impediment to the main plan, nothing more. And he would be eliminated tonight, one way or another.

Looking through the starlight scope he felt just a moment's unease, recalling his conversation with Yegenni Radvonska in Rome. "*I'd go one-on-one with him,*" Spranger had told the KGB *rezident*. "*You would lose,*" the man said.

At first he could make out little or nothing in the drizzle and mist.

"To the left," Lessing prompted at his shoulder.

Then he had it. The *Dhodhóni* was definitely heading away from them, back toward the north point of the island.

Spranger slowly swept the powerful night-vision scope across the open water to the approximate position where the *Thaxos* had gone down in two hundred feet of water. The scope was Russian-made, but the light-intensifying electronic circuitry had come from M.I.T.

There was nothing to be seen in the darkness. But the scope was just a machine and could not perform miracles. McGarvey could be out there in the water, perhaps in a rubber raft, heading this way.

He swept the scope back toward the departing *Dhodhóni,* which had altered course to clear the headland. Somebody had to be piloting it.

McGarvey was returning to Thira.

Spranger straightened up. "He's returning to port," he said.

"Let's go to the chopper now, General," Dürenmatt said.

"Are you frightened of this man? All of you, against one man?"

"After what the Russians told us, and what he did in Tokyo, and now . . ." Dürenmatt let it trail off.

"He's going for help, Herr General," Lessing said.

Everyone was looking at Spranger. He shook his head. "He won't ask for help. He'll show up in Thira, and then come here by land."

"Call the port. Warn Theotokis."

"I think not." Spranger smiled and shook his head. "The Greek owns this island. He's told us often enough. Let's leave it to him. If he kills McGarvey for us, well and good. If not, we'll do the job ourselves when he shows up here."

Dürenmatt started to protest, but Spranger held him off.

"He will come here, Peter. Tonight. And we will kill him. I don't want a big fuss made in town."

Again Dürenmatt looked out to sea. "The sooner we are off this island and safely in Athens where we can disperse, the better I will feel."

"We'll all feel better when we've taken care of this irritation," Spranger said, and he ignored the odd look the other man gave him. "I want one man down here, and the rest up top." He too glanced out to the dark sea. "He's received a two- or three-hour stay of execution, and given us a rest, nothing more."

The only light in the small cell came from the open door to the corridor. Liese Egk, wearing a dark, one-piece nylon jumpsuit, the front zipper pulled low, leaned against the doorframe, an indolent expression on her face. She'd been standing there, unmoving, unspeaking, for the past ten minutes, and Kathleen, huddled on her bunk, had become agitated. Elizabeth, however, standing by the small window, understood that the woman wanted to provoke them. It was a game.

"What do you want?" Kathleen asked in a shaky voice, finally breaking the silence.

Liese grinned, her teeth perfectly even, dazzlingly white. "Your daughter. She and I are lovers, didn't you know?"

Kathleen's hands went to her mouth. She was shivering.

"The drugs have cleared out of my system," Elizabeth said, matching the German woman's grin. It was bravado, but the gesture made her feel a little better.

Liese's smile broadened. "I'm glad to hear it, little girl. I like a partner with, what do you call it? With spunk."

"You'll need to kill me first."

"Elizabeth!" her mother cried.

"Not you," Liese said. She took a nine-inch stiletto from under her jumpsuit at the nape of her neck. "But if I killed your mother . . . If I threatened to carve my name on her chest then you might cooperate. Maybe?"

"My God," Kathleen screeched. "Are you a monster? Are you crazy?"

Liese eyed her calmly. "Yes. I think I probably am both, and more. So, you see, I wouldn't hesitate to carry out my threat."

Elizabeth stepped away from the window, placing herself between her mother and Liese. "You'll have to go through me first."

"Little girl, you can't imagine how easy that would be for me."

Spranger entered the great hall section of the father superior's residence and was headed for the stairs to the dormitory area where the women were being held when he heard his name being called. The sound came from a distance, distorted.

He stopped in mid-stride and turned around, cocking his head to listen.

"Spranger, I'm coming for you."

His walkie-talkie lay on the table, its processing light winking red.

"Spranger, do you copy? I'm coming for you."

It was McGarvey. Spranger cautiously approached the table. He'd never heard the man's voice, he'd never met the American, but he knew it was McGarvey. He started to reach out, but his hand stopped almost of its own volition.

"Do you hear me, you son of a bitch? I'm on my way."

Spranger picked up the walkie-talkie and keyed the talk switch. "I'm waiting," he said softly, and he hit the transmit button.

53

Any lingering doubts McGarvey may have entertained about Kathleen and Elizabeth being on the island left him with Spranger's two words. He resisted the urge to get back on the walkie-talkie and warn the man what would happen if any harm came to them. The German knew of him; undoubtedly he still had connections with the KGB, which maintained an extensive file.

Impatiently he advanced the throttle all the way forward to its stop, and the fishing boat surged ahead, her bows crashing into the rising seas as they rounded the north point.

He'd been stupid to radio them. By now the Germans would have to know that he was on his way back to Thira. They had undoubtedly been watching from the monastery. They would warn Theotokis, who would be preparing a reception committee on the docks.

For a few moments he toyed with Lipton's suggestion that he stand off and call for help. Spranger and his people could be isolated on the north end of the island. They would not be able to escape.

But Spranger was capable of revenge. We would not allow himself to be captured, and before he was cut down he would make certain that Kathleen and Elizabeth died.

McGarvey's jaw tightened. It would do no good to send Lipton's assault force onto the island. Spranger had set this trap to lure

McGarvey out of Japan and kill him. This would be a one-on-one fight. Which suited McGarvey just fine.

Ten minutes later, the seas calmed as he came into the temporary lee of a small uninhabited volcanic island to the west, and McGarvey lashed the wheel amidships so that the boat would maintain its course unattended for a minute or so.

Retrieving his leather overnight bag from a corner of the wheelhouse, he took out a spare clip of ammunition and reloaded his Walther.

Next he took the walkie-talkie out onto the narrow starboard walkway and without hesitation tossed it overboard. There would be no farther communication between him and the STASI leader, nor would the Agency be able to track him any longer.

He was on his own, and it was better like this. "Excess baggage is the bane of the field officer." It was axiomatic.

Back inside, he caught a glimpse of Thira's lights to the southeast. He unlashed the wheel, made sure the throttle was all the way forward, and steered directly for the port, every muscle in his body, every fiber of his being girding for the upcoming fight.

Big swells were running into the harbor, making all the fishing boats on moorings and at the docks work hard against their restraining lines. Even the sleek 180-foot Athens morning ferry tied up along the main quay moved nervously, the car tires dangling from her port side protecting her hull from damage against the concrete dock.

It was very late. No traffic, vehicular or pedestrian, moved along the quay, or along the main street that led up into the town proper. The rain had intensified, and as McGarvey closed with the quay a hundred yards to the north of the big ferry boat, he could see the drops bouncing off the cobblestones and the red tile roofs.

Unaccountably the rain made him sad, and even frightened; not for himself, for his own personal safety, but for Kathleen and Elizabeth and what this experience would do to them.

Their lives would forever be altered. He was less concerned about Elizabeth's mental well-being. If anyone could bounce back it would be she. She was very strong, her will almost as fierce as his own. But Kathleen wasn't so strong. She had been incapable of staying married to him because of the tension his absences caused her. Now she was in the middle of an operation, her life and the life of her daughter in jeopardy. She wouldn't fare so well, no matter the outcome, and he was frankly worried about her.

The rising wind was out of the east, shoving the boats against the docks. Twenty yards out, McGarvey cut the engine, revved it in reverse to slow his rate of approach, then shut the engine off, allowing the *Dhodhóni* to drift the rest of the way. He didn't bother with dock lines, or with the rubber tires stacked on deck, ready for fending off.

On deck he braced himself as the boat slammed into the quay with a sickening crunch. She bounced away; and immediately the wind and swells smashed her into the concrete dock again. Within an hour she would probably batter herself to death. But it didn't matter; Karamanlis was dead, and McGarvey wouldn't be coming back this way.

Timing his move with the motion of the boat, he leaped up onto the dock and darted directly across the quay into the shadows along the line of warehouses. Nothing moved. There were no shots. Only the wind moaning in the rigging of the boats, the protesting squeal of rubber tires being crushed against the docks, and the *Dhodhóni* beating herself against the unyielding concrete, disturbed the night.

Keeping to the shadows but moving fast, McGarvey made his way the block and a half to the taverna where Karamanlis had taken him to see Uncle Constantine. It was the only establishment open on the docks so far as McGarvey was able to tell. No lights showed from any of the windows here, and only a hazy yellow glow spread from the open taverna door.

McGarvey turned and hurried around the block behind the taverna where he found an unlocked gate into a long, narrow courtyard beside what appeared to be an apartment building. The courtyard was muddy and filled with trash. He picked his way down its length, where he had to force another tall gate that opened into a passageway exposed to the sky. A trough had been set into the cobblestones, no doubt for use as an open sewer in ancient times, and, by the smells, still being used for the same purpose today.

Stepping across the trough, he tried the back door into the taverna. It opened silently on well-oiled hinges, as he'd hoped it would. During his interview with Theotokis, McGarvey had watched the comings and goings of the Mafia boss's people. More than half of them had used the back door. It was a regular route for them, apparently, when they wanted to come or go unnoticed by an observer on the docks.

He found himself in a tiny kitchen area, a pantry to his left and a stone urinal trough in a tiny room to the right. A dim light came from behind the copper bar through a swinging door.

McGarvey watched for a moment. Constantine Theotokis was seated alone at a back table. He was reading a newspaper, a bottle of red wine and a single glass in front of him. Obviously he was waiting for someone. Probably Karamanlis and Papagos to return and tell him what had happened.

A thick-necked man with an enormous belly leaned against the bar, apparently reading over Theotokis's shoulder. A double-barrel sawed-off shotgun, its pistol grip stock well used and shining dully in the light, lay on the bar at the man's back. These two were waiting for trouble.

McGarvey took out his Walther, switched the safety catch to the off position, cocked the hammer and stepped through the swinging doors.

The big man spun around and started to grab for the shotgun, but McGarvey was across to him in two steps, the Walther pointed directly at the man's face.

"Stand down," McGarvey said softly.

Theotokis was looking over his shoulder at them, his body absolutely still.

"If need be I'll kill you both. Believe me, I don't care one way or the other."

"Do as he says, Georgios," Theotokis instructed his bodyguard. "I believe Mr. McGarvey is a man who will listen to reason."

54

McGarvey rode in the back seat of the battered Land Rover, bracing himself as best he could as they bounced slowly over the extremely rough dirt track. Theotokis sat in the front passenger seat while his bodyguard drove. As the crow flew it was barely three and a half miles from Thira to the monastery, but the track led over the spine of the island, rising to an elevation of more than 1,600 feet.

It had been simple to convince them to betray Spranger by bringing McGarvey out here. It was either that or be killed. Theotokis had had the intelligence to read that much from McGarvey's eyes.

Georgios the bodyguard, however, had watched McGarvey very closely for any sign of weakness, for an opening, no matter how small, that he could take advantage of. He wasn't a Santorinian. McGarvey would have been willing to bet that the man had learned his trade on the streets and back alleys of Athens or some other big city.

Over the central massif, the stoney path plunged into a valley, and then started immediately up again to the crest of a much lower hill. They were nearing the top.

"How much farther?" McGarvey asked.

Georgios glanced at his reflection in the rearview mirror, but then turned back to his driving, which was difficult along the narrow track and made more dangerous by the wind and rain.

"The church is just on the other side of this hill," Theotokis said. "We will drop you off at the summit, and from there it is only a small walk of perhaps less than a half kilometer."

"Turn off the headlights, and stop here," McGarvey said.

Again Georgios looked at him in the rearview mirror. "What?" he grumbled.

McGarvey jammed the barrel of his pistol into the side of the big man's head. "Do it now," he ordered.

Georgios complied immediately, and as they lurched to a halt, their lights out, they could suddenly hear the wind shrieking around the volcanic rock outcroppings just above them, and the driven rain hammering against the car.

"Do you mean to kill us?" Theotokis asked.

"If I see you again, I will," McGarvey said. "Now you and your friend are returning to Thira."

"As you wish . . ."

"On foot," McGarvey said. "You're both getting out on the passenger side."

Georgios started to turn, but McGarvey jabbed harder with the pistol barrel. "Keep your hands in plain sight, and your eyes forward."

"Do as you're told," Theotokis sighed. "The little walk will certainly be uncomfortable, but considering the alternatives . . ."

McGarvey opened his door on the passenger side and directed Theotokis to do the same.

"Carefully now."

"We will do exactly as you tell us, Mr. McGarvey, you may believe that." Theotokis got out of the car, and his bodyguard slid across the seat behind him and climbed out.

McGarvey got out and stepped a few feet off the track. "Take off your shoes and socks." He had to shout to be heard over the wind.

"That's inhuman," Theotokis protested.

"It's late," McGarvey shouted. "I'm tired. I'm out of patience. And I'm going to kill again for what has been done to my wife and daughter."

"I see your point," the Greek said and he and Georgios removed their shoes and socks.

"Now, go," McGarvey said.

Georgios stared at him for a long time, as if he were trying to memorize McGarvey's face, his eyes narrowed, his lips compressed. "Ernst and his people will kill you," he said. "And in the morning I shall piss on your body."

The rain seemed to intensify as the two Greek mafioso picked their way down the rock-strewn path. McGarvey watched until they disappeared into the darkness. In another age he might have killed them for their part in Spranger's operation. But they were only little people; petty hoods who had no conception of the larger issues, or any desire to know. And McGarvey was finding that he was finally losing his stomach for the business.

He turned and looked up the hill in the direction the Land Rover was pointed. He had lost his stomach for the kill except for Spranger and men of his ilk. He'd been told repeatedly that wherever he turned up trouble would almost certainly develop. Well, Spranger had lured him here. And this night there would be trouble. The man had stepped over the line. Way over the line.

McGarvey holstered his gun, and got behind the Land Rover's wheel. The engine ticked over softly, and for a second longer he hesitated, watching in the rearview mirror for any sign that Georgios or his boss had doubled back. A fleeting thought passed through his head: He wondered how he had gotten to this point in his life from where he had started on his parents' ranch in Kansas.

There were no simple answers, he told himself. Or at least none that he wanted to face just now. But they would come. They would come.

The crest of the hill was about two hundred yards farther up the final slope. He drove to a spot just below it, and picked his way to the top on foot. They knew he was coming and they would be watching for him. He didn't want to be spotted just yet. But there was little or nothing to be seen except for what appeared to be an indistinct mass below.

He checked his watch. It was a few minutes after four, dawn still about two hours off. Even then, if the weather continued overcast and rainy, he'd have an additional half hour or more of covering darkness.

Back at the Land Rover, he popped the hood and, working by feel alone, found the ignition coil and removed the wire between it and the distributor cap. He pocketed it and the keys. Now no one would be able to take the vehicle, but on the way out he could get it started in less than a half minute if need be. There was no telling what shape Kathleen and Elizabeth might be in. It was possible, even likely, that they would not be able to travel very far on foot.

Out of Thira they had driven slowly to the northeast, which meant the sea was now straight ahead and to the right. Coming around the headland earlier this evening with Karamanlis and Papagos, before the weather had completely closed in, he'd seen the tall cliffs that rose directly out of the sea along this section of the island's coast. The monastery was perched on the edge of the cliffs. There would be a path down to the sea, but Lipton's team would be blocking that egress, and the weather was too bad for them to be picked up by air. Which left by land.

They'd be expecting him to show up over the hill along the track, which meant they'd probably be waiting in the darkness on either side of the path. It was time then to even the odds.

He screwed the can-type silencer on the end of the Walther's barrel, made certain a round was in the firing chamber and, keeping well below the crest of the hill, struck off to the east, directly toward the edge of the cliffs.

In terms of vegetation very little grew up here. The ground was mostly broken-up volcanic rock and pebbles ranging in size from a marble to a basketball. Picking his way carefully across the debris field he was reminded of another night in Iceland. The weather was warmer here, but the landscapes were similar; barren, apparently lifeless, almost lunar.

About fifty yards off the track he scrambled silently back up to the crest of the hill, and keeping low peered over the top.

He remained crouched in the darkness for a full two minutes slowly sweeping the darkness left to right for any sign whatsoever that anyone was down there; a noise, the glowing tip of a cigarette, the beam of a flashlight. But these men were STASI-trained professionals. They did not make such mistakes, especially not under Spranger's command. But they were out there. He could almost sense them.

Something moved behind him, and he froze. A rock against a rock. A pebble rolling down the hill, the noise almost immediately swallowed by the shrieking wind.

The sound did not come again, but McGarvey knew it hadn't been his imagination. Someone was back there all right. Probably Theotokis or his bodyguard. Possibly one of Spranger's people.

Still keeping low, but making no indication that he had heard something, he slipped over the crest of the hill, and a few yards on the other side, flattened himself behind an outcropping of rock, his pistol at his side.

A half minute later a figure dressed in black appeared at the top of the hill, hesitated just a moment, then started down.

McGarvey tensed. He wanted this one alive if possible. If he could learn the layout of the monastery and exactly where Kathleen and Elizabeth were being held it would be extremely helpful.

He pressed himself farther back into the deeper darkness as the black-suited figure came even with him. When the man passed, McGarvey stepped out, hooked his free arm around the man's neck and pulled him down, laying the muzzle of the silencer against his cheek.

"Make a noise and I'll kill you . . . ." McGarvey was saying, when he recognized Bob Schade, Lipton's man who'd wanted to tag along.

McGarvey released him, pointing the Walther away as he uncocked the hammer.

"Where is the rest of the team?"

"On the water where you left them," Schade said, sitting up.

"How the hell did you get here?"

"I stowed away on the fishing boat."

McGarvey's eyes narrowed. "You followed me to the taverna?"

"Yes, sir."

"How about up the mountain? How'd you find a vehicle?"

"I didn't," the young man said.

"Well how the hell did you get up here?"

"I ran."

McGarvey sat back on his heels. "You ran," he said, amazed. The kid wasn't even out of breath.

"Yes, sir. But I met the two men who took you up here. They were barefoot and pretty well pissed off. Especially the big one."

"Did you let them pass?"

"I would have, Mr. McGarvey, except I wasn't expecting them, and they spotted me. The old man ordered the other one to kill me. They both seemed to think it was important."

McGarvey glanced reflexively toward the crest of the hill. "What happened?"

"I had to . . . eliminate them, sir."

McGarvey looked sharply at the young man. "I didn't hear any shots."

"My weapon is silenced, sir. But I didn't use it. I had to take them out by hand. There wasn't any time, or room."

"I see," McGarvey said, impressed. The kid was like a dangerous puppy: Innocent and eager, but deadly. "What about your military ID?"

Schade shrugged. "I must have lost it somewhere, I guess."

"Lipton will have your ass."

Again Schade shrugged. "I owe you one."

"Well, there's no doubt that you can take care of yourself," McGarvey said. "But I want you to listen up now. Spranger is holding my wife and daughter to get at me. But he's not a stupid man. He's kept his life and his freedom this long by meticulous planning and ruthlessness. Which means that he's convinced himself that he's going to kill me tonight, and then make his escape. He's stacked the odds in his favor, and we've got no idea what preparations he's made."

"Yes, sir." Schade looked very serious.

"But he's going to make a mistake."

"Sir?"

"He's made this personal. He wants to kill me himself. Or he wants to be right there when I know I've lost."

Sudden understanding dawned on Schade's face. "You tossed the walkie-talkie overboard. You talked to him?"

McGarvey nodded. "You still want in?"

"You bet," Schade said eagerly.

"I want to take them out if we can do it without raising the alarm. Otherwise we'll skirt their positions and take care of them on the way back out. Wherever they're holding my wife and daughter will be booby-trapped. I want to get them out of there first."

Schade nodded. He took out a long, wicked-looking dagger, the blade serrated along both edges, blood at the base of the haft, and headed out a few yards to McGarvey's right, down the hill toward the cliffs. A second or two later McGarvey followed.

Within a couple hundred yards they were able to distinguish the deconsecrated church and a half-dozen other buildings, all of them substantially constructed of native stone, with steeply pitched roofs and battlements. In ancient times people took their religion seriously. This monastery was as much a fortress as it was a church. Faith had been defended here, and now the place was being used for the opposite purpose.

McGarvey pulled up short, motioning for Schade to do the same. He'd heard a muffled cough off to the left. For several long seconds he waited and watched, finally picking out a figure standing behind a pile of rocks that formed a ten-foot-tall obelisk. The guard raised a rifle, equipped with what appeared to be a very large spotting scope, and pointed it up the hill toward the track from town.

Schade edged silently to McGarvey's side and watched for a second or two. The guard's position was about thirty feet from where they crouched.

"A night spotting scope?" he asked softly.

"I think so," McGarvey whispered. "I want him out of there. Can you get in close enough to take him with your knife?"

"Yes, sir," Schade said.

"Keep to his right. I'll cover you from here. But I won't fire unless there's no other choice."

"Right," Schade replied, and he headed across, slowly, silently, like a night animal on the prowl with deadly intent.

There might be others watching, but this one had to be taken out. The starlight scope-equipped rifle made him too dangerous.

McGarvey switched the safety off, cocked the Walther's hammer and centered his sights on the guard's back. The pistol was silenced, but the sound could be heard and recognized for what it was at a respectable distance.

Fifteen feet out, Schade froze.

The guard stepped back, looked toward the church for a moment, then shook his head and leaned up against the obelisk. It was clear he was nervous, but he was probably also cold, wet, tired and bored.

Schade was stuck. The guard had only to turn his head slightly and he would be looking right at the young man.

But they had a second, potentially even more serious problem. The guard had looked up toward the church, as if he'd been looking for *someone*. Another guard watching from a vantage point in the church? Even now that one could be taking a bead on Schade, who would show up in a night scope like a duck in a shooting gallery.

The guard behind the obelisk scratched his nose and started to turn away, when he evidently saw something out of the corner of his eye. He turned abruptly and looked directly at Schade.

For a second he was too startled to move, but the moment

Schade's knife hand began to come up, the spell was broken and the man opened his mouth to shout a warning as he brought the Russian-made Kalashnikov assault rifle around.

McGarvey jumped up and fired two shots in rapid succession, the first hitting the guard in the throat, blood erupting from an artery in a long spurt, and the second hitting his chest, driving him off his feet before he had a chance to utter a sound.

Dropping down, McGarvey immediately switched his aim toward the church, in the direction the downed guard had looked.

Schade did the same, flattening himself against the rock-strewn ground, his silenced .22 automatic pistol in hand.

Nothing moved, and there was no answering fire. If someone had been there, they were gone now, or incredibly, they had seen or heard nothing.

Only the wind and the pattering rain made any noise, until McGarvey started to rise when he heard the distinctive pop of an unsilenced automatic weapon from somewhere in the distance. Below, possibly at the base of the cliffs beneath the church.

"What the hell was that?" he muttered as he and Schade headed in a dead run the last fifty yards or so to the main doors into the church's nave.

55

"What the hell was that?" Lipton demanded. He'd been on the radio copying the latest weather report from Meteorology aboard the *Nimitz* when the sea twenty yards out erupted in a dozen miniature geysers.

"We're under fire," Tyrell answered urgently.

Tony Reid hurriedly started the outboard. Everyone else had their weapons out. Tyrell was studying the base of the cliffs one thousand yards away.

"Belay the motor, Tony," Lipton whispered. "Even with a night spotting scope they can't be sure they see us, but they might be able to hear something."

A little closer, the water to their left, geysered again. This time Lipton estimated fifteen or twenty rounds had been fired, perhaps a few more.

"If he's firing a Kalashnikov, we're at his extreme range," Tyrell said.

"He might get lucky," Lipton said. "Can you spot him?"

"No, but I'd say he was low, maybe right on the water at the base of the cliff."

"A dock?"

"Probably." Tyrell looked up. "It's your call, Ed, but we can't stay here like this. Either pull back, or . . ."

"Or go ashore," Lipton finished it for his number two. They'd been sitting out here for hours waiting for something to happen and now that it had, it was the wrong thing. If Spranger's group was trying to break out, they'd be on the water, a hell of a lot closer, and they'd be using a lot more firepower.

Whoever was firing at them was probably a lookout stationed on the dock. A chance increase in the ambient light level had come at the same moment the guard was looking in their direction, and he'd spotted something. Or thought he had.

They came under fire again, this time the hits coming in a wide pattern off to their right, but much closer. The shooter was finding their range.

They'd received word from Operations aboard the *Nimitz* that the EPIRB signal from McGarvey's walkie-talkie had began to fade before he had reached the port of Thira, and less than a minute later it had cut off completely.

Commander Rheinholtz's best guess was that McGarvey had tossed the device overboard.

"If the sonofabitch wants to do it on his own, then let him," the chief of Air Operations had radioed.

"I'd like to remain on station for a bit longer," Lipton had asked.

The airwaves were silent for a long moment, as Rheinholtz pondered his request. Of course he hadn't told his boss that Schade was missing. There would be hell to pay if the *Nimitz* CAO knew.

"I want you out of there well before dawn, Lieutenant," Rheinholtz radioed. "Acknowledge."

"Aye, aye, Commander," Lipton replied.

"Keep us posted."

"Will do."

Lipton checked his watch. Dawn was less than two hours from now. They were running out of time. Obviously McGarvey had reached the port, but what then? Had he and Schade found a way out to the monastery? Had they attacked from the land side?

The possibilities were nearly endless. But it was very likely that his ex-wife and daughter were still being held. That situation had not changed.

"Ed?" Tyrell prompted.

Another spray of fire from the shooter on the island hit the water, this time close enough to get them wet.

"Bob is probably with McGarvey over there," he said. "We can't leave them."

His men were watching him closely, grim, expectant expressions on their faces.

"We're going in," Lipton said, making his decision. "Secure your weapons and check your rebreathers."

Spranger couldn't see a thing.

He looked up from the starlight scope and glared at Bruno Lessing, who'd done the shooting. The man was a professional;

steady, reliable. It wasn't like him to fire at phantoms. But there was nothing out there.

"I'm telling you, General, that I saw a small dark boat, perhaps a rubber raft, about nine hundred meters out. Three . . . maybe four men."

"I don't see them now," Spranger said, glancing again across the dark sea. If anything the night had deepened as the rain increased, though dawn would be here in less than two hours. He wanted to be gone by then. The pilot had assured him that despite the weather, as long as they had a little daylight he could get them up to Athens. The chopper was ready to fly. All that was needed was to remove the camouflage canopy covering the machine, and undo the tie-downs on the undercarriage and the rotor blades.

"They could be American Special Forces," Lessing was saying nervously. "McGarvey could have called for help."

"Not him," Spranger disagreed. "We saw the *Dhodhóni* heading back to Thira. He's definitely coming here overland."

"Pardon me, Herr General, but you cannot possibly know enough about the man to form such a judgment. Not so soon after you first learned of him."

Spranger had handpicked his people from the survivors of East Berlin. They were the best of the best. All of them, Lessing included, were respectful of his authority, but no one was frightened or intimidated by him, which was as it should be.

But with this now, Lessing could not be right. Because if he was, they were in very deep trouble.

Once again he bent over the scope and peered through the eyepiece. The light intensification circuitry gave the surface of the sea a gray, ghostly cast. But as before there was nothing out there. Absolutely nothing.

"You may be right, Bruno, but it does not alter the fact I can't see a thing now," Spranger said. He stepped aside. "Take a look for yourself."

After a moment, Lessing bent to the scope, and studied the distant darkness for several long seconds. When he looked up he still did not seemed convinced. "I'm truly sorry, Herr General. You are correct, there is nothing out there now. But I did see something."

"Could have been a piece of flotsam, or even a glitch in the little black box." Still Spranger's eyes were drawn to the sea, a slight edge of fear creeping into his head. *With McGarvey, you should expect the unexpected.*

He'd carried the walkie-talkie down with him in case McGarvey decided to make contact again. Dürenmatt came on.

"Ernst, where are you?"

Spranger unslung his comms unit. "On the dock. Bruno thought he saw something, so he fired at it."

"McGarvey is here," Dürenmatt responded so quickly he stepped on some of Spranger's transmission.

"Say again, Peter."

"I said, McGarvey is here. Walther is down. I left my position for less than a minute to take a piss and when I returned, he was down. From where I'm standing I can see that he took at least one hit."

"I'm on my way," Spranger shouted. The detonator was still upstairs in the great room.

"What about me?" Lessing demanded.

"We're getting out of here. If you don't hear from me in the next ten minutes, go to the chopper. But *Gott im Himmel*, Bruno, keep your eyes open down here."

Lipton and his five SEALS were in the water. They'd deflated their boat, and buoyed it just beneath the surface with a sea anchor. Tyrell carried a portable LORAN set, which, although it weighed less than twelve ounces, could bring them back to within fifty feet of the exact spot so they could retrieve their gear.

The antenna mast on Lipton's communications radio was fully extended for maximum range. The LAMPS III chopper would be on station out of visual range somewhere just over the horizon to pick up his radio transmissions and relay them to Operations aboard the *Nimitz*.

"Saturn, Saturn, this is Mercury, acknowledge," he radioed.

Commander Rheinholtz responded immediately. "This is Saturn."

"We're going in."

"Negative, Mercury. Negative."

"We're taking fire, so we must assume that Brightstar is in trouble and the subjects are in jeopardy. We have no other choice."

The radio was silent. Lipton could imagine Rheinholtz on the horn with Washington trying to get a reading on this latest development. But that would take time: Too much time.

Lipton keyed his radio. "Will advise," he said. "Mercury out." He switched off the transmitter, sealed it in its waterproof case, and on signal, he and his four SEALS submerged to a depth of ten feet, and on his lead made their way directly to the island.

At least they didn't have the German woman to contend with, Elizabeth thought as she tried to pick out something, anything, in the black night from her window. But there was nothing out there, nor had there been any further shooting.

Their leader, the one they called Ernst, had taken the woman away. But that had been hours ago. Until the gunfire over the past two or three minutes there had been nothing. They had not been given food or water, but they had not been bothered again.

"Do you see anything, Elizabeth?" her mother asked, in a weak, frightened voice.

Elizabeth shook her head and came away from the window. Her heart was hammering and she was having a little trouble catching

her breath. It was her father they'd been shooting at, she was
convinced of it. Just as she knew that she was going to have to warn
him about the explosives planted in the wall just below their cell.

She put her ear to the door and held her breath to listen. But
there were no sounds from the other side. Nothing. No more
shooting, no sounds of running footsteps, no shouting, not a
sound.

Stepping back she bunched up her fists and hammered them
against the thick, wooden door. "Father," she screeched. "Father!
Are you there?"

56

The sudden cessation of gunfire seemed even more ominous than its start. The first shots had echoed off the church walls nearly two minutes ago, but now there was nothing, no returning gunfire.

McGarvey and Schade pulled up just within the apse where the altar had once stood and looked out the narrow window into a broad courtyard area, what might have been the monastery's kitchen garden in ancient times.

Two men were hurriedly removing a camouflage tarp from a large helicopter with Greek markings. Their weapons, a pair of Kalashnikov assault rifles, were propped against a fuel drum eight or ten feet behind them.

So far as McGarvey could tell there were no others standing guard with them, but it was clear that they were in a big hurry to get out of here despite the rain and the strong winds which tore at the big sheet of canvas. Flying would be an iffy proposition at best.

"Could it have been your team doing the firing?" McGarvey asked.

Schade shook his head. "That was no M-16, sir. Maybe a Kalashnikov. Besides, we've got specific orders to conduct no operations on Greek soil."

The helicopter looked like a stretched version of the old Bell Ranger. She would be capable of carrying a dozen people in addition to her pilot and copilot, and with luck and a skilled crew she'd make

Athens, or almost any point along the nearly deserted Turkish coast
to the northeast.

"If their lookouts are equipped with low-light optics they might
have spotted the raft and opened fire," Schade said.

McGarvey looked at him. "What would Lieutenant Lipton do in
response?"

"That's hard to say." Schade shrugged. "But I'd guess that he
would probably go into the water and come ashore. At least I think
he would."

"If that's the case, this chopper is the only way out," McGarvey
said. "It'd be too bad if something happened to it."

"It would probably upset them a whole lot."

"Enough to kill us, if they get the chance. It's not your fight,
kid."

"It is now, sir," Schade said. "I'll go right, you take left?"

McGarvey nodded. "Watch yourself."

They slipped out of the church through a side door off the nave.
The chopper was at least a hundred feet from them across the
courtyard. The wind and rain continued to worsen, and the two men
who were nearly finished removing the camo tarp were completely
absorbed in their task.

Keeping low, Schade moved away from the church wall, angling
around to the right, keeping his attention completely on the two
men at the helicopter.

McGarvey started to the left, holding back against the wall until
he got to a point directly behind the men, but his internal alarm
system was going off like a fire bell. Something was wrong here.
Some inner sense was telling him to pull Schade back.

Then he had it. The guard outside by the obelisk had looked
back toward the church. Somebody was here. On an upper floor.
With a clear sight line not only toward the path, but down here into
the courtyard as well!

He was about warn Schade when a Kalashnikov opened fire
from above and behind, exactly where he had just realized they were
most vulnerable, and the young man went down in a heap, taking at
least two hits.

The two men by the helicopter dropped what they were doing
and spun around. They'd been well trained. Neither of them hesitated for an instant. One sprinted for the weapons leaning against
the fuel barrel, making himself a moving target, while the other
dropped sideways, to present less of himself as a target, and dug into
his shoulder holster for his pistol.

McGarvey shot him first, one round in the man's right hip,
sending him sprawling off-balance with a cry, and the second in the
side of his head, smashing his mouth so that he aspirated his
shattered teeth.

Immediately switching his aim, McGarvey fired again, the bullet smacking into the second man's chest just as he was snatching up one of the Kalashnikovs. The force of the hit shoved him backwards, the bullet disintegrating inside his heart, killing him instantly.

Except for the wind the night fell silent.

McGarvey moved farther along the wall. The shooter would have spotted his approximate position.

Schade half rolled over and groaned.

"Stay where you are, Bob," McGarvey called urgently, and Schade stopped moving. It was impossible to tell from here exactly how badly he was hurt, but McGarvey figured he couldn't be in very good shape. By rights with two hits he should have been dead.

"Come out into the open, Mr. McGarvey, or I will kill your friend," someone said from above.

"Ernst Spranger?" McGarvey called, but he didn't think it was. The accent was German but the voice was different.

"Do as I say or I shall kill him."

"In that case I would destroy your helicopter," McGarvey shouted.

"You might damage the machine with a pistol, but repairs could be made," the East German said. He had moved too. Now his voice came from directly overhead.

"You would be delayed."

"That is of no consequence, Mr. McGarvey. You would be dead, and we would leave."

"You're forgetting something," McGarvey said, leaning out away from the wall in an effort to catch a glimpse of the man above. But he was able only to see a section of open archway.

"It's you who are forgetting something. There is only you against all of us. In addition we have your wife and daughter."

McGarvey said nothing. Instead he hurried back to the right to a spot just behind Schade. The younger man lay on his side, his gun hand stretched out ahead of him, his left hand clutched to his chest. He seemed to be saying something, but McGarvey couldn't make it out.

"Step out into the open, Mr. McGarvey, and I promise that your wife and daughter will not be harmed. We will have no further need of them once we have you."

A door on the far side of the courtyard opened with a crash and a man carrying an assault rifle burst outside.

"Peter," the man shouted at the same instant he spotted Schade, who had started to rise up on one elbow.

"Don't," McGarvey shouted.

Schade had pulled something from inside his jumpsuit and was tossing it toward the helicopter with his left hand when the man above opened fire and the man across the courtyard started to fall back.

In the last possible instant, realizing what was about to happen, McGarvey threw himself against the church wall, burying his face in the dirt and covering his head with his arms.

A tremendous thunderclap burst in the courtyard, and McGarvey was lifted off the ground two feet by the force of the explosion, the night sky lighting up as if a thousand suns had suddenly switched on.

57

Spranger managed to fall back inside the corridor as the helicopter exploded. Nevertheless a spray of burning fuel burst through the open door, scorching his left arm to the shoulder, the sleeve of his nylon jumpsuit instantly melting, his skin turning an angry red and even black in big patches.

He howled in pure, blinding agony, the searing, white-hot pain rebounding inside his head, threatening to blow off the top of his skull.

Through the momentary haze that clouded his vision, making rational thought all but impossible, he focused on Liese and the others who'd followed him up here. They were bunched in a knot, staring in horrified fascination at him, waiting for him to collapse.

But he wouldn't give them the satisfaction of seeing that their general was human. He couldn't allow it, because if he did they would no longer follow him, especially not where he was leading them and the others when they got off this island.

For a flat-footed instant, standing in the church corridor, the heat from the burning helicopter making sweat pop out all over his body, he found himself wondering if he wasn't making a colossal mistake. He'd been married once, and had one child. But that seemed like another lifetime. They had fled to the West, leaving him to face his suspicious superiors and his contemptuous colleagues.

He had no explanation, he'd told them. But even if they had

crossed to the West to trade secrets for their asylum there was nothing to worry about.

Arbeit macht frei. Work makes one free. It had been the inscription over the gates of the concentration camp at Auschwitz, and it had become the unofficial motto of the STASI.

Thirty-six hours after his wife and child had crossed the border into West Berlin, they were dead. It was winter, and the chimney of the heater in the apartment where they'd been temporarily housed by the West German authorities had backed up, deadly carbon monoxide quickly filling the rooms.

Spranger had never looked back. Never, until now, for just this moment.

He shook himself out of it, conscious that the lapse had lasted only an instant, and must have gone unnoticed by the others under the extreme circumstances. Now, because of the pain, his awareness had become almost preternatural.

"My God, Ernst, is it the helicopter?" Liese cried.

"Yes, it's gone," Spranger croaked, his voice ragged. He struggled to control himself. "But it doesn't matter. McGarvey is dead."

"Ernst, are you there?" Dürenmatt's voice came from the walkie-talkie slung over Spranger's unburned shoulder.

With difficulty he pulled it around and keyed the talk button. "We're in the dormitory corridor across from you." He pushed the transmit button.

". . . thought you were dead. The fire . . . it's everywhere. Did you see him?"

Spranger's gaze turned to his rifle which he had dropped when he'd been burned. Its stock was scorched. "What are you talking about, Peter? Where are you?"

"You don't know?" Dürenmatt screamed. "It's McGarvey, he brought someone with him. He brought help."

"Yes, I know this," Spranger radioed, although he did not, although there had been a shout from across the courtyard, and not from the one who'd tossed the grenade. Two of them out there? The one by the helicopter had surely been incinerated in the explosion. But the other . . . ?

"I'm on my way," Dürenmatt shouted breathlessly.

"We'll meet you in front. We'll have to slip out through Thira."

". . . stupid bastard! It's McGarvey! He's headed your way through the church!"

Down on the dock Bruno Lessing didn't know what to do. He'd heard the explosion, of course, and had monitored the transmissions between Spranger and Dürenmatt, so he knew that escape by air would be impossible. But he was also convinced that someone or something was coming at them from the sea, although he couldn't make out a thing from where he huddled out of the rain just within the rock alcove.

He had seen something on the water, maybe a thousand yards out, more or less, and he had fired at it.

He played with the Kalashnikov's safety catch, switching it on and then off, the metallic snick barely registering in his ears.

But then what had looked to him like a small boat and several men had simply disappeared as if it had never existed. After Spranger had left, Lessing had searched the sea again with the starlight scope with no results.

"But it was there," he muttered to himself, checking his watch again. The ten minutes were up. It was time to go, only now there was nowhere for them to go to. The chopper was no longer an option.

Spranger would get them out of this. He always had in the past, and this time would be no different. The man was nothing short of brilliant. Even though none of them had been able to figure out the real reason why they'd grabbed the two women or had brought them here, they were all equally convinced that the general knew what he was doing. With the Egk woman snapping at his heels, the man had no other choice.

Lessing grinned nervously thinking about her, and the nape of his neck prickled. She was gorgeous, but looking into her eyes was like looking through windows into hell. She might be worth a roll in the hay, but he suspected that an ordinary man would be driven absolutely mad by the experience.

He flicked the rifle's safety catch down, then up, no longer certain in which position the weapon was safetied.

East Berlin in the old days—hell, barely five years ago—had been simpler. There were safe havens. Even now they'd been offered the chance to come to Moscow, but no one was enticed. The Russians were having their problems. No safety there.

No safety anywhere, he thought glumly. Now they were even taking orders from the slant-eyed Japs. It was galling.

He caught a movement out of the corner of his eye, and he jerked to the left in time to see a man dressed all in black, water cascading from his head and shoulders, pulling himself onto the dock.

Lessing started to bring the Kalashnikov around when a noise to his right, like a walrus or a big fish flopping up onto the dock, made him jump nearly out of his skin, and he spun around.

The black-suited twin of the first man stood at the end of the stone dock, an M-16 rifle with a stainless steel wire stock in his hands.

Lessing was swinging the Kalashnikov to the right when a third figure dressed in black rose up onto the dock, a silenced pistol in his right hand.

A thunderclap burst in Lessing's head, and then nothing.

Smoke from the burning helicopter was obvious on the air even in the alcove behind the dock. And it was just as obvious to Lipton and his team that they were smelling burnt aviation gas.

About ten yards out they had surfaced long enough to spot the lone terrorist on the dock. Diving again to a depth of five feet, their oxygen rebreathers leaving no telltale bubbles, they'd split up; Tyrell left, Joslow right, and Lipton down the middle with Bryan Wasley and Tony Reid as backup. The sentry hadn't had a chance.

Tyrell was bent over the man, feeling for a carotid pulse. He'd taken three hits in the head from Lipton's suppressed .22, killing him instantly. The Kalashnikov's safety catch was in the on position. Even if the terrorist had pulled the trigger, his weapon would not have fired.

Lipton and the others were hurriedly pulling off their wet suits and removing the rest of their weapons and equipment from waterproof carrying pouches. Reid and Joslow, weapons up, bracketed the narrow stairway that led steeply up through the cliff into the monastery. On signal Joslow rolled around the corner, his pistol sweeping upward in tight circles.

After a moment he shook his head and turned back. "Clear," he called softly to Lipton. He seemed almost disappointed.

"This one is dead," Tyrell said, straightening up from Lessing's body.

"There was no evidence of a landing strip at this end of the island on the survey maps and flyover shots I saw, which means what we're smelling is probably a chopper," Lipton said.

"McGarvey and Bobby?" Tyrell asked.

"Probably. Which means the bad guys are caught between us, and they're not going to take that lightly." Lipton quickly surveyed the landing dock. "We'll use this as our staging area as planned. We go for the hostages first. Everything else is secondary."

None of his men said a thing.

"Once they're released, Tony and Jules will bring them down here, and depending upon the situation we'll either fetch the boat, or call for help. Commander Rheinholtz is standing by."

"What if we run into heavy resistance and have to fight our way back here?" Tyrell asked quietly. They all wanted to be completely clear on their orders.

"Then that's what we'll do," Lipton answered. "As I said, anything other than the hostages will be secondary. That includes McGarvey and Bobby. If we can get to them, we will. But the safety of the hostages comes first." He looked at his men. "Questions?"

There were none.

"Toss that body over the side," Lipton ordered, starting for the stairs. "The scope and rifle too. I don't want to leave any evidence that we were here."

The stairs were so steep and narrow that only one person could start up at a time. They led five hundred feet into a long, narrow vestibule that opened onto a broad corridor which ran through the main residence and living areas of the monastery.

Lipton silently crossed the corridor and halted at the doorway into the great hall. No one was here, and there were no sounds other than the wind and rain lashing against the thick, lead-glass windows. But the smoke was much thicker up here, and the smell of burning aviation gas was very strong.

"Nobody home, sir?" Wasley asked.

Lipton turned and shook his head. "Go with Ried and Joslow. Check everything to the end of the corridor."

They hurried noiselessly off as Lipton entered the great hall, Tyrell right behind him. They spread out, left and right, and halted for a moment, listening, watching, every sense alert for a sign of trouble.

Somebody had been here recently. There were glasses with dregs of wine still in them on the table. Plates with scraps of food. The Paris, Berlin, Athens and New York newspapers spread out. A sweater tossed over one chair, a black nylon jumpsuit over another.

"They're dealing with the chopper," Tyrell said softly.

Lipton nodded. "They wouldn't have taken the hostages."

"This is a big place, Ed."

Lipton looked at him. "They'll be isolated. Up high, away from everything else."

Tyrell nodded his agreement, and the two of them hurried across the room to a corridor that ran at right angles to the first, deeper into the compound. Immediately to their right spiral stairs led upward.

"Get the others and follow me," Lipton ordered. "But post Wasley down here." He started up the stairs, keeping low and against the inner wall so that he would present less of a target to someone waiting above.

At the top, three stories above the level of the great hall, the stairs ended at a short, narrow corridor, three wooden doors on the right. Isolation cells.

He could hear the scuffle of soft-soled shoes coming up from below. Tyrell and the others. If anyone was up here, it would be the hostages, not the terrorists, he figured. But something felt odd to him. No matter what trouble the East Germans were having they wouldn't simply run off and leave the two women alone. They'd have to know that the hostages were their only real guarantee of success.

His pistol up, Lipton slipped into the corridor and put his ear to the first door. There were no sounds from within and he was about to pull away when he thought he heard something. A murmur, perhaps. A single word spoken, or whispered . . . by a woman. A moment later another woman said something, her voice so low that the words were indistinct, but recognizable as a woman's voice nonetheless.

Tyrell and the others came up, and Lipton motioned for them to check the other two rooms, as he holstered his pistol and gingerly inspected every square inch of the door and thick wooden frame around it for a wire, or any hint that there might be a pressure switch.

If the terrorists had left the woman here, they might have booby-trapped the room. But Lipton found nothing. And the other two rooms were empty.

"Cover the stairs," Lipton ordered. Reid complied and Lipton turned back to the door. "Mrs. McGarvey," he called.

There was no reply.

"Mrs. McGarvey, are you in there with your daughter? Are you all right?"

"Who's there?" A young woman asked softly.

Lipton exchanged relieved glances with Tyrell. "Elizabeth McGarvey?"

"Who is it?" Elizabeth demanded.

"My name is Ed Lipton. U.S. Navy. I'm here with a team to rescue you. If you'll stand back we'll force the door."

"Thank God," Elizabeth cried. "But wait. There was gunfire, and an explosion. Is my father with you?"

"No, ma'am," Lipton said. "Now, please stand back."

Someone said something that Lipton couldn't quite catch.

"Ms. McGarvey?"

"They've planted explosives," Elizabeth said.

"Where?"

"In the stone wall about ten feet below our window."

"Can you see any wires? Maybe something attached to this door?"

"There are wires outside on the wall, but not in here."

Lipton looked over his shoulder at Tyrell. "A remote detonator?"

"Makes sense," Tyrell said. "They wanted to lure McGarvey here. Maybe they figured to let him get this far and then blow the place."

"But he's not here yet," Lipton said. "And Spranger's people have their hands full at the moment."

"Go for it," Tyrell said softly, after just a moment's hesitation.

"Ms. McGarvey," Lipton called. "I want you and your mother to get as far away from the door as you possibly can. Have you got a bed in there?"

"Yes, yes, there are two beds here," Elizabeth called.

"I want you to take the mattress off one of the beds, then crouch down in a corner and cover you and your mother with it. Can you do that?"

"Yes."

"I'll give you one minute and we'll blow this door," Lipton said, and he stepped aside for Joslow, who expertly placed a few ounces of plastique around the door lock, cracked a short acid fuse and stuck it in the explosive.

They all went to the end of the short corridor, and sixty-five seconds later the plastique blew with a respectable bang.

"Get them out of there, on the double," Lipton ordered. They were at their most vulnerable at this point. If one of Spranger's men had heard the explosion and had realized what was going on up here, he might push the button.

Tyrell and Joslow rushed into the cell, and Lipton called to Reid who was halfway down the stairs. "Clear, Tony?" he called softly.

"Clear," Reid answered.

"We're on our way."

Tyrell and Joslow emerged from the cell leading the two very shaken women. For just an instant Lipton was taken aback by their appearance. Their shaved heads made them look bizarre, but they seemed to be relatively unharmed.

"We're taking you out of here now," he told them.

"You have to help my father," Elizabeth cried. "I won't leave without him."

"We'll help him," Lipton promised. "But first we're going to get you and your mother out of danger."

Elizabeth shook her head bitterly. "You're already too late for that," she said.

58

McGarvey crouched in the darkness of the visitor's loft above the nave, his breathing ragged, smoke curling off his clothing. His heart was hammering and his vision wavered, but he was alive and he was sure he'd heard a small explosion, a long way off, perhaps somewhere above.

Flames from the still-burning helicopter illuminated the church with a flickering glow, the air temperature was up at least ten degrees, perhaps more.

It was hard to keep his thinking straight. The concussion when the chopper had blown had knocked the wind out of him. But he was aware enough to know what he'd just heard.

If Lipton's team had come ashore they might have run into trouble by now. He didn't want to give voice to what he feared most, but he couldn't stop himself from working out the possible significance of the small blast.

The East Germans had expected him to rush blindly into the monastery complex in an effort to find Kathleen and Elizabeth. They wanted him to make a mistake so that they could corner him. No doubt they'd booby-trapped the area where they were holding the women, turning it into a killing ground.

With explosives?

But he hadn't done what they wanted. Instead he'd climbed up to the second level and doubled back. Spranger's people would be coming to see about their precious helicopter, and sooner or later they would have to enter the church.

McGarvey's grip tightened on his pistol. The only way he could possibly win against such odds was to pick them off one at a time. Lead them into a blind rush. Cause them to make mistakes.

In the meantime, the one who'd fired on Schade was up here somewhere. He could almost feel the man's presence. Killing him would be a pleasure.

Every joint in his body ached from the concussion, and the ringing in his ears was only just beginning to fade. It felt as if he'd been run over by a railroad locomotive.

But he was lucky to be alive. By some chance the primary force of the explosion had been directed away from him, sending burning fuel from the chopper's port tanks spewing against the buildings on the opposite side of the courtyard, allowing him time to get out of there before he was too badly burned.

It was possible that Schade had calculated the effect that his grenade would have and had tossed it to just the right spot. Every Navy SEAL was trained in the use of explosives. But Schade had been critically wounded. If his toss hadn't been lucky, it had been miraculous.

The kid hadn't one chance in a million of getting out of there alive, of course. The last McGarvey had seen of him, his body was completely engulfed in flames. He hoped the boy was dead before the fire reached him.

The door into the nave from the residence hall crashed open, the sound reverberating loudly in the cavernous hall, and McGarvey edged around a stone pillar so that he could see down onto the main floor.

Nothing moved for a long second or two. The space beyond the open door was in darkness, so McGarvey couldn't see a thing.

He slipped a little farther around the pillar, giving himself a clear shot over the low balustrade at anyone coming through the doorway.

Someone appeared in the doorway for just an instant, and then immediately fell back out of sight.

McGarvey leaned his shoulder up against the pillar for support, and cupped the elbow of his right arm with his left hand, the Walther's front sight lined up just ahead of the doorway. He had removed the silencer for the sake of increased accuracy. There was no longer much need for stealth.

Someone moved off to his left. The shuffle of shoe leather against the flooring planks?

McGarvey froze. Schade's killer? Or had Spranger's people slammed open the door below as a diversion, directing his attention away from the real attack?

The sound came again, and as McGarvey started to drop down and turn left, someone rushed through the door into the nave and disappeared beneath the loft.

A bullet smacked into the stone pillar an inch from McGarvey's head, flying chips cutting his cheek and forehead.

He fired two shots into the darkness as he continued falling back around the pillar, answering fire coming immediately, but hitting just above him. Then he was down, flat on the floor behind the pillar.

At least two other people came into the nave downstairs. He could hear them rushing beneath the balcony. They meant to isolate him up here, and when they were lined up and ready they would rush him.

The problem for him was the two flights of stairs from below; one at either end of the loft. No matter which stairwell he covered, he would be exposed to anyone coming up the other one.

Adding to his immediate troubles was Schade's killer up here pinning him down until the real attack could begin. That, he suspected, would come in a matter of seconds.

McGarvey took the silencer tube out of his jacket pocket, hesitated for just a second, then tossed it off to his left. Immediately he rolled to the right, to the opposite side of the stone pillar.

He got a brief impression of a large man, dressed in a black, jumpsuit, rising up from beneath an overturned pew, and he fired twice, both shots catching the man in the torso, driving him backwards to crash to the floor.

From where McGarvey was lying he could see the East German's right shoulder and arm, the Kalashikov six inches from his outstretched hand. He was not moving.

McGarvey scrambled across to where the downed man lay and felt for a pulse but there was none. One down, time now to give the others something to think about.

Stuffing the Walther in his belt, McGarvey silently dragged the East German's body over to the railing. Nothing moved below. By now they'd be waiting just under the balcony, wondering what was going on up here.

McGarvey heaved the German's body up over the balustrade, balanced it there for just a moment, then rolled it over. It fell the twenty feet and hit the stone floor with a sickening thud. McGarvey wasn't sure, but he thought he heard someone mutter the single sound, "Ah," then nothing.

Seeing their comrade like that would slow them down, McGarvey hoped, just long enough for him to prepare himself for the coming assault. He had hoped to take out Schade's killer, then pick off the others as they came into the nave. But they'd anticipated him.

He understood why when he retrieved the East German's rifle. The same type of walkie-talkie he'd tossed overboard on his way into the port of Thira was propped up against the overturned pew. The others had been warned about the ambush.

His only hope now was that Lipton had brought his team

ashore. Short of that he would hold them off here. The longer he did that, the longer they would remain away from Kathleen and Elizabeth.

He'd made a mistake coming up here. The bitter thought rankled as he dragged another solid oak pew over to the first, and muscled it over onto its side. The bench was at least fifteen feet long and had to weigh several hundred pounds. The thick seat bottom would stop just about anything short of a grenade or a LAW rocket, neither of which was beyond the STASI's ability to acquire.

But he had run out of options by stupidly forgetting that Spranger was a professional. His men would be well trained, well disciplined, well armed and well equipped. They would communicate.

Hunkering down between the pair of overturned pews which offered him protection from both stairwells, he ejected the Kalashnikov's curved magazine and quickly counted the bullets. There were only eleven, and there were no spare clips lying around. He had reloaded his pistol on the road, on the way up here from town. He ejected the clip. It was empty, which left only one round in the firing chamber.

Twelve rounds with which he not only had to defend himself, but with which he had to prevail and then rescue Kathleen and Elizabeth.

He smiled grimly as he holstered his pistol, and made sure the Kalashnikov's safety was switched off, the selection lever in the single fire position.

Impossible odds, he thought. But still manageable.

59

Lipton stood with the others at the head of the stone stairs to the dock, listening, but the gunfire had stopped for the moment. The young woman seemed to be in better condition than her mother, but neither of them would be able to withstand much more. They seemed weak, and more listless than they should under the circumstances. Lipton suspected they'd been drugged.

"Tony and Jules will get you ladies off the island, and then call for help," Lipton told them.

Elizabeth clutched his arm. "My father is here. He's looking for us, but they know he's coming. It's a trap."

"As soon as we get you to safety we'll see what we can do to help him."

Elizabeth looked at Lipton's team, and laughed, the sound short and sharp. "I'm sorry, but I hope you brought more men with you than this."

Lipton glanced at Tyrell. "Why is that, Ms. McGarvey?"

"Because there's a lot more of them than there are of you. And they're very good."

"We'll take care of it," Lipton said. "But first, you and your mother are getting out of here."

Elizabeth looked at him for a long time. "Then good luck," she said, and she took her mother's arm and they started single file down the stairs.

* * *

McGarvey held his breath as he tried to distinguish sounds other than the shrieking wind and the annoying ringing in his ears. He thought he'd heard someone on the stairs behind him, and he had looked over his shoulder, but there was nothing yet.

The flames from the burning helicopter in the courtyard had finally begun to die down, and there was much less light up here in the loft, which was just as well. If he couldn't see his attackers, then they couldn't see him either.

Both stairwells were in darkness, and he kept switching his gaze from one to the other, his eyes barely above the level of the over-turned pews, so that he almost missed the movement in the west stairwell.

His heart froze, then steadied, as he switched his attention to the opposite stairwell, bringing the Kalashnikov up and resting it lightly on the pew.

"Take a peek," he muttered softly. "Just a little peek to see what's going on up here."

A head and shoulders appeared in the stairwell, and McGarvey fired once, driving the figure violently backward and out of sight.

Switching his aim immediately back to the west stairwell he was in time to see a figure dart left into the shadows toward one of the stone pillars.

He squeezed off a single shot, catching the man in the side, flipping him over the stairwell railing with a desperate cry, and McGarvey heard him crashing down the way he'd come.

Spranger could hardly believe what was happening. Dürenmatt was dead, his body lying in a pool of blood on the stone floor where McGarvey had flipped it over the chorus loft balustrade. Scherchen was crumpled in a heap at the foot of the east stairwell. And Magda was shaking and crying silently with rage over the body of her husband lying in the west stairwell.

Their chopper was destroyed, their pilot and maintenance man dead, and aside from Lessing down on the dock, that left only three: Him and Liese at the east stairwell and Magda on the opposite side.

Liese was staring at him, a slight smirk on her beautiful lips, as if she were saying, I told you so. He had the urge to reach out and slap the look off her face.

Tiny flashes of light were going off inside his head, like police cameras in a morgue, each burst illuminating some morbid scene in the recesses of his mind.

Radvonska's warning in Rome about McGarvey kept coming back to him, and he kept pushing it away. This operation was falling apart at the edges. Monaco, Japan, the States . . . all unraveling. All because of one man.

He looked up into the darkness of the loft. The two shots that had been fired had come from a Kalashnikov. Dürenmatt's, which in itself was so galling he could hardly stand it.

Who was he?

Intense pain from his burns threatened to blot out what little sanity was left to him. Only through sheer force of will was he able to hang on. To think.

They were going to have to leave this place soon. It wouldn't be long before the Greek authorities began to sit up and take notice that something was going on out here. And Dürenmatt had said that McGarvey had not been alone in the courtyard. Which meant the man had help. Who?

Maybe Lessing had seen something out in the water after all.

He pulled the walkie-talkie around and keyed the talk button. Liese was still staring at him, the same fixed expression on her face, in her eyes. She was, Spranger thought, an enigma even to him.

"Bruno, what is your situation down there?" he said softly into the microphone. "Have you seen anything else?"

He keyed the transmit button, and waited impatiently for Lessing's reply. But there was no response.

"Bruno, do you copy?"

Still there was no answer.

"Bruno, come back," he transmitted.

"What's the matter, Ernst, are your friends deserting you?" McGarvey's voice drifted down from the loft.

Spranger stepped back a half pace, as if he expected an apparition to appear at the head of the stairs, guns blazing. A ghost, incapable of being harmed, and yet supremely able to inflict death and destruction.

"Ernst . . . ?" Liese said softly.

Magda was looking across at them, the big Russian assault rifle clutched in her arms.

Spranger dropped the walkie-talkie on the floor. "Get them," he told Liese.

"The women?" she asked, blinking.

"Yes. Bring them here."

Liese looked up toward the loft. "What do you mean to do, Ernst?" she asked. "Let's leave now, while we still have the chance."

"It would be the end of the project."

"Fuck the Japanese," Liese said urgently. "But we can take the women with us. At least the young one. She's fit to travel."

"Liese," Spranger said. "Get them."

She looked directly into his eyes for several long moments, a test of wills, but then her gaze dropped and she turned and hurried off.

When she was gone, Spranger laid his rifle down, took out the detonator, and motioned for Magda to take a position at the top of the stairs. She nodded her understanding and went up.

Spranger gave her a half minute to get into place, and then called up to McGarvey.

"I'm going to come up the stairs, Mr. McGarvey. Unarmed. I want to talk to you about saving the lives of your ex-wife and daughter."

"What do you want out of it?" McGarvey answered.

"There are only four of us left. We would very much like to walk away from here with our lives."

"Then go. Turn around and walk away."

"Ah, but it's not going to be that easy," Spranger said, much calmer now that he had a plan. He started up the stairs. "Here I come, and as I say, I am unarmed. But I am carrying a small electronic device in my right hand. My thumb is on the button. If the button is pushed a powerful explosion will destroy the room in which your wife and daughter are being held. There would be no chance of their survival in such a case. Do you understand?"

"No," McGarvey said harshly.

Spranger stopped halfway up. "Do you believe that I am not serious, Mr. McGarvey?"

"What do you get out of it? You still haven't answered my question."

"I propose to give you the detonating device in exchange for Peter's rifle and your pistol," Spranger replied, smiling.

"Then you'll kill me."

"On the contrary, we will need you alive to effect our escape past your friends."

The church was silent for a long time. Even the wind howling around the eaves seemed to have calmed down for that instant.

"Mr. McGarvey?" Spranger called.

"Come," McGarvey said.

"I need your assurances that . . ."

"Come," McGarvey repeated.

Holding the detonator away from his body, Spranger went the rest of the way up to the loft. "Here I come."

He hesitated for a beat on the last stair, then stepped up, out of the deeper darkness. At first he couldn't make out much except for a few vague shapes. Something had been piled up in the middle of the loft.

"Put the detonator down," McGarvey's voice came from the darkness, but Spranger couldn't pinpoint it. Had he made another mistake with this man?

"I cannot see you. Show yourself."

"Do it," McGarvey said, and this time Spranger was sure that the American was at the far end of the loft where he would see Magda if she showed herself.

"All right, I'll do it," Spranger shouted hastily. He had to distract the man's attention for just a crucial second or two. "I'm putting it down, but you must lay your weapons aside." He started to crouch down to place the detonator on the floor when Liese shouted at him from the nave, her voice desperate.

"Ernst! They're gone!"

Magda Schey rose up out of the dark stairwell at that moment and brought her rifle up.

"Nein . . ." Spranger cried when McGarvey fired once, driving Magda backward, her weapon discharging in a long burst, the bullets ricocheting dangerously off the stone walls.

Then McGarvey fired again, this shot hitting Spranger in the right shoulder before he had time to react, shoving him off balance down the stairs, every fiber in his being raging at the surprise and injustice. It wasn't supposed to end up like this!

60

Spranger's horribly burned left arm and collarbone broke in the fall down the stairs, and at the bottom his face smashed into the stone floor, crushing his nose and both cheekbones with a grinding agony.

For a seeming eternity he just lay there, sounds echoing interminably in his head.

But he was alive and conscious, though just barely, his world spinning, a deep nausea rising up making him gag and almost vomit.

"*Christus, Christus,*" he muttered wetly, spraying the floor with blood as he tried to push himself upright with his wounded right arm.

The instant shot of sharply localized pain was like a burst of adrenalin to his system, momentarily clearing his head and his vision.

The detonator, its plastic case cracked, lay on the stone floor about two yards away. Spranger started to pull himself toward it, everything within his being concentrating on the one thing: On the electronic device, on revenge.

McGarvey had brought him to this. The one man. And he would suffer the consequences of his actions. If he was still alive. If Magda hadn't killed him: She'd managed to shoot.

He cocked an ear, but there was no gunfire for the moment. If McGarvey were dead, killing his wife and daughter wouldn't matter.

But he would do it anyway, and in the doing he would be striking a double blow—at McGarvey, and at that bitch Liese. If she'd simply kept her mouth shut about the women being gone . . .

Spranger stopped for just a moment and turned that stray thought over in his head. Liese had said something about the women being gone. But that was impossible. They could not have escaped from their cell. And even if they had, they couldn't have gone anywhere.

She was mistaken. It couldn't be.

Suddenly Liese was there, above him, concern written all over her face. "We must get out of here now, Ernst," she told him. "There are others coming."

"Get the detonator," Spranger croaked, blood slobbering down his chin and the front of his tattered jumpsuit.

"What are you talking about?" she cried, glancing nervously up the stairs.

"I want to blow the tower."

"They're gone, you fool!"

"No," Spranger growled, the single word torn in anguish from the back of his throat. "I won't allow it." He looked up into her eyes. "Liese, please. It's all I ask. We'll push the button and then we'll get out of here. Together. We'll regroup and finish the Japanese project. It's all still possible, but you must help me."

"I'll help you," Liese said, resignedly. She got the detonator and then helped him to his feet. "We'll go overland, and hide in the mountains until it's safe."

"Do it, Liese. Do it!"

McGarvey huddled behind the overturned pews, the breath knocked out of him. He had taken two hits from behind, one in the left shoulder, the bullet exiting cleanly just below his collarbone, and the other, much more painful wound, in the meat of his right thigh.

Once again he understood that Spranger had outthought him, although he was certain that he'd hit the East German general at least once.

The ringing was back in his ears, and between that and his ragged breath whistling in his throat, it was becoming increasingly difficult to concentrate on anything. He wanted simply to close his eyes and sleep. He wanted peace, something he'd not had for a very long time.

As he went down he'd managed to get off a second burst before his weapon either jammed or ran out of ammunition. He was too tired to find out which. But he'd got the impression of Spranger falling back. At least that's what he thought it had been, but lying here in the darkness he wasn't sure of what he'd seen; or, in fact, if he'd seen anything.

He'd heard a woman's voice. But just now it was difficult to recall exactly what she'd said.

"McGarvey," someone shouted from below, on the floor of the nave. Spranger? It was a man's voice.

McGarvey struggled to sit up. He pulled the Kalashnikov over to him. The ejector slide was locked in the open position, the breech empty.

"Mr. McGarvey?" someone else called from below. This time it was a woman. Her English had British intonations, but the accent was definitely German.

"Bastards," McGarvey shouted, the effort causing a shooting pain in his side.

"Listen," the man called. "*Sagen Sie, aufwiedersehen.*"

"Bastards," McGarvey shouted again, when a huge explosion a long way off shook the very foundation of the church. Kathleen and Elizabeth. McGarvey was galvanized.

Dropping the Kalashnikov, he clawed the Walther from his holster, switched the safety off, cocked the hammer and clambered to his feet.

"Come back," he shouted, lurching toward the balustrade.

Something crashed into one of the pews behind him, and he swung around, getting off a snap shot with his last round at a black figure rising up, as it fired its assault rifle on full automatic.

61

A thirty-foot section of the residence building's outer wall was simply gone, the upper floors of the tower, including the area in which the women had been held, gone also.

Lipton and Tyrell huddled behind a pile of smoking debris just off the great hall waiting for Wasley to report back. He'd gone down to the dock to make sure that no one had been hurt in the blast, and see if that avenue of escape was still open to them.

The gunfire they'd heard just after the explosion had stopped, and the only sounds now were the wind howling through the jagged opening and the sea crashing against the rocks five hundred feet below.

"I don't like it," Tyrell said, "McGarvey has to understand the significance of the explosion, if he heard it. But there's been no response."

"Don't write him off yet, Frank," Lipton replied. "You didn't see his file. I did, and it's damned impressive. Bob is no slouch either."

"They're only two."

Wasley came through the corridor door and hurried across the great hall, crouching down beside them. He was winded from the climb. "A section of the dock was buried, but they're okay," he said. "Joslow said he's going to hold up there, unless you tell him differently. He's called Ops for help."

"Good," Lipton said. They'd decided against using walkie-talkies because they'd not counted on being separated, and they'd wanted to keep unsecured communications to an absolute minimum. He could see that it had been a mistake. "How are the women holding up?"

"Joslow and Reid have got their hands full, sir. The younger one says she's not leaving the island until she finds out about her father."

"What's Ops' ETA over the dock?"

"Unknown. Joslow thinks they're waiting for authorization. Word from Athens is that the Greek authorities are beginning to stir."

"Then we'd better get the hell out of here on the double," Lipton said.

They crawled over the pile of debris, their weapons at the ready, and ducked into the corridor that ran the length of the monastery complex toward the courtyard and the desconsecrated church at the front.

Leapfrogging, Lipton first, Wasley second and Tyrell taking up the rear, they hurriedly worked their way forward. Every doorway, every corner, every set of stairs were places of possible ambush and had to be approached with extreme caution.

But nothing moved. There was no gunfire, no signs, except for the lingering stench of the burning chopper, that the monastery was anything but a abandoned center of study and worship.

Lipton held up at the final junction, the corridor ending in a *T*, the intersecting hallway much narrower. Directly across from where they crouched, a window looking onto the courtyard had blown out. The last of the flames were dying down, nothing identifiable left of the helicopter except for a section of the tail and tail rotor.

The heat had been so intense that lead holding the window panes in place had melted and formed small gray pools on the floor. Even the stone walls inside the corridor had been blackened, and the thick framing timbers in the walls and ceilings had caught fire and were still smoldering in places.

To the right the narrower hallway ended at a door that opened into the nave of the main church.

Lipton pointed that way, then keeping low, darted across the corridor, to a spot just beneath the window, and motioned for Wasley to follow.

Tyrell was the first at the doorway, and he held up until Lipton joined him, this time with Wasley acting as backup.

On signal the two of them rolled into the nave, left and right, Wasley immediately taking up a position to cover them from the corridor.

But nothing moved here either, except for the wind and rain that came through an open door at the front of the church.

Crouching in the darkness Lipton stared at the open door for a moment or two. Someone had left the church? In a hurry?

Turning back, he spotted the three bodies just beneath the balcony; one in the middle and one at the foot of the stairs on either side. It was obvious even from a distance of twenty-five or thirty feet that they were dead.

Lipton zigzagged to the east stairway. When he was in place he motioned for Tyrell to take the west stairway, and for Wasley to remain where he was.

Whatever had happened here was bloody and final. Lipton wasn't at all sure he wanted to know what was upstairs on the balcony, but he figured that McGarvey had probably made his stand here . . . and lost?

He pointed up, and he and Tyrell started up the stairs at the same time; silently, their weapons at the ready.

The balcony was mostly in darkness now that the flames from the courtyard had died down, so it took Lipton several moments to regain his night vision. When he did he nearly staggered backward off-balance.

McGarvey, blood streaming from several wounds in his neck, face and body, stood in the shadows, the heavy Kalashnikov assault rifle held over his head like a club, ready to smash Lipton's head.

Slowly, he lowered the rifle, and managed a slight smile. "Kathleen and Elizabeth?" he asked, his voice barely audible.

"Safe," Lipton said.

"Then let's get out of here. I could use a drink."

BOOK FOUR

62

LANGLEY, VIRGINIA
JULY 16, 1992

Roland Murphy watched from his seventh-floor office at CIA Head-quarters as the sun came up on what promised to be a beautiful day. His mood, he decided, should be expansive, instead it was dark with worry.

Unable to sleep, he'd had his driver bring him back at four this morning, and he'd had the overnight supervisor bring him up to speed. The world situation was reasonably calm; no major wars or conflicts involving American interests, no serious threats to any of their in-place networks, no crises needing immediate attention.

Nothing doing, in fact, except for the situation they'd hired McGarvey to investigate. It had not changed. The threat still existed, but no one had so much as a clue what to do about it.

Murphy's secretary wasn't here yet, so he got an outside line himself and called the fifth-floor isolation ward at Bethesda National Naval Medical Center.

"This is Roland Murphy. If you need to confirm that, I'm at my office. I'll instruct the Agency operator to put your call through."

"I'm Dr. Singh, and that won't be necessary, Mr. Director, I recognize your voice."

"How is your patient?"

"We've had him here for less than twelve hours," the doctor said cautiously. "But he is by all appearances a singularly remarkable man. He is already on the mend."

"How long?"

"For what, General?"

"Until he will be fit to resume his . . . duties."

"Under normal circumstances, three months, perhaps four," Dr. Singh said. "But if his presence is of vital importance, all other considerations secondary, I would say six weeks at the minimum."

"Is he conscious?" Murphy asked, masking his bitter disappointment. McGarvey was a man after all, not a superman.

"Oh, yes, he is very much conscious. He refuses all pain medications and sedatives."

"Someone will be along this morning to interview him," Murphy said.

"Seven days."

"This morning."

"General, I could refuse you."

"I think not," Murphy said. "But we'll wait until this afternoon. We'll give you that much time."

"Him, General, not me. You need to give him time to heal."

Murphy called a meeting for his top three at 8:30 A.M. in the small dining room adjacent to his office. Besides the Deputy Director of Central Intelligence Lawrence Danielle, the Deputy Director of Intelligence Tommy Doyle and of course the Deputy Director of Operations Phil Carrara, CIA General Consul Howard Ryan was at the breakfast gathering.

Murphy dropped the bombshell.

"I was told earlier this morning that McGarvey will recover from his wounds, but he'll be out of commission for at least six weeks, perhaps longer."

"Shit," Carrara swore crudely, but he noticed out of the corner of his eye that Ryan had a smug look. "Then whatever did or did not happen on Santorini, K-1 was successful. They wanted him off the case, and that's what they got."

"It would seem so," Murphy answered heavily. "He's awake and apparently coherent. Phil, I want you to go over there this afternoon and talk to him. He must have seen or heard something that'll be of use to us."

"Yes, sir," Carrara said. "In the meantime we've come up with a tentative identification on the woman that Elizabeth described for us." He took several black and white glossy photos from a file folder and passed them across the table to Murphy. "Her name is Liese Egk."

"Former STASI?" Murphy asked, studying the photos, then passing them over to Danielle.

"Yes. Her speciality is assassination."

Danielle's eyebrows rose, and Ryan took the photos with interest. "Still no trace of her or Ernst Spranger?"

"None," Carrara said. "The Greeks are, needless to say, oversensitive just now. Apparently there were two local businessmen who somehow got involved, and got themselves killed, in addition to the two fishermen whose boat was found abandoned in the port of Thira."

"The Navy wants to be keyed in to what we're doing," Danielle said softly. "Admiral Douglas telephoned yesterday afternoon after you'd already gone for the day. One of their boys was killed on the island."

"What did you tell him?"

"That we'd get back to him, but that the young man definitely did not give his life on some fool's errand."

"That'll have to do for now," Murphy said. "If he presses, invite him over for lunch. I'll talk to him then."

There was a momentary silence that Tommy Doyle finally broke.

"Which brings us back to Tokyo. We're getting a lot of mixed signals from the Japanese on the official as well as the unofficial level."

"What about the news media?"

"So far they've been relatively silent about the killings, which in itself is spooky."

They were all looking at Doyle.

"What are you trying to say, Tommy?" Murphy asked.

"It's my guess that whatever is going on has at least the tacit approval of someone at ministry level or higher."

"Tough charge," Ryan suggested, but Murphy ignored the comment.

"It's time we pulled Kelley Fuller out of there," the DCI said. "With McGarvey out of commission she's on her own."

"You don't mean to write off our Tokyo station," Carrara said. "Not now, General."

"We'll have to restaff. There's not much else for it. In the meantime it's possible that McGarvey's action on Santorini scared them off, or at least delayed their plans."

"Six weeks is a long time," Doyle said.

"Send someone else," Ryan suggested.

"Who?" Murphy asked bluntly.

"I don't know. We must have a Japanese expert on staff somewhere who could make some quiet inquiries for us."

No one said a thing.

"We don't have to send a maniac whose solution to every problem seems to be shooting up the local citizenry."

"Right," Murphy said. He turned back to Carrara. "As soon as you talk to McGarvey get back to me, would you, Phil?"

"Yes, sir," Carrara said. "Maybe we'll have something by then."

63

The morning was beautiful. McGarvey stood at the window, his body cocked at an odd angle, his neck, right arm and shoulder and his right leg swathed in bandages. He'd gone from night into day; from danger to safety, but the assignment wasn't over.

A CIA psychiatrist who'd examined McGarvey after a particularly harrowing operation early in his career had come to the conclusion that though McGarvey had a low physical threshold of pain response, he had an extremely high psychological threshold. He felt pain easily, but he was able to let it flow through and around him without it affecting his ability to function.

He was in pain now, but he continued to refuse any medication, preferring to keep his head straight. Spranger and the woman with him were gone. Lipton had admitted it before they'd left Santorini. And as long as that monster was still on the loose none of them would be truly safe.

McGarvey's right shoulder had stiffened up and his burns still hurt, but his biggest problem was the flesh wound in his right thigh. Walking was difficult at best. If he found himself in a situation where he had to move quickly to save his life, he might not make it.

But lying in a hospital bed fretting wouldn't help despite what the doctors told him. They'd backed up their warnings by posting a guard at the door. At least he hoped the hospital had ordered the security and that it hadn't been done at the Agency's request.

Someone knocked at the door and he turned around as Kathleen came in. Her left eyebrow arched when she saw him standing at the window, but she said nothing, closing the door.

"Good morning," McGarvey said. He decided that she didn't look any the worse for wear, except in her eyes, which seemed to have lost their usual haughtiness. She was dressed in street clothes, a blue scarf on her head.

"How are you feeling?" she asked.

He shrugged. "I'll live. You?"

"I'm all right."

"Elizabeth?"

"She wants to see you."

McGarvey tried to read something from his ex-wife's expression, her tone of voice, but he couldn't. He'd never been able to predict her.

"How is she holding up?"

Kathleen shook her head, but she made no move toward him. "I honestly don't know, Kirk. She's definitely your daughter. She stood up to them, and probably saved my life in the doing despite what they . . . did to her. But she won't talk to me about it. She just sidesteps the questions. Says she'll live, whatever that means."

"What now?"

"You tell me," she said. "The FBI is guarding us. They said something about temporarily placing us in the Witness Protection Program. Either that or taking us into protective custody."

"Not such a bad idea . . ."

"For how long, Kirk?" Kathleen cried. "From the day I met you this has been going on. How much longer must I endure it?"

"I'm sorry . . ."

"We're divorced. Stay away from me and Elizabeth! Please! If you love your daughter, as you profess you do, then leave us alone!"

He felt badly for her, but he knew that there was nothing he could do to alleviate her pain and fear except do as she was asking: Stay away from her, and in the meantime go after Spranger and what remained of his organization.

"If you think it's for the best."

"I do," she replied.

McGarvey nodded. "Will you let me talk to her now, for just a minute?"

Kathleen stared at him for a long second or two, her rigid expression softening a little. "I don't think I could stop her," she said. "The doctor certainly could not."

"Get out of Washington, Katy. Let the Bureau take care of you."

"My name is Kathleen," she corrected automatically. "And Elizabeth and I are going to do just that. No one will know where we are. No one."

She turned and left the room, giving McGarvey a brief glimpse of

Dr. Singh in the corridor before the door closed again. He hobbled back to the bed and got in. A moment later Elizabeth, wearing faded jeans, a pink V-neck sweater, and a head scarf, came in.

For a long time she stood stock-still, looking at her father, the expression on her face even less readable than her mother's, except that she was frightened.

"Liz?" McGarvey prompted.

"Daddy," she cried and she came into his arms, a sharp stab of pain hammering his right side.

He grunted involuntarily, and Elizabeth immediately reared back.

"Oh, God, I'm sorry," she apologized, her hands going to her mouth.

"It's okay, Liz," he said. "It's okay." He held out his hand to her.

She hesitated. "I don't want to hurt you."

"You won't. Now come over here and sit down. I want to hear everything that happened to you and your mother, and then I want you to do me a favor."

"Anything," Elizabeth said, gingerly sitting on the edge of the bed.

"I'm going to need some clothes."

She looked sharply at him. "What do you mean?"

"I'm getting out of here."

"But you can't. You're hurt."

"It's all right," he said, patting her hand. "Believe me. But first I want to know about Ernst Spranger and the woman with him."

A dark cloud passed over Elizabeth's features and she flinched. "Her name is Liese. The others are murderers, but she's worse. Much worse."

"What happened?"

Elizabeth turned away. "I can't . . ."

"Your mother said you won't tell her."

"I'm afraid."

"You're safe here."

She turned back to her father. "Not for me," she said. "For you."

Suddenly McGarvey was cold. He'd been told what condition Kathleen and Elizabeth were in when Lipton's team had found them but he'd not seen either of them until this morning. They both wore wigs beneath their scarves, and although they seemed pale they appeared to be uninjured. Yet he wondered, his mind going down a lot of dark corridors he wanted to avoid.

"I'm sorry," he said.

Elizabeth's eyes widened, and she shook her head. "No," she blurted. "That's wrong. Mother's wrong. You're not responsible for the bad people in the world. It's not your fault. You didn't do anything wrong."

"If I hadn't been involved none of this would have happened to you and your mother."

"Don't say that," she cried, tears suddenly filling her eyes. "Don't ever say that."

"It's okay, Liz," McGarvey said, reaching for her.

Elizabeth stared at him for a long time, as if she'd never seen him before. "If not you, who can I believe in?" she asked finally.

A battered Volkswagen van with Italian plates pulled up at the Villa Ambrosia overlooking Monaco around five in the afternoon. So far as Liese could determine the compound was just as they had left it. She'd half-expected to see yellow *Do Not Pass* tapes across the doors, or an Interpol surveillance unit parked nearby. But she'd made three different approaches to the house, and had spotted nothing.

"How does it look?" Spranger asked from the back of the van. His voice was muffled but recognizable, which was, as far as Liese was concerned, enough for the moment.

"Clear," she answered. "I'm going to release the alarms and open the gate."

"Watch out for a trap."

They'd been over this same ground for two and a half days all the way from Athens, across Italy and along the Riviera. Spranger's intense hatred and desperate need for revenge had distorted his perception of everything. He had ranted and raved about striking back, getting even, killing.

More than once Liese had been brought to the brink of putting a gun to the back of his head and pulling the trigger. But each time she'd backed off at the last moment because she needed him. Needed his voice for what remained to be done. Their field officers were in place and ready to go to phase two, but they would only move on Spranger's direct orders. Without him the entire operation would fizzle and die.

Checking the rearview mirror again to make certain no one was coming up the road, Liese got out of the van and cautiously approached the tall wooden gate in the thick concrete wall that surrounded the compound.

None of the three hidden switches that activated the villa's extensive alarm system had been tampered with, and she released each of them, the gate's electric lock cycling open, and the gate swinging inward.

Back in the van she drove into the compound, and parked at the rear of the house. Before she helped Spranger out, she closed and locked the gate, and reset the alarm system.

Spranger was a mess. The Greek doctor on Santorini had been an incompetent fool, his methods and most of his equipment 1940s-vintage war surplus. He'd dug McGarvey's bullet out of Spranger's shoulder successfully, but he'd done too much cutting and when the wound healed, scar tissue would be bunched up as big as a clenched fist.

He'd set Spranger's broken arm and collarbone poorly, and

whatever salve he'd used on the extensive burns had a terrible odor. Within twenty-four hours noisome fluids were freely suppurating from it, horribly staining his clothing and bandages.

His broken nose and cheeks had swollen up and discolored black and blue and yellow.

But he was alive, and coherent, and therefore still useful.

Inside the house, Liese poured him a brandy, then made the first of four telephone calls, this one to a number down in Monaco. It was answered on the first ring by a man speaking French with a Japanese accent.

"*Oui.*"

"Mr. Spranger calling for Mr. Endo, please," Liese said. Spranger was watching her closely.

A second later their Japanese contact came on. "Yes, you have something to report, Ernst?"

"This is me," Liese said, and she caught the slight calculating hesitation in Endo's voice.

"Yes, I understand, please proceed."

"Mr. McGarvey has been eliminated as a problem.

"I see. And will you now be able to make your deliveries as contracted."

"Within seventy-two hours," Liese said, and Spranger nodded, his hand gripping the brandy glass so tightly she thought it would shatter at any moment.

"Very well. We look forward to concluding our business then."

Liese hung up, got the dial tone again and called the first of their three teams standing by in the field; This one outside of Lausanne, Switzerland, and Spranger put down his drink, ready to do his part.

64

Elizabeth was back a few minutes before one in the afternoon with a change of clothes for her father. This time she was dressed in a sheer blouse and skimpy knit miniskirt. She looked like a healthy, extremely sexual young animal, and the sight of her like that took McGarvey's breath away.

"Mother is waiting downstairs," she said, laying the straw bag in which she'd brought the clothes on the end of the bed. "We're leaving this afternoon from the Baltimore airport."

"Did you have any trouble getting back in?" McGarvey asked, getting out of bed, and pulling the clothes out of the bag. "Turn around."

She turned away as her father got dressed. "No. I think they like my smile out there."

McGarvey chuckled to himself. She was a little girl playing with fire, he thought. But then something else struck him and he looked up at her. She was only a girl in his mind. In reality she was a vital, intelligent young woman.

"Is the guard still out there?" he asked.

"Yes."

"Can you get him away from the door for a minute so that I can get out of here?"

"Where are you going?" she asked in a small voice after a moment.

"To finish what I started," he answered her. There was no use lying now. Not after what she'd been through.

"If something happens . . . I may never see you again."

"You will," McGarvey said, his throat suddenly thick. "Count on it."

When he was finished dressing, he took his daughter into his arms and held her closely for a long time. "It'll be okay, Liz."

She looked up into his eyes. "You'll make it, won't you, Daddy?"

"Sure." He kissed her on the cheek. "Now, go wiggle your tush at the guard and get him to show you the way to the cafeteria."

She smiled demurely, and left.

McGarvey waited for a half minute then carefully opened the door a crack. Elizabeth and the guard were gone, and for the moment no one else was in sight. He slipped out into the corridor and headed toward the stairwell door in the opposite direction from the nurses' station.

At any moment he expected someone to shout for him to stop, and then come running. But no one did, and a few minutes later he had made his way painfully down three flights of stairs to the ground floor, then along the main corridor to the entry lobby and information desk.

Otto Rencke, his long hair flying, his sleeveless sweatshirt dirty, and his sneakers untied, came through the front doors and started toward the information desk when he spotted McGarvey. He came over, his expression falling as he got closer.

"Holy cow, Mac. Do you know that you really look like shit?"

"What are you doing here?"

"I came to see you, but wow, I didn't think you'd be ambulatory, you know. The hotshots across the river have got you half dead."

"Did you bring your car?"

"Sure."

"Then get me out of here."

"Where to?"

"I'll tell you on the way, and in the meantime you can fill me in."

Rencke's face brightened again. "Kiyoshi Fukai."

They were on their way out and McGarvey stumbled and nearly fell on his face. "What?"

"The bad guy. His name is Kiyoshi Fukai. As in Fukai Semiconductor. Fourth richest man in the world. Worth in excess of twelve billion U.S. But I don't think that's his real name."

Kathleen was waiting in a cab in front of the hospital, and when McGarvey emerged with Rencke she sat forward in the back seat, her eyes wide. McGarvey nodded to her, but hobbled after Rencke to the parking lot across the driveway. As long as Elizabeth joined her soon she wouldn't make any noise. And within a few hours they'd be out of the Washington area and relatively safe for the time being.

Rencke's "car" was a beat-up green pickup truck, the U.S. Forest Service logo faded but still legible on the doors. Heading away from the hospital, McGarvey caught another glimpse of Kathleen waiting in the taxi, Elizabeth just coming out to her, and he allowed himself to relax a little.

"Where are we heading?" Rencke asked.

"You can take me to the Marriott across the river. I'll catch a cab from there."

"Are you going out to Langley?"

McGarvey nodded. "Now, what makes you think that Kiyoshi Fukai is our bad guy?"

"Well, it's actually quite simple once you get on the correct side and look back. But you've got to think about all the elements. Sorta like a big jigsaw puzzle, only in four dimensions. We've got to add time, you know."

McGarvey said nothing.

"Start out with the man who says he's Kiyoshi Fukai right now. If you talk about Japanese electronics and research his name will come up every time. For the past few years, he's been buying up American and British electronics companies . . . or at least he's been trying to do it. The feds—our feds who art here in Washington— have been putting the kibosh on his efforts to take over TSI Industries on the West Coast. Silicon Valley. Guess they're doing too much research in sensitive areas. Word is that it won't be long before they're—TSI that is—the number one chip producers worldwide."

"If Fukai owns TSI, then he'll maintain his dominance of the world market."

"Owns or destroys," Rencke said. "So, we've got a possible motive, and a man with the money to do something about it. On top of that, Fukai hates America and Americans, and he doesn't care who he tells it to. Tokyo has tried to shut him up on more than one occasion. And it was probably him, or someone he controls, who is writing anti-American books and distributing them to all the top Japanese businessmen and government honchos. See where I'm going with this?"

"So far," McGarvey replied.

"Of course that profile also fit a number of other fat cats, but Fukai caught my interest because of the background he claims. He says that before and during the war he was nothing more than a humble chauffeur. His is sort of a rags-to-riches story. Only it doesn't wash."

Rencke concentrated on his driving for a minute or two as they entered the District of Columbia at Chevy Chase, the traffic heavy.

"First of all, humble chauffeurs do not rise to become industrial giants. At least they didn't in the Japan of the late forties and fifties. But if Fukai had actually done just that he would have crowed about his achievement. But there's never been a peep out of him."

"Then how'd you find out?"

"Army records. Fukai surfaced at a verification center in Matsuyama in December of 1945, claiming he was Kiyoshi Fukai, the chauffeur. He was friendly and cooperative with the occupying forces, and no one thought to question his identification."

"Whose chauffeur was he?"

Rencke grinned. "Ah, that's the point, isn't it? His boss was a man by the name of Isawa Nakamura. A designer and manufacturer of electronic equipment. A black marketeer. A staunch supporter of the Rising Sun's military complex. A regular user of Korean and Chinese slave labor."

"There's more?" McGarvey asked, knowing there was.

"You bet," Rencke said. "Guess where Nakamura's wife and kiddies were killed?"

McGarvey shook his head.

"Nagasaki."

McGarvey telephoned Phil Carrara from the Marriott Hotel.

"I'm coming out by cab. Meet me at the gate."

"Where the hell are you?" the DDO demanded. "Your doctors are screaming bloody murder, claiming we've kidnapped you, and the FBI wants to know what's going on."

"I'm going to need my gun, my passport, and some clothes and shaving gear."

"What the hell are you talking about?"

"I'm going back to Tokyo. I know who's behind all of this."

65

McGarvey flew first class from Washington to Los Angeles, and then the long haul across the Pacific to Tokyo. The cabin attendants wanted to fuss over him, but on his insistence they left him alone for the most part.

He took sleeping tablets to make sure he would get some much-needed rest, yet he dreamed about the monastery on Santorini. It was night again, the wind-swept rain beating against the stained glass windows, and Elizabeth's screams echoing down the long, dank stone corridors. But he couldn't do a thing to help her; he'd been crucified. His hands and feet had been nailed to the cross above the altar, while the congregation of STASI killers watched him bleed to death.

Elizabeth was going to die unless he could help her, but it was impossible and he knew it.

"I'm sorry," he mumbled in his sleep. "Please . . . Elizabeth . . . forgive me."

McGarvey looked up into the eyes of a flight attendant, an expression of concern on her face. "You must have been having a bad dream," she spoke softly to him.

"What time is it?" he asked, still half in his nightmare. He felt distant, almost detached.

"Seven-thirty in the morning. Tokyo time. We're about forty minutes out. Would you like a cup of coffee?"

"Yes, please," McGarvey said, and the girl helped him raise his seat.

"The restroom is free," she suggested.

"I'll have the coffee first. And put a shot of brandy in it."

"Yes, sir," she said, smiling.

When she was gone, McGarvey raised his windowshade, the morning extremely bright and nearly cloudless. They were flying west, nothing yet but the empty Pacific beneath them. But he got the feeling that somebody was waiting and watching for him to show up. Ernst Spranger or Kiyoshi Fukai. He knew that he would have to fight them both, sooner or later, but he wasn't at all sure of the outcome.

Narita International Airport's Customs and Arrivals hall was a jam-packed mass of humanity. All the Japanese officials, airline representatives and redcaps were courteous, efficient and even outwardly obsequious, though, handling the jostling crowds as if they couldn't think of anything that would give them more pleasure.

All a sham, McGarvey wondered, presenting his passport, their smiles no more than a facade over their real emotions? The old newsreels came immediately to mind of the smiling, bowing Japanese diplomats in Washington on the day before the attack on Pearl Harbor. It was an unfair comparison, then and now, yet he couldn't help but make it.

"The purpose of your visit, Mr. Fine?" the passport officer asked, looking up.

"I have business in Nagasaki," McGarvey answered. "With Fukai Semiconductor."

"Yes, very good," the official said, smiling. He handed back McGarvey's passport. "Have a pleasant, profitable stay in Japan."

"*Arigatò*," McGarvey answered, and the official shot him a brief scowl that changed instantly back into a smile.

In three hours flat Technical Services had come up with a passport and legend for McGarvey as Jack Fine, a sales rep for DataBase Corporation, a small but upcoming competitor of TSI industries. If anyone called the Eau Claire, Wisconsin number, or asked for information to be faxed, they would be told that McGarvey was indeed who he presented himself to be. DataBase Corp was a legitimate company that sometimes acted as a front for the FBI's CounterIntelligence Division, and in this case as a special favor to the CIA.

Of course if Spranger was here, and got a look at McGarvey, the fiction would immediately fail. The confrontation would come then and there. He almost hoped it would happen that way.

Kelley Fuller was waiting for him on the other side of the customs barrier after he'd retrieved his single bag and had it checked. Dressed in a conservatively cut gray business suit, her hair up in a bun in the back, and very little makeup on her face, she looked like somebody's idea of an executive secretary for an American or Canadian firm.

He hadn't expected her to be here like this, but he had to admit he was pleased to see her, and to see that she seemed none the worse for wear.

"I have a taxi waiting for us," she said in greeting. "Our train does not leave for another three hours, but we may need that time to reach the train station."

"Where are we going?"

"To Nagasaki, of course."

"But you're not coming with me."

"Yes I am, I have taken a great risk to speak on the telephone for so long with Phil. He thinks the Japanese are becoming sensitive just now about such calls between Tokyo and the U.S."

"There'll probably be a fight. You could get hurt."

"Yes," she said outwardly unperturbed. "Afterwards you will need someone who understands Japanese to speak on your behalf to the authorities. Now, let's hurry, please."

He shuffled as fast as he could to keep up with her across the main ticket hall to the taxi ranks outside. She didn't say anything to him about his condition, but he noticed her watching how he limped and favored his right side.

Something had happened to change her in the week since he had left her at the Sunny Days Western Ranch in Shinjuku's Kabukicho. She was still frightened. He could see that in her eyes, but fear no longer seemed to dominate her as it had before. She'd gained self-confidence; either that or she had, for some reason, resigned herself to her fate, whatever that might be.

The cab was pleasantly clean and very comfortable. The doors automatically opened and closed for them, and when they were settled the driver took off toward the city at a breakneck speed through the unbelievable morning traffic.

"What happened while I was gone?" McGarvey asked as they careened onto a crowded freeway.

Kelley looked over at him. "I could ask you the same thing."

"If need be I'll telephone Phil and force him to keep you here, or better yet, order you back to Washington."

"No," she said so sharply that the cabbie looked at them in his rearview mirror.

"Tell me what happened, then," McGarvey gently prompted.

Kelley's hands were in her lap. She looked down at them, her upper lip quivering, but her eyes remained dry. It was obvious she was trying to hold herself together.

"I had this friend in Washington. Her name was Lana Toy. We used to work together at the State Department. We were roommates too. Even fought over the same boyfriend a couple years ago."

McGarvey thought he knew what was coming.

"She's dead. Burned up in a car accident. But it was no

accident, you know. That's how they killed Jim and Ed Mowry . . . with fire."

"Who told you about it?"

She looked up. "Phil Carrara," she said. "How else did you think I'd find out?"

66

Hermann Becker was running late, and he was getting the feeling that someone was following him, though he'd been unable to detect any signs of it. He parked his rental car in the Cointrin Airport Holiday Inn parking lot, and walked directly from it, stopping a hundred yards away in the shadows to look back. No one was there.

It was coming up on 2300 hours, and his Swissair flight to Tokyo was due to take off at midnight. He couldn't miss the plane because there was no other flight out until tomorrow afternoon, and he had to be in Japan by evening, Tokyo time. But he was worried about more than time.

Liese Egk had sounded strained on the telephone, but Spranger had sounded worse; so bad in fact that Becker had hardly recognized his voice. But the general's orders had been clear and concise. The time was now.

"You must make delivery as planned. There can be no delays for any reason whatsoever. Are you perfectly clear in this?"

"Yes, of course," Becker had replied, his mind already racing ahead to the various steps he would have to take to insure his unimpeded arrival in Tokyo and then Nagasaki.

But the scenario had been worked out in beautiful detail months ago. They'd even made several dry runs with absolutely no difficulties. This time would be no different. Except that Becker was worried about how Spranger had sounded on the telephone, and he had become jumpy.

Carrying his leather purse under his left arm, Becker, a small, dark-complected intense-looking man, entered the hotel, crossed the lobby and took the elevator up to the eleventh floor. His room looked out toward the airport terminal a little over a mile away. He was assured that the hotel shuttle would run until the last flights arrived and departed.

It would take ten minutes to get downstairs and check out. Another ten minutes for the shuttle ride over to the terminal and another ten minutes to check in, which gave him something under twenty minutes to finish here if he wanted to be five or ten minutes early for his flight.

He threw the deadbolt on his door and slipped the security chain into its slot, then telephoned the front desk.

"This is Becker in eleven-oh-seven. I'll be checking out in time to catch a midnight flight. Please have my bill ready."

"Yes, *mein Herr.* Will there be any further room service charges this evening?"

"No," Becker said irritably, and he hung up, turning his attention next to the Grundig all-band portable radio receiver.

With a small Phillips head screwdriver he removed the six fasteners holding the radio's backplate in place. It unsnapped out of three slots at the top, slid down a fraction of an inch and then pulled directly off, exposing the outermost printed circuit boards.

Selecting a small nut driver, he loosened four fasteners holding the power supply board in place, and carefully eased it outward to the limit of its soldered wires. Using a tiny propane torch about half the size of a ballpoint pen, he unsoldered three of the wires, and swung the power supply board completely out of the way, exposing the circuit board containing the first and second IF stages, and a series of low- and high-pass filters.

Working again with the torch, Becker unsoldered fourteen of the filters and removed them. The tiny devices were each housed in a pale gray metal container a little less than a quarter-inch long, and half that in thickness and width.

These he took into the bathroom, wrapped them in tissue paper and flushed them down the toilet.

Back at his work table he took a small plastic box out of his purse, opened it and from within drew out a tiny device to which a pair of wires were attached. Oblong in shape, the triggering device, which had been designed and manufactured by the Swiss firm of ModTec, was not much larger than the filters he'd removed from the radio.

Working with extreme care he soldered the glass-encased trigger into one of the slots that had held a filter, making certain he did not allow the device to get too hot, or for any solder to splatter the board.

Providing the selector switch was not turned to the shortwave band, the radio would work normally.

When he was finished with the first trigger, he soldered in the remaining thirteen devices, then resoldered the power supply wires to the proper connections, refastened the power supply board, and closed the back cover, replacing all six screws.

He was sweating lightly by the time he had cleaned up his tools and equipment and finished packing his single bag.

Making sure he had his airplane tickets and passport, and that he was leaving nothing incriminating behind, he left his room and took the elevator down to the lobby.

The time was just 2332.

Wind was gusting to forty miles per hour, sending spray a hundred yards inland from the waves crashing on the rugged rocky shoreline, and snatching away most sounds except for the wind itself.

A panel truck, its headlights out, materialized out of the darkness on a narrow dirt track that ran down toward the water and disappeared on the stoney beach. A long time ago local fishermen had maintained a cooperative dock here. A few years after the revolution, however, government forces had occupied the nearby town of Dalnyaya on Cape Krilon at the extreme southern tip of Sakhalin Island. Japan was barely thirty miles south, across the Soya Strait, and this area had been abandoned.

The beat-up, dark gray truck stopped twenty feet off the beach, and Franz Hoffmann switched off the engine. He was a huge, rough-featured man with a pockmarked face and a thick barrel chest. His eyes, however, were small and close set.

He glanced over his shoulder at the four animal cages in the back. Now that they were this close he was becoming nervous.

"Let's get the little bastards down to the beach," Otto Eichendorf said.

Hoffman looked at the other East German. Spranger had ordered them to take refuge inside Krasnoyarsk three months ago. Neither of them had liked the assignment, and he could see that Eichendorf was just as nervous and just as anxious to get away as he was.

"Take the light and make the landing signal first, Otto. I don't want to get caught here."

Eichendorf nodded, and got out of the truck. Hoffman watched as the man trudged down to the beach and raised his flashlight.

They were a half hour early, but if the boat was out there waiting for them as planned, they would see the light and signal back.

Again Hoffmann glanced into the back of the truck. Two of the cages contained a pair of wild sables, and the other two each held a pair of wild Siberian mink.

They were vicious animals, and any border patrol prick or naval rating they might encounter would certainly think twice about sticking his hand in those cages. But if he did, and if he survived with his hand intact, he would find eighty pounds of refined plutonium 239 encased in lead containers beneath the false bottoms in each cage.

They had brought it overland from the nuclear facility at Khabarovsk, where, incredibly, they had purchased it in small lots from a local black marketeer who boasted (and rightly so) that he could get them anything for the right price. On the coast they'd hired a fishing boat to take them across the Tatar Strait onto Sakhalin Island . . . simple fur animal smugglers that everyone was happy to deal with for a few hundred rubles.

The idea was a to commit a visible crime for which the authorities were willing to take a bribe, in order to hide their real action. So far it had worked beautifully.

Now, however, if they were caught by the KGB, or by a Japanese Coast Guard patrol, they would have a more difficult time explaining themselves. Internal smuggling was one thing, but trying to take sables out of the Soviet Union was another crime, serious enough to expect, if they were stopped, that the cages would be searched.

A pinpoint of light out to sea flashed once, then twice, and once again, and Eichendorf hurried back up to the truck.

Hoffman climbed out. "I saw it," he shouted over the wind.

"I'll be glad to get off this rock," the taller, thinner man said. "Now let's get the cages down to the beach."

They went around to the back of the truck and opened the door. The animals went wild, hissing and snapping and banging against the wire mesh, their teeth bared.

Hoffman pulled the first cage out by the handle, careful to keep his fingers as far away from the mesh as possible. One of the sables was madly biting and chewing at the wire.

Eichendorf took the other side and between them they carried the sixty-pound cage over the rocks the rest of the way down to the beach, setting it down a few feet from the water's edge.

They could see nothing out to sea, no lights, not even the dark form of the boat. But they'd seen the light signal in reply to theirs. So it was there. Nevertheless Hoffman was starting to get very jumpy. It was the tone of Spranger's voice. The general had sounded . . . worried, upset. Hurt. It had been disconcerting listening to him.

It took them several minutes to haul the other three cages from the truck, and by the time they were finished they were both winded, and sweating lightly despite the breeze and the chill.

Hoffman held up a hand for Eichendorf to keep silent for a second as he cocked an ear. He had heard something over the wind, an engine noise perhaps.

He stepped closer to the water and held his breath to listen. The sounds were definitely there, but not out to sea, he realized with horror.

He spun around, and looked up toward the dirt track.

Eichendorf was hearing it now too. "Christ, is it a KGB patrol?"

"I don't know, maybe not," Hoffmann said. "Get the rifles."

"Right." Eichendorf raced back up to the truck, as Hoffman snatched the flashlight and turned back to face the sea. Under these circumstances he was supposed to send five short flashes, which meant there was trouble on the beach, and that the pickup was off.

But they were so close. To be caught here on the beach like this would mean certain arrest, and almost certainly death by firing squad after a very brief trial for espionage. Never mind they were ex-STASI, and had once worked for the KGB. That old alliance would not protect them now.

Eichendorf came back with the Kalashnikov rifles. "Did you send the signal?"

Hoffman threw down the flashlight and grabbed his rifle, levering a round into the firing chamber and switching the safety off. "No," he said. "We're getting off this beach tonight, or we're going to die here."

The sound of the engine faded, came back and then faded again and was gone. Hoffman took a few steps toward the road, but he could hear nothing now, other than the wind.

"Franz," Eichendorf called urgently.

Hoffman turned as a big rubber raft, carrying two men dressed in rough dungarees and thick sweaters, surged onto the beach. One of them immediately hopped out.

"*Macht schnell,*" he shouted. "We have a KGB patrol boat on our ass."

Hoffman and Eichendorf exchanged glances, and Hoffmann shook his head slightly. Whatever had been heading toward them on the road had apparently turned around and left.

Between the three of them it only took a couple of minutes to load the cages aboard the boat. Eichendorf and the sailor clambered aboard, leaving Hoffman to push them off.

"What's going on down there?" someone shouted in Russian from behind them on the road.

Hoffman snatched his Kalashnikov and in one smooth motion turned around. He had only a moment to catch sight of two uniformed soldiers above, on the rocks, and he opened fire, cutting both of them down before they could utter another word.

For a long second or two, the night seemed suddenly still. Even the wind seemed to lessen for that time, but then Eichendorf grabbed Hoffman by the back of his jacket and dragged him into the boat.

"I hope they were alone," one of the sailors said. "Because if someone is still alive up there, and can use a radio, we're dead men."

"I didn't have a choice."

"No," the sailor said. "And now neither do we."

Thoma Orff presented his passport and customs declaration form to the uniformed officer when it was his turn. Tokyo's Narita Airport was jammed to capacity, but the noise level was surprisingly low.

"What is the purpose of your visit to Japan, Mr. Orff," the customs official asked. He had difficulty pronouncing the name.

"Tourism. I've had no holiday in years."

"How long will you be here?"

"A week, maybe a little longer."

"Have you nothing else to declare?"

"Only the brandy," Orff said, holding up the cardboard liquor box by its handle. "Three bottles. Good stuff. French." The nuclear weapons initiators were hidden in two of the bottles, which were in turn wrapped in lead foil that had been sandwiched between thin layers of ordinary-looking aluminum foil.

"Welcome to Japan, Mr. Orff," the official said, stamping the passport. "Have a pleasant holiday."

67

The morning on the mountain overlooking the port city of Nagasaki on the south island of Kyushu was pleasantly cool, the air sweetly fresh. McGarvey indulged himself in the luxury of coming slowly awake, careful to steer his thoughts away from the reasons he had returned to Japan.

Kelley was up already. She sat outside in the garden sipping green tea, and watching the sun over the mountains just beginning to illuminate the city below.

From where he lay on his tatami mat, he could see her in profile. Her dark hair was down, spilling around her tiny shoulders, and she was dressed only in one of the snow white *yukatas* or kimonos that the *ryokan* (a Japanese inn) supplied its guests. She was beautiful, he decided, yet she was a contradiction. On the one hand she was a frightened little deer, with large dark eyes and the sudden tiny movements of the animal that is always ready to bolt at the first hint of trouble. While on the other she had a surprising depth of character, of fortitude, that made her stay.

As she'd explained yesterday afternoon on the train, she had nowhere to go. "I can't hide for the rest of my life, so I am with you to finish the assignment."

There was an Oriental simplicity about her. Everything she did, or said, seemed to be clear-cut and obvious. Her life had been sad, and she was doing everything within her power to lay the groundwork for a big change. Like everyone else, she only wanted to be at peace, and happy.

But he was beginning to believe that that was *all* she wanted. She seemed to have no other ambitions, and in that she was completely opposite of his ex-wife Kathleen.

A tiny table had been set up next to his tatami mat, steam rising from a pot of tea, a cup beside it. McGarvey rose stiffly on one elbow and poured a cup of tea.

Kelley turned and looked at him, a slight smile coming to her lips. "How do you feel this morning, McGarvey-san."

"I'll live," he said, returning her smile.

"I am truly glad to hear that, because today we will make our move against Fukai."

Kelley had arranged to rent a car yesterday, and at 8 A.M. it was brought up from the city and left for them in the tiny parking lot, across the garden beyond the hotel annex. She drove because she could read Japanese—none of the road signs, what few there were, were in English—and because McGarvey's right leg had stiffened up, making it difficult to walk, let alone manipulate the pedals.

Only a few puffy white clouds sailed over the hills and mountains ringing the city, but the sky was a hazy, milky blue, illuminating the lush green countryside with an almost magical light. This region was like a fairytale land: Important in the mid-sixteenth century when Nagasaki was the only port open to foreigners; again in 1945 when the atomic bomb was dropped here; and now because of some insane plot for revenge.

Fukai Semiconductor's vast factory complex and world headquarters were located northeast of Nagasaki on Omura Bay. McGarvey's briefing package had contained extensive diagrams showing the installation's layout and something of the sophisticated security systems designed not only to detect the presence of intruders, but in some instances to neutralize them, even kill them. Fukai himself was apparently paranoid about security; and he was rich and powerful enough to maintain a substantial armed force of guards without the federal government lifting a finger to stop or in any way control him.

The compound was built like a fortress. McGarvey had spent a considerable amount of thought on exactly how it could be breached, coming to the conclusion that he would have to get close enough for a firsthand look before he could make any plan.

He had briefly discussed the problem with Carrara and the Technical Services team that had been hastily assembled to brief him, and they agreed, with one reservation.

"If Spranger is actually working for Fukai—and we don't have any direct proof of that yet—he probably told them about you," Carrara had cautioned.

"No doubt," McGarvey replied. "But they won't be expecting me to show up so soon, nor will they be expecting me to come in the front door with the proper credentials."

"I'd like to send someone over to back you up, but it's not possible." Carrara shook his head. "There's going to be hell to pay for this. A lot of political fallout."

"I stay out of politics," McGarvey said.

"Right. Just like a surgeon stays out of the operating theater."

Traffic was heavy along the narrow highway until they were well clear of the city, and even then there was no time when they had the road to themselves. Kelley was a good driver, and she apparently knew the local customs and rules of the road well enough to get along without incident.

She had dressed again in the plain gray business suit she had worn at the airport, making her look like the executive secretary and translator her legend said she was. McGarvey had let her study the briefing package he'd brought out from Langley, and afterwards he had filled in whatever gaps he could, though there were holes a mile wide in the plan.

"What happens if something goes wrong out there?" she asked.

"We play it by ear."

"I meant what if they recognize you, or me?"

"I don't know," McGarvey had told her, and they'd not discussed it any further. This morning she'd made no comment as she watched him reassemble his gun and then place the holster at the small of his back, but he could see that she was troubled. There was nothing he could say to reassure her, so he said nothing about the possibilities they would be facing.

They topped a rise and suddenly Omura Bay was spread out below. Fifteen miles across they could see a jetliner taking off from the Nagasaki Airport. But directly below, spread out along the western shore of the bay, the Fukai Semiconductor compound ran for at least five miles, and included the main administration area, a huge research facility, seven large processing and assembly buildings, a landing strip and several hangars for the fleet of business jets and two Boeing 747s, and an extensive dock and warehouse area for the fleet of ships the corporation maintained.

Satellite antennae were located throughout the vast compound. Several years ago Fukai had begun putting up its own communications and research satellites, buying boosts into space from the European Space Agency as well as NASA until recently, when the Japanese themselves (with a lot of Fukai money behind them) started launching their own rockets.

Carrara admitted that the National Security Agency's current guess was that at least two of the Fukai satellites were probably being used as surveillance platforms. Parked in geostationary orbits some 22,000 miles over the western hemisphere, there was little doubt about just who was the likely surveillance target. But nothing could or would be done about it.

"Space, as it was explained to me," Carrara said, "is still free. That means for *anyone*, not just any government."

Also evident, even from a distance of several miles, were the outward signs of Fukai's security arrangements. An inner and an outer wire mesh fence (no doubt electrified) surrounded the entire compound. Separated by a twenty-five-yard-wide no-man's-land, the fence line was punctuated every hundred yards or so by tall guard towers.

As they watched, they could see Toyota Land Rovers patrolling the perimeter not only inside the fence, but outside as well.

The place looked like a prison. Only in this case the guards were not trying to keep people in, they wanted to keep intruders out. It made one wonder what they were doing down there that they had to go to such extreme measures.

"It's bigger than I thought it would be," Kelley said, her voice and manner subdued.

"Yeah," McGarvey said absently, his thoughts racing. He pulled over to the side of the road and studied the vast compound for several long minutes.

"What do we do now?" Kelley asked.

McGarvey looked at her. Security might be tight, but he thought he knew how he could get in undetected tonight.

"We'll present our credentials," he said. "I need to take a look at something."

68

Liese Egk tossed her Louis Vuitton bag in the back seat of the Jaguar convertible parked next to the Volkswagen van in the garage. She stood in the darkness for several long moments, her hands gripping the edge of the car so hard that her knuckles turned white.

Ernst was asleep in the house, and if he'd taken the sedatives she'd laid out for him he wouldn't feel a thing for another twelve hours. Plenty of time for her to make it down to the waiting private jet at the Rome Airport.

But she could not leave. Not like that. Not knowing what Spranger, even in his present condition, was still capable of doing. The man was half dead, and he was a maniac, yet he was the best and most ruthless operative she'd ever known. And he still had the loyalty of the group, the contacts around the world, and the respect of a great many people who would be willing to hunt her down if it came to that.

She walked slowly to the door and looked across the compound toward the dark house and shivered even though the night was warm.

If she left like this tonight, Ernst would recover eventually and he would come looking for her. Even Fukai's promise of protection would do her no good. Ernst would find a way to get to her. And when he did he would kill her . . . unless she killed him first.

She turned that thought over in her mind. On the way up from Greece she had toyed with the idea on several occasions; putting a gun to his head and pulling the trigger would have been child's play. But in her heart of hearts she'd known that she wouldn't do it.

That was then. Now that she was abandoning him, she'd come back to her original decision; to kill him, when the time was right, for everything he'd done to her. For everything he'd made her do.

She shivered again.

Spranger had taught her about sex—sex with men, that is—in East Berlin when she was still a teenager. And when he was finished with her, he'd used what he called her "certain charms" to help the STASI's aims. She'd been ordered to sleep with Russians, with West Germans, Americans, and even Frenchmen.

The worst had been the most recent. She'd slept with Fukai himself on four different occasions, each time worse than the previous, because each time the old man had come to learn more and more about her body, exactly what made her respond, and she hated him and Spranger for it.

Stepping out of the garage, Liese moved silently across the courtyard and into the house. She halted just within the great room, a light breeze billowing the window shears at the open patio doors.

In the distance she heard a train whistle, and in back the pool pump kicked on. Other than those sounds the night was still. Not even insects were chirping, a fact that somehow did not register with her.

She was dressed in a short khaki skirt, a sleeveless blouse, and sandals without nylons. Reaching down she undid the sandal straps and stepped out of them.

The tile was cool on her bare feet as she moved across the great room, down a short corridor and stopped just outside the open door into the master bedroom wing.

This part of the house faced the opened veranda, and the glow of Monaco's lights provided enough illumination so that she could see the big bed was empty, the sheets thrown back.

Going the rest of the way in, she went to the night table where she'd left the glass of water and sedatives. The water was down and the pills were gone, which meant he'd be unconscious by now. He'd probably gotten out of bed and had collapsed somewhere.

She hurriedly checked the bathroom and dressing alcove, but he wasn't in either place and as she started back to the corridor, thinking he might have gone to the kitchen, she spotted him standing on the veranda at the low railing, his back to her.

Careful to make absolutely no noise she went back to the nightstand, opened the drawer and took out the big Sig-Sauer automatic he kept there. She switched the safety off, cocked the hammer, and went to the open glass doors.

Either he'd thrown the pills away, or he'd just taken them and the sedatives had not had a chance to effect him.

In any event he seemed awake and alert enough to still be a significant danger to her if he realized that she was planning on abandoning him.

She stepped out into the night and padded softly around the end of the pool, stopping barely three yards away from him. If she shot him now, his body would pitch over the rail and plunge three hundred feet onto the rocks and thick bush. If no one heard and pinpointed the shot, which she didn't think they would, it might be a very long time before his body was discovered.

"Do you mean to shoot me now, and leave me for the carrion eaters?" he asked, his voice barely rising above the gentle breeze.

Liese was so startled that her hand shook and she nearly fired the pistol. But she got control of herself.

"You won't be missed," she said.

Spranger turned around to face her. He leaned back against the rail for balance and smiled wanly. "Haven't you realized by now, my dear, that alone you are nothing? Even less than nothing, because your sexuality gets in the way of any sort of rational thought?"

Liese raised the pistol and started to bear down on the trigger. Spranger's smile broadened.

"You have been the means to many ends," he said. "You must understand that you are only a very pretty tool; of no value without the hand of the craftsman to guide it."

"I would rather it be Kiyoshi Fukai than you."

"That's not true," Spranger said. "You hate the man even worse than you hate me."

"He is a means to my end."

"That's possible. If you could leave here and catch the plane in Rome."

"What's to stop me . . ." Liese asked when she suddenly realized what Spranger had done. She pulled the trigger and the hammer slapped on an empty firing chamber. He'd foreseen what she would do, and had unloaded the gun.

He reached into the pocket of his robe and started to withdraw a pistol, when Liese suddenly came to her senses. With a small scream she leaped forward, raising her hands, her elbows stiff.

Because of his condition he was too slow to react. Liese hit him squarely in the chest with the palms of both hands, the Sig-Sauer still in her right hand, shoving him backwards over the low stone railing.

He fell without a sound, his body hitting the face of the cliff about ninety feet down, and, turning end over end, finally landing in the rocks at the bottom.

For a long time she just stared down at him, unsure of what she felt. But then she dropped the Sig-Sauer over the edge, turned and went back through the bedroom and out to the great hall where she retrieved her sandals.

Before she left the villa she washed her hands in the guest bathroom. One more job and Fukai would pay her. After that no man would ever touch her again.

69

A polite young man in a three-piece business suit was sent over to escort McGarvey and Kelley from the main gates to the administration complex overlooking the bay. They had to leave the rental car parked outside and take an electrically powered shuttle across the compound.

"We employ more than eighty thousand people at this location alone, Mr. Fine," their escort explained. "Traffic would be worse than Tokyo's if we allowed everybody to bring their personal vehicles inside."

"Where do your employees park?" Kelley asked.

Their escort smiled. "Very few of our employees feel the need to drive, Ms. Fuller. Fukai Semiconductor provides bus service for the majority of employees, limousine service for some, and helicopter shuttle service for others. It is very efficient."

"How about Mr. Fukai himself?"

The young man's smile broadened. "Ah, Mr. Fukai maintains a private residence here on the grounds."

"Will we be able to meet with him this morning?" McGarvey asked.

"I'm sorry, Mr. Fine, but that will not be possible. Mr. Fukai will be involved with meetings all day."

"Tomorrow, perhaps?" McGarvey pressed.

"Bad luck. Mr. Fukai will be out of the country tomorrow. Paris."

"I see. Then I will have to try again the next time I come to Nagasaki. My company hopes to do much business with Mr. Fukai in the future."

"Yes, I have seen the preliminary proposals. We are most anxious to do business with your firm."

Evidently Fukai had contacted DataBase, and they'd upheld the legend. McGarvey made mental note to pass along his thanks through Carrara.

The world headquarters of Fukai Semiconductor was housed in a mammoth, sprawling building of glass, polished aluminum and native rock that seemed to be a hybrid design between traditional Japanese architecture and something off the drawing board of Frank Lloyd Wright, though there was almost nothing Western about the place. Situated along the shore of the bay, the massive structure rose in some places five stories above the water, each level cantilevered at a different angle thirty and sometimes fifty or sixty yards without apparent support. In other places the building was low, and followed the sinuously twisting shoreline as if it had grown out of the rock.

About a half-mile north, still along the bay, the end of the main runway was marked by a cluster of hangars, a 747 jetliner with Fukai's stylized seagull emblem painted in blue on the tail, parked in front of one of them.

On the way across they were stopped four times by red lights. Electric cart and truck traffic was very heavy.

"Is it like this all the time, or just on weekdays?" McGarvey asked.

"All the time, Mr. Fine," their escort said. "Twenty-four hours per day, seven days per week. We must be ready to accommodate all of our offices and branch factories worldwide . . . in every time zone."

"Almost looks like a factory on war footing," McGarvey said.

Their escort glanced sharply at him, then smiled again. "Business is war, one's competitors the enemy, don't you agree?"

"Of course," McGarvey said.

They left their electric cart with one of the security people in front and went up a broad wooden walkway to the headquarters dramatic main entrance. There were no doors, only an opening thirty or forty yards wide and a couple of stories tall blocked by a shimmering curtain of water. Whether it was falling from above or being pumped straight up was impossible to tell, but as they approached the entry the curtain of water parted, leaving them a dry opening wide enough to pass through.

The entry hall was just as dramatic, with curtains and ribbons and tubes of water angled through the air as if to defy gravity, multicolored laser beams piercing the flowing water in seemingly random patterns.

"It's beautiful," Kelley said.

"It represents the inside of one of our new computer chips," their escort said. "It has the same architecture."

They followed their guide along a series of moving ramps and walkways, to a reception area on one of the cantilevered floors jutting out over the bay. Docked just below was a sleek pleasure vessel that McGarvey figured had to be two hundred twenty feet or longer.

"If you will just rest here for a moment, I shall return," their escort said, and left them.

They were in a large open area, furnished with groupings of couches and chairs. Flowers, living trees and other plants were everywhere in profusion. It was almost like being in a futuristic greenhouse.

McGarvey moved down the line of windows until he could read the vessel's name. She was the *Grande Dame II* out of Monaco. Another connection between Fukai and K-1, who were said to be based somewhere in the south of France? The Japanese flag flew at the stern, and Fukai's blue seagull ensign was hoisted on the port halyard.

But the boat was docked here, not at Monaco, which was half a world away.

A hostess dressed in a traditional kimono offered them tea, or anything else they would like to drink, but before they could order anything their escort returned, an apologetic expression on his face.

"I am very sorry, Mr. Fine, but the gentleman who was to have met with you this morning has been unavoidably detained. He asked me to convey his sincerest apologies, but he asks if you could postpone your business until tomorrow. A helicopter would be sent for you."

McGarvey remained by the windows. He looked down at the boat, and studied the line of the dock running south, until he had his answer. He turned.

"Regretfully I will have to first check with my company. I was supposed to return to Tokyo first thing in the morning."

"We could arrange for your meeting here, and still get you to Tokyo faster than you could get there on public transportation."

"We will see," McGarvey said. "I will telephone from my hotel in the morning."

"Very good, Mr. Fine."

"Who shall I be calling?"

"Mr. Endo, " their escort said. "He is in charge of special projects."

70

The highly modified Sea King helicopter touched down on the rooftop landing pad of Fukai Semiconductor's headquarters building a few minutes before nine in the evening. The strobe light on the machine's belly flashed across the registration numbers and the stylized blue Seagull painted on the fuselage.

A short, slightly built Japanese man, dressed impeccably in a suit and tie, had been waiting in an elevator alcove. He hurried across the pad to the chopper as the hatch slid open. A pair of technicians in white coveralls came directly after him, guiding a motorized hand truck.

"Any trouble?" he called up to the helicopter crewman at the hatch.

"None getting down here, Endo-san. But they had to shoot their way off Sakhalin."

Endo wanted to hit something, anger instantly rising up like bile in his throat, but he restrained himself. "Was the boat spotted?"

"No."

Franz Hoffmann's bulky frame filled the hatch opening and he shoved the Japanese crewman aside. "Is Ernst here yet?" he demanded in German.

Endo looked mildly up at the man. "Not yet, but I expect him to come for his payment very soon."

"Well, let's get this shit unloaded and verified. I want to get out of here."

"Very good," Endo said, and he stepped aside to let his technicians move in with the hand truck.

Hoffmann and the other East German, Otto Eichendorf, unstrapped the animal cages from the restraining rings in the chopper's cargo deck, and carefully passed them out the hatch one by one, the sables and minks hissing and snapping wildly as they threw themselves against the wire mesh.

The Japanese technicians handled the cages with extreme caution, and when all four were loaded, they maneuvered the hand truck around and headed back to the elevator.

Endo had remained to one side, an unreadable expression on his face, the strobe light making him look pale, almost ghostly.

Hoffmann jumped down from the helicopter, and reached back inside for his Kalashnikov rifle.

"There'll be no need for that here," Endo said.

Hoffmann looked at him, startled, but then he relaxed and put the rifle back. "Right," he said, and he stepped back as Eichendorf jumped down.

"Just this way, gentlemen," Endo said graciously pointing the way toward the elevator.

The two East Germans turned and started across the landing pad. Before they got ten feet, Endo pulled out a Heckler and Koch VP70, nine-millimeter automatic, and fired two bursts of three rounds each, Hoffmann and Eichendorff stumbling and going down. They were dead before they hit the deck.

"Strip their bodies and dump them at sea," Endo said, without bothering to turn around as he headed toward the elevator. "And have someone clean up this mess immediately."

"What about the others, Endo-San?" the crewman from the helicopter called.

"They have already been taken care of," he said. The elevator came and he took it down to a sub-basement, still much work to be done before this night was over.

The pit had been carved out of the living rock three hundred feet beneath Fukai Semiconductor's headquarters. Sixty feet on a side and fifty feet deep, the room and anything that happened within its confines was totally undetectable from outside, and from anywhere within the normal areas of the building above.

It had been built nearly thirty years ago for just the purpose it was finally being used for this night. All during that time Fukai's most trusted aides and scientists had continually updated its equipment so that at any given time the place was a state of the art laboratory-factory for the assembly of nuclear weapons.

Endo watched from behind thick Lexan plastic windows in an upper gallery as one of the technicians wheeled a small equipment cart over to the four cages set side-by-side on a long steel table. The restless animals paced back and forth, stopping frequently to see what the human was doing.

The tech flipped a couple of switches on the piece of equipment that looked like a heart-cart. Two leads snaked from the front panel. The tech clipped one of the leads to the wire mesh of one of the cages, and poked the second lead inside that cage, the probe barely touching the side of one of the sables.

The animal leaped straight up, its back violently arching. Endo had the speaker on, and he heard the sable scream once before it fell dead.

There was pandemonium in the cages as the other animals went berserk, understanding instinctively what was happening. But within a couple of minutes all eight of them were dead, and the technician turned off the machine, unclipped the lead and pushed the cart away.

A pair of technicians, these dressed in radiation suits, came from behind a lead shield in the assembly area across the lab. One of them opened the cages and removed the animals' bodies, handing them to the other tech who dumped them in a lead-lined bin. It was a simple precaution in case the animals had somehow become contaminated. The bin would be buried in a hole bored one thousand yards into the bedrock beneath the laboratory level so that no radiation would ever be detected here, even if someone managed to penetrate this far.

Endo had turned that thought over many times, and he'd discussed it once with Fukai, who'd agreed that extraordinary measures would be taken to discover who was behind the . . . attack. Therefore every effort would have to be made to thwart the ensuing worldwide investigation.

When the last of the animals' remains had been disposed of, the technician removed the false bottom from the first cage, and from within gingerly withdrew a gray cylinder about the size of an ordinary thermos flask, and cradling it in both hands very carefully handed it to the second technician.

There was little or no danger of harmful radiation at this point, because the cylinders they were handling were lead-lined containers for the weapons-grade plutonium.

But there was always the possibility of accidents, and every man working on the project understood that the amount of material they would be handling this evening constituted a critical mass.

It would take the precise mechanism of the bomb itself to cause the material to actually explode. But if a critical mass were to be accidentally assembled, a meltdown would occur that would kill everyone in the lab, and possibly burn as much as ten or fifteen yards through the solid rock. Nothing would live down here for a very long time to come; possibly as long as ten thousand years. So the technicians were all taking extreme care with their work.

Endo leaned forward on the balls of his feet, practically pressing his nose against the window so that he could get a better look. Power had always impressed him. It was one of the reasons he had gone to work for Fukai in the first place, and one of the reasons he'd become the old man's right hand. For power, Endo would do anything. Literally anything.

But this, now, below in the assembly laboratory, was the ultimate of powers on earth. A few pounds of dull gray metal; not so heavy that a man couldn't lift the weight, was enough to kill 100,000 people. Powerful enough to change the course of world events—witness what had happened because of Hiroshima and Nagasaki.

Endo felt the flush of his bitter shame reach his neck, and he rocked back.

That would change, after all these years. The score would be evened.

Kelley Fuller watched as McGarvey pulled on the single scuba tank, adjusted its weight on his shoulders, and fastened the Velcro straps holding his buoyancy control vest in place.

They were huddled out of the wind behind some rocks twenty-five yards below the highway, and barely six feet above the waters of the bay. In the distance, to the north, they could make out the lights of Fukai Semiconductor. It was 11:00 P.M.

"You still haven't told me what you hope to find over there," she said. "Or how you're going to get inside. There'll be security on the docks."

"I'm going to get aboard the boat first, and then go ashore as one of the crewmen," McGarvey said, checking the seals on the water-proof camera case which they'd picked up at the dive shop where they'd rented the scuba gear. Earlier in the afternoon they'd purchased a compact Geiger counter from a scientific school supply house in Nagasaki. The unit fit perfectly in the camera case.

"What if the crew is all Japanese?"

McGarvey looked up. "It's possible," he said. "But I saw a good number of Westerners in the compound this morning. So it stands to reason there'll be Westerners as crew aboard a pleasure boat that's registered out of Monaco."

"Once you're ashore, what then? It's a big place."

"If there's a lab to handle nuclear material, it'll be beneath ground. In a sub-basement or even lower, which means it'll have to be equipped with an elevator, perhaps an emergency stairwell, or access tunnel, and probably an air shaft or two. I've seen these sorts of things before."

"If you don't find it?" she persisted.

He smiled. "I don't give up that easily. Especially now that we've come this close. Besides, I owe this one to someone I'm very close to."

Kelley's eyes narrowed slightly. "What if you don't find it?"

"Then I'll find Kiyoshi Fukai, and ask him to show it to me."

"He won't tell you anything."

"Then if I can prove that he's involved, I'll kill him," McGarvey said evenly, and Kelley shivered because she believed him.

"Good," she said, and she helped McGarvey pick his way across the rocks and into the water. His leg was giving him trouble because of the weight of the equipment he was carrying.

McGarvey spit on the inside of his mask, spread it around with his fingers, then rinsed it off in the bay. "If I'm not out of there by daybreak, I want you to call Carrara and tell him what's happened."

She nodded. "Is she beautiful?"

McGarvey donned the mask. "Very," he said.

"Who is she?"

"My daughter."

He had timed his entry into the bay to coincide with slack tide. Even so he briefly surfaced twice to make sure he was swimming a straight line underwater. The *Grande Dame II* was at least a mile from where he'd started at the edge of the Fukai compound, and being off by one or two compass degrees he could have swum past it in the pitch-black water.

But he was right on course, and the second time he surfaced he was close enough to pick out a lot of activity on the dock.

From the window of the headquarters building this morning he had spotted closed-circuit television cameras and what he took to be proximity alarm detectors along the line of the docks, which meant they were more concerned about someone coming ashore than anyone in the water.

Storm sewer openings would be screened and equipped with integrity alarms. And although he'd hoped to find the ship dark, and possibly even unattended, the unexpected activity would serve his purpose just as well, distracting attention away from the bay side of the ship's hull.

The other thing he'd seen from the waiting room above the dock was the *Grande Dame II*'s anchor chain. Apparently because of tidal currents, the anchor had been dropped to keep the ship from swinging too hard against the docks. It would also provide a way aboard.

Of course there was still a high probability that he would be spotted and challenged. But if it happened, it happened, he told himself, biting down so hard on his mouthpiece that he nearly severed the thick rubber.

The expression in Elizabeth's eyes that night off Santorini had not faded days later when she came to him in the hospital. He didn't think it would ever go away, because she had become a frightened woman. Her self-confidence had been taken away from her by these people. And now if someone got in his way . . . it would be too bad.

Twenty minutes later the ship's hull loomed up out of the darkness, and McGarvey reached out and touched it. He could feel the vibration of machinery through the bottom plates, probably a generator or generators supplying the ship with power. A vessel this size never truly shut down unless she was in dry dock.

He followed the line of the hull to the bows, then turned away, to the right, coming at length to the anchor chain leading at an angle through the murk. Some of the light from the dock filtered a few feet down into the water, sparkling on the suspended particles of mud, like dust motes in sunlight.

Slowly he swam up the angle of the chain, breaking the surface ten or fifteen yards away from the looming white hull.

At this point he was practically invisible from the dock, but as soon as he started up the chain, anyone looking up from shore would be able to see him. There was no other way.

Careful to make absolutely no noise, he pulled off his BC vest and scuba tank, then unclipped his weight belt and draped it around the harness. It floated on its own until he opened a valve in the vest and released the air it contained and the entire assembly slowly sank.

He took off his fins and pushed them away, and, making sure that the strap holding his Geiger counter to his side was secure, started up the chain, one link at a time.

For the first three feet or so, he nearly lost his grip on the slimy chain several times, but when he reached the part that had never been in the water, or hadn't been in the water for a long time, the going became easier.

Twice he stopped, holding himself absolutely still, stretched out along the chain as a security guard came to the edge of the dock and spit into the water.

The second time, the man looked up directly at McGarvey for several long seconds as he scratched himself, but then he turned away and walked back out of sight.

At the top, McGarvey was just able to squeeze his way through the hawse hole onto the bow deck, behind a thick bollard, where he crouched in the relative darkness. His leg and arm were throbbing, and it felt as if some of his stitches had broken open. He thought he might be bleeding.

Five decks above and forward of midships the bridge was lit up, and as he watched he could see several people moving around.

It was possible, he thought, that the parts for the nuclear device had already been delivered and assembled, and would be transported aboard this boat to wherever Fukai intended on igniting it. It would mean the target would probably be somewhere on the U.S. West Coast.

But it would take ten days or more for the ship to make that distance. And somehow McGarvey didn't think Fukai would be willing to wait that long. Because of what had happened to the STASI on Santorini, and what had happened up in Tokyo, the Japanese billionaire had to realize that someone would come poking around his operation sooner or later. Every hour he had possession of the bomb parts, especially the weapons-grade plutonium or uranium, he was risking detection.

McGarvey unzipped the front of his drysuit, took out his Walther and cycled a round into the firing chamber.

Next, he unsealed the camera case and took out the Geiger counter. He flipped on the switch, but there was no reading above ambient on the dial, nor had he expected any. If the bomb material was here, it would be well enough shielded to avoid detection except at close range.

Certain that no one on the well-lit bridge deck would be able to see him down on the dark foredeck. McGarvey darted out from behind the bollard and took the first hatch into the ship.

What he needed now was to find a crewman willing to give up his uniform.

72

The Fukai shuttle helicopter touched down on the rooftop landing pad of the headquarters building around midnight. As the rotors began to slow down, a crewman opened the hatch, fitted the aluminum steps over the edge and helped Liese Egk climb down. He'd stared up her short skirt all the way down from Tokyo's Narita Airport, and his hand shook when he touched the bare flesh of her arm.

She smiled back up at him when he passed down her single bag. "*Dōmo arigatō*," she said.

"*Dō itashimashite*," the young man said breathlessly.

"Your charms are still intact, I see," someone said, coming from the elevator alcove.

Liese turned as Endo, still dressed in a crisp suit and tie, came across the pad. He said something in Japanese in a very sharp tone to the crewman, who immediately answered, "*Hai*," and closed the hatch.

"I assume all of our shipments arrived on time and intact," she said, coldly.

"Yes, we are most pleased. Now, I imagine, you have come here to arrange for payment. Your situation must be very difficult after Santorini."

"We are reorganizing. Within the month we will be ready to accept new assignments."

"What about Ernst? How is he faring?"

"I killed him."

"I see," Endo replied, smiling faintly. "It must leave you short-handed."

"Besides my couriers who made deliveries . . ."

"They have been eliminated," Endo interrupted, but instead of reacting the way he thought she might, Liese continued smoothly.

"Besides the couriers, I have twenty frontline officers, plus the usual network. We lost some very good people in this operation, but of course we expected as much. It is one of the reasons, as you may recall, that you agreed to pay so dearly."

Endo had to admire the woman's coolness. It was almost a pity, he thought, that she would have to die tonight.

He took her bag, and pointed the way toward the elevator, but she stepped back a half pace.

"You first," she said. "I wouldn't want to get lost."

Endo stared at her for several long seconds. He could take out his pistol and kill her, here and now. Fukai-san understood the danger she presented. But she reached inside her shoulder bag, as if for a compact or a handkerchief . . . or a gun . . . and he forced a smile.

"No, we wouldn't want anything to happen to you," he said, and he led the way across the landing pad to the elevator and held the door for her.

"I'll stay the night," Liese said on the way down. She took a handkerchief out of her purse and dabbed her nose. "We can conclude our business in the morning and I will be out of Japan by noon."

"You may stay the evening, of course, but we'll have to make our business arrangements immediately. Unfortunately Mr. Fukai leaves for Paris first thing in the morning."

"That's just as well. Your shuttle can take me back to Narita."

"Yes, of course."

The elevator opened to a broad empty corridor of very low ceilings, scrubbed wooden floors and rice paper sliding doors. Traditional Japanese music played softly from hidden speakers, and from somewhere they could hear the sound of water gently splashing as if on rocks at the bottom of a small waterfall. The fragrant odor of incense was on the pleasantly warm, moist air.

Near the far end of the corridor, Endo slid open a rice paper door and went in. The room was sparsely furnished as a tea place or as a waiting area in a traditional Japanese home. Putting her bag down, Endo went to the sliding doors along the opposite wall and opened them onto a broad rock garden, beneath a fake sky that was made to look like dusk, just after sunset or just before dawn. Water tumbled down a pile of rocks that rose at least thirty feet into the sky, falling into a pool in which a dozen large golden carp lazily swam. The sandy areas had been carefully raked, and a cedar tub filled with steaming water was ready on the broad, low veranda. Even birds were singing.

"You may refresh yourself, Ms. Egk. Mr. Fukai will see you in one hour. If you have any needs in the meantime, just speak out loud, and you will be attended to."

Liese had been here to Nagasaki before, but she had never seen this place. "It's beautiful," she said.

Endo smiled. "It is restful," he replied, and he bowed and left.

For a full minute Liese remained standing in the middle of the room, drinking it all in; the sights, the smells, the sounds, all carefully engineered to seem authentic, and all designed to promote a feeling of peace and security. Nothing bad could ever happen here.

This place had obviously cost Fukai a great deal of money. But as a business tool it had to have paid for itself dozens of times over each year by disarming those who came here seeking to do hard, fast business.

She crossed the room and stepped out onto the veranda. A very gentle breeze was blowing from the left, and it smelled faintly of the sea.

The evening (she decided the atmosphere was meant to be sunset) was balmy. Perfect.

She stepped out of her sandals as she unbuttoned her blouse and padded down the veranda to the shower head just beyond the tub. She wore no bra, and already her nipples were erect in response to the sensuous surroundings. She took off her skirt and panties, and layed them over the low wooden rack provided for just that purpose, and stepped under the shower head, the weight of her body on some hidden control beneath the floor boards turning on the water.

The spray was perfect in strength and temperature, and she turned slowly beneath it as she lathered her well-tanned, almost athletic body.

Endo stood just within an alcove at the far end of the veranda watching Liese take her shower, and he felt aroused. She was a beautiful creature, he decided. More's the pity that he would have to kill her tonight.

Ernst Spranger had hinted that the woman was a lesbian, but watching her lather herself, he found that hard to believe. And, recalling the occasions she'd spent with Fukai-san, Endo felt that Spranger had hoped to gain something by such a lie. Now that he was dead, it had become a moot point.

When she was finished under the shower, clean and well rinsed as was the Japanese tradition, she moved gracefully, like a cat or some night animal, off the veranda, and across the stepping stones to the pool. She hunched down and dabbled her fingers in the water.

From where he stood, Endo had a perfect view of the curve of her haunches, and the delicate line of her backbone merging with the crease of her buttocks. He fought an almost overwhelming desire to go out there and touch her.

"She is a lovely animal, isn't she," Fukai said from within the alcove's entrance hall.

Endo turned to face his master. Fukai was nearing eighty, but his hair was still jet black, his eyes still dark and clear, and his lean, compact body still well muscled because of the workouts he did every day of his life. But there was a cruel streak to his face; the set of his mouth, the expression in his eyes. Each time Endo looked at Fukai, he felt like a prize butterfly in the presence of a ruthless master collector.

"Yes, indeed she is," Endo said. "Do you wish for me to kill her now, or would you like to watch her for a while?"

"Perhaps it won't be necessary for us to kill her this evening," Fukai said. "We shall see." He was dressed in a spotlessly white kimono, wooden block sandals on his feet.

"Ernst Spranger is dead."

"It is of no consequence."

"Possibly . . ." Endo said, but Fukai silenced him with a glance.

Liese straightened up, watched the fish swim beneath the waterfall for a long time, then turned and lanquidly went back up to the veranda where she slowly lowered herself into the scented, very hot water.

Fukai stepped around Endo onto the veranda. "You look like a fawn at peace in the forest."

Liese turned. "Kiyoshi-san," she said, apparently with pleasure.

Endo backed out of the alcove and left, certain that Fukai was making a mistake with the woman that might cost him his life.

73

McGarvey stepped through a hatch onto a dimly lit catwalk that looked down into the engine room. The generators were humming, and one of the main engines was turning, but there were no crewmen.

Except for the few people on the bridge, the *Grande Dame II* seemed to be deserted. Below decks should have been alive with activity if the ship was being readied for departure, as she seemed to be. Yet the passageways were empty, as were the cabins he'd looked into, the galley, the crews' dining area, and now the machinery spaces.

It made no sense unless something had happened ashore that had drawn the crew away.

Something incredibly powerful slammed into his right shoulder, sending him crashing against the railing, a tremendous pain rebounding throughout his body, nearly making him lose consciousness. Before he could recover, his pistol was snatched from his hand so violently his body was spun around.

Heidinora Daishi, the squat bulldog of a man from the Imperial Gardens in Tokyo, stood grinning at McGarvey, whose heart was hammering painfully in his chest. He was having trouble catching his breath and his vision was blurring.

"I hoped that I would see you again," the Japanese killer said, his voice low-pitched and rough, and his English difficult to understand. "This time you have lost your weapon, so the fight will be equal." He casually tossed the Walther back into the passageway, sending it clattering along the deck.

McGarvey's head was spinning as he desperately tried to work himself fully conscious. Under the best of conditions this fight would have been unequal; the man he was facing was built like a Sherman tank, probably was an expert in any number of martial arts, and, more important, seemed to want to vent his power here and now.

"Stand up now," Heidinora said, taking a handful of McGarvey's drysuit and shaking him like a rag doll.

McGarvey feinted left, then came in under Heidinora's right arm, and hammered three quick blows with every ounce of his strength to the man's chest just over his heart.

Heidinora grunted in irritation, not pain, and batted McGarvey away like an insect, sending him sprawling on the catwalk, stars again bursting in his eyes.

Before he could move out of the way the Jap was on him, kicking him viciously in the side with his steel-toed shoe.

The pain was exquisite, and he knew that he could not take very much more punishment before he became totally helpless.

Heidinora kicked him again, this time on the hip, nearly dislocating his back.

Christ! The man meant to kick him to death. It could not continue. But he had no way of defending himself.

Heidinora kicked again, but this time McGarvey managed to rear up and deflect the blow with his left arm, momentarily pushing the man off-balance.

Rolling right, McGarvey pulled himself under the catwalk railing, and before Heidinora could react, twisted over the edge, and dropped the ten or twelve feet to the engine room floor, the hard landing knocking him temporarily senseless.

When he finally looked up, Heidinora was gone, on his way down to finish the job. His head still spinning, McGarvey frantically looked around for something to use; anything. But the engine room was spotlessly clean. Not even an oily rag lay out; no empty coffee cups, no ashtrays, no tools.

He managed to get to his feet, where he had to support himself against a piece of machinery for a long moment until he regained his balance. The entire ship seemed to be spinning around, the decking heaving and bucking as if they were at sea in a heavy storm.

Straight ahead was a thick steel waterproof door on massive hinges. The sill was high, so that whoever came through would have to lean forward to step over it.

McGarvey stumbled as quickly as he could to the door and pulled it all the way open. As he'd hoped, it was well-balanced, and swung easily.

Someone was coming down the stairs at the end of the short

passageway, and McGarvey stepped back behind the door, out of sight.

A moment later Heidinora started through the doorway, his right leg first, his right hand on the doorjamb, and his head and shoulders bent forward.

McGarvey heaved the door closed with everything he had, the thick steel smashing into the Japanese killer's face, driving him backward, and then catching the man's leg against the jamb, crushing his kneecap.

Heidinora roared in pain and rage, and he shoved the door back, and tried to pull his way through.

McGarvey smashed the heavy door into the man's face and forehead again, pulled it back, and shoved it again with all of his might, this time hitting the top of Heidinora's skull with a sickening crunch, and then closing on his hand, severing all four fingers at the roots.

Heidinora was in trouble. His eyelids were fluttering and his breath came in big, blubbering gasps as if he were a drowning man trying desperately for one last breath of air. Blood pumped out of a wicked rent in his skull. The man's chest heaved once, and then he slumped back. He was dead.

McGarvey hung on the doorframe for a long time, catching his breath, pain coming at him in waves, but the blurred vision and dizziness finally subsiding.

A plastic security badge was clipped to the lapel of Heidinora's coveralls. McGarvey peeled off his drysuit, stashed it in a dark corner behind some machinery and back at the doorway took the security badge from the body and clipped it to his jacket.

The ruse would not stand up to close scrutiny, but all he needed was to get off the ship, across the dock and into the main building.

Careful not to step in the blood, McGarvey made his way down the corridor and painfully up the stairs to the catwalk where he retrieved the Geiger counter. Its case was cracked, but otherwise it seemed undamaged.

He found his gun in the upper passageway, and from there worked his way up to the main deck. He held up at the portside hatch. Ten feet away the rail opened to the boarding ladder down to the dock. The moment he started down he would be in plain view of everyone below, as well as anyone watching from the bridge. But there was no other way ashore.

Shoving the Walther in his belt beneath his jacket at the small of his back, he stepped across the covered passageway on deck, and started down the boarding ladder, making every effort not to limp or in any way show that he was in pain.

Two men in white coveralls, Uzi submachine guns slung over their shoulders, stood talking on the forward dock, near the ship's bows. They looked up as McGarvey descended, said something to each other, then looked away, apparently uninterested, even though they could not have seen the security pass from that distance.

At the bottom, McGarvey crossed the dock without hesitation, and entered what turned out to be a ship's stores and holding area within the main building. Someone was working with a forklift to the right, at the end of a long file, but there was no one else in sight.

Moving quickly now, McGarvey went to the far end of the warehouse, and through a door which led down a short corridor to a freight elevator.

The elevator was up one floor. He called it down, and then pulled out his pistol, switching the safety catch off, stepping to one side as the doors slid open on an empty car.

Inside, he studied the board. This floor was indicated by a light. There were four floors beneath it. He punched the button for the lowest floor and then moved back and to the side.

Something was nagging at the back of his mind. Something about the ease with which he'd gotten off the ship, across the dock and this far into the building.

The elevator opened on the fourth sublevel to a T-intersection of two corridors that disappeared both ways into the darkness. This place was deserted too; another fact that was somehow bothersome.

A few yards down the left corridor a pair of tall wire mesh doors led into a high-voltage electrical distribution cabinet. McGarvey glanced inside. This set up could accommodate the power needs of a big skyscraper, yet he didn't think it was the main distribution center for the headquarters complex. No, this supplied power for some specific section of the complex. Some installation. Something that required a huge amount of amperage.

The elevator doors closed and the car started up. McGarvey turned and hurried back to the head of the corridor to watch the floor indicator. The car stopped one level up, and almost immediately started back down.

McGarvey turned and looked both ways down the corridor, but there were no doors, nowhere to run. Nowhere to hide.

In desperation he rushed back into the darkness to the electrical distribution cabinet, yanked open the door and crawled inside, taking extreme care not to brush up against any of the yard-long bus bars that carried so much power. He could feel the hair on the back of his neck standing up.

He closed the door and eased back into the deeper darkness as the elevator slid open and two men armed with Uzi submachine guns stepped out into the corridor, sweeping their weapons left to right, as if they'd been expecting trouble.

Moments later one of them said something into a walkie-talkie, and when he had his reply, said something to the other man who sent the elevator back up.

McGarvey could not make out what they were saying, but it was evident they were nervous. They kept a wary eye on both branches of the corridor.

The elevator returned and two white-suited technicians got off with a motorized cart. Without hesitation the four of them started down the left corridor and as they came even with McGarvey's hiding spot, his Geiger counter began to react, the volume just loud enough for him to hear the crackle.

He pulled the device off his shoulder and stared at the gauge. The needle was jumping well above ambient.

On top of the cart was an oblong metal box about one yard on the long axis and half that on the short side. It was marked in French: PORTSIDE SEWAGE LIFT PUMP.

As the technicians disappeared with the cart into the darkness, the Geiger counter reading rapidly subsided. Whatever the box contained, he decided, it definitely was *not* a sewage lift pump.

74

Roland Murphy sat at his huge desk listening to what his Deputy Director of Operations, Phil Carrara, was saying. It was coming up on noon, and besides Carrara, the DCI had called Ryan and Doyle in to listen. The general was tired, and he had every right to be. He'd been going almost twenty-four hours a day since the Japanese crisis had come up, and he wasn't as young as the others.

"She won't do anything foolish, will she?" he asked his DDO.

"I don't think so," Carrara said.

"How'd you get her to stay?" Ryan asked.

Carrara sighed. "I told her a lie."

"Her friend, Lana Toy?"

"We have her in protective custody. Told her that we needed her cooperation if we were going to save Kelley's life."

"What happens if they blow the whistle when this is all over?" Ryan asked.

"I don't know," Carrara said wearily. "But in the meantime Kelley is damned frightened. I think McGarvey has made a believer out of her. She'll stick, no matter what happens."

"Which gives us just a few minutes before she calls back. What time is it over there now?"

"A little before 2:00 A.M.," Carrara answered. "Dawn will be in another three hours, which will put her in an exposed position if we order her back to Fukai's perimeter."

"No word from McGarvey?" Murphy asked. "Not so much as a sign?"

"I'm afraid not, General," Carrara said. "She told us that he went into the water around twenty-hundred hours their time, about four hours ago, with the intention of somehow getting aboard a ship tied to the Fukai docks, and from there getting ashore."

"What do we have on the boat?" Murphy asked, turning to Doyle, his Deputy Director of Intelligence. Doyle had worked with the National Photo Reconnaissance Office over the past days. He opened a file folder and withdrew a satellite shot of the Fukai compound. He passed it to Murphy.

"She's the *Grande Dame II*, one of the two Feadship pleasure yachts in Fukai's fleet. The other, sister ship, the *Grande Dame*, has been sailing in the Mediterranean for the past year. Evidently number two is being made ready to replace number one for the fall and winter season. They're identical; 243 feet at the waterline, twin MTV diesels, state-of-the-art electronics. Either ship is capable of crossing any ocean in style at cruising speeds in excess of twenty knots."

"Impressive toys," Ryan mumbled taking the photograph from the DCI. "The bomb, if one exists, could easily be transported aboard either ship."

"Of course," Doyle said. "But I don't think it's likely. By now Fukai has to realize that he's come under suspicion."

"Especially with McGarvey poking around," Ryan put in.

"If he has the bomb parts there in Nagasaki where his technicians are putting them together, he'll want to get rid of the device as quickly as possible."

"He could load it aboard the ship at his dock in under an hour, I would suspect," Murphy said.

"I don't mean just get it out of Japan, General. I meant deliver it to its target and . . . fire it . . . as soon as possible."

"By air," Carrara said. "Fukai Semiconductor maintains a fleet of jetliners. They've even got a pair of Boeing 747s."

"One of which is currently on the ground at Fukai, for routine maintenance," Doyle said. "Kiyoshi Fukai himself is scheduled to fly out to Paris in a few hours."

"Paris as a target?" Murphy said. "That doesn't make sense. Nor would he risk riding on the same plane with a bomb. He'll want to keep his distance."

"Pardon me, General, but I don't agree," Carrara said, sitting forward. He turned to Doyle. "He's going to Paris by what route Tommy? East or west?"

"East," Doyle replied. "With a stopover for fuel in San Francisco."

"Where the bomb would be off-loaded," Carrara said, turning back to the DCI. "A customs check on a man such as Fukai would be perfunctory at best. He could drop the bomb off, set on a timer to explode after he was well on his way to Paris. There'd be no evidence left behind to connect him with the device."

"Then we stop the plane from taking off," Murphy suggested.

"That wouldn't be so easy," Ryan cautioned. "As you say, Fukai's stature puts him above that of an ordinary citizen."

"I can convince the President."

"And if we were wrong, what then?" the Agency's general counsel asked. "Maybe McGarvey's presence has been detected and the bomb would *not* be loaded aboard that plane. There'd be an international stink if we convinced the Japanese government to go after its richest man and nothing was found. I suggest we wait until the plane lands on U.S. soil and make a routine but thorough customs check. If a bomb is aboard, we'll not only find it, but we'll have Fukai himself in custody."

"Unless he's insane," Carrara said softly. "If he's cornered mightn't he trigger the bomb anyway?"

"That's a cheery thought," Doyle said. "But it's a possibility we should consider."

"What do you suggest?" Murphy asked.

"Let me call my office first," Doyle said. "There's been a satellite pass within the past few minutes. Photo Recon has got a realtime link." Doyle picked up the phone and called his chief of Analysis. He had his answer almost immediately.

"Well?" Murphy demanded impatiently.

"The 747 that was parked on the apron has been moved to a hangar near the Research and Administration complex. We caught a view of her tail section, but nothing else." Doyle looked at the others then back to Murphy. "Call the President, Mr. Director, and lay it out for him. Our alternatives, as I see them, are to stop the plane on the ground now, before it leaves Japan; let our customs people take care of it in San Francisco; or . . ." Doyle hesitated a moment. "Or divert the flight to a deserted airport somewhere well away from any civilian population so that if the bomb is triggered, casualties will be at a minimum."

"If the pilot refuses?" Ryan asked.

"Then we'd better be ready to shoot it down over the ocean."

Kelley Fuller called two minutes later from a roadside phone three miles from the main gate into the Fukai compound, but still within sight of the airfield. She sounded bad.

"There is still no sign of him," she said, obviously at the edge of panic. "I think he must have drowned. There were small boats swarming all over the harbor until just a little while ago."

"Listen to me, I want you to do one more thing for us," Carrara said. The call was on the speaker phone so everyone could hear.

"Yes, I'm listening," she said.

"Can you see that big airplane from where you are?"

"Yes," she answered uncertainly.

"I want you to keep watching it. The moment it moves toward the runway I want you to call us. Then you can get out of there. But only then. Do you understand?"

"Yes, I do," Kelley said. "But what about Kirk?"

"We'll help him," Carrara said. "Trust me."

75

One hundred yards from the intersection, the corridor ended at an elevator that could only be operated with a key. There were no indicators on the outside telling if the car was on the way down or up, or even if the elevator went both ways.

McGarvey figured it was a fair bet that the car only went to some lower level where he supposed the bomb was being assembled now. But there was no indication of any radioactive source nearby, nor could he hear anything from below by putting his ear to the elevator door. It was as if no one had ever come this way, yet the technicians with the cart had to have used this elevator. There were no other doors in the corridor.

Which meant that unless there was some other underground passage out, which he doubted, the assembled bomb would have to be brought out this way.

He looked back the way he had come. His position was exposed here. If someone else came down the corridor from the freight elevator, he would have nowhere to run. He would have to shoot his way out, which would alert Fukai's security people that he was here.

He had found what he had come looking for; evidence that Fukai Semiconductor had in its possession material that was radioactive. Enough evidence to launch an immediate investigation.

All he had to do was turn around now, and retrace his steps. He didn't think he would have much trouble swimming down the bay, past the Fukai perimeter to where Kelley Fuller was waiting.

Together they could return to the hotel, or even Tokyo, and take refuge in the U.S. Embassy.

But that wasn't enough. The look in Liz's eyes, and the expression in her voice back in Washington was still very fresh in his mind. Fukai and Spranger were going to be held accountable for what they'd done. He was going to make sure of it.

It was past 2:30. The technicians had been down here at least a half hour. To do what? Make some final assembly? Perhaps install the initiator into the bomb itself, assuming that the sewage lift pump contained it. Unless he misunderstood the relatively simple construction of a nuclear device, he didn't think that sort of an operation would take very long. A few minutes at the most.

And, if the assembled bomb was to be installed aboard the ship, it would probably be done under cover of darkness. Except for the people on the bridge, and the man he'd fought with, the ship had been deserted.

The time was now. The bomb was going to be put aboard tonight. In the morning the regular crew would come aboard and the *Grande Dame II* would sail east; perhaps for San Francisco, where a nuclear explosion would wipe out TSI Industries. Perhaps Honolulu, as a reprise of the start of World War II. Or perhaps even the Panama Canal, which would isolate the Pacific Basin, making an eventual Japanese takeover more feasible.

Once the body was found just outside the engine room, however, there was no telling what Fukai would do. Obviously he would have to change his plans.

The elevator door rattled slightly with a change of air pressure inside the shaft. McGarvey again put his ear to the door, and this time he could definitely hear the car coming up.

He sprinted down the corridor and slipped back into the electrical distribution cabinet, softly closing and latching the mesh gate, then easing farther into the shadows.

A minute later the same technicians and guards came down the corridor with the motorized cart, but as they passed McGarvey's hiding place he got a good look at what they had brought up. It was an oblong metal container about the same size and shape as the one they'd brought down. But this unit was marked in English: HYDRAU-LIC DISTRIBUTION SYSTEM–SECONDARY, beneath which were the letters TBC. The Boeing Company? It was a Boeing 747 they'd seen parked on the ramp to the north of the headquarters building.

Perhaps the parts had arrived by boat, and would be leaving by plane.

The group turned right, past the freight elevator, and disappeared from McGarvey's view down the opposite corridor. As before, the Geiger counter went crazy, but unlike earlier, the guards were not so jumpy. As they'd passed the electrical distribution cabinet McGarvey had gotten a close look at them. They'd been wary, alert, on edge, but definitely not jumpy. They'd learned something in the past half hour. What?

McGarvey waited a full half minute then carefully opened the gate and stepped out, his pistol still in hand. At the corner he flattened himself against the wall and eased around the edge.

This corridor was in darkness too, the light fading thirty yards away. One of the guards switched on a flashlight and led the way. Within a minute or so they had disappeared in the distance. And unless it was an optical illusion, McGarvey thought that the corridor sloped upward at a very slight angle.

Like the other wing, no doors led off this corridor, and within seventy or eighty yards he came again within sight of the four men. He slowed down so that he just matched their pace, keeping well back so that even if they did stop and turn around, he would be outside the range of their flashlight and would have plenty of time to get back to his hiding spot.

But they didn't turn or alter their pace and fifteen minutes later McGarvey thought he could see the first faint glimmers of light from somewhere well ahead.

He figured they had come at least half a mile or more from the freight elevator, which had to put them at the edge of the main building, and probably near the airfield. He was also certain that the corridor was sloping upward at a gentle angle, and what he had guessed at before was not an optical illusion.

An assembled nuclear device was going to be loaded aboard a Fukai jetliner, probably one of his 747s, which would take him to Paris via the West Coast of the United States. When they stopped for refueling in San Francisco, the bomb would be off-loaded and stored at an in-transit warehouse, timed to explode after Fukai was well clear of the area. Possibly even days later.

But Fukai was too brilliant to leave anything to chance. The bomb would probably be equipped with some sort of a proximity detonator, or certainly a tamper-proof firing mechanism. It could possibly even be fitted with a remote control, the triggering impulse sent by radio, or perhaps cellular telephone.

The problem was there would be no way of knowing any of that for certain without actually being aboard the airplane.

McGarvey stopped fifty yards later when he could make out the end of the corridor, which seemed to open into a large room or open space of some sort.

The technicians turned left through the opening and disappeared, leaving McGarvey alone in the dark corridor. It struck him again how simple it all had been, getting off the ship and following the technicians here. Almost as if they had been expecting him, and this was a setup.

He glanced up at the light fixtures on the ceiling. They were spaced every fifteen feet or so, and had they been lit the corridor would have been so brightly illuminated he could not possibly have followed the technicians this far.

But it changed nothing, he thought, tightening the grip on his pistol. He still had to find out what Fukai's exact plan was, and he didn't want to back off until he had extracted his own revenge for what they had done to Kathleen, and especially to Liz.

Also, when it came down to it, he too had been backed against a wall and left for dead. It was no love of country (though he thought he loved his country) that motivated him. Nor, he supposed, was it simply revenge.

He had been in this position before, where backing off would have been the most sensible option, but where each time he not only hadn't turned away, he found that he could not.

In the end it was shame, he supposed, that made him who he was. Who he had become. Though he seldom had the courage to admit it, even to himself.

The sins of the fathers shall visit their sons, from cradle to grave. That would be chiseled on his tomb should the truth ever be known.

"Good evening, Mr. McGarvey," a man's voice came from an overhead speaker.

McGarvey stepped back against the wall as the corridor lights came slowly up.

"It's all right, no one will harm you for the moment," the man said. His English was heavily accented with Japanese, but clearly understandable.

"What do you want?" McGarvey asked, again looking back the way he had come. The corridor was fully illuminated now, and he could see no one back there.

"For you to be my guest this morning. We're flying to Paris, and it would only be correct of me to take you as far as San Francisco."

"How did you know I was here?"

"We've been following your progress all evening, Mr. McGarvey. The only time you had us confused was when you slipped into the electrical distribution box. Our motion detectors lost you. But we figured it out. Now, come along please."

76

Two Fukai Air Transport Division crewmen, armed with Ingram Model 11 submachine guns, relieved McGarvey of his pistol and the Geiger counter, then stepped aside and motioned for him to go first.

The corridor opened onto a broad balcony that looked down into a vast aircraft hangar, easily large enough to accommodate two 747s. One of the gigantic airplanes was parked three-fourths of the way into the building, with only its tail section outside. Its hatches and cargo bay doors were open and from what McGarvey could see it looked as if the plane were in the final stages of being loaded and readied for takeoff.

A jetway connected the front passenger door of the plane to a spot one level below this balcony. The armed crewmen motioned for McGarvey to cross to an open freight elevator just at the end of the balcony, five yards from the corridor.

Dawn was only a couple of hours away, and from here McGarvey could smell the odors of the sea and even the mountains. Freedom.

Below, on the floor of the hangar, there was no sign of the white-suited technicians and the cart containing the bomb, but there was little doubt they were already aboard, or soon would be, and by the time morning came they would be well on their way east, into the rising sun. It would be a dramatic moment; fitting, in Fukai's mind, after forty-seven years of waiting for revenge.

The crewmen let McGarvey ride alone down the one floor. They were taking no chances being with him in such a confined space. He had hoped for such an opportunity, but he hadn't thought they'd be that dumb.

Two other armed crewmen waited for him on the lower balcony, at a respectful distance, and they motioned for him to proceed down the jetway into the airplane.

He hesitated only a moment before complying, and they followed him the thirty feet or so to the hatch. He wondered at what point they had spotted him tonight. Getting off the ship, perhaps. Which meant they'd followed his every move.

The flight across the Pacific to the West Coast of the United States took nine or ten hours. He didn't think they would kill him until they were almost there, which would give him time for an opening.

He smiled grimly to himself, his gut tightening. There *would* be an opening. He would make sure of it.

Traditional Japanese music played softly from loudspeakers aboard the airplane. A pretty young japanese stewardess dressed in a flowered kimono smiled demurely and bowed slightly.

"Welcome aboard, McGarvey-san," she said in a lovely sing-song voice. "If you will please take your seat, the others have been waiting for you for some time now."

A crewman armed with an Ingram blocked the stairs up to the flight deck. He wore shoulder tabs with three stripes. The copilot, no doubt, doing double duty for the moment.

To the left, in the area that was normally laid out as business-class seating, a door was ajar, and McGarvey could see what appeared to be an extensive communications console. Wherever Fukai went in the world, he would have to be connected with his business enterprises, via satellite. Just then, however, no one was seated at the console, though its lights and gauges were lit, indicating that it was functioning.

"Just this way, please," the stewardess prompted, pointing aft. The armed guards from the balcony stood at the open hatch.

"Domō arigatō," McGarvey said pleasantly, and went aft, the young woman opening a sliding door for him.

The main cabin was furnished Japanese ultra-modern, in soft leathers and furs, muted tones, delicate watercolors, and beautifully arranged living plants.

A compactly built Japanese man dressed in a three-piece business suit was seated next to a stunningly beautiful white woman. They both looked up when McGarvey came in, and the man got lanquidly to his feet. He did not smile, nor did he seem pleased. But he definitely did not appear to be concerned, and he wasn't holding a gun.

"Ah, Mr. McGarvey, we have been waiting for you," the man said.

"You have me at the disadvantage," McGarvey said conversationally. There was something about the man that reminded him of a cobra.

"You may call me Mr. Endo."

McGarvey nodded and turned to the woman, knowing who she was even before Endo said a word, and he had to hide his almost overwhelming urge to step across the cabin, pull her off the couch and snap her neck.

"Liese Egk, permit me to present the infamous Kirk Cullough McGarvey," Endo said dryly. "I believe you two have much to talk about."

McGarvey controlled himself, although he was shaking inside. "You were at the monastery on Santorini with Ernst Spranger and the others?"

She nodded. "Yes. But I'm surprised to see you here so soon. We all thought that you were dead, or close to it."

"Spranger isn't aboard yet?"

"I killed him," Liese said.

"That'll make my job so much easier, then," McGarvey said, sitting down across from them.

Endo warily took his seat. "Although you are not armed, I believe you still constitute a threat to the safety of this aircraft, Mr. McGarvey. Be advised that I am armed, and quite a good shot. In addition, you are being watched at all times by at least one of our crewmen, also armed, and also an expert marksman."

A stewardess came in, took McGarvey's drink order, and until she came back with it, Endo and Liese said or did nothing except stare at him, as if they expected him to jump up at any moment and strike at them.

When the young stew returned with his cognac, Endo said something to her in Japanese. She replied politely and then left.

"We will be taking off within the next few minutes," Endo said.

"The bomb is already aboard, I presume," McGarvey said.

Endo ignored the question. "If you make no untoward moves during the flight, no immediate harm will come to you. But again I warn you that you are being watched."

McGarvey rudely crossed his legs and sipped his drink as Endo talked, his eyes on the woman.

"What did you mean?" Liese asked. "What job of yours will be so much easier now that Ernst is dead?"

"Killing you, of course."

"Rich," Endo said. He got to his feet. "If you'll excuse me for a moment, I'll see to our final preparations."

Liese was about to say something, but then bit it off as Endo turned and left the main cabin.

McGarvey sat absolutely still. He'd spotted the armed crewman at the partially open sliding door.

Nervously, Liese reached for her purse and took out a small automatic; what looked to be an Italian-made .32-caliber. Probably a

Bernadelli Model 60, McGarvey thought. Very effective at close range. She pointed it at him. "Buckle your seatbelt."

He put down his drink and complied. "If you're going to shoot me, I suggest you do it now. If you're using steel-jacketed ammunition, or if you miss when we're at thirty-five thousand feet, you might kill everyone aboard."

"I use soft points, Mr. McGarvey, and I don't miss," she said, more confident now that the odds, at least in her mind, had tipped in her favor. "I am really surprised to see you here."

"Not staying to make sure I was dead was the second biggest mistake of your life."

"What was my first?"

"You know," McGarvey said, his voice suddenly very soft.

Liese flinched. "You mean the little girl? Your daughter? You and she have talked?"

McGarvey could feel every muscle in his body tensing. He had buckled his seatbelt, but he had made certain the latch hadn't caught. He could be out of his seat in a split second. She would fire, and miss, and he would be on her before she could recover, her body blocking any shot from the crewman at the door. But he continued to maintain his control, though the effort was costing him dearly.

"Yes," he said, still softly, his eyes locked into the woman's.

She began to shiver, her nostrils flared, color coming to her bronzed, high cheeks, and a blood vessel throbbed at the side of her neck. McGarvey figured she was on the verge of firing and he got ready to spring.

The sliding door opened all the way, and an old, but very well built, almost athletic man came in. He wore a light polo shirt, slacks and Western-style loafers. Endo, a Heckler and Koch pistol in hand, was right behind him.

"That won't be necessary just yet, my dear," the old man said.

Slowly Liese dragged her eyes away from McGarvey's, and looked up. "He is a very dangerous man, Kiyoshi-san. He means to kill us all."

"Yes, I know."

McGarvey made himself relax. "A pleasure to meet you . . . Nakamura-san," he said.

The old man's expression darkened.

"You do understand, of course, that my government will block you because they know your true identity . . . Isawa Nakamura, a favored son until the defeat in 1945."

77

Deputy Director of Intelligence Tommy Doyle knocked once then stepped into the darkened room just off Roland Murphy's seventh-floor office. The general was asleep on the cot that had been brought up.

"Mr. Director," Doyle called from the doorway.

Murphy looked up immediately. "What is it?"

"Fukai's 747 took off thirty-two minutes ago and headed east as it climbed to altitude. The pilot filed a flight plan direct to San Francisco."

The DCI sat up. "What time do we have?"

"Coming up on one-thirty in the afternoon," Doyle said. "Three-thirty Tokyo time."

"What's their ETA in San Francisco?"

"Another nine and a half hours would make it eight tonight, their local."

"All right, it gives us a little time." Murphy shook his head and looked up. "No word from Kelley Fuller about McGarvey?"

"No, sir."

"Tell Phil to pull her out of there right now. Bring her back here to Washington. Then have my secretary call the President for me. We'll get the FAA and, I suppose, the Air Force started."

"Pardon me, Mr. Director, but I have a better idea. Their ETA over Honolulu is around six this afternoon, local. It'll still be daylight. Why don't we have the Navy send up an intercept from one of their carriers out there? Seventh Fleet. The *Carl Vinson* is five hundred miles west of the islands right now."

"You've done your homework," Murphy said. "I'll check with the President first. But he's going to want to know what happened to McGarvey."

"Yes, sir, we all want to know."

"Who was Kiyoshi Fukai, or was that just a fictitious name?" McGarvey asked conversationally.

They had raced east into a brilliant sunrise, after which the two stewardesses served them breakfast of tea, steamed rice, fish, raw eggs and other delicacies, which everyone but Liese seemed to enjoy. The dishes had just been cleared.

"Actually he was my chauffeur, Mr. McGarvey," Nakamura said. "A loyal, if somewhat unimaginative fellow, who was killed in Hiroshima in the atomic blast."

"You would be well advised to curb your tongue, McGarvey," Endo warned, the automatic on the couch at his side, but Nakamura held him off with a gesture.

"Actually I am curious about one thing. Perhaps Mr. McGarvey will tell us how his government has supposedly uncovered our little adventure. If they have."

"I wouldn't be here otherwise," McGarvey replied.

"I don't think that's the case," Nakamura countered. "If the CIA had its proof we would not have been issued clearance to land at San Francisco, or to overfly the entire continent. No, I think that you were here for two reasons: To get the proof, and for revenge."

McGarvey shrugged. "In any event my absence will be reported."

"By the woman who visited headquarters with you?" Endo asked. "My people will soon find her. And kill her."

Again Nakamura held him off with a gesture. "Let us spare Mr. McGarvey the details. For now, my curiosity remains about how my real identity was guessed."

"It was simple, actually," McGarvey said, watching Liese out of the corner of his eyes. She'd put away her gun, but she was still very nervous. The armed guard was no longer at the forward door, which meant only Endo's weapon was close at hand.

"Yes?" Nakamura prompted.

"We understood early on that some organization or individual was assembling the materials to build a nuclear device, using General Spranger's group of losers as mules. That's why I was hired in the first place, and that's why they kidnapped my wife and daughter—to lure me away from you. Of course, it didn't work. They're not very good at what they do."

"At least you won't survive this flight," Liese said sharply.

"And do you think you will?" McGarvey asked. When she didn't respond he turned back to Nakamura. "It left two questions: Who could afford to finance such a big project, and who would have the motive? In other words, what was the target?"

"Why did you turn to Japan?" Endo asked, his right hand resting loosely on the pistol.

"We wouldn't have, except for the murder of Jim Shirley in Tokyo. It was a mistake on your part."

Endo said something in Japanese to Nakamura, who responded in English. "We will be perfectly open and aboveboard here. The murder of Mr. Shirley was a mistake, at least in its timing. But we were given reliable reports that James Shirley was involved in financial dealings with the same party we were using to transfer funds into Ernst Spranger's European bank accounts. It was a most unfortunate coincidence. But it still does not explain how you connected what was happening with me."

"I was in Paris when the Airbus was shot down. I recognized one of the terrorists as an ex-STASI hitman. During the investigation the French found one of your encrypted walkie-talkies, and the same sort of device was found in Tokyo after Ed Mowry was killed."

"There was more?"

"The French Action Service told me that they'd been investigating Spranger's organization for some time, and with the cooperation of the Swiss they learned that Spranger had been recently paid a substantial amount of money in yen."

"My name?" Nakamura asked.

"You could afford it, you have been very vocal and outspoken about your hate for America, and if TSI Industries were to be destroyed in a nuclear blast, you would stand to gain billions of dollars." McGarvey smiled blandly as he tensed. "And, you stupid, vain little man, humble Japanese chauffeurs do not rise up to become multi-billionaires. It's the fatal flaw in your system."

Nakamura reared back as if he had been slapped in the face.

"If you think you'll get anywhere near U.S. territory with this aircraft, you are even more foolish than I thought."

Liese grabbed her purse and started to pull out her gun. But Endo, his face a mask of rage, snatched his own weapon and leaped up, blocking her line of fire as McGarvey hoped he would.

Nakamura shouted something in Japanese, but it was too late.

At the last possible instant, McGarvey shoved aside his seatbelt, jumped up, body-blocked the charging Endo, and brought his left knee up into the Japanese's groin with every ounce of his strength.

All the air left Endo's lungs with a grunt as he fell back on top of Liese. She had managed to get her pistol out and it discharged, tearing through the man's back into his heart, killing him instantly.

Nakamura jumped up from his seat with surprising agility for a man his age, and scrambled on the deck for Endo's gun.

McGarvey roughly pushed him aside at the same moment Liese got herself untangled from Endo's body, and brought up her weapon.

McGarvey was on her in two steps, snatching the gun out of her hand before she had a chance to fire, and nearly breaking her wrist in the process.

She was like a wild animal, hissing as she shoved Endo's body completely away with almost inhuman strength. She jumped up directly at McGarvey, who managed to sidestep her charge. He hit her in the jaw with his right fist in a round house punch that snapped her head back, knocking her unconscious.

McGarvey spun on his heel, swinging the Bernadelli in a short arc, left to right. But Nakamura was gone. Probably up to the flight deck to warn the crew. They were still hours from the U.S. West Coast which gave them a little leeway, but as desperate as they might be, Nakamura's people would be very careful about firing any weapon at this altitude.

One of the stews screamed and an instant later there was a shot, and then a second, from somewhere forward and above.

McGarvey braced himself for the explosive decompression, but after a second or two, when it didn't occur, he went to the half-open sliding door and cautiously looked out into the galley, toward the stairway and the door to the communications center.

The two young stewardesses were huddled together in the galley, a look of abject terror on their faces. They shrank back when they spotted McGarvey.

For a long beat McGarvey couldn't make sense of what was happening. Two shots had been fired. At whom? The crew on the flight deck? Why?

But then it came to him in a rush, and he had the very bad feeling that it was already too late. Nakamura was insane, but he was also dedicated and brilliant.

Shoving the sliding door the rest of the way open, McGarvey stepped across to the stairway. There was no sound from above, only the dull roar of the jet engines.

He turned back to the young women. "Did Fukai-san go upstairs to the flight deck?"

The women shrank even farther back into the corner. They were shaking, tears coursing down their cheeks.

"This is important for all of us. We may be killed. Did he go upstairs?"

One of the stews nodded. "*Hai*," she whispered.

"Is there anyone else up there except the pilot and co-pilot?"

The young woman shook her head.

"Where did the guards go?"

"They did not come with us."

"What about in there?" McGarvey asked, motioning toward the communications bay.

"No one there. Fukai-san operates the equipment. No one else."

"Hide yourself somewhere," McGarvey said. "And no matter what happens do not come out until we have landed."

Making sure that the Bernadelli's safety catch was in the off position, McGarvey made his way upstairs. At this point it didn't seem likely that any of them would survive this flight, but he'd at least wanted the young women out of the way for now.

Except for the light coming from the open door to the flight deck, the upper level was in darkness, all the windowshades pulled down.

He could see the pilot and copilot still strapped in their seats, slumped forward. They were not moving.

Nakamura had killed them, leaving no one to fly the plane.

McGarvey cautiously came up the last two stairs at the same moment Nakamura stepped out of the shadows to the right.

"Don't shoot or the bomb will explode," the Japanese billionaire said. His voice was gentle, almost dreamy. In his right hand he held Endo's Heckler and Koch, in his left a small electronic device like a television remote control, his thumb poised over the button.

McGarvey pointed the pistol at him. He could not miss at this range. The bullet would kill the man, but it would not exit his body to penetrate the pressure hull of the airplane.

Nor would it stop Nakamura from pressing the button, even if it was only by reflex action. If the man was telling the truth, and there was no reason to think he was not, the bomb would explode.

But before they made it to the West Coast, if they got that far with no one flying the plane, McGarvey told himself that he would have to take the chance. There was no other choice. But for the moment, at least, there was still a little time.

"What do you want?"

"Drop your gun."

"I won't do that," McGarvey said. "You won't shoot me, because I might manage to fire back, and the bomb would explode. Out here over the Pacific, it would do no harm. Nor will I shoot you first. I don't want to die. So it's a stalemate."

Nakamura thought about it for a moment. "They're dead in there. The crew. But what about Endo, and Ms. Egk?"

"He's dead, she's out of commission. Put down your gun and I'll put mine down. You'll still have the detonator."

"As you wish," Nakamura said, and he uncocked his pistol and casually tossed it aside. "Now yours."

"I lied," McGarvey said.

"I'll push the button," Nakamura shouted, raising the remote control.

"Go ahead," McGarvey replied calmly. "Push it, you crazy bastard. It's just us now. Push it. Do it."

78

Lt. Commander Donald Adkins, chief of the Combat Information Center aboard the CVN *Carl Vinson*, was in a foul mood. He figured that from the captain on down, every line officer aboard the carrier was going to end up in deep shit if this mission somehow got away from them, or if the slightest screwup were to occur. The White House is watching: It was the word of the day.

Adkins stood just behind the senior operator's console in the Air Search Radar Bay, watching the inbound track of the Japanese civilian aircraft. A decision was going to have to be made, and soon. They were expecting it topsides right now.

"Talk to me, Stewart," he said.

Chief Petty Officer Stewart Heinz adjusted a control on his console. "No change, Commander," he said. "She's still losing altitude at a very slow rate, and still inbound at 603 knots on a 281 radial."

The *Vinson* was steaming west, into the wind, nearly 435 nautical miles north-northwest of the Hawaiian Islands. The moment the airliner had come up on their Long Range Radar system, the captain had ordered them into the wind at their best launch speed of 38 knots. A pair of F/A-18 Hornets were waiting in position on deck for the go-ahead.

Adkins glanced over at his chief plotting officer, who shook his head. Nothing had changed. Their best estimate at this point was that the 747 was probably on autopilot, on an easterly course, and descending, that would put it at an altitude of about 5,000 feet somewhere over San Francisco.

"Perfect for a maximum damage nuclear airburst," Air Wing Commander Roger Sampson had replied when told.

"If he doesn't stand down, we nail him," the captain said. "It's going to be as simple as that."

"How far out is he now?" Adkins asked.

"He's just coming across my 125 mile ring," Heinz said. "If nothing changes, he'll be overhead in just under thirteen minutes."

Adkins turned and went immediately to his console, where he picked up his direct line phone with the Air Wing Command Center. "Adkins, CIC," he said. "The time is now."

"Red Dog One, ready to launch on my mark," the command came from Air Wing.

Lt. Joe Dimaggio, in the lead F/A-18 on the steam catapult, sat well back in his seat, bracing his helmet against the headrest. "Red Dog One, ready," he radioed.

"Three, two, one," and it was as if a gigantic foot had kicked him in the ass, as the steam-driven ram accelerated his aircraft down the short length of deck, off the bow of the carrier.

Immediately he hit his afterburner, pulled back sharply on his stick, and a second later hit the landing-gear retract button.

Before he passed five thousand feet, his wingman, Lt. (j.g.) Marc Morgan joined him just below and behind his port wing.

"Intercept course coming up," Dimaggio radioed, as the data was relayed from the Vinson's CIC directly into his aircraft computers, and flashed on his HUD (Head-Up Display). Among other information, he was given the best course and speed to his target. Time to intercept, in this case, was less than four minutes.

"Let's take a looksee," Morgan radioed. They were friends, and like most pilots enjoyed an easy comradery, even in combat missions. They'd both flown in the Gulf Crisis.

"Good idea," Dimaggio replied, and they pushed their throttles to the stops in unison.

"I won't push the button, unless I'm forced into it, until we reach our destination," Nakamura said. "But you won't shoot me, you'll wait for me to make a mistake so you can take the detonator."

"We're heading for San Francisco," McGarvey said. "But how do you intend on landing the plane . . ." He cut himself off, and turned to look across at the flight deck and the dead officers. He took a step in that direction.

"Stay away from there or I'll detonate the bomb now," Nakamura warned.

"We're on autopilot heading for San Francisco. But you don't intend on landing. Once we're over the city . . . what, five, ten thousand feet? . . . you'll push the button."

Nakamura's eyes were mesmerizing. He was a powerful, purposeful man, and had been all of his life. But he was insane, and therefore unpredictable.

"Do you believe that I will do this thing?" he asked.

McGarvey nodded.

"I will, but it is good that you know it. It will make the remainder of the flight more pleasant." Nakamura motioned toward the stairs. "We'll go down to the lounge. I would like to have a drink."

"We should be near Hawaii," McGarvey said. "The Navy will probably send someone up from Pearl to check us out."

"We're on a legitimate flight plan, approved by your traffic control authorities. No one will bother us."

"I'm missing."

"You won't be connected with this flight. In any event your government would not dare interfere with me." Nakamura shrugged. "Even if they are suspicious, they will wait until we land to ask any questions, or to seek my permission to search the aircraft."

The bastard was right.

"Even in that unlikely event, it wouldn't matter," Nakamura was saying, but McGarvey wasn't really hearing the man. Somewhere between here and the West Coast he was going to have to take the detonator, no matter the risk.

"A drink," McGarvey said. He uncocked the pistol and stuffed it in his pocket, then turned and went downstairs, Nakamura right behind him. The women were gone.

Nakamura stopped at the galley. "Where are they?"

"They're hiding. They think you're crazy."

"Different," Nakamura said wistfully. "I've always been different."

There was no answer to that statement. McGarvey led the way into the main cabin.

Liese had evidently regained consciousness long enough to shift position. Her eyes were closed now and her breathing was labored, but she was lying on her back a few feet away from Endo's body, her left arm twisted under her head as if she were merely lounging. Her long, tanned legs were spread, and her skirt had rucked up over her thighs, exposing a thin line of dark pubic hair. She wore no panties.

"She was a lesbian," Nakamura said looking at her. "Ernst Spranger told me that at the beginning, though he said she would do my bidding." He smiled fondly. "And she did. Once she unlearned her bad, Western habits, she became quite good."

"You'll miss her," McGarvey said, going around to a wet bar at the rear. He poured himself a cognac. "You?" he asked over his shoulder.

"A cognac will be fine," Nakamura said. "Yes, I suppose I will miss her, but at my age I'll miss almost everything."

It was the most human statement the man had made, though it was the direct opposite of what most eighty-year-olds might say. In his life he had gotten everything he wanted, and he had wanted practically everything. Now that he was at the end, he wanted even more.

McGarvey turned with the drinks, but then froze. Nakamura was kneeling at Liese's side, the detonator still in his left hand.

"Liese," he said gently. He touched her thigh with the fingers of his right hand, then traced a pattern on her skin.

Nakamura was looking at her legs and pubis, but McGarvey had seen her eyes flutter. She was feigning unconsciousness.

"Liese," the old man cooed softly. His fingertips flitted lightly over the lips of her vagina. He slowly bent forward and kissed her there.

Liese moaned softly, her legs spreading slightly, and Nakamura leaned even farther forward.

Her right hand came down to his face to guide him, and her touch spurred him on. Suddenly she was holding a long, wicked-looking stiletto in her left hand, and before McGarvey could move or say a thing, she plunged the blade all the way to the haft into the back of Nakamura's neck, angling it upwards into the base of his skull.

McGarvey's breath caught in his throat. If the bomb went off now, he wouldn't feel a thing. The entire airplane would be vaporized in a matter of milliseconds, much too fast for his senses to react in any way.

But Nakamura simply relaxed down on top of Liese, every muscle in his body instantly going limp, the denotator slipping out of his hand, the weight of his body pressing against her thighs.

McGarvey dropped the drinks, and sprinted forward to grab the detonator at the same moment Liese shoved Nakamura away and grappled for it.

She reached it first, and held it up in his face, a triumphant look in her eyes, then pushed the button.

Dimaggio came in from above and to the north of the eastbound 747, made a tight nine-G turn, cutting back on his engines and almost instantly dropping his speed out of the supersonic range.

Morgan dropped in on the starboard side of the big jetliner and together they matched speeds, hanging just a few yards off the big plane's flight-deck windows.

For a moment or two Dimaggio wasn't sure what he was seeing, although the tail numbers and dove insignia matched his intended target. But he could see the pilot and copilot.

"Fukai Semiconductor aircraft on an easterly heading, north of the Hawaiian Islands, please come back. This is the U.S. Naval warplane off your port side," he radioed.

There was no answer. His communications would be monitored and recorded aboard the *Vinson*, just ahead of them now.

He pulled out his motorized drive Haselblad camera and took a half-dozen shots of the 747's flight-deck area, then got back on his radio.

"Red Dog Two, this is One. Marc, what do you see over there?"

"I see the crew, but they look . . . dead to me, Joe," Morgan radioed.

"Brood House, this is Red Dog One, you monitor?"

"Roger."

"What do you advise?"

"Stand by."

Dimaggio dropped a couple of meters lower, and mindful that the 747's wing was just aft of his own tail, he eased in a little closer.

From here he could definitely see that the crew was dead.

"Brood House, this is Red Dog One. The crew are definitely dead. I see blood on the back of the pilot's head."

"Roger," the Air Wing CO radioed. "You are authorized to arm and uncage your weapons. Designator, Yellow Bird three-easy-love."

Dimaggio quickly flipped through his authenticator book. "Wild Card seven-one-delta."

"Roger," the *Vinson* radioed dryly.

"Red Dog Two, I'll take aft and starboard."

"Right," Morgan radioed back, and they both peeled away, making looping turns right and left, as they climbed to get above and behind the big airliner. They both uncaged their AIM-7F Sparrow air-to-air missiles.

Nothing happened. Liese pushed the button again, but still nothing happened. Nakamura had been lying. The bomb was evidently set on a timer, or there was some sort of a coded sequence in which to push the button.

McGarvey yanked the device out of her hand and got up. But again she was like a wild animal, driven by some inner compulsion to attack and kill. She viciously yanked the stiletto out of Nakamura's skull and leaped up.

McGarvey stepped aside, pulled out the Bernadelli, cocked the hammer with his thumb and shot her point-blank in the face.

The bullet entered her skull just above and to the left of the bridge of her nose, destroying her face and snapping her head back. She was dead before she crumpled to the deck.

McGarvey turned and sprinted back up to the flight deck, manhandling the pilot's body out of its chair in time to hear someone on the radio.

"Fukai Semiconductor aircraft on an easterly heading north of the Hawaiian Islands, this is your last chance to respond before we fire."

79

"Brood House this is Red Dog One, negative response, advise," Dimaggio radioed.

The jetliner was one mile ahead and five hundred feet below them. Dimaggio had illuminated it with his doppler radar and had a positive lock for the Sparrow.

"Red Dog One, you have permission to fire," his confirmation came. "Repeat, you have permission to fire."

"Roger," Dimaggio said, and he reached with his thumb for the air-to-air weapon-release button on his stick.

McGarvey scrambled into the pilot's seat, snatched up the microphone and frantically searched for the proper transmit frequency selector. Outside, the afternoon was beautiful, with only a few low clouds beneath them, and the pale blue of the Pacific Ocean lost in the haze on the horizon. There were no signs of any warplanes, but McGarvey figured they would by now be above and behind, ready to shoot.

He pushed the microphone button. "U.S. warplanes about to shoot at the Fukai Semiconductor 747 aircraft, do you copy?"

The radio was silent. McGarvey leaned forward as he tried to get a look aft, but he still couldn't see anything but blue sky. Of course the warplanes did not have to be within sight in order to attack. Some of their missiles were accurate forty nautical miles out.

"U.S. warplanes, this is the Fukai 747 north of the Hawaiian Islands, do you copy?"

"Roger, we copy. You are required to immediately break away from your present heading, do you understand? If so, acknowledge."

"Negative," McGarvey radioed. "You're going to have to get confirmation of what I tell you, but we've got to get this aircraft on the ground and soon."

"Repeat, you are required to immediately break away from your present heading. This is your last warning. If you do not comply immediately you will be shot out of the sky."

"Listen to me. My name is Kirk McGarvey. I am an American intelligence officer, something you can verify by calling Washington. Everyone else aboard this airplane is dead, including the crew. We're carrying a nuclear device that is probably set on some sort of timer. It's hidden in a unit marked hydraulic distribution system—secondary. Have you got that?"

There was no answer.

"Goddamnit, ace, I asked, did you get that?"

"Stand by."

McGarvey sat back in the seat for a long moment, closing his eyes and trying to let his mind go blank. He wanted to crawl away and curl up in some dark corner somewhere, to lick his wounds—both mental and physical. But it was not possible now, nor had it ever really been possible ever since his parents had been killed in Kansas . . . a century ago? Ten lifetimes?

And, as before, the death and carnage that always seemed to surround him solved nothing, offered no satisfaction. Even the woman's death, for what she had done to Elizabeth, had been empty. Liz's life would not be changed for the better because of it. Nor would his. The deaths were nothing more than another chapter in his continuing nightmare.

Minutes later the F/A-18s showed up just off both sides of the 747.

"Mr. McGarvey, you still with us?" Dimaggio radioed. McGarvey could read the pilot's name and rank stenciled on the Hornet's fuselage beneath the canopy.

"That's a famous name you got there, Dimaggio. Any relation?"

"I wish," Dimaggio said. "You're it aboard?"

McGarvey was looking directly at the young man. "Except two female flight attendants," he said. "That's the good news. The bad is that the biggest plane I've ever flown was a V-tail Bonanza, and that was fifteen years ago. I never did get my license."

"Did you land it?"

"Badly."

"But you walked away from the landing," Dimaggio said. "So things aren't as bad as we thought they might be. Now listen up, Mr. M, this is what we're trying to work out for you."

* * *

Twenty-three U.S. Navy and Marine Sea Stallion helicopters out of Pearl and off the *CVN Nimitz* showed up almost simultaneously along the west coast of Niihau, the most isolated island in the Hawaiian chain, and immediately began announcing the evacuation of all residents.

Eighteen miles long and five miles wide the island was home to less than two hundred people who spoke only Hawaiian, though they understood English, who did not use electricity, plumbing or telephones, and who got around by bicycles and horses.

During the Second World War an airstrip had been laid down on the island's arid interior, and although it had been lengthened to take jets almost twenty years ago, it had never been used except in emergencies.

Even before the evacuation had begun, a C-130 Hercules was touching down on the strip with fire fighting and medical units out of Pearl, while another C-130 circled overhead, ready to lay down a thick blanket of foam along the entire runway and surrounding area the moment the supplies and personnel were secured and the first C-130 took off.

Also among the personnel were two Air Force nuclear weapons specialists on loan to the Navy at Pearl. Everything humanly possible to secure the bomb aboard the 747 when the jetliner landed was being done. McGarvey's survival was secondary, even though it was up to him to bring the big jet in.

"Ten to one he doesn't make it," one of the technicians aboard the circling AWACS commented. "But the device should survive a controlled crash landing with no real problem."

The 747's controls were surprisingly light, the jetliner even easier to fly, in some ways, than the small four-place Beech Bonanza.

Ted Kinstry, a veteran 747 pilot for United Airlines, had been brought out from Honolulu aboard the AWACS to talk McGarvey in, and although he figured the chances of pulling off a survivable crash landing were far less than ten to one, he instantly established a rapport with McGarvey and talked him through the motions, step by step.

"I have the island and the runway in sight now," McGarvey radioed. On instructions he had dumped most of the 747's fuel out over the ocean before changing course for the nearly five hundred mile straight-in approach.

While still well away from any land, Kinstry had McGarvey make two simulated landings, using an altitude of twenty thousand feet as the imaginary ground level. On the first landing, McGarvey managed to pull up and level off at eighteen thousand five hundred feet; the second time at nineteen thousand seven hundred.

"You crashed and burned both times," Kinstry had told him. "But there was an improvement."

"Let's try it again," McGarvey suggested.

"No time or fuel. Sorry, Mac, but the next time is the big one." Which was now.

"We're going to start using flaps now," Kinstry's voice came into McGarvey's headphones.

"Why so soon?" McGarvey asked.

"Because we need to slow you down sooner. This time we're not using landing gear. You're going to belly her in. It'll tear hell out of the aircraft, but the landing will be easier."

"You're the boss," McGarvey said, trying to blink away the double vision that was coming in and out now, at times so badly he could barely read the instruments. He hadn't told that to Kinstry. It wouldn't have helped.

"You don't have to reply from now on unless you have a question," Kinstry said calmly. "Reduce throttles to the second mark."

McGarvey pulled back on the big handles on the center console, and the aircraft's nose immediately became impossible to hold.

"Don't forget to adjust your trim each time you change a throttle or flap setting," Kinstry cautioned, and McGarvey did as he was told, the jetliner's nose immediately coming up, the pressures on the control column easing.

"Now we're going to five degrees of flaps. Again, watch your trim."

McGarvey lowered the flaps which acted as huge air brakes, slowing the plane even more, the roar of the wind over the added wing surface suddenly loud.

Ahead, the runway seemed impossibly narrow and much too short.

"I have you in sight. Come right slightly to line up with the runway."

McGarvey turned the wheel very slightly to the right as he applied a little pressure to the right rudder pedal. The big jet ponderously swung on line, then passed to the right. He had to compensate left, then right before settling in.

"You're at eight thousand feet, glide path a little high. Reduce throttles to the third mark, and flaps to ten degrees."

McGarvey did both, remembering to adjust the trim each time, and the plane slowed even further, the roar now very loud.

"Looking good," Kinstry said. "Reduce throttles to the fourth position, and increase flaps to twenty degrees—maximum."

The big jetliner was no longer so easy to handle even with the trim tabs properly adjusted. The controls seemed sluggish and unresponsive, and McGarvey got the unsettling impression that the jetliner was hanging in the air by the very narrowest of speed margins just above a stall.

"Your glide path is a little low, pull up the nose."

McGarvey eased the wheel back, and the stall horn began

beeping shrilly, a red stall-indicator lighting on the panel flashing brightly.

"I'm getting a stall warning," McGarvey radioed.

"Don't worry about it. Your glide path is looking good, bring it right a little more. From now on you'll probably have to hold a little right rudder, looks as if you have a slight crosswind."

The plane came right and lined up perfectly this time. The stall warning continued to buzz.

"At one thousand feet, glide path is a little low, pull up," Kinstry said.

The stall warning continued to buzz, and now the runway was definitely too small by at least a factor of ten, maybe more.

"At eight hundred feet, glide path still a little low, pull up."

The jetliner began to shudder, the control column vibrating in his hands. McGarvey knew enough to understand that the wings were on the very verge of stalling.

"Four hundred feet," Kinstry said. "Three hundred feet, your glide path is perfect."

The end of the runway was less than one hundred yards out.

"Two hundred feet . . . one hundred feet . . . You're over the end of the runway, chop power now!"

McGarvey hauled back on the throttles, cutting all power to the engines, but instead of dropping out of the sky like a stone, the ground effect between the wings and the runway took effect and the 747 seemed to float for a second, or longer, then it touched down with a terrible crash. The big airliner bounced once, hit on its belly again, and then the controls were yanked out of McGarvey's hands, everything outside his windows turning opaque white as the plane plowed through the fire retardant foam.

He could do nothing but brace himself against the inevitable crash, and he finally let himself succumb to his wounds, his loss of blood, and lack of rest over the past weeks.

Slowly the big jetliner began to decelerate, turning almost gently to the right. And finally something crashed against the portside wing, the plane slewed sharply left, and came to a complete halt.

For a long time McGarvey allowed himself the luxury of breathing, and of not having to think or concentrate for his own life, and his world collapsed around him into an indistinct but pleasant grayness.

80

Very early on the morning of the seventh day of McGarvey's hospitalization at San Francisco's General, Kelley Fuller, wearing a pretty knit dress and sandals, showed up. She was still deeply frightened, and when she touched his lips with her fingertips she was shaking.

"Phil said he pulled you out of there just in time," McGarvey said. Most of the past week had gone by in a blur for him. Until today the doctors had kept him sedated most of the time to hold him down.

"I was going crazy," she said. "I didn't know what had happened to you. I thought maybe you had drowned."

"I found the bomb."

"I know, and Fukai is dead. All the papers are saying he died of a heart attack when his plane crashed-landed on that island. They're calling him a national hero in Japan."

"It doesn't matter," McGarvey said. "He's dead and it's over."

She was staring at him, an odd expression in her eyes. "You're really an extraordinary man," she said softly. She went to the door and closed it, then propped a chair under the knob so that no one could come in. "I came to see how you were, and to thank you for saving my life," she said, coming back to the bed. She stepped out of her sandals, and then pulled the dress off over her head. She wore nothing beneath it.

"If you pull my stitches my doctors will have your hide," Mc-
Garvey said, throwing back the covers.

"So let them sue me," she said, gently slipping into bed with
him, and easing her body on top of his. Her skin was like silk against
his, and the nipples of her breasts were hard, her breath warm and
fragrant.

He let his hands run down her back, along her hips and the
mound of her buttocks, feeling himself responding almost immediately.

The bedside telephone rang, and he reached over and picked it
up. "Later," he said, "One hour." He broke the connection, but left
the phone off the hook.

"I don't know if that will be long enough," Kelley said, kissing his
forehead.

"Let's try," McGarvey said. "We can at least do that."

"Who was that on the telephone?" Kelley asked when they were
finished. She'd gotten out of bed, used the bathroom and then put
on her dress and stepped into her sandals.

All through their lovemaking she had asked him questions
about what he had seen and done while in the Fukai compound.
Each answer had seemed to spur her on, almost as if she were
playing some sort of sexual game with him.

"It was Phil Carrara," McGarvey said tiredly. Because of his
wounds he had no energy, no stamina. He felt very weak.

Kelley's breath caught in her throat, but McGarvey didn't see it.
"Get some sleep before you call him," she said. "You need it."

"Are you going to stay?"

"I have to go. But I'll come again tomorrow."

McGarvey was beginning to drift again. He watched as Kelley
pulled the chair away from the door. She blew him a kiss and then
was gone.

For a long time he let his mind drift, his eyes half closed. Odd,
he thought, that she had left so suddenly. Odd that she hadn't even
kissed him goodbye.

He turned that over in his head, worrying it like a dog might
worry a bone. Something wasn't adding up, but it was hard to make
his brain work.

A nurse bustled into the room, a stern look in her eyes. "Are you
awake?" she demanded.

McGarvey opened his eyes. "Just barely," he answered, smiling,
but something was bothering him. Something he couldn't quite put
a finger on.

"Well, your telephone is off the hook, and somebody from
Washington wants to talk to you," she said. She replaced the phone
on its cradle, and almost immediately it rang. She answered it. "Yes,
he's awake." She handed the phone to McGarvey. "As soon as you're

done, I want you to get some rest." She breezed out of the room, shaking her head.

"Kirk, is that you?" Phil Carrara asked.

"Sorry I hung up on you before, but something came up," McGarvey said, his attempt at humor as weak as he felt.

"They said Kelley Fuller was out there to see you. Is she there now?"

"Just left."

"I wanted to tell her that her friend Lana Toy is all right."

"She's not dead?"

"No. We have her in protective custody."

"But you told Kelley . . ." McGarvey let it trail off.

"We needed her help, Kirk. In the meantime how are you feeling?"

"I'll live," McGarvey said, understanding now what was wrong with Kelley. It was the business. There was no honor to it.

"The general is grateful, I mean that sincerely. And the President will be calling you in a couple of days to thank you."

"What about Kathleen and Liz? Are they all right, Phil?"

"They're back in Washington. Your daughter insisted on coming out to be with you, but we convinced her to stay here for the moment. Just in case."

McGarvey's heart was jolted. "Just in case what, Phil?"

"We finally came up with some answers in Switzerland. *Two* sets of triggers were taken from ModTec, not one. Which means it's very possible there's a second bomb floating around out there somewhere."

McGarvey closed his eyes, and tried to make his muddled brain work. Something just outside his ken was nagging at him. Something Nakamura had said to him aboard the airplane. He tried to bring it back.

Carrara was saying something about tracking down the British-made initiators, but McGarvey was back on the 747.

". . . *your government would not dare interfere with me,*" the Japanese billionaire had said. "*Even if they were suspicious, they would wait until we landed to ask my permission to search the aircraft.*"

McGarvey remembered having thought that the man was probably correct, but then Nakamura had said something else. Something odd.

"*Even in that unlikely event, it wouldn't matter.*"

McGarvey opened his eyes. "Was the bomb aboard the plane set on a timer?"

"Yes, it was," Carrara said. "But we had all the time in the world to disarm it, because it hadn't been set to go off for another 98 hours."

McGarvey did the arithmetic. A little over four days. "What day would it have gone off?"

"Thursday."

"I mean the date, Phil. What date was it set to explode in San Francisco?"

"The sixth of August."

McGarvey was suddenly very cold. He had no idea what the date was now. "What day is it today, Phil?"

"It's Sunday, August ninth . . . Oh, my, God."

"On August 6, 1945 we dropped an atomic bomb on the seaport city of Hiroshima. Three days later, on August 9th, we dropped a second bomb on a seaport city, Nagasaki, south of Hiroshima. Nakamura's first bomb was set for San Francisco. His second is set for Los Angeles."

"Today," Carrara said, amazed.

"What time was the Nagasaki bomb dropped?" McGarey asked. He looked up at the digital clock in the overhead television. It was 8:47 A.M.

Carrara was back a few seconds later. "The bomb was dropped on Hiroshima at 8:05 on the morning of August sixth. Nakamura's bomb was originally set to go off in San Francisco at exactly that time."

"What about the second bomb?"

"This morning at 11:02," Carrara said. "Your time, I hope, which gives us less than two and a half hours. But where the hell is it?"

"Call the FBI," McGarvey said, throwing off his covers and painfully crawling out of bed. "Have them standing by with the fastest plane they have to get me down to Los Angeles. I'm leaving here immediately. I know where the bomb is located—exactly where."

"Where?" Carrara shouted.

"Aboard the *Grande Dame II* disguised as a sewage lift pump."

Kelley Fuller was just climbing into a cab when McGarvey emerged limping from the hospital. He'd found his freshly laundered clothes in the closet and over the doctor's protestations and threats had bullied his way out. Kelley fell back in shock.

"What's happening, Kirk?"

"There's a second bomb down in Los Angeles," McGarvey shouted, shoving her aside and climbing in.

"What's this about a bomb?" the cabbie demanded.

"Never mind, just get me to the airport as fast as you can. The general aviation terminal."

"I'm going with you," Kelley said, trying to climb in after him, but he pushed her back.

"You're staying here."

"I have to go with you," she cried.

"Your friend Lana Toy is not dead.

She looked at him, her eyes suddenly wide. "What?"

"She's in protective custody. She's not dead, I swear it."

"Was it Phil Carrara?" she asked in a small voice.

McGarvey nodded.

"Why?"

"He needed your help, and he was willing to tell you anything."

"Now you?"

"I'm different."

She looked into his eyes. "Yes, you are different," she said, stepping back. After a moment she turned and walked away.

A Learjet with the FBI seal emblazoned on its fuselage was warming up on the apron for McGarvey when he arrived at the airport and paid off the very impressed cabbie. Special Agent Sam Wilke helped him aboard and even before he was strapped in they were taxiing toward the active runway, Special Agent Richard Conley piloting.

"We'll be in L.A. in about an hour," Wilke said as they started their takeoff roll. "Washington wasn't real specific about what was going on, except that you're CIA, you need help, it's damned important, and we need to go like a bat out of hell."

"All of the above," McGarvey said, sitting back. "Can you have a helicopter standing by for me?"

Wilke nodded. "Where are we headed?"

"To wherever the *Grande Dame Two* is docked. She's a pleasure vessel out of Nagasaki, but registered in Monaco. Should have pulled in yesterday or maybe even this morning."

"Do you want her and the crew impounded?"

"Negative," McGarvey said, opening his eyes. "Under no circumstances is that ship or her crew to be approached by anyone."

Wilke was looking at him. "I'll take care of it."

"Good," McGarvey said, lying back again as they climbed. He closed his eyes, and he could see the look on Kelley's face when she'd learned that Carrara had lied to her, and that her friend was still alive. Relief. Hurt. Finally, fear.

An FBI 206 JetRanger helicopter was waiting for them on the pad at Los Angeles International Airport. Wilke came along with McGarvey and Kelley, and minutes after they stepped off the Learjet they were airborne toward the waterfront.

"The *Grande Dame Two* came in last night, and just cleared customs about two hours ago," Wilke shouted over the roar. He'd been on the radio most of the way down.

"Where?" McGarvey asked.

"The Long Beach Marina. About twenty miles from here. We'll make it in a few minutes. But would you mind telling me what the hell is going on? Your boss said he's on the way out."

"What's nearby?" McGarvey asked.

"Huntington Beach, Long Beach, of course."

"Strategic targets."

Wilke's left eyebrow rose. "Long Beach Naval Shipyard, Los Alamitos Naval Air Station."

"Anything high tech?"

"TSI Industries is building a new research unit somewhere down there, I think."

McGarvey looked at him. "There's an atomic bomb aboard that ship."

Wilke didn't know whether or not to believe him. "Set to explode when?"

"Two minutes after eleven, this morning."

"Christ," Wilke swore. "Are you sure?"

"Yes," McGarvey said. "I think I'll be able to find it, but the problem might be the crew. Could be someone aboard who'll push the button if we show up in force."

Wilke was shaking his head. "It won't matter," he said. "At least it won't in another fourteen minutes. That's all the time left."

The *Grande Dame II* was tied up at the end pier, and although the marina was very busy there was no one to be seen on deck.

The chopper had set down in a parking lot a quarter mile from the ship, and they'd commandeered a delivery truck from a confused, angry UPS driver.

Wilke remained with his walkie-talkie in the truck parked at the side of the office about fifty yards from the ship. He'd called for a SWAT team, a hostage negotiator, and the Bureau's Interpol liaison man. A pair of nuclear weapons experts had already been dispatched from nearby Travis Air Force Base on Carrara's orders and were expected on the scene at any minute.

McGarvey walked directly down to the ship and climbed the ladder, absolutely no time now for explanations or any sort of delicacy. Even if they tried to run, they couldn't possibly get far enough away to escape the probable blast radius.

At the top he halted for a moment, listening, his ear cocked for sounds aboard. Some machinery was running below decks, but there were no other noises.

Nakamura's people would have abandoned ship in time to get well away. At least they would have if they knew what they carried and when it would explode.

Wilke had given him a 9-millimeter Ruger automatic, which McGarvey pulled out of his belt an cocked. He didn't bother checking his watch; knowing exactly how much time remained wouldn't help.

He ducked through the hatch, and hurried as best he could down the stairs into the machinery spaces where he'd had his confrontation with Heidinora back at Fukai's docks. The big Jap had been doing something down here. Maybe making sure that the area was clear so that the sewage lift pump could be readied for the bomb.

Stepping out on the same catwalk he stopped. Below, the

engines had been shut down, but a generator was running, and the lights had been left on.

There were pipes and lines running everywhere in a seemingly jumbled maze. Nothing seemed to make any sense, nothing seemed familiar.

Time. It always came down to time.

The same Company psychologist who'd once told him that he had a low threshold of pain had also told him that he was a man who did not understand when it was time to quit.

"I suppose I could study you for ten years and still not find the answer to that one," the shrink had said. "If there is an answer."

He spotted the oblong metal container, marked in French, PORTSIDE SEWAGE LIFT PUMP, attached to a series of pipes on the interior of the hull.

But there was no time left. It had to be nearly 11:02, and he could see with a sinking feeling that it would take a wrench or a pair of pliers to open the cover of the bomb. Two nuts held it in place.

Now there were only seconds. No time to search for tools. No time to call for help.

"Goddamnit!" McGarvey shouted in frustration.

He stepped back, raised the pistol, turned his head away and fired a shot nearly point blank at the left-hand nut holding the cover in place.

The bullet ricochetted off the metal, bending but not breaking the nut and bolt assembly.

"Goddamnit!" McGarvey shouted, and he fired a second shot, and a third, and a fourth, bullet fragments and bits of jagged metal flying everywhere.

But the bolt was off. Tossing the pistol aside, McGarvey pulled the left side of the cover away from the case, bending the metal back by brute strength, three of his fingernails peeling back.

The inside of the device was simple. A long, gray cylinder took up most of the space, while tucked in one corner was the firing circuitry and timing device.

The LED counter showed three seconds.

McGarvey reached inside to grab one of the blue wires, when someone came out onto the catwalk behind him. He looked over his shoulder as the LED counter switched to two.

A short, wiry man with bright red hair, wearing an Air Force master sergeant's uniform, came up, reached over McGarvey's shoulder into the bomb's firing circuitry, and as the counter switched to one, pulled out a yellow wire.

The counter switched to zero, and nothing happened.

"Sorry, sir," the sergeant said. "No time to explain. But you had the wrong wire."

THE END